International Praise for *Bethlehem Road Murder*

"Marked by keen psychological insights and well-developed characters, Gur's latest also offers a valuable portrait of a divided, contemporary Jerusalem." —*Library Journal*

"Through the investigative techniques of her fictional detective Michael Ohayon, Batya Gur finely lays bare the contradictions that tear modern-day Israel apart. She tells us about racism, fear, hatred, the conflicts between European and Oriental Jews, and the violence linked to the second intifada. But also—and better than newspaper reports convey—she reveals the incredible love of life in this little country that dances on a volcano." —*Elle* magazine (French edition)

"There is a substantial measure of courage and talent here, hidden under the pretext of an amiable detective novel."
—*Le Monde*

"Batya Gur is a skillful observer of various milieus and the sensibilities within Israeli society. . . . It takes an uncompromising analyst like Gur to make an outsider understand the complicated nuances of a seemingly homogeneous society."
—*The Standard*

Praise for Batya Gur's Mysteries

"*Murder Duet* is not only a superb murder mystery but also a subtle study of the relationships between creativity, ambition, love, and possessiveness. A warm book, full of skillful modulations."   —Amos Oz

"*The Saturday Morning Murder* is a splendid mystery. . . . Intriguing. . . . A therapeutic whodunit."   —*Time*

"Both Jerusalem scenery and the psychological scenery of *The Saturday Morning Murder* are wonderfully presented. Like all good mystery novels, this fascinating, pleasurable book is difficult to put down: curiosity propels you from page to page until what seemed unlikely ends in being inevitable."
                                                    —Shimon Peres

"*Murder on a Kibbutz* is an enormously satisfying read, suspenseful and layered with colored details about everyday life in Israel."   —*Cleveland Jewish News*

Isolde Ohlbaum

BATYA GUR lived in Jerusalem, where she was a literary critic for *Ha'Aretz*, Israel's most prestigious newspaper. She earned her master's in Hebrew literature at the Hebrew University of Jerusalem, and she also taught literature for nearly twenty years. Her five other Michael Ohayon mysteries include *Murder Duet, The Saturday Morning Murder, Literary Murder, Murder on a Kibbutz,* and *Murder in Jerusalem*. She passed away in the spring of 2005.

ALSO BY BATYA GUR

Bethlehem Road
MURDER

~·~

· *A Michael Ohayon Mystery* ·

BATYA GUR

TRANSLATED BY VIVIAN EDEN

HARPER

NEW YORK · LONDON · TORONTO · SYDNEY

HARPER

This book is a work of fiction. The characters, incidents, and dialogue are drawn from the author's imagination and are not to be construed as real. Any resemblance to actual events or persons, living or dead, is entirely coincidental.

A hardcover edition of this book was pulished in 2004 by HarperCollins Publishers.

HarperCollins books may be purchased for educational, business, or sales promotional use. For information please write: Special Markets Department, HarperCollins Publishers, 10 East 53rd Street, New York, NY 10022.

First Dark Alley edition published 2005.
First Harper paperback published 2006.

Designed by Nancy B. Field

The Library of Congress has catalogued the hardcover edition as follows:

Gur, Batya.
    [Retsah be-Derekh Bet Lehem. English]
    Bethlehem Road murder : a Michael Ohayon mystery / Batya Gur ; translated by Vivian Eden.
      p. cm.
    ISBN 0-06-019573-8
    1.Ohayon, Michael (Fictitious character)—Fiction. 2. Police—Israel—Fiction. 3. Jerusalem—Fiction. I. Eden, Vivian. II. Title.

    PJ5054.G637R3913   2004
    892.4'36—dc22   2004042444

ISBN-10: 0-06-095492-2 (pbk.)
ISBN-13: 978-0-06-095492-5 (pbk.)

06 07 08 09 10 ❖/RRD 10 9 8 7 6 5 4 3 2 1

To Ariel

Bethlehem Road
MURDER

Chapter 1

There comes a moment in a person's life when he fully realizes that if he does not throw himself into action, if he does not stop being afraid to gamble, and if he does not follow the urgings of his heart that have been silent for many a year—he will never do it.

Chief Superintendent Michael Ohayon did not say these things aloud, but this is exactly what he thought as he listened to the grumblings of Danny Balilty, the deputy commander of the intelligence division, who grumbled incessantly while Ohayon leaned over the corpse. He knelt to get a better look at the silk fibers that dangled from the rip in the scarf around her neck, beneath the face that had been smashed into a pulp of blood and bone.

Ada Efrati, who had called them, was waiting for them on the landing of the second floor, in front of the apartment she had bought. The moment they arrived Balilty had battered her with questions that he ultimately assured her would be pursued extensively the following day by Chief Superintendent Ohayon. He'd failed to notice the look of astonishment on Michael's face as he climbed up the twisting external stairs behind him to the second, and top, floor of the building. Even then, when he first saw her in the twilight, Balilty had looked over his shoulder and wondered about her ("Is she worth it or not? What do you say?" and without waiting had answered himself: "She's a tough one. She's got pretty lips, but you see those two lines near her mouth? They say: Not interested. But did you see that body on her? And those nerves she has? Nerves of steel. We've seen ordinary people after they find a body and she—look how she stands there.").

Balilty kept up his grumbling as Dr. Solomon, the pathologist who had just come back from a monthlong special training course in the United States, leaned over the body. In intervals between murmuring to himself as he examined her, Solomon told them about the latest innovations in the field of DNA that he had brought back from America. He palpated the corpse's feet and ran a fingernail over the skin of her arm as he recited data on body temperature into the little microphone of the recording device hanging around his neck. From time to time he looked over at his balding assistant, a new immigrant from Russia who followed his superior's every move and kept wiping his damp hands on his light khaki pants.

The two people from Forensics were also on the scene. Yaffa was taking photographs from various angles around the huge water tanks between which the body sprawled.

"Get a load of this," muttered Balilty as they climbed up the creaky wooden ladder to the narrow opening that led out to the attic under the tiled roof. "There's still water here from the siege of Jerusalem in 1948."

Then Yaffa knelt down, and through a rip in her jeans peeped a bit of white skin as from close up she photographed the smashed face and then the skeletons of the pigeons and the desiccated dead cat that had been thrown on top of them. Alon from Forensics, who had been introduced to Michael as a chemistry student ("They say he's some kind of genius, a prodigy, ab-so-lute-ly brilliant," mocked Balilty skeptically; "What he wants with us, I don't know"), shook the cramps out of his legs, rolled the white chalk between his fingers and ran his hand along the yellow marking tape. It was evident that he was waiting impatiently for the pathologist to finish and allow them to mark the scene.

When the call from headquarters came in, Balilty and Michael had been in the car on their way to the Baka neighborhood to have a look at the apartment Michael had just bought. When they arrived in front of the building, just around the corner from Michael's new place, Balilty looked at the rounded balcony and at the arched windows on either side of it, and with astonishment that he concealed behind pursed lips he said: "Is this a castle, this thing? And they've bought it now? Look at the size of it." Then in the yard they floundered among wild sorrel and weeds and he pointed to a tree that spread large limbs up to the second floor and said: "That's a dead tree. It should be uprooted."

Linda, the real estate agent, whom Michael had picked up in their car so she could show Balilty the apartment he had bought, gave him a dirty look. She stopped in front of the tree and stared at Balilty. "What are you talking about? This tree is the most beautiful tree in the neighborhood. It's a wild pear that has simply shed its leaves for the winter."

But Balilty, who never liked to be corrected, hastened up the outside staircase where Ada Efrati was waiting for them at the top. Even before they reached the landing, she said in a shaky voice: "Up there on the roof, there's a woman and she . . . she's . . . she's dead. They smashed her face in. It's horrible . . . I've never seen . . . It's awful . . . awful."

Balilty exchanged a few sentences with her and hurried into the apartment. He advanced through the spacious corridor into the large room from which the shaky wooden ladder led up to the space under the tile roof.

"Have you called the ambulance?" asked Michael, who hadn't meant to get into a conversation with Ada just then, but she said: "No, she's dead. I saw that right away . . . I . . . I've seen dead people before. We realized we had to call the police immediately."

Then, as he lowered his head to the walkie-talkie and told headquarters to send out the Forensics people and the pathologist at once, Ada Efrati said: "Michael? Is that you, Michael?"

She was standing under a lamp that was already lit even though it was not yet dark, and behind her stood a short, skinny woman clenching her arms around herself as if in an embrace. "This is my architect," explained Ada Efrati.

The lamplight cast a glow on her face as her pupils contracted and emphasized the deep brown of her startled eyes. Her voice sounded familiar, like a weak echo. "I know her," Michael said to himself, and gazed at her slim hawk nose, the delicate line of her lips and the pale tan skin against her white blouse. I certainly do know her, he said to himself in astonishment.

"You don't remember me," she said with an embarrassed smile, and she twined her hands together as if trying to control her reactions.

"Who says I don't remember? How could I not remember you, Ada? Ada Levi. Of course I remember, and you have the same face . . . exactly the same . . . eyes." He went silent and looked at the corner of her mouth, which twisted into a kind of smile that did not reach her eyes. Now, too, as they stood under the roof, for a brief moment the scene of the crime vanished, the voices of the people from Forensics vanished and everything was gone—except for a sharp memory of the smell of grapefruit, sore hands and a ladder with Ada Levi perched on top; he saw the smoothness of her arms and her shins, the olive skin that tanned in the sun, a sudden, stolen, hasty kiss at the bottom of the ladder. The taste of grapefruit. And then the nights at the kibbutz summer camp, his clumsy fingers, excited and stupid, faltering among the buttons of her blouse and into the tiny cups of a white brassiere. When they returned to the city, it was all over. He couldn't remember the details exactly: She had a boyfriend, in the army, older than them.

"Thirty years," he said to her. "You haven't changed a bit. You have the same—"

"Thirty-one," she corrected.

He looked at her questioningly.

"Thirty-one. It was the summer work camp after eleventh grade. We were seventeen. In fact I was sixteen and a half and you were almost eighteen. Already . . . they said that you . . . they said things . . . and I was . . . well, how should I say it."

"Naïve," suggested Michael. "You were naïve."

"Even then you were a gentleman." She smiled. "Thirty-one years . . . I remember exactly . . . I've always been good at remembering dates . . ."

"Ohayon!" yelled Balilty from above. "Come, come see. Are you coming up or not?"

"I'll wait here," said the architect, who was standing at the foot of the shaky ladder. "I can't go up and see . . ." And she immediately moved away from the ladder toward the large window that looked out over the neglected front yard.

"I knew that you were in the police force," whispered Ada as she followed him into the apartment. "I even thought of looking for you, a long time ago, but not now, because when you find . . . when you find someone dead like that, you don't think anymore. I came with the architect and with the renovations contractor to see . . . to take measurements . . . Never mind . . . I knew that you were important—that is, that you had a high position in the police force. When I called the police it didn't occur to me that they would send someone like you . . ."

"I was in the neighborhood, nearby," he heard himself apologizing. "Sometimes it happens that if you're right in the neighborhood, and especially if you're the duty officer . . ." He wanted to ask her what she meant by thinking of looking him up, but then he heard the Forensics laboratory vehicle pull up on the sidewalk in front of the house and directed the two Forensics people into the apartment.

"Don't you even have a good word to say about how quickly we got here?" asked Yaffa as she climbed the stairs.

"Good for you, really," said Michael as he gazed after the long stride of Alon from Forensics, who followed Yaffa and stared skeptically at the old ladder that creaked when he placed his foot on it.

"I haven't seen an ambulance," said Yaffa without looking back at him. "Did you call us first?"

"Dr. Solomon is on his way here. He's been at headquarters for a meeting about that boy from Kfar Saba," Michael assured her.

"Ada Levi," he said slowly and contemplatively. "Small world."

"Efrati," she corrected. "I got married right after the army."

"Are you coming up, or what?" yelled Balilty from above.

"The contractor is waiting in the car outside," said Ada. "He . . . He . . . We were here, the three of us. We didn't know what to do. He's not . . . He's Arab, Palestinian," she finally blurted. "We thought . . . he didn't want to get involved . . . Does he have to stay here?"

"Yes, he has to," said Michael, holding on tight to the ladder. "Everyone who was here has to stay now. Wait down here. We'll talk later."

He climbed the ladder. She remained standing on the ground floor, with the architect.

During the forensic examination, between Balilty's talk and Yaffa's reports and the questions they asked him, Michael asked himself why he hadn't seen Ada since that work camp in eleventh grade, and why he hadn't tried to find her or asked any of their acquaintances about her—even though long afterward he would sometimes recollect her face, her lips, the sweetness of the scents of the grove, the softness of her skin and her shy smile. He vaguely remembered that at the end of that year she left the boarding school they attended in Jerusalem, but he couldn't remember where she went, and in any case she had a boyfriend. And then she got married. Of course she got married—everyone got married. Even he, and many people also got divorced, like him, and now she has a husband and most probably children, too. Maybe even grandchildren. If there was a husband, where was he now? She had said: "I bought this apartment," and not "We bought."

In the attic, Dr. Solomon the pathologist was working slowly and thoroughly, humming a tune to himself. Even though the main examination would be carried out at the Forensic Institute, there wasn't an inch of the corpse he did not inspect, ignoring the rustle of the roll of yellow tape that Alon from Forensics was winding around his finger as if to hasten the process of the examination. Danny Balilty, the police intelligence officer who had arrived at the scene completely by chance, was deep in his own concerns, the same matter with which he had been so heatedly concerned previously.

"I want to show you something," Michael had said to him after they had eaten lunch together. "Don't ask questions, just come with me." He had intended to show him the apartment, and to tell him only afterward that he had bought it, but when they stopped at the traffic light at the corner of Bethlehem Road and Emek Refaim to pick up Linda the real estate agent ("Who? Who is it you need to pick up?" demanded Balilty as they'd approached the intersection), the police radio began to squawk. Thus, it was only as they were on their way to the scene that Michael had told Balilty, briefly, about the apartment he had bought.

From that moment Balilty kept badgering him, and now, too, in Michael's ears the complaining whisper buzzed ("Why didn't you consult me? You know that you shouldn't do things like that alone. Has Yuval seen it yet?"). Michael did not respond. He did not take his eyes off the corpse and suppressed a wave of nausea at the sight of the black and red pulp that had once been a face. Judging from the silk scarf that had not been ruined and the fine woolen dress that clung to her breasts and her slim hips, it was possible to conjecture that the face had been well cared for and perhaps even beautiful; her legs, which had already become rigid, were folded under her in a strange, crooked fashion.

Now Balilty's endless talk about the apartment embarrassed him. Even after years of standing at the scenes of murders and looking at corpses, he had not yet learned to take this equably; he could not manage to seal himself off from the fragility of the body and its temporariness, nor could he steel himself to the crude presence of death, which time after time made mockery of the illusion of the permanence of the soul, of the very thought of the *existence* of the soul. Each time he stood over a corpse, as he was standing now among the water tanks beneath the exposed roof tiles, he imagined he felt every bone of his body and his skull laughing derisively beneath his flesh. He thought about his own death, and he thought about it with curiosity, and about how this death would render superfluous all his efforts to change his life. It took time for these thoughts to change, from a strong acknowledgment of the force that destroys and changes decisively—even though this was not formulated clearly—to continued action. This urge to act arose in him in reaction to the impotence that attacked him whenever he saw a corpse at a murder scene.

Over the years he learned that in the first moments his face froze. His expression then would not reveal his feelings even in the slightest, and the people around him would interpret this freezing as anger that he restrained with effort and his slow movements and his silence as signs of concentration. He was always embarrassed by the thought of the special powers of concentration attributed to him, which he himself did not recognize.

The dozens of times Danny Balilty had stood beside him at a murder scene had not blunted the embarrassment that attacked Michael when he heard him talk there (and usually about things having to do with life, which had nothing to do with the case they had been called to investigate). Balilty would look at the murder victim's corpse as if at a slaughtered steer. Sometimes Michael felt as if the dead had imposed on him the responsibility for preserving their dignity, and then he would withdraw into silence and pretend to be listening; sometimes he revolted and tried to silence Balilty. This time, there was the additional burden of the matter that Balilty refused to stop chattering about, as he had long taken upon himself the role of Michael's quasi-patron.

The soles of Linda O'Brian's clogs clattered on the gray ceramic tiles of the first floor, and he listened to the clicks as he stared at the dead doves that had been trapped in the space under the roof and at the cigarette butts that had been tossed among the scraps of paper and the burnt matches and a dry orange peel, which Yaffa collected carefully into a small plastic bag.

"I'm coming up," called Linda from the bottom of the ladder. Michael shrank when he felt the touch of her finger on the back of his shoulder. He turned around and saw the long cigarette she offered him with a typical placating gesture. Even though he usually refused them because of the menthol taste he loathed, he took it this time because his senses were dulled by the musty air. Linda the real estate agent, who knew Michael as a hesitant but impetuous client, leaned toward him, and while taking care not to look at the corpse she lit the cigarette that was decorated at its tip with a stripe of gold.

"It would be better if you waited below," said Michael. "Are you also connected to this building?"

She shook her head. "I know it, but they gave it to a large agency, in town," she whispered.

"You can go now, and I'll call you later."

She nodded obediently, taking care to turn her head away from the corpse, and went down the ladder.

Balilty's harangue about his hurt feelings echoed in the space enclosed by the tile roof. It was possible to stand upright only in the center of the attic; any step away from the center meant having to hang your head so it would not bump into the sloped ceiling. Motes of dust floated in the beam cast by the spotlight, one of the three that the Forensics people had positioned in the corners of the attic to illuminate the scene and the corpse lying there. Balilty gave Michael respite only in those moments when something attracted his attention. Then he would come back and stand beside him and mutter sentences like the one he was uttering now: "People go and buy houses! You see, here's a case. This woman bought a house and found a corpse."

"Are you done?" the pathologist asked Alon from Forensics.

Alon nodded. "I've just finished photographing," he said, and laid the camera very gently between his feet.

Dr. Solomon tried to stretch the woman's legs. Even when they were folded beneath her, in shiny stockings with gold threads that gleamed in the beam of the spotlight, it was possible to see how long and shapely they were. She lay on the dusty concrete surface in a close-fitting gray woolen dress, in the pose of a film actress asked to play dead. In the smooth black hair that covered her head like a dark halo shone ends dipped in blood, and it was easy to imagine that the pulp of the face was only the sophisticated makeup of a horror film. The beams of the spotlights directed straight at the crime scene sharpened and reinforced the shadows, which gave the water tanks the look of primeval monsters.

"You know her," said Balilty. It was both a question and a statement. He nodded his head in the direction of the ground floor, where Ada Efrati was waiting.

"We went to high school together," Michael replied quickly, before Balilty could ask whether he had "something going with her too."

"Did you have something going with her too?" asked Balilty.

"Don't talk nonsense," said Michael sharply.

"Okay, so don't tell. Who's talking nonsense?" protested Balilty with a kind of crooked smile. "There aren't any women left in this city anymore who haven't gone down on their knees to you. They say that you're . . . you know, they talk about your eyes and all that. I could see the way she was looking at you. And also that real estate agent who—"

"Enough already," said Michael with a wave of his arm.

"Who found the house for you? Her?" Balilty gestured with his head at the ladder Linda O'Brian had descended, and laid his hand on the yellow tape that surrounded the scene.

Michael did not reply.

"I don't know about her. What is she? She looks completely cuckoo. Is she a serious person? Like that? With that nightgown she goes around in? Is she listed in the Board of Realtors?"

Michael nodded and rolled the menthol cigarette between his fingers. "She just looks that way . . . and it's not a nightgown. And anyway, it's irrelevant. She's a real estate agent who specializes in this neighborhood," and he immediately reprimanded himself for attempting to convince Balilty of her bona fides. And to go into details about the way she dressed? What did he care what Balilty thought?

Balilty gave a derisive snort. "Don't you know that all real estate agents are crooks?" he demanded. "Do you call that work? Anyone could do it. Couldn't I sell a house to someone? It's, like they say in Yiddish, *luftgescheft*. Just think how much money they make, from something you were too lazy to find out for yourself."

Michael leaned forward, the better to follow the movements of Alon, who was now holding the dead woman's rigid palm in his left hand— even from a distance it was obvious that rigor mortis had set in—while with his right he dug with delicate tweezers under the long red fingernails. One might have thought that a skirt chaser like Balilty would be concentrating on the shapely body inside the gray woolen dress, and the shiny, long black-red hair spread around her like a train, and the pulp of the face, and would suggest all kinds of hypotheses about beauty that had been destroyed. But Balilty did not pause in his tirade (though the moment after he saw the body he had said: "Some chick! Wow, what a body! What would you give her—twenty-five?" and Dr. Solomon had shrugged and remarked, to the same tune he had been humming throughout the examination, "There was some work here on the nose, and she has dieted a lot.").

"Did you win the lottery or something? What got into you? What's so urgent—have you come into an inheritance? What does Yuval say about it? Have you even shown it to him? Let me understand—have you gone completely crazy?" demanded Balilty.

"I showed it to him. Of course I showed it to him, but he isn't going to live here—he moved to Tel Aviv. What are you worried about? It'll be all right," Michael said in a tense, low voice, and looked down, at Ada Efrati—in his mind she was still Ada Levi—who was now standing at the bottom of the ladder. With a tanned and slender long-fingered hand, she pushed aside a lock of her short, dark hair, which was threaded with gray. The beam of the spotlight under which she was standing wrapped her face in a cloud of webs. She was still standing beside the architect.

"You see," chided Balilty, "tomorrow morning they had planned to start renovating, and now their whole timetable has been disrupted. You see, you mustn't plan anything around things like that."

The architect climbed the ladder, and halfway up she stopped and cleared her throat as if waiting for her turn to talk to Michael, who was watching her ascent. Repeatedly, she tried to attract their attention, until Balilty shut up for a moment. "Excuse me," she said in a thin, shaking voice. "Are you Chief Superintendent Ohayon?"

Michael nodded.

"They told me that you're . . . that you're in charge of the . . ."

Michael nodded.

"Forgive me for bothering you with our problems. I know this isn't the time and place, but a lot of people are depending on this and I have to . . . There's the matter of a schedule here . . . We had intended to start the renovations tomorrow morning, and I have to know . . . approximately . . . what to tell the contractor. We still have to . . . Never mind. Would it be possible to know when, more or less . . . that is, not definitely . . . how much time it will take until we can . . ." She cleared her throat again. "Are you, um, going to close the house up? How much time will it take before we can start to work? That is, would it be a matter of days, or weeks, or months?"

Michael took a drag of his cigarette and looked over at Dr. Solomon and at Yaffa from Forensics, whose ponytail cascaded down her back as she knelt on the floor and felt the rough, dirty concrete with her hands, searching for some small, invisible object. The fading daylight was not penetrating the cracks between the roof tiles, and Michael had not allowed Balilty to break even one of them to let in more illumination, in case the rain came in and destroyed evidence. "Wait until it's absolutely necessary," he had ordered.

"I already told the contractor that everything would be delayed in the meantime," the architect explained, "and of course Ada also understands this, but we do need to have some idea, because we can't keep the people on like this. This is a pretty big job."

"There you go," said Balilty victoriously. "Now you see what renovations are. You have no idea what you're getting into." He turned to the architect: "Are they all Arabs, the workers?"

"The contractor is from Beit Jalla," she replied, "but I always work with him."

"Always," grumbled Balilty. "'Always' doesn't apply anymore. We've seen their true face. They fire on Gilo, slaughter people . . . In any case they won't be able to get to work because of the closures . . ."

"I even worked with him during the intifada," she protested limply.

"That intifada was Disneyland compared to this," said Balilty dismissively. "You shouldn't work with Arabs. It would be better if you brought Romanians."

"Drop it now, Danny," said Michael. "There are more urgent things right now." And to the diminutive architect, who was hugging her skinny body as if to conceal the trembling she could not control, he said: "I will be able to give you an estimate only after everyone's finished here. Not before tomorrow morning." She nodded, and with small steps retreated back down the ladder.

But Balilty did not let go: "I know this building. Not this one," he hastened to say, indicating his surroundings. "I mean the one that you want, the one you've supposedly bought . . . I've known that street ever since I was born . . . When we were little, my grandmother lived in the new housing projects in Baka, on Bethlehem Road. We used to go there—it's not far. Lots of times we played in the yard behind the building, over there . . ."

Michael, who was not looking at Balilty's face, suddenly heard a new tone that concealed a smile, and because of that he turned toward him.

"I played doctor and patient there, with this girl . . . What's 'er name. I don't even want to say her name out loud. Today she's a very important woman, in the Prosecutor's Office . . . We know her, so do you. Today she's called Aster," he blurted derisively, "but then they just called her Estie. And I'm sure that she remembers very well, and is just pretending . . . Okay, so she's really become a celebrity. Do you know her? Do you know who I'm talking about?"

Michael nodded slightly, in limp acknowledgment.

"There, in the basement of the building. It's the corner building, isn't it? Between Yiftah Street and Bethlehem Road, right? So there," continued Balilty, "there's where we played doctor and patient, and that was the first time I'd ever seen . . . Never mind . . . I'm telling you, I know that building. You can't move in without renovating—electricity, pipes, floor tiles. You have to knock down walls, change windows—the renovations alone will cost you a bundle. How much did you settle for?"

In front of them, in the middle of the attic, the pathologist was watching his intern, and in an authoritative voice that had dropped the tune he said to him: "Write it down, write it down just to make sure, even before the autopsy. I don't trust this device." He glanced at the little microphone hanging around his neck and immediately continued to speak: "A fracture in the back of the neck, in the second vertebra . . . bruises on the neck . . . apparent strangling . . ." Again he looked at the intern, who wiped his hands on the side of his pants and put an open notebook down on one of the water tanks and wrote.

Michael bent down and examined one of the plastic bags into which Alon had put her pointy-toed gray shoes. He touched the edges of their narrow high heels and peeked inside them, feeling the inner sole, where, though blurred, the manufacturer's label was legible.

"This is an expensive Italian shoe," said Alon from Forensics. "It's all leather, even the outer sole, and this dress, it's not just any old dress. From what I can see it's good wool. I just don't understand," he said, looking at Balilty, his immediate superior, "how a girl like this, with shoes like these and a dress like that, climbed up into a place like this." He indicated the opening in the ceiling and the ladder that was leaning on its rim. "Was she holding her shoes in her hand? How did she lift her legs to reach the rungs of the ladder?"

"*Nu,*" said Balilty. "It's not such a big mystery. For this you don't need a doctorate in chemistry. You hold the dress like this"—with both his hands he rolled up an imaginary dress and tucked its hem into the waistband of his trousers—"and you hold the shoes here"—he indicated his armpits—"or you give them to someone to hold for you. Have you forgotten that she wasn't alone here?"

"She has a run in her stocking," noted Alon.

"It's a big hole, not a run," corrected Yaffa, who was still kneeling on the other side of the body. "It had to have happened here. Someone like this, with a dress like this and shoes like these, wouldn't go around in public for half a minute with a hole like that in her stocking. She would have died of embarrassment." Yaffa suppressed a sly smile and hastened to blur the impact of her remark: "The stockings, too. They must have cost at least forty-five shekels. Not cheap."

"Yaffa," Michael said, and moved closer to her. "Tell me, Yaffa, in your opinion, is it possible that she wasn't carrying a purse? With a dress and shoes like that, no wallet?"

"Unthinkable," shot back Yaffa without pausing to think. "In the pocket of her coat, here"—she indicated a small plastic bag—"there was a tissue and a piece of an ATM slip. I tried to identify it, but you can only see yesterday's date and the hour. Look," she said as she removed the tape and a tiny piece of paper from the plastic bag with her gloved fingers. "Don't touch it yet," she warned, and pulled back her hand. "You aren't wearing gloves, and there's no sign of the account number or the name."

Michael, who in any case had not intended to touch it, didn't say anything.

"And there's also no sum and no bank branch or anything, just the date and the time—ten P.M., so we already know A, she was still alive at ten, and B, she had some cash on her. So where's the money? Where's that lipstick she has on?" She glanced at what had once been a face. "It's certain that she had a lipstick and a comb and makeup and even perfume. There's no question—a woman like that doesn't go out without her purse."

"The ATM slip doesn't necessarily have to be hers—there's just a date, and it could be that it wasn't she who withdrew money, but someone else," suggested Alon, "and it could be that the person who was with her took the money."

"Not just the money, but the whole purse. It's a sure thing that she had a handbag. It's a sure thing it was gray like the shoes," said Yaffa, and to his astonishment Michael heard the hint of envy that had slipped into her voice. "Just her coat alone—it's pure silk and brocade. Look at this. If she had a coat like this . . ." Her voice faded as she smoothed the brocade collar and ran her finger around the petals embroidered on the glossy fabric. "It's a lightweight coat, and it's definitely not from here," she said as she fingered the label. "Look. 'Made in France.' Not from Taiwan, from Paris. What did I tell you?" Softly she folded the coat into the large bag she had spread on the concrete floor. "Even the lining is pure silk, and this is how she threw it on the floor . . . Maybe she was even lying on it at the beginning"—she sighed—"and maybe he was the one who threw it down there. He, what does he care about a coat, if he doesn't care about a person's life?"

"Maybe we'll find the purse tossed away somewhere, maybe even up here," Michael indicated a circle in the dark space. "We'll have to do a search all around here. And also downstairs and in the yard, because she must live somewhere."

"What do you mean?" asked Alon. "Of course she lives somewhere."

"I'll tell you what he means." Balilty twisted his thick lips. "Keys. The boss is talking about keys. Does a person leave home without keys? To the car, to the house, to the office, God knows what. Everyone has keys. Were there keys in the coat pocket?"

"No," said Alon, "but maybe the person she was with has them. Maybe they live together."

"Tell me," said Balilty with evident impatience, "how long have you been working for us?"

"A month. Why?" Alon's Adam's apple bobbed up and down his long thin throat.

"So they haven't taught you to think yet?"

Alon was silent, and Michael looked at Balilty and said to him: "Enough, Danny. That's enough, okay?" But Balilty continued to examine the fellow from Forensics who was shifting his weight from one foot to the other, and it was clear that he had absolutely no intention of stopping.

"Because," he drawled, "I'm wondering how you see it. People who live together, what would they be doing in a hole like this? A woman like that on dirty concrete like this? What would she be doing here if she had a house to be in?"

The prominent Adam's apple in Alon's throat rode up and down, and he lowered his eyes. "I don't know," he said in a barely audible voice. "I don't have much experience, but I've heard that people like . . . variety, and Dr. Solomon thinks that before he . . . that they . . . fu . . . that there was a quickie here. He doesn't know for sure yet, but it looks that way, so maybe they came for a change of scenery."

"Can you say whether she was alive when she got here, or that she was strangled first and then dragged up here?" Michael asked the pathologist.

"I think she was completely alive here," said Solomon, "but I'll be able to tell you definitely only . . ."

"Okay, okay," soothed Michael. "I won't make you commit yourself."

"Tell me," said Balilty to Alon from Forensics. "Are you crazy? Is this a place they would come to for a change of scenery for fucking? Does this look like a romantic place to you? With all the . . ."—he took in the musty air with a wave of his arm—"all the water tanks from the year one, with the dust and the spiderwebs and the dead pigeons? For that they would take a hotel room or something. They'd come to this place only if there were no alternative or if they had to go into really deep hiding."

"These aren't ordinary people," pleaded Alon. "You're already dealing with a strangler. He smashed her face. He's a pervert, isn't he?"

"To strangle someone and smash her face in is one thing, and to fuck is another thing," said Balilty. "And only one person does the strangling, and the other comes here with all her Italian shoes and her cashmere and her silk, right?"

Alon was silent for a moment, then suddenly said: "And with Poison."

"What's that?" asked Balilty, confused.

"Perfume. Very fashionable," explained Alon. "You can still smell it. I can."

"Okay, so you have a sense of smell. But they didn't live together, that's for sure," said Balilty. "Maybe we need more manpower to make a search here. There has to be a purse. With keys and lipstick and everything. Let's just pray he didn't take it with him. In my opinion this whole thing could be connected to the security situation . . ."

"You think there was an Arab . . . ?" asked Alon.

"I say this: There's a tense situation now, right? Never mind tense, there's a war on, right? So we have to take into account that—"

"I've noticed, in fact, that there have been fewer break-ins and murders recently. Since this whole mess began there have hardly been any complaints about break-ins . . . ," insisted Alon.

"*Nu*, it's hard to work like this, with squad cars at every corner. That's why there are fewer burglaries," dismissed Balilty.

"That's exactly what I'm saying," said Alon.

"But one or two can get through, especially if there are Arabs here doing renovations," Balilty said, and looked down the opening at the ground floor. "Where's that contractor? I want to talk to him."

"He's waiting outside, in his car. The boss said it was okay if he waited for—" Alon said.

"So let him wait. Because he isn't leaving here before I clear up a few points with him."

"Yair is on his way here. He'll be here any minute," noted Michael.

Balilty was annoyed. "What's Yair?" he demanded. "Some kind of Buddha? I don't have the patience for his serenity. Where, oh where, is Eli Bachar?"

"On vacation. Don't you remember? You told them to go to Turkey, so they listened to you and went. They're coming back tonight," replied Michael, crushing the cigarette butt with the heel of his shoe.

"So we've decided that it's a man?" asked Yaffa.

"Why, who would she fuck with? With a woman?" said Balilty derisively. "With a woman it doesn't leave traces." He roared with swift laughter and cut it off with the question: "Didn't you hear Solomon talk about a fuck?"

"It is not certain that there was sexual contact," said the pathologist, who had approached the top of the ladder with the brown leather valise. "For now, it's just an intuition. Only in the laboratory, with a smear, will we be able—"

"Okay, okay." Balilty flung up his arms in a gesture of submission. From the small tin box he held in his right hand he took out a cigarillo and tapped its end. "Tomorrow all of us will be the wiser."

"Even if someone took her wallet or her purse from here," said Michael Ohayon, "we'll find it in the end. No one would take a thing like that home. Anyone who doesn't want to incriminate himself throws things like that away or hides them, and doesn't keep them at home."

"There's always a first time," warbled Solomon, who had already begun to gather his implements into the leather case.

"You won't find anything if they took it home to Beit Jalla or Beit Sahur," said Balilty decisively. He turned to the pathologist and said: "So what do you say?"

"I can't swear to it," said the doctor as he shut the leather valise, "but it looks to me like she's been here maybe since yesterday, but late at night. I don't think it was any earlier than that. And you're also saying that there's this slip from an ATM from ten o'clock last night, so it couldn't have been before then. But we'll be wiser tomorrow, after the autopsy at the Institute. I'm telling you, this is just from what I can see, gut feeling and experience, and because of the rigor mortis." He addressed Michael as if Balilty weren't there, and Michael recalled how the two had been at loggerheads in the case of the cabdriver who was found with his throat slit next to his vehicle. It turned out that it was the pathologist who was mistaken then, but now Balilty, who usually preferred to act as if he didn't hold a grudge, completely ignored the way the pathologist was ignoring him and asked: "Strangulation? Is that final? With this delicate rag?" He pointed to the red silk scarf that Yaffa had deposited in a plastic bag. "This would have torn in a minute, wouldn't it?"

The doctor shrugged. "That's the way it looks now, strangulation, but maybe not with this rag, as you call it, but with two hands over the scarf, without touching the skin directly. There are some bruises on the neck—you'll see the photographs." He placed his foot on the first rung of the ladder.

"There are two things I want to know," said Balilty. "First of all, how did they get in here in the first place, and secondly, what did he crush her face with? With a blunt instrument?" There was scorn in his voice as he enunciated the cliché that gives absolution for the need to be precise about a murder weapon.

"How can I tell now, without an autopsy? We'll find traces on her skin and we'll tell you. Did you find any instrument here that crushes faces?" replied the pathologist crossly. "It would help us if you did find it. That's something he didn't take home, whatever it was."

"We'll find it," promised Balilty "If necessary, we'll find it. And how did they get in here?"

"A few years ago there was an office here," pondered Michael, "high-tech or something. Most probably keys were floating around everywhere. It's your job to find out who had a key," he said to Balilty.

"Who's going to take the valise down for me?" asked the pathologist. "Vlodya is already downstairs, and I'm not sixteen anymore," he added joylessly. "For me it's a major project to climb down like that—and they're also going to have a problem with the body. How are they going to get it out of here?"

"We've already moved more complicated things," said Balilty. He lit the thin cigar and sent up a thick, gray cloud of smoke from it.

"I need her in one piece," warned the pathologist, "if you want all kinds of answers to all kinds of questions."

Alon approached the top of the ladder, holding the brown valise by its handle. Solomon, who still had gloves on, held on to the sides of the ladder. "You'll be at the autopsy," he said. It was both a question and a statement of fact, and Michael Ohayon nodded affirmatively.

"When will you get there?" asked Solomon. His foot was already on the third rung. "When they get her out of here," promised Michael. "This is going to take a bit more time."

"So I'm going home to sleep," warned the pathologist. "I need a few hours of sleep a night, and tonight I'm not going to get any. I'm not a youngster anymore. Let me know when you leave here. I'll be waiting for you there."

"Can you already say more or less when you'll know the details? How long will it take for you to finish there?" Balilty called out to Dr. Solomon on his way down the ladder. Without waiting for a reply, Balilty turned to Michael to scold him again about the apartment, and again the amazement was heard in his voice: "Even God consults. Read the Bible and you'll see—even God," and he waved his hands at the roof tiles.

"Sure God consults. Where? In the Book of Job? And did you notice who he consults? And did you see what came of it?"

"Don't change the subject. We're not discussing the Bible now, and you don't do a thing like that on your own," hectored Danny Balilty. "Did you sign? Just tell me if you've signed any papers. Did you give them any down payment?"

Before he got an answer to his question he was diverted by Alon, who for the past few minutes had been bending and searching among the water tanks. "I've found it!" he cried. "Here, inside the water tank! I checked the tanks one by one and suddenly . . ." From the large water tank inside which his head was hidden, he pulled out a broken board, and Balilty's mutterings stopped at once.

"I think this is it," Alon said, and moved toward the spotlight, holding the board in both hands and examining it closely. "There are stains, but we'll only know when we get this to the lab whether it's blood and whether it's her blood and all that . . ."

"Of course it's blood, and not so old," said Balilty, who had moved to take a look at the dark board with Michael, thus releasing him from the obligation of admitting in a noncommittal way that indeed he had signed a memorandum of intent, though he had been warned that such a signature had the validity of signing a real contract. After admitting a thing like that, there would have been no point in reminding Balilty of his own impetuousness: Balility suffered from it only in his relationships with women, never in money matters.

Alon was wrapping the board in plastic sheeting pulled from the roll on the concrete floor when Balility started to speak again: "I told you: I know that building, and not just from my childhood. And I know about all kinds of complications, if you don't check with a lawyer and the Land Registry. Look, not long ago I told you about the case of my Sigi's boyfriend. His parents were looking for an apartment and they found one and signed, and then it turned out that the mother there was still alive and only the father had died and there were troubles with the inheritance and the probate. They put it up for sale after the father died, but the mother has Alzheimer's and she could easily live for another ten years and no lawyer will be able to get it registered in their name at the Land Registry and they've already paid a third and now they're stuck. Did you know that?"

Michael nodded, but Balility ignored this. "You've signed and you've also given them a down payment? How much did you give them?" And without waiting for a reply he said angrily: "What's got into you, and who have you spoken to, anyway? With her?" he nodded in the direction of the ladder that Linda had descended a while ago, and his nod was accompanied by a derisive snort and a cloud of gray smoke. "That woman? She'd never tell you things like that. She has her own interests, that one. As far as she's concerned, you just buy it and she gets her percentage and then you can bang your head against the wall, and until they put it in the Land Registry the worms will have eaten you."

"In fact, she did tell me about all kinds of difficulties and even warned me about complications, and we checked everything at the Land Registry," said Michael.

The corpse with the smashed face and the red scarf wound around its neck, and the way he was standing there next to the spot where she had been murdered, spared him for a moment the necessity of explaining why he was acting out of character—he, who for many long years had never contemplated the possibility that he might have a home of his own. He had ignored all the pressures applied to him by the people closest to him and his friends—and Balility was among the most forceful of them—and he had never considered moving out of his rented apartment and getting himself "out of all this already" (in the words of Balility, who had several times dared to mention the woman upstairs, saying that every time Michael went up or down the stairs he expected to hear her door opening and then her voice calling him back). And when the pressures increased—Yvette, Michael's older sister, who couldn't stand his rented apartment anymore, had sent his friend and commander Shorer to talk to him—he insisted that the location and shape of places to live were external matters and unimportant, and in any case he never spent much time at home. ("Look at the kind of person you are," Emmanuel Shorer had said to him. Shorer felt himself responsible for him and for directing his life, not as a father, but as a big brother or a close uncle, because he was the one who had brought Michael into the police force. "You always come up with theories that suit the conditions and justify them," and Michael ended the discussion with silence or with the excuse that he didn't have enough money and strength, and certainly not for an apartment he would really want.)

Were it not for Alon from Forensics, and were it not for Yaffa, who now stretched her arm under one of the water tanks, Balilty would not have let him alone, and finally he would have been dragged into answering and telling him about the family council that convened at the beginning of the summer, and the way all his brothers and sisters rallied, and their decision to ignore all his refusals ("He can't move into another rented apartment in one of those projects in those new neighborhoods," said Yvette, the eldest, who moderated the discussion. "Ever since he got divorced—How long ago was it? Twenty years ago?—he lives like a gypsy. What is he, a student? He's not a little kid anymore"). They had put together, jointly, each of them according to what he or she could afford, half of the sum needed for an apartment that would suit him.

Until now, he hadn't shared his thoughts about retiring with Balilty. He hadn't yet explained to him that a revolutionary step like buying an apartment was also connected to the possibility that he might be spending more time at home, and maybe he would even conduct his investigations from there, if he followed his own hankering and the urgings of Eli Bachar, his veteran assistant, who wanted the two of them to start their own private investigations firm.

But the explanation to Balilty could be postponed, he thought morosely: There are people who get insulted if you don't accept their opinion. He did not hold a grudge against Balilty, whose vulgarity and irritability had been exacerbated by the dieting regime he had finally imposed on himself, after he'd experienced symptoms of a heart attack.

Until the doctor had warned him that his insurance premiums would go up, he could not give up the stuffed vegetable and meat delicacies in which he especially delighted late at night, and now he had distanced himself from them and had devoted himself to exercise and to "rabbit food"—peeled carrots and washed lettuce leaves that made him sigh every time they passed near the market, where he used to relish, even late at night, a skewer of cow's udder or stuffed spleen.

For a long time they stood silently by the corpse and watched Alon carefully put the contents of the coat pocket into small plastic bags, which he sealed and wrote on with a purple marker.

"Who knows what else there is in those water tanks," muttered Balilty. "For years they've been standing here. So, you've bought an apartment? That's it? It's final?" He returned to his crossness and Michael nodded and turned to look behind the water tanks, in case a wallet or a purse with something that would identify the corpse was there after all.

"What do you mean you bought an apartment?" Balilty burst out again. "What sort of thing is it to buy an apartment just like that? Did you check it out? Did you ask? Has anyone even seen it? Even if he lives in Tel Aviv you could consult him. He's not a child anymore, your son. Why didn't you come to me? You know I know about these things. Why didn't—"

Michael sighed. "Later, Danny. We'll talk about it later," he promised. "Now we have a job to do here, don't we?"

"If we hadn't come to have a look before the renovations, this body would have rotted here for another month," said the architect suddenly. She was standing beneath them, at the bottom of the ladder. "It was only because of Ada, who's a thorough person and wanted to see the space again, before they break through the ceiling once and for all. If it weren't for that, we wouldn't have found her so quickly."

Michael went down to the bottom floor. "Do you have any idea who she is?" he asked the architect, who shook her head.

"How? Without a face?" She trembled and turned her face toward the ladder. "And they haven't got a clue either," she added, gesturing toward Ada and the contractor. The two of them were whispering together in the corner of the room, into which large sacks of sand had already been brought. "This apartment has been empty for years," explained the architect. "There were problems with the transfer of ownership and squabbles between heirs, and all kinds of drug addicts hung around in the yard."

Balilty went quickly down the ladder. "Tell me," he said to the architect in a threatening tone, and Michael, who knew what was coming, tried to calm him down with his hand. "Can you explain how a person buys a house in this neighborhood, half of which is abandoned property and the other half—"

But something interrupted him, and it wasn't Michael; loud and clear from the entrance to the apartment came the voice of Sergeant Yair ("Where is it?" he asked), whom Balilty called the "bucolic Buddha" because of his serene temperament, and sometimes "the farmer" because of the examples from the world of agriculture that he would add to his explanations. Eli Bachar, who had reluctantly brought Yair into his most recent cases, called him "Miss Marple" because of his stories from the moshav, the cooperative village where he was born.

"Where are you?" Yair now called. "Downstairs they told me upstairs but I don't see any upstairs here and there isn't any electricity."

"Look up," Balilty snorted, and stuck his head into the rectangle that had been torn into the ceiling between the ground floor and the roof. "Up here it's illuminated like a basketball court. Usually your head's in the clouds, isn't it? But be careful when you come up, so you won't scare her away."

"You want me to climb up that ladder?" asked the sergeant, moving toward them.

"Like ivy," replied Balilty, and even in the dimness it was obvious how much pleasure this retort gave him.

Michael glanced at the renovations contractor, who was standing by the large window overlooking Bethlehem Road. He was stroking his short beard and sneaking glances around him. He had never seen her in his life, he said in English. He had returned here only a few months ago after years of living in the United States.

"Do you still need us here now?" asked Ada Efrati. Her voice sounded lower than he remembered.

"Yes," said Michael after thinking a moment. "I think you should come with us to make a statement right now. Also about the keys—who had keys and who didn't, because they didn't break in here. They opened the door with a key."

The renovations contractor retreated backwards.

The architect, who was looking at the contractor, went up to him and touched his arm. "Does he also have to come?" she asked.

"He most certainly does!" said Balilty.

"But he doesn't have anything to with—," tried the architect.

"But he does, he most certainly does," said Balilty, pursing his lips. He turned to the contractor and said something quickly to him in Arabic.

"What did he say?" whispered the architect.

"He's taking him in the squad car," explained Michael.

"So he's also taking us in the squad car," declared Ada Efrati. "He's with us, we're together. Don't you have anything to say about this?" she demanded of Michael.

"I'll come after you in my car. I've got a few more things to do here," he said, without looking at her.

"Leave your vehicles here," ordered Balilty, and they proceeded down the long corridor to the front door.

"Are you saying you have no idea who she is?" ascertained Balilty.

"I told you," burst out Ada Efrati. "I've never . . . And with that smashed-up face . . . Even if I had happened to see her once by chance, how could I . . . No, I really don't know."

"I need all your phone numbers, and also his," said Balilty, gesturing toward the contractor with his eyebrows. "Was anyone here planning to go abroad for the holidays?"

"No one here is going anywhere," declared Ada Efrati. "These aren't times for trips abroad."

"Are you trying to say that everyone has stopped living because of the new intifada?" Balilty gave a challenging look to the contractor. "If that's the case then we can close down the shop, if we live by the situation, isn't that right? Are you from Beit Jalla?" He turned to the contractor.

"Beit Jalla," he affirmed.

"I live in Gilo. Maybe it was from your house that they sniped at our neighborhood. Huh?"

"Leave that to the army and the border police," Ada Efrati said, and laid her fingers on the contractor's arm, as if trying to protect him.

"Those leftists," snorted Balilty as they went out. "They spit on them, they get wet and they say it's raining."

Chapter 2

D r. Solomon wiped his hands on his gown and stretched the rubber
gloves over them. *"I'm dressing in your honor, see? In your honor I've
put a new long gown on me,"* he warbled in the direction of Sergeant
Yair, and pulled the cuffs of the gloves up his forearms. Then he went
over to the gleaming table where the body had been placed and touched
the raised head, the hair spread over the stainless steel headrest. On the
smooth surface, which glittered in the metallic light, the mane of hair
surrounding the skull looked like the silken tassels of a black scarf inter-
woven with threads of red. Without pausing, he peeked into the crushed
mouth and then raised his head and said: "A few teeth have remained
whole—we've taken a print, and of the gums as well. There are two fillings in the wisdom teeth. Who puts fillings in wisdom teeth nowadays?"

He went silent and held his hand out to his assistant, who wiped his
brow, which shone in the blue neon light, and handed him the scalpel. Its
long, sharp blade glittered as it was placed on the metal shelf, to the right
of the raised head, in synchronization with the notes of the Hasidic tune
the pathologist was humming to himself. Even when the pathologist
swiftly rolled up the white sheet to reveal the naked corpse—the yellowish grayness looked like a kind of scum that disfigured the tawny skin of
the living woman—and even when he scolded Yair and the others for
their tardiness, he did so in the melody of a yeshiva student arguing a
Talmudic question. Now, as he began the incision along the width of the
brow, very close to the frame of hair, he stopped humming and was
silent.

"It wasn't our fault," explained Sergeant Yair when they arrived, following instructions from Michael. "It was the American Powell and the day
before the holiday. We were stuck at the exit from Jerusalem, stuck like—"

"The eve of the holiday isn't until tomorrow. Trust the Jews—they begin a holiday on the eve of the eve of the holiday. Because of you I slept only three hours. Why didn't you sound your siren? Also because of the eve of the holiday? What are you police for? I thought the police force was above holidays. Isn't the police force above everything?" He continued to address all these questions to the crushed head of the corpse, whose mouth remained wide open.

"Even sounding the siren wouldn't have helped. Gridlock, I tell you, really gridlock," Yair explained as he fixed his eyes on the blue edges of the white sheet that Solomon was rolling up. Along its edges were written the words "Ministry of Health—The Forensic Institute." "You can't drive through there as if you were an ambulance. We had to help them clear the road, no?" There was no embarrassment evident in Yair's voice because of this excuse, the obvious feebleness of which he had pointed out on the way to the Institute.

"Not if I'm waiting for you," Solomon answered, and glanced at Michael, who was continuing to look at the smashed face, at the neck and the belly, and was trying not to avert his eyes from the narrow waist and the curve of the hips and the dark tangle of pubic hair. He preferred not to apologize to Solomon, whose yellow-brown eyes glistened cold and cunning and cruel through the thick lenses of his horn-rimmed glasses. Michael preferred leaving the job of conciliation to the young sergeant, whose simplicity and frankness vaporized even Solomon's acrimony. He gazed distractedly at the blue bruises on the stiff thighs, at the toenails that had been lacquered bright red, his mind troubled by the confrontation with Balility. He heard Yair say: "You can't imagine how many cars we saw there, one on top of the other, and two traffic policewomen who were simply incapable . . . Just to get a bit of order there took me twenty minutes, and there wasn't enough personnel and—"

"The main thing is that you're here," muttered Solomon, and after he had tossed the white sheet far from the operating table, he spread his arms and with a half-bow he said: "Voilà."

Sergeant Yair, who was standing very close to Michael, looked at the corpse. From head to foot he looked at it, then mumbled: "Isn't it a waste of all that beauty?"

"*Isn't it a pity, the loss of something pretty,*" chimed Solomon, "and why aren't you wearing gloves?" With two fingers he adjusted his thick horn-rimmed glasses, and then with his arm he rubbed the hooked chin that gave his profile the look of an old witch and with his right hand he fin-gered the surgeon's mask that drooped around his neck.

"I . . . I didn't think that . . . I don't intend . . . I don't need to touch anything," replied Yair suspiciously.

"You never know," said Solomon, with an amused glint in his eyes at the sight of the scared expression on the young sergeant's face. He pulled the mask up onto his face and nodded to the assistant who was standing at his side, his body taut in the green gown, and then strode quickly to the corner of the room. The door of the tall steel cabinet groaned and creaked under his hand as he opened it, and he rummaged among the shelves and came back with two pairs of latex gloves and two white masks. Without a word he handed them to Sergeant Yair and Michael.

"You're new here," commented Solomon after he glanced at Yair. "Where's Eli Bachar? I miss his pale cheeks. How pale he went the last time he was here—and Balilty?" he said, and snorted. "Our terrible macho man who is even afraid to come in here." He pressed the button on the recording device, and after he checked the microphone that dan-gled from his neck, he quietly stated the date and described the body prior to the autopsy.

It was in the silence that now prevailed, as the pathologist passed the knife along the forehead, that Michael allowed himself to feel how annoyed he was by the melodious humming that had become one of Solomon's trademarks ("For this he became a pathologist?" Balilty once complained. Balilty usually explained his absence from the autopsy as being caused by both a terrible headache and this annoying humming. "Even the dead don't stop him from singing. This one even sings when he eats. He should have been a cantor."). Michael, who was now listening to the sound of the blade and the sounds of the recording device, which the intern had switched on the moment the scalpel touched the bluish, dark skin, thought that the humming was aimed at distracting attention from the tic that every few seconds distorted the left side of the elderly pathologist's face from the corner of his mouth to his eye, which would shut tight and then open again at brief intervals. Now he cut behind the scalp, and with a single motion pulled away the skin of the scalp with the cascades of hair. "You see, I'm not detaching it entirely," he commented to Sergeant Yair. "It remains attached, and then we'll put it back."

"Yes, yes," the intern hastened to say, as if this were directed at him, and in a heavy Russian accent, which was not muffled by the mask, he added: "This I have already seen more than once."

"Take the magnifying glass out of my jacket pocket, and the tweezers," said Solomon sharply, and the assistant hastened to where the pathologist's jacket was hanging next to the steel cabinet. He took a magnifying glass out of a pocket and then he rummaged among the implements on the tray and held out a delicate forceps. "There's no tweezers, just this," he said in alarm. "That's fine," the pathologist replied, and leaned over the pulp of the face. "Here," he cried, and waved the forceps. "Didn't I tell Balilty that I would find it before you? Did I or didn't I?"

The repeated mention of Balilty's name annoyed Michael. His conflict with the intelligence officer was still echoing in his mind. Balilty was in fact the reason they were late for the autopsy. When he'd arrived with Sergeant Yair at Jerusalem police headquarters in the Russian Compound, after he had supervised the removal of the body from the roof space, Ada Efrati was waiting for him at the entrance to the building. "Have you already given a statement?" he asked her.

She shook her head in negation. "I waited for you," she said in a trembling voice.

"But for that you don't need me. Anyone can . . . ," he said in astonishment.

"I," said Ada Efrati, shaking her head, "am not speaking to that Balilty. I simply don't want to see that creature, and not his assistant, either. And no one is going to make me." Her voice grew sharp and she was obviously angry when she said: "For years I've been hearing that this is the way things are conducted here, but I didn't believe it."

Michael looked at her with concern, trying to control his breathing, which had accelerated. "What happened? Maybe you'll explain to me what happened?"

"He," she said in a strangled voice, "he took him into a room downstairs and we didn't want him to take him alone and . . ."

"Take it slowly," said Michael. "Who? Who took whom?"

"That creature, Balilty, with another fellow he said was his assistant, took Imad to a room downstairs and—"

"Imad? The contractor from Beit Jalla?"

"Imad Abu Salah, just because he's a Palestinian. They took him to a room downstairs. Shoshi the architect and I went with them. She stayed downstairs and I waited for you here because—"

"What do mean 'downstairs'?"

"I don't know. I just know that he separated us from him and told us to wait upstairs but we went down anyway. That Balilty person came out of the room after three minutes, and his assistant two minutes later, and Imad stayed there in the room, with the door shut. And an hour later—we were standing by the door, in the corridor—nothing had happened. I try to open the door—and it's locked. They locked him in like that, for an hour, without saying anything . . . And Imad is just like me—he was there by chance. And I just opened the door. That is, I tried but it was locked, and I spoke to him through the door and he said that they had gone to check his papers and his situation with the income tax people and whether he had paid value-added tax and so on, and whether there was anyone in his family who had been convicted or suspected of membership in Hamas or hostile activity. Do you understand? A person comes to testify that he found a body in a house before renovations, and those are the things they ask him! They're just giving him a hard time, for no reason. So I left Shoshi by the door and I came to wait for you and—"

"Wait for me inside," Michael said, and led her quickly to the bottom floor. The architect stood there in the faint glow of the corridor lightbulb, pale and trembling, and looked at him as he tried to open the door to the room that during his first years on the police force had been his office.

"It's locked," she whispered. "You can only hear."

Michael knocked on the door and called to Balilty. Total silence prevailed behind the door. After a long moment, it opened and Balilty came out quickly and closed the door and stood in front of it. "Excuse me," Michael said, and moved him aside with a swift movement—Balilty obeyed, silenced by surprise—and went in.

A young policeman with freckles and red cheeks stood over the contractor, who was sitting with his face buried in his hands. "What happened?" he asked the policeman, who shrugged.

"Routine," he answered. "Nothing."

Michael repeated the question and this time he looked at the contractor, who had taken his hands away from his face and directed an exhausted look at his documents, which were spread out on the table. "I don't know what they want," said Imad. "I gave them my ID card, I gave them my license. I gave them my business permit—no good. Everything is no good."

"Get out of here," said Michael to the ruddy policeman, who was looking at him with astonishment, anger and fear. "Get out, get out!" he roared. "And I don't want to see you here ever again. This is the end of you here, the end! What's your name?"

"Sergeant Yaron Levy, sir," answered the policeman in a parched voice. "Chief Superintendent Balilty told me—"

"Get out," said Michael in exasperation, and waited for him to leave. "Filth," he spat before the door was completely shut.

"Come closer, Ohayon," called the pathologist now. "You're too far away." Michael moved closer to the forceps and looked at the blood-covered splinter of wood.

"Do you remember what old Dr. Kastenbaum used to say?" asked Solomon.

"Every contact leaves a trace," recited Michael obediently.

"Good for you," muttered the pathologist. "And look, you can see just how right he was. Were there red fibers from the scarf inside the cuts in the neck? There were. Now there is also this little splinter, and it's not from a broomstick," he promised. "This, I think—just from superficial observation but we'll send it to Forensics to make sure—is actually from that piece of wood you found. Construction lumber, maybe from scaffolding, maybe even in the attic where they found it. You have to check that thing—there will be traces of blood on it. I've told you time and again that everything leaves traces on everything."

"But we found them," cried Sergeant Yair. "Don't you know we found them? Didn't they tell you that the CID found bloodstains on the board we took out of the water tank?"

"So then we're fine," said Solomon. "Did you write down that the jaw is broken, and the cheekbones?" His assistant nodded, and above the mask his startled eyes darted back and forth between the pathologist and Sergeant Yair.

"Write it down, write it down, don't worry," said Solomon to him gaily. "I'll correct your mistakes in Hebrew. They send them here straight off the airplane," he explained to the air in the room, "and I have to correct their autopsy reports. He writes everything in Cyrillic letters, Hebrew but in Cyrillic letters. What do you say to that?"

No one answered.

"You can saw now," Solomon said, and moved aside. His assistant, who held the handle of the long saw in large fingers to which the latex gave an unreal look, began to saw around the skull. "Gently!" cried Solomon. "Look how much dirt there is here, and you," he said to Yair, "move aside. It makes sparks fly!" And Yair moved.

Michael's face lifted to the wall of its own accord as Solomon removed the brain from the skull cavity and placed it gently, as if it were alive, on the scales that stood next to the metal table.

"Why is he doing that?" whispered Yair anxiously. "Why is he weighing it?"

"To find out whether it is of normal weight," answered Michael.

Solomon said into the microphone: "Five hundred and-sixty-one." Then he turned to Michael: "Okay, we have here hemorrhages as well as cracks in the skull. So they hit her on the head, beat it, hit her in the face but they apparently didn't throw her down on the floor. In any case I hadn't thought that was how it went. I thought that first they strangled her and then they smashed her face in. Here, look at the tongue." He held the tip of the tongue and wiggled it from side to side. "Do you see how it's loose? It's already clear that there was strangling here. Give me forceps," he said impatiently, and the assistant hastened to hand him forceps. "That's too big. Give me the medium size." The assistant obeyed in silence, and Solomon lifted the tongue and pointed with the tip of the forceps. "Broken, you see," he said, and wiggled the tongue. "It's completely free."

Michael nodded.

"And without checking, I'm sure there's a break in the cortex, but we'll see in a moment. Do you know what a broken cortex looks like?"

Even though he hadn't directed his question at anyone, Yair answered him, if hesitantly: "I think it's when the upper vertebrae, the ones nearest the skull, are affected, then—"

"That's where the medulla oblongata is," interrupted the assistant, in his heavily accented Hebrew. "The lowest part of the brain is responsible for breathing and the cardiac system and the blood vessels. If it is affected—there's death."

Yair nodded with the expression of a student, and Solomon ran the scalpel from the chin down to the sternum, and while he was making the incision deeper he said to the corpse: "Take some new chewing gum out of my gown pocket for me." Immediately the intern peeled off his gloves and extracted a green packet from the pocket of Solomon's gown.

"Anybody want some?" asked the pathologist.

No one answered.

"Later, when we get to the stomach, you'll change your minds," warned Solomon. "Put it in my mouth," he ordered his assistant. "*Nu,* slip it under my mask and then take new gloves." Solomon spread out the tawny skin of the neck and with a victorious glance indicated the upper vertebrae. "You see? Broken, just like I said, and look at the trachea. Crushed. Did you see?" Without waiting for a reply he ordered, "Forceps," and this time the assistant hastened to hand him large forceps. A moment or two later Solomon pulled a dark lump out of the neck cavity and muttered: "We'll open the esophagus. Open it, but carefully. There are scissors over there." He gestured with his shoulder toward the tray. "Take the big ones, but first weigh this. What would we do without this Russian immigration? We'd be lost," he said, and fixed the assistant with his eyes. "Do you realize that we have only four Israeli doctors here, and one of them is a woman, and all the rest, all the helpers and the interns, are Russians or Arabs?"

Michael was silent.

The assistant weighed the lump that had been extracted from the throat and told Solomon its weight, and the pathologist repeated the figure into the mouthpiece of the microphone. Michael followed the motion of the scissors that cut into the esophagus, and the hands of the assistant that spread it open carefully and flattened it out on a stainless steel tray. "Everything is fine," the assistant said to Solomon.

"There are no lumps, and no flaws, either," Solomon explained to Michael, as if he had never been there, and Yair cleared his throat from behind.

Now Solomon palpated the sternum. Michael, as he looked at the metal table, again forced himself to detach the scene from the whole body and the life that had been in it. If Solomon, whose skinny body leaned over the corpse and whose small round bald spot gleamed at the back of his head, had looked back he would have discovered to his satisfaction how pale Sergeant Yair had gone. But Solomon did not turn around to check up on "the boy"—that is how he referred to Yair over the phone, when he recommended not bringing along "some virgin boy who is going to faint here"—who wavered on his feet for a moment, then steadied himself as the pathologist sketched with the scalpel a thin incision from the sternum to the pelvis. Then the pathologist sketched a parallel incision, and then made them both deeper, one after the other.

"First I cut into the cartilage," he explained to the air in the room.

"Have you already taken out a sample of fluid from the skull?" The assistant nodded in alarm, and his light eyes darted from the corpse to Solomon's face. He hurried to the implement tray and put the ladle that he took from it into the cavity of the skull and dipped out some turbid liquid that he poured into a clear plastic container. Then he tightened his mask, wrote the date and time on the container and set it aside.

"Come, help me get this out," said Solomon to the assistant. "Did you know that all the internal organs from the tongue to the larger intestine are attached to one another, huh?"

Michael sensed Yair's obedient nod and thought about how keen the young sergeant had been about coming to the autopsy.

"It's part of the job. Right from the outset I should have been there, only you said I didn't need to yet," he had argued on the way here, when Michael warned him about the sight of the naked body in the autopsy theater.

"It's not just the body they operate on," he had warned him then as he lit a cigarette—already with the thought of the exposed and gleaming metal surface and the stiff body lying there, bringing the disturbing smell of decay to his nostrils—"it's also all the rest. Outside on the lawn everything's very pretty, and in the lobby, too, but if you go down a few steps to the basement, you see all the bodies lying there waiting for autopsies, and they're not always covered."

"I've already seen so many cows and mares. Believe me, it's not so easy to see a mare that you've raised spread her legs and die. And haven't I been at autopsies to see what happened to them?"

In a fatherly way Michael commented that there was nevertheless a certain difference between animals, no matter how beloved, and human beings.

"I didn't even know her when she was alive," insisted Yair.

Michael wondered whether to persevere, since sooner or later the sergeant would have to be present at an autopsy. Yet nevertheless he heard himself say: "You'll begin to think that it's you under the flesh," and, again in a fatherly way, he tried to explain to the youngster, who was exactly the same age as his son: "You can't remain indifferent to it."

"Why should I remain indifferent?" wondered Yair. "There's no need to be indifferent. Why indifferent? After all, it's shocking, and she's a young woman. If you get shocked, so you have to be shocked, and that's normal. You don't die from being shocked."

The simplicity of this statement silenced Michael and led him to think about his own first years on the force, when he tried time after time to "take it like a man" at autopsies, especially during their first moments. He attributed the alienated concentration and the almost scientific curiosity he had ultimately developed to his strenuous war against shock, which he wanted to distance from himself as fast as possible. Yair's words and his way of looking at the world with an innocent and contented gaze amazed him, and he often wondered why this young fellow from the moshav in the Jezreel Valley happened to become a police detective. Twice he had asked him this directly, and Yair had found it hard to explain. In reply to Balilty's crude questions—"If you're such a farmer, then why didn't you go study agriculture?"—Yair would reply with his dreamy smile, which spread his tanned face and narrowed his dark brown eyes. "It just worked out that way," he said at most, and shrugged.

Hearing this answer Balilty would snort loudly, which meant: "That's no answer." And Yair would smile again and say nothing.

"He's a little cuckoo, your agricultural Buddha," Balilty once said at a special investigation team staff meeting, a moment after Yair had left the room to fetch coffee.

"He's a sweetie," Tzilla had said then, "just adorable."

Eli Bachar stared at her: "Adorable?! What's so adorable about him? Anyone can keep quiet a lot and smile. What's so adorable?"

But Tzilla just giggled, shaking her head in a coquettish way that shook the long silver earrings she wore. "You're all just jealous, that's the thing."

"Jealous!" said Balilty dismissively. "What's there to be jealous about? Am I your husband or something?" His head indicated Eli Bachar. "He can be jealous all he wants—that's why he's a husband. But me? Why should I be jealous of a baby who's never been abroad, who doesn't know anything and who hasn't seen anything. What have I got to be jealous about, tell me."

"Of his innocence," said Tzilla. "Yes, his innocence, that looks at things from a different angle."

"He'll get over it," promised Eli. "Believe me, a year or two, and maybe even sooner. Once or twice at Abu Kabir, and when he finds someone who has shot his children and afterward the wife, too. The first time he sees a burnt family, he'll get over it, this joie de vivre and the innocence, both."

"He's already seen such things," said Tzilla. "Don't forget that he was the one who found the little girl that pervert left to dehydrate beside the wadi with all the signs of rape. And all the change I've seen in him? He just became sadder and—" Then Yair came back into the room holding a plastic tray of glasses and coffee and milk and sugar, with the proud look in his eyes of someone who had managed to overcome all obstacles.

"I promised Hannah at the cafeteria that I'd bring it back the moment we're done, because she doesn't have enough cups," he explained as he set down the tray, and to Balilty he said with satisfaction: "I even got sweetener for you, and she doesn't let *anyone* take it out of the cafeteria."

Michael was careful not to express his opinion. It seemed to him that his own affection for the youngster, and not Tzilla's, was what had aroused the jealousy in Eli Bachar, who usually got along with the people on the special investigations team without any difficulty (apart, of course, from Balilty, with whom he had a long-standing grudge and with whom each case provided only a temporary truce). Eli Bachar, who was devoted to Michael with all his heart, especially since he had shared his deliberations about whether to marry Tzilla—he had even insisted that he, Michael, and not Tzilla's father be the godfather to their two sons— never managed to conceal his suspicion of those whom his chief liked. Michael watched him as he slowly and deliberately stirred his black coffee, his chin propped on his left hand, his green eyes staring at some invisible point. It was amazing to see that an experienced investigator like Eli Bachar could see the new sergeant as a threat.

From the very first moment Michael had felt a deep affection for the youngster, perhaps because of his eager look, except for those moments he withdrew into himself, and maybe the affection was stirred because he was out of the ordinary—his calm naiveté and the contemplative expression with which he would offer weird examples from the field of agriculture to demonstrate some police problem. Now, too, as he looked at the corpse, there was neither shock nor disgust in his soft brown eyes, but rather a kind of quiet, inner sorrow. He had not even told Shorer about his liking for this youngster, because he thought that he would again tell him—as he had told him when he had first introduced Yair to him—"But he's not like Yuval at all, haven't you noticed? Your son resembles his mother, and this fellow—maybe he reminds you of yourself when you were a youngster. Everyone has been telling me how much he resembles you. Maybe there's something in it, his height, and the eyes, and even his eyebrows. But the facial structure is completely different. He doesn't have those cheekbones of yours . . ."

Michael, to whom the definition of his feelings as fatherly sounded crude and simplistic, protested. He thought of Yair as a kind of pupil—a student from whom something could be learned about innocence that wasn't sentimental. The naturalness with which Yair learned about the new world, the curiosity and the naturalness with which he related to everyone—he did not even develop suspicion toward Balilty, and he also totally ignored Eli Bachar's demonstrations of hostility—captivated him, as if Yair's mere presence on the special investigations team was itself comforting.

"My father wanted me," Yair once told him, "to find something new, different, just to be sure, as there's no future in agriculture here, and it's clear that we won't be able to live from it. How can you make a living from it, with all the droughts and the dry years and the foreign workers and all the economic problems? At first, I went to study at university, but I didn't know what I wanted. That is, I wanted to be a veterinarian, but you can't study veterinary medicine anywhere in Israel and I didn't want to study in Holland or Switzerland. I didn't want to leave here. I love . . . Never mind, I didn't want to. It was also impossible economically. So I did a general BA and I started criminology. I don't know why, because what would I do with a general BA? What kind of job can you find with that? And just at that time a friend of mine told me that you were recruiting and the work is interesting, so I just gave it a chance." He had only confided these things to Michael, but even him he had told nothing about his life in Jerusalem on weekends, when he always went back to his parents at the moshav.

Nevertheless he blanched now facing the corpse, and stepped back, and as he rushed out of the operating theater he held the mask over his mouth. And Michael, too, felt the familiar wave of nausea, when the buckets were placed at the foot of the corpse, and Solomon and his silent assistant spread the stomach cavity wide open and working together pulled out the internal organs, like anchors on long, heavy chains. Together they placed them on the table, and the sweet stench of decay flooded the large room and penetrated through the mask he hastened to pull up on his face. In face of the death that filled the entire room and flowed into all his pores, to what avail were all the preparations and methods of alienation (a woman he once knew, an amateur painter, had told him that she had sat at the bedside of her dying mother, whose legs had been amputated because of a complication of diabetes, and had drawn in pencil all the smallest details of the stump)? Yair, who came quietly back into the room, wiped the skin of his face, which had gone gray, with the back of his hand and looked with suspicion at the pathologist, who continued with what he was doing.

The heart, red and moist, was laid on the scales and weighed, and then the assistant passed it to Solomon, who cut it open and examined the valves and the ventricles and muttered: "The heart is perfectly normal; she would have lived to be a hundred." The lungs were also spread out, one after the other, on the stainless steel surface. "Nothing special here, either," Solomon summed up, "so we'll check the stomach. Have you put out the bucket?"

In the momentary silence came the sounds of the dripping of the stomach fluids into a black plastic bucket. Solomon raised his head and said: "According to this, it was even earlier than we had thought. What was it you said to me earlier about an ATM?"

"There's a piece of receipt from ten P.M.," said Michael cautiously.

"Going by what I see here," said Solomon, indicating the contents of the stomach, "by ten o'clock she was no longer with us."

"So when?"

"I would say six or seven, no later. Don't forget that we've gone off daylight saving time, and it's already dark by five, five-thirty, if you see what I mean. And there in the attic it was black as Egypt, and the temperature had already gone down. It's October."

"But the receipt," said Michael musingly, "the slip from the ATM. That means that—"

"That's already your job, not mine," remarked Solomon with satisfaction, "and permit me to remind you that such things have already happened: People don't need to be alive for money to be withdrawn from an ATM with their cards."

"Yes," mused Michael, "the slip was in the pocket of her coat, and the hour is still visible. But it could be that it's someone else's account, or that someone knew her secret code number. How many people know someone else's PIN?"

"Not a lot," agreed the pathologist.

"What this means," added Michael, "is that someone left there shortly before ten, withdrew money and came back and planted the receipt in her pocket. Does that sound reasonable to you?"

He had addressed the question to Yair, but Solomon hastened to reply: "Like I told you, it's not my field, thank God. I don't deal with hypotheses, only facts. And that," he said, pointing to the stomach that was spread out on the large tray, "very simply, is a fact."

"It couldn't have been later? After six or seven?"

"Maybe eight, tops," said Solomon. "Definitely not after ten."

"So we found her almost twenty-four hours later?"

"Be grateful. You could have found her two months later, or never, if it weren't for the renovations."

"Somebody would have looked for her," said Michael.

"And if they were looking for her?" argued Solomon. "If they were looking for her, would they have gone there? Into that tile roof? I heard that the house has been neglected for years."

"No, not years, just months, since it was sold," said Michael, "and no one had gone into the space under the roof for more than forty years now."

Sergeant Yair, who did not appear to be listening to the two of them, moved closer to the wide-open corpse. "Don't touch anything," Solomon warned him in a nasal voice that indicated he too was breathing only through his mouth.

"I'm not touching anything," said Yair. "I'm just looking at all those puddles inside. Look how much blood there is at the bottom around the spine."

Michael looked at the blood that had collected in the bottom of the stomach cavity, and involuntarily he blinked at the sight, but he did not turn his face away.

"It seemed to me . . . ," said Yair, "when I saw the uterus—this is the uterus, isn't it?" He pointed to the large tray with the internal organs over which the assistant was leaning. "It seemed to me that it was too big."

Solomon froze to the spot. "Very good, young man," he said without astonishment. "Come here, Ohayon. Get closer a moment, please. I have a surprise for you."

Michael moved closer to the tray on which the internal organs were spread.

"Before we spread the lungs and analyze the contents of the stomach," said Solomon severely, "before anything else, there is one thing that is very clear. Do you see this uterus? We opened it very carefully, we didn't cut it in half and we didn't make lateral incisions, because it is very enlarged. More than seventeen centimeters without measuring, just eye-balling it. This is a uterus of pregnancy, maybe ten or even twelve weeks. What a waste, what a waste."

Michael looked without saying a word. He remembered that Solomon and his wife were childless.

"I knew it!" whispered Yair. "Right away I saw that it was very enlarged."

"What are you, a gynecologist? You, who until you vomited were a virgin?" thundered Solomon.

"No, of course not. I don't know anything about women. But I had a mare—"

"Here we aren't talking about horses. Here we have a fetus in the third month, which is about nine or ten centimeters long. It is already the size of a fist. Look, I'm taking it out." Solomon used scissors to separate the tissues. The color returned to Yair's face. In his large palm, on the surface of the glove, Solomon held a lump of tissue covered in mucus. "I would estimate, nine centimeters without the placenta. Weigh the placenta," he said to his assistant. "We already had something like this once, the fifth month, with a really developed fetus, almost a person. Do you remember?" Michael, to whom he had turned his head, nodded. "That was the one you found inside the carpet in a car, right?"

"Yes," said Michael, "but then we knew who she was. No one had taken away the documents or the purse."

"You'll know this time too," said Solomon. "No matter how long it takes, in the end you'll know. This isn't someone off the streets. Disgraceful," he muttered. "Disgraceful. A pregnant woman. What a waste."

"Yes. Definitely," said Michael. In the bottom of his heart he had never managed to feel certainty in his ability to solve crimes, the certainty that everyone around him seemed to have, especially Balilty. Only with Emmanuel Shorer, who eighteen years ago had convinced him to leave his doctorate in history and join the police and who since then had moved on to command a district and then the entire police force—only with him did he speak of his panic, and Shorer would listen seriously to his anxieties, year after year and case after case. And the last time, when he was already police commissioner, he summed them up by saying: "I'm not trying to tell you that it's not like that. Sometimes there are things we don't solve; I don't need to tell you that. But maybe it's best that you are never certain. Maybe it keeps you from getting burnt out. Would you rather be like . . . like Danny Balilty? Pleased with yourself all the time? Because you know, Balilty isn't really self-satisfied. He just looks that way."

The thought of Balilty now made him clench his jaws again.

"What do you want?" Balilty had said to him the night before, while they were still in his office. "There are Arabs around there. Maybe they raped her. Those Arabs, if you don't scare them, you can't get anything out of them. Furthermore, if they left the door open, anyone could have gone in, isn't that so? And also since when have you become such a goody-goody? I know them, don't I? I work with them all the time, and you don't."

"I didn't know that that was called 'work,'" said Michael coldly. "I call it something else."

"What? What do you call it?"

"Shameful behavior," said Michael.

"Do you hear yourself?" protested Balilty. "Look at how you're talking to me, as if I were some . . . What self-righteousness! Am I to blame that he's an Arab? Huh? If he's an Arab I can't interrogate him? In a minute you're going to file a complaint against me, huh?"

"You know that he was with the two women. He has an alibi. He met them—"

"Don't talk nonsense," yelled Balilty. "This phony leftist talk of yours is worse than . . . than that corpse that is already two days old, and where did we find it? In a house that he was going to renovate with his workers, also Arabs. You know that he has a battalion of workers? And that all of them are from Beit Jalla? He'd already been in that house, and maybe he had already seen the corpse and kept quiet so as not to get involved."

"And you," said Michael in fury and despair. "What have you done? You've taught him that it really isn't *worth* it for him to get involved."

He looked at the corpse again. The sight calmed his anger. Despite his anxieties, he knew that this woman, whose corpse they had found in the attic of the house that was about to be renovated, was not one of those missing persons for whom no one was going to look. And even if no one looked for her, it was clear that through systematic work that would not even take a very long time they would arrive at a definite identification: a chic woman, young and pretty, who was certainly not homeless, a woman with a steady job, who had friends and acquaintances. She was not just some streetwalker or drug addict.

"Do you see any drug use here?" he asked.

"Not in this examination," mumbled the pathologist, who was again examining the arms closely. "Maybe in the analysis of the blood and the fluids. But there's also no sign in the pupils."

It could be positively assumed that her identity would be ascertained, but nevertheless Michael was still disturbed by her anonymity, and even more disturbed by his anxiety about the next stage, once her identity became known and they would have to find out who had murdered her. This feeling, which came back to haunt him time after time at the sight of an unidentified corpse with no clue to lead them to the murderer, usually faded once the investigation began to roll and they began to reconstruct the story in which the explanation lay hidden. And if it didn't really fade, at least it shrank into a corner that released him from grappling with it, at least during his waking hours, because in his sleep he would grind his teeth, sometimes until his jaw hurt.

"Can you tell whether there had been sexual contact before the murder?" asked Yair.

"Not without a smear," said Solomon. "Only after we check the smear we took from the vagina, because she's not a little girl any longer. At a very young age, or very old, when there are signs, it is possible to tell just by looking because . . . Never mind. We'll know. What is certain"—the smile in his voice could be heard from behind the mask—"she wasn't a virgin anymore, unless she's a new Mary."

Of three or four in a room, thought Michael, remembering a poem by Yehuda Amichai, there is always one who will prefer vulgarity as a defense against . . . Against what did Solomon have to defend himself? Michael knew that five years before retirement, Solomon's heart was already hardened against the corpses in which he rummaged. But in fact what else did he really know about the pathologist? A few crumbs of information he had picked up during the course of autopsies, each of them containing a surprise: for example, that he had been brought to Israel from Hungary after World War II, a year-old baby, and that during the first years he grew up in a kibbutz; or that during the period that preceded his medical studies, he lived in Mea Shearim and tried to be a yeshiva student and "fled from that, too," as he'd put it, while pointing at the corpse he was dissecting, "from the frying pan into the fire." And

Michael also knew about his long marriage: Solomon's wife, a distant relation of his and older than him, had come down with Parkinson's disease years ago. Michael was once at their home and had met her and had shaken her trembling hand, hesitantly and fearfully. Years ago, when Solomon had been called to an autopsy on the first night of Passover, right during the hours of the festive meal, he told Michael, "We don't have anything, the two of us, my wife and I, no siblings and no brothers and no anything. We're free as birds. We don't have to give an accounting to anyone: 'Yes we're coming, no we're not, yes we'll invite them, no we won't,'" and a moment later he began to hum slowly and quietly, reconstructing the catchy melody from the Passover liturgy, *"Dai daiyenu, dai daiyenu"*—"It would suffice us . . ."

Now Sergeant Yair's face evinced evident curiosity. He stood very close to them as they spread open the lungs and he observed every stage and followed the large Latin letters the Russian assistant wrote on the caps of each plastic container into which he poured the fluids from the stomach cavity.

"Who wants to do the sewing?" asked Solomon. "Do you want to sew?"

The assistant nodded.

"So sew, and put everything in right. Maybe I'll just . . ." And he replaced the scalp, sewed it in back and sewed it on the forehead. "I just have to do this myself, so it'll be nice."

The assistant shrank in silent protest.

"Fine, now you can put everything back," said Solomon. He moved aside and pulled the mask up onto his forehead, where it stayed like a loose cloth ribbon.

"You've forgotten the brain," said Sergeant Yair. "You've already sewn her up and it's still here in—" He went silent all at once, as he followed the movements of the assistant, who was pushing everything, including the brain, into the stomach cavity.

"Don't worry," Solomon said dryly, and pulled off his gloves. "When the dead are resurrected, the brain will also go back to its place. The main thing is that it's here, and anyone looking from the outside won't see a thing. Anyway, there are people whose brains are in their bellies. She will be as if she were newly dead," he said sarcastically. "Believe me, she's ready for Our Lord the Messiah."

"So what did we have here?" Despite himself, Michael was pulled into the pathologist's cynicism. "A smashed face and strangulation—that is, vice versa—a break in the tongue bone, a broken cervix, a torn main artery and a twelve-week pregnancy?"

Solomon took off his gown and nodded.

"About six or seven in the evening? The day before yesterday? That is, approximately"—Michael looked at his watch—"if it's now two A.M., then thirty or thirty-one hours ago?"

"Exactly right," replied the doctor, taking off his horn-rimmed glasses. His eyes stared at the white wall opposite him as if what was beyond it would be revealed there. "But you'll get the printed report." And then he returned to the tune he had been humming and polished the lenses of his glasses with a paper towel that he pulled from the dispenser near the steel cabinet. "You'll get it in the morning. First thing in the morning."

Chapter 3

For nearly half an hour Netanel Bashari had been waiting at the entrance to the Vayashuvu Banim Legvulam Synagogue at the corner of Railroad Street and Naftali Street, and the whole world was getting on his nerves. He was waiting for his sister Zahara, for whom he had canceled an important meeting, and Zahara hadn't shown up. Maybe she had made a mistake about the time or the day, because Zahara wasn't a person to cancel an appointment without letting you know, nor was she forgetful. Nevertheless, he was sorry that he had not reminded her this morning about the appointment they had made for two o'clock in the afternoon. This meeting was important to her, because she wanted to check out, together with him, the acoustics both in the synagogue hall and in the front courtyard, where the temporary sukkah tabernacle, with all its decorations, was already standing. Now, during these long moments at the gate, her plan to sing this evening—the eve of the seven-day holiday Sukkot, the Feast of Tabernacles—seemed even more absurd than it had when she'd first proposed it.

He wondered what had gotten into Zahara, who for months had been arguing with him about a solo concert for inhabitants of the neighborhood. First she had considered holding it at Linda's house and afterward, when she had decided on the synagogue, she had presented the idea to Netanel with great enthusiasm, and was insulted by his dismissive response and got angry. Even after he had apologized for the ridicule and made do with merely expressing mild reservations, her anger had not subsided, until he had given in and agreed that on the eve of the holiday she could put on what he called her "folklore spectacle." And it was just because of that quarrel—if that's what you could call her outburst, to which he tried not to react—that he was now even more disturbed:

Maybe Zahara really was censuring him inside herself, and maybe even distancing herself from him.

The "spectacle" included the establishment of a small neighborhood museum in a room of the synagogue where Zahara planned to display "the splendor of Yemenite culture"—that is how she defined it—"a culture that monsters like the murderer of the prime minister and Rabbi Meshullam"—who not long ago had led a violent but abortive Yemenite "liberation movement"—"had caused to be completely forgotten because of their deeds."

In the large basement of the synagogue, she had already stored cartons full of photographs she had collected since her childhood from her grandmother and her mother and her aunts (and which she had also purchased on occasion), lengths and scraps of cloth and embroidered dresses, furniture and kitchen equipment, goldsmiths' tools and tailors' tools and cobblers' tools (among them old pliers and a small mallet), and tin wires and a small drill that were used by pot menders to repair cracks in earthen vessels. Zahara intended to display all these in rotating exhibits in the back wing of the synagogue, and through them show "varied facets of Yemenite life."

He swallowed without a word her application to the members of the synagogue board, and the plans they had approved in his absence, despite his known reservations, and he tried to logically explain to her his theoretical position and his fears that a museum of the Yemenite heritage might blur the synagogue's progressive image. He held back and did not say to her that her absorption in the study of the community's roots and her family looked like a kind of perversion, which of late had aroused his concern as well as his opposition.

He felt a modicum of pleasure when he mused on the new spirit he had breathed into the synagogue, which had stood half-empty for years, during which nobody came to pray there except a few oldsters from among the Persians and the Iraqis who were still in the neighborhood. It had been he himself who had initiated the move to persuade the neighborhood elders to open the synagogue to others as well and to make it progressive and integrative ("modern" was the word he had used with the handful of old men who were faithfully in attendance there on Friday nights and holiday eves), a place that Ashkenazim would also attend, and especially the new inhabitants of the neighborhood, the ones who had arrived after the Six Day War from the United States, from

South Africa and from Europe (on condition that they were "traditional" and not "really black"—which he had no hesitations about calling the extreme ultra-Orthodox in front of the board).

Why was Zahara so angry at him? All he wanted was to turn the desolate building into a social center that would also host cultural events and family celebrations. It had taken a lot of effort to overcome the objections of the regular worshipers, who were leery of an Ashkenazi takeover; and he had maneuvered among them with diplomatic patience until he obtained their agreement. "American and French Jews," he promised them, "aren't ordinary Ashkenazim. It's not like the old-timers here from Poland and Russia. They're not really Ashkenazim at all"— thus he argued, and he had even invoked the name of his father, who was a favorite of the congregation and whose indifference was luckily interpreted as a positive stance.

He had fulfilled all his promises: He had promised to renovate the building and "make a palace of it," and now, five years later, even if it wasn't quite a palace, no one could deny that it had been splendidly renovated; he had promised that the building would be "a home for all the residents of the neighborhood," and indeed almost every night it was the venue for cultural and social activities, like the Community Center in the upscale neighborhood of Rehavia. Even now, five years after he had persuaded the dozen elderly worshipers to give him his way, an occasional sigh of satisfaction arose in him when he recalled the agreement he had managed to extract from them, be it because he was from a Yemenite family or because the years had taught them that they could not fight the changes the neighborhood was undergoing.

And how could Zahara accuse him—him!—of "social indifference," after he had invested most of his spare time in the renovation, and had also gladly taken upon himself the job of sexton and had even—without even revealing a glimpse of his burning desire to sing—taken on the role of cantor during the High Holy Days. And after all that, Zahara was accusing him of utilitarianism. The accusation was really hard to understand, because all in all, what did he want? To strengthen the ties within the neighborhood? Anyway, this was a neighborhood where everyone knew everyone else, so why did he have to unite them into a single congregation?

It was simply hard to believe the kinds of complications faced by those trying to change something—Rabbi Stieglitz, for example, who had come to them from the ultra-Orthodox community of Kiryat Mattersdorf. You could go out of your mind when you came up against this insensitivity on the part of the Ministry of Religious Affairs and the Jerusalem municipality, who sent them a rabbi like that who entirely ignored the unique spirit of the place, who wouldn't even allow every Jew, provided he observed traditions, to participate in the cultural-religious experience offered by the neighborhood synagogue. Stieglitz had come just an hour ago and announced that the sukkah, which everyone including the children had been so busy building since the moment Yom Kippur was over, was not a strictly kosher sukkah! And why? Because only half of it was covered with branches, and therefore a pious Jew could not sit in it. "A bridegroom of the Torah," ruled Rabbi Stieglitz, "will not sit in a sukka that is not kosher." And now, at two in the afternoon, two hours before the holiday was to begin, who was there to put branches over the half of the sukkah roof that was left open to the sky? And it wasn't just the missing branches—Rabbi Stieglitz had also condemned the artistic program and had suddenly remembered that it was "forbidden to listen to a woman sing lest she stir lust." It was a good thing that at least these comments had been spared from Zahara, who was late for their meeting.

Everything annoyed Netanel Bashari today. As he was standing in front of the sukkah while the rabbi was examining its branch roof, he had seen Linda in the silver Rover—and he'd known very well to whom it belonged. And indeed, after a moment Moshe Avital stepped out of it, opened the door on her side, extended a hand to her in a courtly gesture and carried her shopping bags to the door of her house. You might think, Netanel had said to himself, that any divorced woman here was easy prey and that any filthy vermin could just snatch her up. And how he worked her over with his courtly manners, that Avital, a Moroccan pretending to be French, and an irresponsible skirt chaser. And how Linda had looked at him, at that Avital-Abutboul, with such grateful eyes, and when she saw Netanel standing there she had waved gaily to him with her white arm, as if he were some mere acquaintance. And he, Netanel, just stood there across the way with Rabbi Stieglitz, furious at the sight of the brown gate that shut behind the two of them as they walked up the path through the front yard to the little house with the flat roof. And how many times had he warned Linda not to trust anyone who changes his name from Abutboul to Avital and acts French! Just thinking about it was enough to nauseate him. And he, Netanel, who had never even thought about changing his name—his own sister accuses him of trying to become Ashkenazi.

And Linda? How easily she had waved away his warnings, with all the wolves circling her house from the moment she'd got rid of that drunken Russian! How she had giggled and asked whether he, God forbid, was jealous, as if she hadn't heard the story of Avital who had destroyed, but completely destroyed, the Shalevs' marriage, and as if she had not seen Avigail Shalev going around at night with that Avital, when her husband was working alone day and night in their architects' office on the bid for the new Hilton.

Because of Rabbi Stieglitz, who had transferred his gaze from the car to his interlocutor, Netanel stayed where he was and did not cross the street and did not open the gate and did not follow her into the house, as he had done several times during recent months in similar circumstances. From the looks Rabbi Stieglitz was giving him, it appeared that the rumor about the latest neighborhood scandal had also reached his ears. Hagar had caused it one night before Rosh Hashanah, when she banged on the brown gate and called out his name so that the whole street could hear. No one had opened the gate for her, and it could not be proven that he had really been there at Linda's house. Afterward, instead of "being entirely open," as he had promised to Linda he would do at the first opportunity, and as a decent person should do, he found himself conciliating his wife with a declaration that he had just been out for a walk because he couldn't fall asleep. And to make the story believable, he also told her how he had happened to run into David Baruch, a friend of his since childhood, and how the two of them had sunk into a nostalgic conversation, and how this conversation had stretched out from their past to their future.

Now, waiting here for Zahara, Hagar's sarcastic comments rang in his ears. She swore she would never forgive herself that, at the time, she had agreed that he go study history, and Russian history at that, instead of trying all kinds of successful possibilities that had been open to him then, when the two of them had got out of the army. "It's all because you're so busy being not-the-son-of-Yemenites. Otherwise, why would you choose to specialize in Russian history?" And right away she had voiced her old complaint about his "fateful decision" not to study economics. "You could have had a high position by now at the Bank of

Israel or at least a high-tech company, and all our problems would have been solved." She had repeated this complaint in the midst of their quarrel this morning, which began with the question of whose turn it was to do the shopping for the holiday.

It was Hagar who had encouraged Zahara to insist on her plans and stood by her in their latest argument. She hadn't hesitated to stir up the members of the congregation against him, and had even enlisted the women from "The Committee for the Other" to urge him to allow her to sing traditional Yemenite songs on the eve of the holiday. He was more and more annoyed by Zahara's Yemenite vision, which was so contrary to the openness for which he was active, so that the synagogue would be a kind of neighborhood melting pot that blurred the barriers between the ethnic groups. It was very strange, really strange—he looked at his watch again, and at the nearly empty street—that a young girl, especially one as talented and beautiful as Zahara, would be so deeply involved for the last few years in researching her family's past. And with that voice of hers, instead of agreeing to the offers of impresarios and musicians who heard her and had already talked about a solo appearance or a compact disc, she insisted on singing songs from Yemen, where she had never been, all of which she had learned from her grandmother, who used to sing them on holidays and at family celebrations. It was hard not to see this as criticism of—and even profound revolt against—his way of life, and in fact against him personally.

It was from Hagar that Zahara had learned to keep pressing on his weak point, criticizing him in words she had learned from Hagar for all his efforts to become like an Ashkenazi. Zahara of all people, whom in fact he had raised. He had read to her when she was a child and had spent hours talking with her about serious things in order to get her off the intended track that was taken for granted by their parents—a woman's only purpose, they thought, was marriage and children. She of all people had taken to rummaging around in the old family stories he wanted to ward off and bury. When he tried to say that "ethnic identity has no meaning nowadays," Zahara responded angrily and argued that the entire course of his life and his status demonstrated exactly the opposite; yes, because look at the price that had been demanded of him to "climb up the rungs of Israeli society"—the submissive eradication of his roots.

"Nowadays there isn't discrimination on an ethnic basis," Netanel told her. "What was true of our parents is now a total anachronism. What good does all this rummaging do, all this messing around with ancient tragedies?" he asked her when they met a week ago, after she told him that he amused her ("What irony," she had said with a toss of her head). She taunted him that as a historian he should really be interested in solving mysteries from the past. "That is, if you love history," she challenged him, "because maybe twentieth-century Russian history isn't exactly history, and maybe what's important to you is something else entirely . . ."

"What? What else?" he asked her, and she cocked her head and said, "Forget it, never mind," and no matter how he begged her she wouldn't say.

In recent months, their meetings had always ended sourly, after she insisted upon what she called her way and crassly commented to him about "the way you're becoming an Ashkenazi, which in the end is going to cost you dearly." She would regard him with a skeptical expression, and sometimes the skepticism was replaced with scorn which sharpened into anger when she asked him about "Big Zahara," as if he knew more about her than she did. At their last meeting, last Thursday, she had lectured him about the importance of the "miniconcert"—that was how she defined her evening of song—that would take place at the synagogue on the eve of the holiday, and lectured him on her theory about the gradual introduction of Yemenite culture "in an experiential-emotional way, yes, in a way that will awaken excitement and pluck at the heartstrings and make everyone curious about this cultural world, which has been lost almost entirely." Zahara hadn't explained why it was important to revive that world and especially for the Ashkenazis from western Europe who had taken over this neighborhood she had never left. And Netanel, who valued family ties and really didn't want to muddy these meetings with arguments, stopped insisting that she explain.

Again he looked at his watch and at the bend in Naftali Street, and again he looked over at the brown gate across the way—the silver Rover was still parked there—and decided to get his sister together with Benvenisti, whom he saw as the spiritual guide who had shaped his way in life. On the Eve of Rosh Hashanah, when he came to give holiday greetings to Benvenisti as he did every year, he noticed the tremor in the professor's hands. Even though he was not yet seventy, it looked as though old age was already upon him. And then he was assailed by a gnawing worry: What if he had to resign from the directorship of the Institute, or if heaven forbid something happened to him, and then immediately the flock of young heirs would swoop down, most of whom spoke Russian as their mother tongue. It was Benvenisti who had brought Netanel close to Russian when he was a BA student, and had influenced him to concentrate on eighteenth- and nineteenth-century Russian history, and had appointed Netanel as his teaching assistant in his third year and had seduced him—yes, seduced him, with compliments and flattery and promises of the glorious career that awaited him in a field that was just emerging, and from this seduction Benvenisti had also benefited considerably—to follow in Benvenisti's footsteps and help him establish the Russian Studies Institute he was slated to head. Now, if God forbid something should happen to Benvenisti, Netanel, his veteran deputy, would have to struggle for his place without any support.

But this wasn't the issue now; Zahara was. If he introduced her to Benvenisti, maybe she would understand and respect the strange choice he had made when he was younger and would stop accusing him of trying to be Ashkenazi. Furthermore, if the professor listened to her plans to gather testimonies from people who had lived in Israel at the beginning of the Yemenite immigration, maybe she would drop her plan to rummage in the affair of Kinneret, the agricultural settlement that had expelled the Yemenites in the 1930s. And smitten by his personal charms, she might also give up her desire to solve, "once and for all" (as she had declared, with pressed lips that gave her face a fanatical, almost ugly look), the affair of the kidnapped Yemenite children who were given over for adoption at the end of the 1940s.

The conflict between him and Zahara, which had initially looked merely like differences in outlook, was sharply revealed upon his research into the Jews who had come to Palestine from Russia in the Second Immigration. That led him to research into the economic flourishing in the kibbutzim during World War II, and thus he learned about the role that was played by young people from the Yemenite community, about which he told Zahara. She was so excited by this discovery that she urged him to write about it.

No one before him, she argued heatedly, had investigated the role of the Yemenites in the kibbutz economy at a time when more working hands were needed to provide for the needs of the British army. Together, said Zahara, the two of them could gather data for an entire book. "Not some boring academic study," she said with that burning, fanatical excitement in her eyes that had been worrying him so much recently, "but a real book that will show what happened and how it happened and how they planned everything. It was a real conspiracy."

And again, as at all the family meals and at all the weekly meetings between the two of them, she reminded him how important it was to discover historical documents that would reveal the plan by the country's founders, Ashkenazim of course, to eradicate all the distinguishing characteristics of the Yemenite Jews and assimilate them and marry them off to the descendants of the eastern European Jews until they became sabras in every respect.

"This book will cause an even bigger stir than the one you wrote about the Russians," she promised him, and he grimaced dismissively; the very fact of the comparison between that study, which dealt with Stalin and Hitler and had caused a great stir and led to his international reputation, and the affair of the enlistment of a "Yemenite workforce" in the kibbutzim aroused protest in him. Zahara chose to ignore the courageous things he had said in an interview to *The Times of London* when his book came out: He had spoken there not only about Stalin's attitude toward Britain, but also about the Jews who had immigrated to Israel recently from Russia and their hatred of their past, and the popular press was furious at his revelations. He also spoke forthrightly about the Russian immigrants' role in Israeli politics, and explained their leanings to the right and their capitalist views, and how they had distorted and revised the history of the Soviet Union. For months after that interview he was still subjected to terrible attacks in the British press, was shocked by the vilifying letters sent to *The Times* and also faced explicit threats to his life.

Although he knew very well that the research itself demanded no special courage or intellectual integrity, but only persistence and a lot of time at the archives that had been opened to researchers into Russia, he nevertheless had been praised for his courage by Benvenisti and senior colleagues at the Institute. But this praise, which assuaged Hagar's complaints for a while, did not help him with Zahara, who challenged him at the table and demanded time and again that he also display his courage with respect to the Yemenite problem. "This concerns you personally," she argued, but he did not feel that way, and after he did not comply with her wishes she began relating to him with aggressive scorn.

Only an objective individual as intelligent and charming as Benvenisti could get her to loosen up and stop those charges, which were becoming more and more spiteful, as when they met last week and she spoke about "this pathetic attempt"—his attempt—"to be like Hagar and her parents. And soon you're going to invent a new biography for yourself, as if your parents had also founded some kibbutz. Look at them, at Hagar's parents whom you admire so much, and see what has become of their lives!" she'd shouted suddenly, pushing the plate of hummus away in disgust. "Look at who you want to be. They founded a kibbutz and now they're always busy trying to hide the fact that they're living in poverty, just like beggars. And they never even mention that not a single one of their children has remained in the kibbutz. Never mind in the kibbutz—in the country. Only Hagar has remained in Israel—and her sister Einat? Even after it turned out that her Finnish husband was an alcoholic and beat her, she didn't come home, and she's stuck there in Finland. And her elder brother? He's a little guru in some ashram in India. And Yotam makes a living as a real estate agent in Florida. And Father and Mother—aren't they obsequious to the Beinisches?" With what spite she spat out the name of the hated neighbors. "They go out into the yard with their Ashkenazi in-laws, as if to show them the garden, but really so that the Beinisches will see them and bust a gut. And how Hagar's mother says, 'Show me your row of herbs and medicinal plants,' and Mother goes and shows her the basil just so she can hear again 'How beautiful the *khadi* leaves are,' just like that, with a kind of accent, like she heard from Mother. And you, it's all because of you, all because you intentionally married a sabra girl, and one from a kibbutz yet, a blonde with blue eyes. And you went and became a professor of Russian history. Who ever heard of such a thing?"

"What's happened to you, Zahara?" He was alarmed, and he also noticed a small, light brown mark under her eye, but he did not dare ask about it. "What's gotten into you? I thought you liked Hagar and—"

"So you were mistaken!" said Zahara. "Or maybe I was mistaken. You can't trust Ashkenazim," and he had never heard such bitterness from her before. "Look at her. A few days ago I suddenly saw your wedding picture, the one in the living room on the television. When was the last time you looked at it? Look at Hagar there—a perfect Israeli girl with all those freckles, certain that the world belongs to her, with her long hair and blue eyes. Look, and you'll see why you really married that woman."

"What has she done to you?" Netanel himself was astounded by the anger that rose from the depth of his throat. It was one thing to be tired of your wife and to see her weaknesses and faults day after day, and another to hear other people condemn her, especially if the other person was your baby sister.

"She hasn't done anything to me personally," Zahara had said to him then, "but as a learned historian, you should know by now that not only personal things count."

Netanel kept quiet. In truth, he thought that it was only through personal interest that an individual arrived at ideas, but he kept his mouth shut and didn't tell her that it was only through personal injuries and hurts, or because of a specific conjunction of circumstances as in his case, that a person arrived at any theoretical occupation, and even historical research.

"Don't you see how materialistic she is? And the . . . Have you seen how she shops all the time?" Zahara demanded to know.

"That's enough, Zahara," said Netanel.

"It is not enough!" Zahara said, and looked around at the other diners in the small restaurant. "Have you seen the way your house looks? Like a smugglers' den in Istanbul—Russian and Czech dinner services and samovars from Uzbekistan . . ."

"They were bargains at the neighborhood flea market. New immigrants from Russia were selling them, and it was a good deed to buy them . . . ," he mumbled uncomfortably.

"Oh? Really?" scoffed Zahara. "And the sets of towels and the linen sheets from the fancy stores at Kikar Hamedina in Tel Aviv? And the microwave? This is already the third one she's—"

"What do you care?" said Netanel with irritation, precisely because he also hated those endless purchases and was ashamed of them. "What do you care what Hagar buys?"

"I don't care. Let's just say that I don't care if my big, successful brother is married to a woman who . . . who is the essence of the ugly Israeli. She's proof that there's no such thing as 'Israeli culture.' How can there possibly be spirituality in the present if you deny the past like that? Look at how you're living a lie and—"

"Zahara," interrupted Netanel. "Why are you so hard on us? Hagar is even helping you against me about the museum and all that and—"

"Sure she's helping me, and do you know why? Because now she wants Mother's silver objects and her embroideries, that's why. All that interests her is getting all those things from Mother before . . . while Mother is still alive, so that I won't get them. So that I'll be glad if she gives them to her, that's why."

"Enough," Netanel protested, and put his hands over his ears. "I don't want to hear any more." And when he saw that Zahara had no intention of stopping, he changed the subject to Sukkot: Not only had he come to terms with the evening of song, but he also spoke about it as if he really wanted it despite the fact that he didn't even know either the *Nashid,* with which she intended to open (*"If you desire a man chosen for secrets,"* she chanted in a low voice. "Do you know this?") or *"Wazil man jaman wamahna"*—*"O, from the place where thou sittest observe and see / A poor people exiled weak and oppressed").* But he did know "In the Shade of the Sukkah" and *"Ya Grada."* His grandmother used to sing them ("She used to sing them to you when you were little. Mother told me").

"Maybe my parents are right," he had said to Linda after that meeting. "Maybe we have to find a man for her who will calm her down, with all that hot blood. She should get married and have children and stop driving us crazy."

"How you talk, Netanel," protested Linda, tapping him on the nose. She explained that what was necessary was to talk to Zahara seriously about the University of Indiana and remind her what a pity it was that all her talent was going to waste.

"'A pity' is putting it mildly," said Netanel musingly. "It's really criminal, this waste."

Then Linda concluded that they had to talk to his father, and that if he didn't agree to pay for Zahara's studies, they had to take a loan. In the rapid English to which she switched, she said that the problem began with the fact that their parents were not prepared to part from their baby, but it was clear that she could not be allowed to live with them anymore. It's absolutely clear, she said, because they're just driving her crazy and recently even she, Linda, who had been closer to Zahara than anybody, could no longer manage to talk to her. It's as if she's been haunted by a dybbuk, she went on, if it weren't for all that nonsense about the Yemenites you might think that Zahara is head over heels in thwarted love or that she has something going with a married man and on second thought, yes, she is beginning to think that that's really the case, that she has had some disappointment in love and she's hiding it.

• • •

It had, in fact, been thanks to Zahara that the relationship between him and Linda had begun. At the age of thirteen, when Zahara had still been fat and awkward, her hair always a mess and her chin dotted with pimples, she'd baby-sat every morning one summer for Linda's twins and had fallen in love with them, and had fallen even more deeply in love with their mother. Linda was the first to take her musical talent seriously, and by the middle of the summer she had come to Netanel—"because it's difficult to talk to your parents," Linda had said in her accent that rolls 'R's—and swore that she would not give up until they sent the girl to a serious teacher, because "talent like that doesn't grow on trees."

It was then that Netanel noticed the luxuriance of her reddish curls, the blue glow in her eyes, her rounded limbs, the glimpse of her thighs revealed by the wide *jalabiyya*—the long garment resembling a tailored shirt that forgot to stop, usually worn by bedouin men. And all these were in addition to her generous warmth.

One night, after he had seen her earlier that evening leaving Nissim's grocery store on Bethlehem Road, and after he had played with his children and eaten with them and exchanged a few words with his wife as well, he had dreamt about her. In his dream, the grocery store was a broad expanse and in its center was a small pool or fountain or well or maybe a large container or even a barrel of the sort that was used during the siege of Jerusalem, and Linda stood there in her *jalabiyya* holding an overflowing pottery jug or pitcher of water. When he got close to her and touched her face, she smiled and tipped the vessel to his mouth.

Netanel Bashari, who only rarely remembered his dreams, awoke with a great sense of clarity and realized that he had fallen in love. And when he wondered about how he had known to dream such a romantic biblical scene, he recalled how he himself had once defined Nissim's grocery as the neighborhood well, around which the inhabitants of the neighborhood gathered and exchanged neighborhood or national news.

Five years ago he had taken Linda to the old synagogue building to share his vision with her, and when she expressed delight in the classical symmetry of the square windows with the crumbling frames and the height of the ceiling and the original doors—"I've never noticed. It's perfect Bauhaus"—he found himself caressing her smooth, milk-white arm, and then he confessed how attracted he was to her. That visit led to a prolonged relationship, and the guilt feelings it aroused in him were replaced by currents of fear every time he thought about the future and his increasing dependence on Linda. But because she did not pressure him to change his life, and asked nothing of him, he had no idea whether she was jealous of his wife and whether she wanted to be together with him. He often asked himself whether his sister realized the nature of their relationship, but Linda dismissed this question with a laugh, made a little speech in praise of discretion and asked about whether in fact he would like her to talk about him with Zahara.

As he approached the synagogue gate, he saw that there was a cardboard sign hanging on it with two handwritten lines saying that due to the situation, the farmers' market would be canceled and would not be held as planned in the space behind the synagogue. Maybe it was better—he continued to gaze at the sign—that Zahara not sing this evening. In any case, he knew many people would rather stay home because of the fear of terror attacks, and even those who came to services would be in a lousy mood. It would be better if she sang in a week's time, at Simhat Torah, because maybe by then the situation would ease up and the disturbances would stop. The carob tree in the yard looked sick, but instead of the diagnosis made by Netta the gardener, who had volunteered to advise them, he now thought about the words "the plague of leprosy," and upon hearing his voice in his head he got alarmed and entered the building.

He stood before the holy ark and looked at the little bags of surprises for the children that had been placed in front of its doors, in anticipation of the last day of the Sukkot holiday week, Simhat Torah. This is how a life in which there is tradition and harmony should look, he reflected, a life that makes it possible to prepare little bags of surprises for the children in the synagogue, like at birthday parties, and place them at the foot of the holy ark with bright red apples and flags with which the children will march around the Torah scrolls. He bent down and picked up the flag on top of the pile, and distractedly he opened the cardboard window in the front of it and touched the sparkles of gold and silver that were revealed within. They were sprinkled over the face of a boy wearing a skullcap and holding a tiny Torah scroll, and for a moment Netanel wondered what this boy had to do with the children who would look at him, children who passionately collected Pokémon cards. Then he turned to the screen that separated the main hall from the women's section and pulled back the lace curtain on which golden butterflies had been embroidered, that too by volunteers, and covered up the openings one by one. On Simhat Torah, he mused, the building will be full of people and the men will take the Torah scrolls out of the holy ark and dance with them in a circle and carry the children on their shoulders and the women will pull aside the curtains on their separate section and watch them with glowing faces.

Of all the Jewish holidays, Simhat Torah was his favorite, perhaps because of that memory of his father carrying him on his shoulders and the memory of the painted cardboard flag he waved with the apple stuck on top of its stick. He also remembered the sweet taste of the autumn air during Sukkot, when they'd race home from the synagogue and he and his little brothers would carry pots and copper bowls out to the sukkah, which would be filled with the scent of the *etrog*, the large yellow citron used in the holiday ritual (every year his father would take him to the market to choose strictly kosher citrons). Their grandmother would hobble after them, leaning on her cane and supervising so that they would not drop anything, neither they nor their mother, who carried out the delicacy most beloved of everyone—orange quinces cooked in sugar.

When he went back to the top of Naftali Street, he smelled the pungent, disturbing scent of the blossoming carob trees he remembered from his childhood, and at the corner of Railroad Street he gazed again at the brown gate in the stone wall and looked at his watch, wondering whether to knock on Linda's door (he used his key only when he knew she was alone) and ask her if she knew where Zahara was. But Moshe Avital's silver Rover was still parked in front of the gate, and because he did not want to look like a suspicious lover, he also refrained from calling her on the phone. And he didn't want to call his parents, either, to ask about his sister, because a question like that would just make them worry, and anyway, he had left his mobile phone at home. Thus he found himself walking up Shimshon Street to Bethlehem Road, and then he went into the neighborhood butcher's shop when he remembered that he had promised to buy the meat for the holiday meal Hagar was planning.

Straightaway Moshe, the senior butcher, announced that the shop was closed and hurried to lock the door behind Netanel. "We also have to get ready for the holiday," he muttered heavily to the large refrigerator. A thick gold bracelet gleamed on the wrist of the younger brother, who was brandishing a butcher's knife over a leg of lamb while waiting for the customer opposite him to nod in agreement. Then, with a practiced motion he began to cut the meat, and the client turned around to see who had come in. Seeing Netanel, he hurried to turn his face away. Neither did Netanel look directly at Beinisch. On the contrary—he felt an urge to walk out of the store. Nevertheless he stayed there, and from the corner of his eye he saw how Beinisch was watching the younger butcher's hand as with a swift moment he removed the layer of fat from the meat, and between cut and cut he criticized the way Israel was perceived internationally and those people at the Foreign Ministry to whom it never occurred to present the state in a positive light, and that after all the restraint toward the Palestinians' provocations.

"Take Arafat," Joseph the butcher said, and pushed aside the pieces of white fat. "Look at how they're exploiting that picture of the boy that was shot. Believe me, they're sending their children out to get killed only so they can film it and broadcast the pictures to the whole world. I'm leaving a bit of fat on for you, otherwise the meat will come out dry and Mrs. Clara will kill me."

"Do whatever you think is best," Beinisch said to him. "I rely on you."

Netanel, who had turned his face away from the glass counter, minutely inspected the large, gleaming refrigerator. The mere thought of the Beinisches was enough to arouse paralyzing rage in him and now, as he stood so close to the man who had caused him and his family such prolonged anguish, even the air that he breathed in his presence became bitter and dry. He was just a neighbor, but neighbors who embittered a person's life with everyday trivia—what could be done about them, apart from setting their house on fire?

Years ago, when he was still serving in the army and was a young officer and proud of his rank, he tried to talk to Mr. Beinisch and reach a truce with him, if not a comprehensive peace, to make life easier for both families. But Mr. Beinisch, whose small, light eyes darted here and there in his large, fat, freckled face (back then his head was still covered with red hair), would not look at Netanel, and as he fiddled with the ends of his light blue tie he rejected the suggestion to even commit himself to a truce: "We aren't doing anything. Talk to your mother. She's the one you have to talk to." Even his uniform and the rank of first lieutenant that Netanel had earned had not diminished by one whit the sense of superiority Netanel saw in every one of Mr. Beinisch's looks.

Because of that conversation, Netanel hit his little sister for the only time in his life; the thought of those blows, which Zahara often mentioned in their conversations, and sometimes even in jest, now—a whole hour after their appointment that had not been kept—made him feel strangely ashamed. At the time, he had already been an MA student and Zahara was two or three. He found her one afternoon in the wooden shed behind the house, yelling and playing inside a large wooden crate with Yoram Beinisch, the neighbors' son. He could not understand how the two tots— only their heads, the dark one and the light, peeked out of the crate, and their eyes glistened with fear when he looked in and saw that they had taken their clothes off—had dared to disobey the prohibition imposed on them by both families: not to speak to each other. Now, as he recalled how he had pulled Yoram Beinisch out of the crate and thrown him into the next yard like a naked kitten and then immediately pulled Zahara out and smacked her, he was attacked by discomfort. His sister had not run into the house to complain to their mother, but stayed standing at the door of the shed crying quietly to herself for a few minutes before she asked: "What have you done to Yoram? Did you kill him?"

The Beinisches had bought the empty part of the two-family house in 1958, the year Netanel was born, and even as a child he was aware of the scornful looks of the couple, who were still childless then, every time they passed him in the yard. (During the first years, before they had split its area between them, the yard had not been divided by a stone wall.) Mr. Beinisch had no respect for the seniority of the Basharis, who had been living in the house since 1948. The Beinisches had paid full price for the house, had not had any discount at all—so said Mr. Beinisch in that single conversation Netanel had forced on him—whereas the Basharis were "living here only because they were sent there from the transit camp in Rosh Ha'ayin."

In 1948, when the Arabs had abandoned their homes in the neighborhood, Netanel's grandfather and grandmother had been transferred there from the transit camp with his parents, who lived with them, and with other immigrants from Iraq, Morocco and Romania, and housed in the buildings that had been abandoned. For several years it had been possible to buy the houses for pennies, as the Beinisches did—"right at the last moment," as Netanel's father often said bitterly—before the prices began to rise and before anyone imagined that this would ever become a prestigious neighborhood. Netanel's parents had believed that the neighbors would eventually become human beings, if only they had a child, but even after their only son Yoram was born (a year before Zahara) the quarrels between the two households did not end. They reached their height when Mrs. Beinisch accused his mother: "By us, we know how to think about the future. Anyone can make babies like an animal. That's the way they are. That's the way they brought them from the caves. They brought them down from the trees. Asiatics. If she did not"—Clara Beinisch never addressed his mother directly, but always addressed some invisible audience—"have all those children, then she would not need more space." Netanel's mother never forgave her for those remarks, and kept quoting them to her children and forbade them with vows and threats of excommunication ever to speak with the people who lived in the house next door, to go past it or even to look at it from their yard or through the windows.

Until his own children were born, Netanel Bashari had not known real worry. But from the moment his first child was born and even when the four of them had grown up, and especially now, when two of his sons were serving in the army, he was in a constant state of disquiet, and only on Friday evenings when all of them gathered for the family meal and he counted up his little tribe with his eyes, only then was he calm for a moment, until he thought about his sister and his brothers and also Linda, or any other people who were important in his life and whose whereabouts he did not know. Now, as he left the butcher shop—Moshe had opened the door for him and locked it quickly before another client could come in—Netanel listened anxiously to the thunder that rumbled in the distance. For a moment he thought it was the thunder of shooting, but immediately afterward the sky clouded over and became heavy and low to the tops of the tall cypresses, and a bleak mood came over him. A line of cars stretched in front of the shops on Bethlehem Street. In another hour the holiday would begin and the rain would get into the sukkahs and interfere with their meal.

At the entrance to the grocery store, Nissim stood rubbing his hands together and looking gleefully at the sky. The narcissi in the garden had already begun to come out, he informed Netanel: "Like clockwork, they are." If only the rains weren't late again, he added, like last year, the cyclamens would also begin to do their work.

"Jews," said Netanel to him. "They're never satisfied. Give them rain, and they'll say it's too soon, it comes into our sukkahs. Don't give them rain, and they'll start wailing about drought."

Nissim smiled, and after a moment he looked at Netanel and said that for a while now he had been meaning to ask him, as a professor at the university, that is, whether he had noticed that there is always a connection between the political situation and the seasons of the year because he, Nissim, even though he is just the proprietor of a grocery store, has noticed that the wars always break out here in the summer or the fall. Even though this was an obvious fact, Netanel said that this was a significant and interesting observation.

"Tell me," Nissim suddenly said, "where's your sister Zahara? I've been keeping this wine for her that she ordered for three days now. I brought it for her specially and I've been holding it since Tuesday and she hasn't come for it."

"Haven't you seen her today?" said Netanel in alarm.

"Neither today nor yesterday. I thought maybe she'd gone away somewhere. Do you want to take it for her? Because if not, I do have someone to give it to, believe me. This is a Yarden Merlot from 1997. It won a prize, and if Yoram Beinisch just hears that I have some of this, he'll take it on the spot."

"Give it to me. I'll see her today," Netanel said, and then, bottle in hand, he walked slowly down Bethlehem Road to his house.

At the door, where a ceramic plaque bore their name as if they were still a happy family, he heard the phone ring, but by the time he had opened the door it had stopped. He put the package of meat in the refrigerator and paused for a moment in the kitchen, which smelled, as the whole house did, of chlorine bleach and other cleaning products that his wife bought on sale, and which filled the shelves in the laundry nook. The dining chairs were still turned upside down on the table to let the floor dry and the deaf-mute cleaning woman (a Peruvian who had settled in Israel without a work permit; Hagar said it was a good deed to employ her) was absorbed in scrubbing the kitchen sink.

Only afterward did he blame the cleaning woman—he did not like to be in the house while she was working; he was bothered by her suspicious looks, as if she were afraid he would attack her—for his forgetfulness: He had not listened to the voice-mail messages and therefore they could not find him before the holiday began. On the way to his parents' house to wish them a happy holiday he decided to go via Naftali Street past the synagogue, where no one was waiting for him, and the where sidewalk across the way was also empty. Moshe Avital's silver Rover was no longer parked by the brown gate, and he decided to drop in on Linda for a minute, and because she was so delighted at the sight of him, that minute stretched into two hours, during which no one knew where he was.

Chapter 4

Nessia gazed at the pattern of lines and squares in the narrow sidewalk beneath her feet. Rosie, sniffing excitedly, pulled her into the squares or toward the bushes, but Nessia was wary of the lines, as if they were part of a trap, and pulled the dog back to the edge of the sidewalk. For a girl like Nessia, whose body felt so heavy and whose inner thigh was itching and turning red and burning, it was hard to run after her dog twice a day: once early in the morning before school, and once in the evening before bed. Not that Nessia suffered from these walks; she liked them, and she knew very well that for Rosie they were the best parts of the day. But Rosie—couldn't she at least show that she was happy? Say thank you that they were walking like that, so fast, and that Nessia was so patient, even when the leather leash cut into her hand? Two folds of flesh humped over the leash, because even her wrist was fat, and it might have been expected that Rosie would notice that for a change today she was having her walk in the afternoon. She could at least wag her tail or bark happily. Or something. But Rosie seemed to have been infected by Nessia: On her, too, you couldn't see anything anymore. Rosie's bark, when she bothered to bark, was always the same, and all she bothered to vary were her pulls on the leash, sometimes forward, sometimes to the side, sometimes insisting on this way, sometimes insisting on that.

Today was a special day, and not only because it was the eve of a holiday, but also because of the troubles with the Arabs and the terrorists, because of whom she wasn't allowed to go out after dark, even if she explained to her mother that the dog protected her ("That dog?" snorted her mother scornfully. "Could she protect anyone? That dog would sell her mother for a slice of salami."). There wasn't a chance that they'd let her go out after dark, even if there wasn't a single Arab roaming the street (apart from Jalal, whom she met at the grocer's, but Jalal didn't count because he was Yigal's friend).

"Sure," said her mother yesterday. "Sure there are no Arabs now. During the day they're afraid to stick their noses out, and only at night they come out of their holes." The air was cool and clear, and Nessia took deep breaths as she looked at the bits of peel and the shoe and the newspapers the garbagemen had left behind on the sidewalk. And she whispered to Rosie to stop getting so annoyed, yes, and she should say thank you. Because she was lucky, she simply didn't grasp how lucky she was that she, Nessia, was healthy and could take her out like this twice a day. Yes, because what if she were sick? Or gone on a school trip? There wouldn't be anyone to take her out, no matter how much she whined.

Even before they got Rosie, her mother said that they could not expect her, after a day's work and with her varicose veins, to walk a dog as if she were some fine lady who had time. Such fine ladies do exist, of course they do, she acknowledged, but she wasn't one of them. So sometimes she would send the dog out on her own, and then Nessia, who for some reason or other was not allowed to go out at the moment, was afraid that Rosie would get lost or run over. (Rosie had a weakness for cars, and she liked to rub up against the tires of parked cars and squat and pee against them, and she especially liked to wet the wheels of Yoram Beinisch's red Toyota, which for the past two days had not been parked by the sidewalk.) Usually Nessia managed to go out with the dog, holding on tight to the leash and stopping when necessary next to trees and fences. Rosie, who was not especially large, always pulled hard in the direction of her sniffing nose. Sometimes she really had to struggle with the dog, especially if Nessia insisted on a certain route and Rosie was involved in her own business. Like now, for example, when she was pulling so hard in the direction of the bushes that she practically made Nessia step on the lines, and that was exactly what she was avoiding because of her secret plan.

The leash cut red cracks into her hand. If she'd had delicate hands with long fingers, like Talia from 5-C, who adorned them with small silver rings and made them dance, and whose long nails gleamed with green and blue polish, everything would look different. She glanced at her swollen red hand and her bitten nails and sighed.

You could never tell when a charm would begin to work; but anyone who understands these things—that is, truly believes in the power of spells—knows that only patience can effect the change. For more than a year now Nessia had understood that true desire was tested by patience and persistence, by dedication to a distant goal, even if you didn't know when, or even if, anything would come of it. If again today she didn't step on any lines (the path from the building to the sidewalk didn't count), and if she crossed the street and walked to the end of Bethlehem Street, as far as the haunted house at the corner of Railroad Street, and walked around it three times, and went into the yard and burnt the things she had hidden in her sweatshirt, and recited the spell, and then dug a hole and buried the ashes in it—if she did all that, maybe the change in her would begin. And supposing she walked like this now, with her left foot in the street and her right on the edge of the sidewalk, and went around the whole block three times that way, then maybe she would even get taller all at once. Yes, why not. And the stiff brown curls that her mother struggled with every morning until they were braided into two stubby, babyish pigtails would become blonde waves. And if not blonde, at least smooth. Why not? Completely smooth and black like perfect Zahara's hair.

She had invented the spell herself. She always had to invent things for herself, because otherwise who would invent them for her? Once, by chance, she'd heard Zahara's magic charm, behind the nearly closed shutters: "To get anything you want, do everything I tell you." Nessia had written it all down on a piece of paper. "Write with rouge and saffron and rosewater on two clean pieces of flaxen cloth and put one into a green candle and dip it in oil of bane and light it. And put the second one beneath your head and sleep for one hour . . ." and after that she couldn't hear any more. At the natural foods store and at the pharmacy she got saffron and rose water, and she already had a candle, a green one, even. But she had not succeeded in finding out what exactly flaxen was—or bane. The dictionary at school said it was a poison or a toxin, and where would she get poison?

Instead, she collected things that belonged to Zahara: a paper tissue that Zahara had dropped as she got into a cab, a leaf from the tree by her windowsill (Nessia had pressed it between pages of the Bible), a hairpin and even a bra of Zahara's she had taken off the clothesline. Some strands of Zahara's hair had also come into Nessia's hands; that had been the most difficult mission of all, because morning after morning she had crouched under Zahara's window and waited for her to get up and get dressed and comb her hair and throw the strands of hair that got stuck in her comb out the window. For four days Nessia waited—she was already familiar with all of Zahara's habits, but she hadn't hit the right moment—until one morning the green shutter on the window facing the back yard opened, and a long and slender tawny arm emerged and dropped a small tangle of black hair.

Nessia looked at the cars that were parked close together at the sides of the street. Yoram Beinisch's red Toyota stood there somewhat distant from the family parking place, without the white cover that usually protected it from the sun. Apparently he had come back late at night again, and his parents' two cars had taken up the covered carport. Two days ago his fiancée had arrived from America with five blue suitcases and a large yellow handbag. Not that his fiancée was so pretty, and she wasn't special, either. Just a little bit tall and with platinum-blonde hair. And ever since she'd arrived all they did was drive away and come back all the time.

A little red light twinkled inside the Toyota, the automatic security lock light. And Nessia liked to look at this light that went on and off like the beating of her heart at night. But even more, she liked to hide behind the fence and peek at Yoram Beinisch when he washed the car, wearing only shorts and the upper part of his body bare and the setting sun lighting it up then with scarlet and gold, like he was a prince whom a magic bird had dropped into the yard. It seemed to her that his bare legs were sprinkled with golden powder, as were the hands that scrubbed off the stains left on the roof by the fruit of the ficus.

Yoram Beinisch coddled the new car he had received from his job: He scrubbed and washed and dried it and caressed it with his hand and walked around it and checked whether there were any scratches before he pressed the key ring and locked it (two beeps came out of his palm then). Every Friday afternoon he soaped it down with a yellow cloth and sprayed it with the rubber hose he pulled out of the garden like a trained snake. This was his vehicle from his workplace, as his mother, Mrs. Beinisch, told Mrs. Jesselson, the neighbor from the second floor, explaining that the car hadn't cost him a thing, not a cent. "It is part of the benefits package of the high-tech firm he's with," she said, and fingered the clasp of her pearl necklace, as if confirming it was still there.

They hardly ever noticed Nessia, and if they did, they paid her no attention. Maybe because she was just a girl, and maybe because she looked like nothing to them. Yoram Beinisch, for example. He didn't even know she existed. He was twenty-three, not yet really a man you called "sir," but in his eyes she was just a baby. And until his fiancée arrived from America, he had so many girlfriends! Almost every night, when she peeked out her window that overlooked the street, she saw his silhouette attached to the silhouette of some girl—until the fiancée came from America. It would be most suitable if he married Zahara. Yes, Nessia thought, this could be perfect: the two of them the same age, and neighbors—they wouldn't have to go anywhere. But he wasn't on speaking terms with Zahara, certainly not near the house. Because if he were to speak to her near the house, and his mother or Zahara's mother saw this, what a fuss there would be.

Her mother once told Mrs. Jesselson—the Toyota had just pulled into the parking space—that the children, that is to say Zahara and Yoram, used to wave to each other over the fence, and it was so obvious that they wanted to play with each other, but their mothers wouldn't let them. And the upbringing, her mother told Mrs. Jesselson, does its job: That's the way it is, what can you do? "That's the way it is," agreed Mrs. Jesselson. "What you bring from home is for your whole life. This one doesn't look at her, and that one hates Ashkenazim. And they don't even look at each other. And you know what? Maybe it's better that way. It's better than all those hypocrites here, who say hello-hello and then talk about you behind your back." If anyone noticed Nessia they immediately scolded her and sent her away, no matter who, even Zahara. Yes, the way they told a cat to scram was already more gentle than that.

When Nessia was still in first grade, too small to know her place, she once stood by the yard and looked at Zahara, who came out of the house in her white dress and high-heeled shoes. Her black hair gleamed, and the sweetness of her perfume hung in the air of the street even after she got into the cab. And Nessia, she just wanted to see her, at most touch her hand for a moment or even not her hand, just the white dress, but Zahara said: "Go away, little girl. Can't you see you're getting in the way?" That's what Zahara said to her, and closed the window of the cab as if she wanted to erase her completely. And what was it, after all, that Nessia wanted? To look at her, and maybe to touch her a little. And also to do things for her, yes, all kinds of things—even to go to the grocery store for her—yes—because if she were close enough to her, maybe some of Zahara's beauty would stick to Nessia.

But Zahara, before the cabdriver had honked even once, looked at her in disgust, as if it was Nessia's own fault that she looked the way she did, and as if Nessia was going to infect her with her fat and her pimples and who knew what. As if Nessia had some infectious disease. "Go ahead and perfume yourself as much as you want," Nessia said to her silently afterward every time she saw her, and she nursed her revenge slowly.

It wasn't that Nessia hated her, really not—really, really not—because it wasn't like the way you hated someone who hit you and called you names and you could tell on him afterward. But that look, which she never forgot, was still stabbing and hurting. Hurting, yes, but not like when they hit you, but in a different way, and therefore it wasn't right to think that she hated Zahara, because she didn't. She really didn't. She was just insulted, yes, but not like when they call you names, but in a different way. To the depths of her soul, yes, because she also had a soul, under all the pimples and fat.

If they didn't notice Nessia, this also had great advantages—she saw not only what they wanted to show, but also things that none of the other people who lived on the street imagined she took in. She spent entire days all alone and she began to conduct observations the way she had learned in nature lessons, when the teacher taught them how to observe insects and flowers and document what they saw in reports. When Nessia listened to the teacher's explanation, she realized that she had been conducting observations for years, and when she learned how to write an observation report she scrupulously did this every night before she went to sleep, when she came back from her walk with Rosie. These were observation reports on the street, and every day, in the special notebook bound in brown leather, she noted the weather and the people she had seen, if she knew them by name, and also the license numbers of the parked cars.

Under the heading "Unusual" she would sometimes describe special events in a short sentence. For example: "The police came and searched the Muallems' in entrance D." Or: "Mrs. Je. threw out the Arab who came to ask for money." Or: "Mrs. Bash. came home in a cab this evening and didn't have money to pay the driver."

Sometimes she wrote: "A dead white cat in the middle of the street," and sometimes: "They didn't collect the garbage," or: "Today they came from the municipality to get rid of the rats that were walking on the electric wires."

The longest report was about Mr. Avital, who came one day with his new, silver-colored car to pick up Zahara and there, in the backseat, sat his daughter. (It was for good reason that Nissim from the grocery store said of her: "Poor thing, God knows what will become of her. She's already thirteen and acts like a two-year-old.") And how did Nessia remember this? Only thanks to the report she had written: "Mr. A.'s daughter came home for a vacation from the institution and Mr. A. took her in the car to pick up Zahara from the house with his new car."

Day after day, during the evening hours, she sat on the stone fence of the apartment block and watched the inhabitants of the street as they came and went: who stopped to talk at the entries to the buildings, who returned plastic bottles to the big recycling bin up the street or dumped trash at the edge of the sidewalk (first they glanced right and left). Who started their cars, who parked, who carried home bags of purchases from the greengrocer or the grocery store. Attentively, she listened to fragments of conversations she heard, and also wrote them down: who said what to whom and when and where.

Once, a long time ago, when she was little, she used to go into the neighbors' yards and listen under the windows and sometimes even peep inside. Yes, it wasn't that she had no shame, she did have, but she wanted to know more about life, because she didn't have enough from her mother anymore. And she didn't have enough from herself, either. Yoram Beinisch, for example—the window of his room overlooked the backyard—or Mrs. Beinisch or Mrs. Bashari, and most of all Zahara aroused her curiosity, yes, because she wanted to discover what made her so perfect. Now, when Nessia was too big and Rosie went every-where with her, it was a bit hard to go into the yards, but sometimes she took the risk anyway. Not always, but now and then. Through the win-dows you could hear all kinds of things, for example the conversations and fights between Zahara and her mother.

Zahara had three older brothers, and she was the only daughter of the Bashari family. The whole street knew how her father spoiled her but only Nessia, hunkering in their yard under their kitchen window, heard Mrs. Naeema Bashari, Zahara's mother, say: "Do you know what kind of reputation a girl who comes home at five in the morning has? Do you know what they call a girl like that? A whore, that's what. Where were you?"

And Nessia also heard Zahara's peals of laughter, the happy gurgle when she said: "Come on, Mother, I'm already twenty-two, not your little

girl. All I did was sing at a wedding yesterday. You knew about it, and you
know that—"

"I don't know anything," said Mrs. Bashari. "Nothing. A wedding
doesn't last till five o'clock in the morning. At the latest, eleven or
twelve, not five in the morning. You're just lucky that your father sleeps
soundly and doesn't hear when you come in."

Nessia was amazed by Zahara's laughter and because she didn't get
scared or insulted by her mother. Nessia herself was insulted by her tone
of voice: Mrs. Bashari didn't speak to her daughter, the only girl she had
after all those boys, the youngest and the best-looking, the way you
speak to a daughter, but as if she hated her. And as Nessia rose to peek
into the window, she heard Mrs. Bashari crying "Zahara! Zahara!" and
saw her slap her daughter on the cheek with the tips of her fingers three
times.

"You have a lot of nerve, Zahara," she said.

And Zahara laughed and said: "If you take a female mouse and the
heart of a goat and put them in water and sprinkle the water around the
house, the beatings and the quarrels in that house will never cease."

"I've told you a thousand times," screamed her mother, "stop messing
around with all those spells and the evil eye, like a primitive person. A
pretty young girl like you—don't you have anything better to do?"

In her pocket notebook Nessia wrote down only "Mrs. Bash. yelled at
Z. because she came home at five in the morning." If she had understood what Zahara had said about the mouse and the goat, she would
have written that down too, but in any case she would remember it, just
as she had written down only "Z.—silver car at the corner" and remembered quite well which car she meant.

Nessia's mother once said to Mrs. Jesselson that the Yemenites place
more importance on the family and the children than even the
Moroccans, and gave the Bashari family as an example: how they gave
everything, but everything, to their children even when times were hard.
"Even when they had nothing, the children lacked for nothing, and that's
four children, not two."

Before that, Mrs. Jesselson had boasted, in a very loud voice, about
her son's wonderful report card, and about her daughter who had
received a promotion at the Interior Ministry and was now in charge of
the passport department. "I've known them since 1948, even before they
built the addition to the house," her mother said, "when they just had

one room and a toilet in the yard, and the other half of the house was a ruin. Pigeons and cats lived there, before Beinisch bought it."

"Of course, when the Beinisches came we were already here," said Mrs. Jesselson, and the beginnings of a nasty smile glinted in the corners of her eye.

It was obvious that she was about to start recounting in detail the story of the war between the Beinisches and the Basharis, but her mother paid no attention and continued: "And especially to Zahara, who from the very beginning they dressed like a princess, and kept giving and giving and giving to her . . ."

"I'm against spoiling," Mrs. Jesselson announced, and tightened the edges of the flannel housecoat she was wearing over her flowered dress. "This will end badly," she promised Nessia's mother. "Zahara is heading for trouble."

"Heading for trouble? How?" protested her mother. "She's pretty and she has a good heart. She's wonderful. And what a voice she has! I also know she works for Mr. Rosenstein the lawyer, in his office, and he says that Zahara—"

"That girl is heading for trouble," said Mrs. Jesselson decisively, and narrowed her small eyes at the setting sun as with the back of her hand she wiped her broad face, which gleamed as if it were floating in a layer of fat. "Mark my words." She waggled her finger. "That girl is spoiled rotten and heading for trouble. She's so full of herself, Zahara, that she doesn't even say hello, and at the grocery store when I asked her how her mother was she turned her head aside as if I was air. I'm telling you, you can see it on her forehead that she is thinking bad things. Really the evil eye, heaven help us."

Mrs. Jesselson looked around and whispered: "The evil eye against Ashkenazim. Did you know that Zahara hates Ashkenazim?" and an evil look appeared in her faded blue eyes. Like a ray, that faded blue look touched Nessia, and she shrank, because Mrs. Jesselson looked like she was going to talk to her mother about "a new diet for the girl" and about Nessia's skin, "where in a little while there are going to be adolescent pimples with pus if you don't watch her diet."

If it weren't for the cake that Mrs. Jesselson baked every week— Nessia waited from one Thursday to the next for the moment when Mrs. Jesselson would call her in the high voice that could be heard in the yard: "*Nu*, so do you want some cake?"—she would long ago have put a curse on her. But she could not give up the golden cake and the warm sweetness that filled her mouth and the sweet vanilla icing and the raisins she found inside like treasure. It amazed her how Mrs. Jesselson's fat ugly fingers, with the red nail polish that was always flaking, could prepare such a wonderful delicacy, and how her sour expression and her mean little eyes did not spoil the perfect taste of her cakes.

Nessia's mother said that Mrs. Jesselson wasn't a bad person, just a gossip you had to be careful of and not tell anything. You just mustn't tell her anything, her mother would say; yes, even if she asks how Zion is doing and how much longer he has in the army, or whether Yigal already has a girlfriend, or when Peter is coming from America (he was supposed to be coming from Australia, from Sydney, but Nessia did not correct her) or how school is and what your grades are. And every Thursday evening Nessia went upstairs to the second floor and entered the spotless apartment after she had wiped her feet on the floor rag in front of the door, and sat down in Mrs. Jesselson's kitchen and didn't say a word while she generously sliced the cake and certainly not when her mouth was full of the cake as across from her Mrs. Jesselson followed every bite she took and made sure that no crumbs fell on the floor. Not for a moment did Mrs. Jesselson stop asking her about her mother's job and her brothers, about Mrs. Rosenstein and school and everything else. Below her gleamed the floor tiles that Mrs. Jesselson had just put down, like her mother wanted to do "so that there will be a bit of light in here instead of how dark it is with those old gray tiles," but that was one of those things Mrs. Jesselson could allow herself, because she had a husband who did whatever she said.

Not only did Nessia know every single one of the people who lived on their street, she also knew things about them that no one imagined she could know. And these, too, she sometimes put down in the reports she wrote, but in code or a shorthand that only she knew how to decipher. All the residents of the street knew about the long feud between the Basharis and the Beinisches, who lived right opposite the apartment block where Nessia and her mother lived. Before the War of Independence, an old Arab woman had lived in the two-family house, and once a year, when she came to visit, Mrs. Bashari would bring a stool outside and give her a glass of cold water, full to the brim, so that she wouldn't bother her anymore. Everyone knew that Naeema Bashari had not agreed to let the Beinisch family build a second floor on the single-story house, and everyone knew that there was nothing in the world that Mrs. Beinisch wanted more, because she intended to build a small apartment there for her son. She was even prepared to buy the agreement of the Bashari family, and to allow them to build a second story as well. And Mr. Bashari, who Nessia's mother said was a good person who didn't even become snobbish after he became the manager of the entire Co-Op supermarket chain in Jerusalem, had been prepared to give in long ago, and build a room there for Zahara, but his wife didn't agree. ("Naeema Bashari would cut off her nose to spite her face," Nessia's mother had said once.)

Everyone followed the sequence of quarrels between the two families—once because of a leak from the Basharis' water tank, and once because of a section of the yard that Mrs. Beinisch took from the Basharis to build a stone barbecue, and once because of the people from the cable television company who left their filth in the yard. On the eve of Rosh Hashanah, everyone had come outside of their houses upon hearing the sounds of yelling, and were in time to see how Mrs. Beinisch's head was rolling from side to side from the slap Mrs. Bashari had given her, and how Mr. Beinisch, who always wore suits because he was an important accountant (Nessia did not understand what "accountant" meant. Did he count ants? She could also count ants, but it wasn't that interesting), called the police on his mobile phone from the middle of the street. Everyone watched him, but only Nessia had seen Naeema Bashari dump a sack of garbage in front of the Beinisch family's door in the middle of the night. Everyone had heard her shouting "Damn you" and waving her fist at the Beinisches' door, but only Nessia, while walking Rosie early in the morning, had seen Mrs. Beinisch break Naeema Bashari's rosebush; for a moment she glanced right and left, and after she broke the rosebush she lifted the edges of her housecoat and trampled the white flowers of the jasmine with her feet.

And she, Nessia, was the only one who knew the two families' deepest secret of all, because only she knew how to see everything, not only in the neighborhood but also outside the neighborhood, far from home. Nessia had not told anyone. She hadn't told anyone anything, because she realized that anything could cause trouble. Even with Peter, her brother's best friend (apart from Jalal, who didn't really count because he was an Arab), with his funny talk in English, half of which she didn't understand, she spoke only a little, and never told him anything really important.

Peter was the first person in the world who had said to her, "We're friends," as if an adult could really be friends with a girl of nine and a half—and a fat and ugly one at that. Her brother Yigal didn't really like it when she came to their place—"You again? That girl is like glue," he would say—but Peter insisted on hosting her, and once he even gave her a lift in his green Fiat, when she was little, maybe just eight. He stopped at the corner of Bethlehem Road and Yiftah Street and opened the door for her as if she were already a lady, and said: "Get in, get in, so the dog doesn't get sick from the rain." In the little Hebrew he knew he asked her whether she walked the dog every day, and then he said to her very slowly in English, so that she would understand, that it was easy to see that she was a good girl and a few more things that sounded to her like compliments, and if he wasn't being flattering because of Yigal, he was very smart and already saw her the way she really was.

"You're a girl who sees things," Peter said to her in the car. "You see a lot." And Nessia didn't know what he was aiming at. When he stopped in front of her house, she quickly said, "Excuse me, thank you, good-bye," and ran after Rosie, who was already pulling her out. What was it he thought she saw? What had she said without noticing? If he knew things about her, maybe he also knew that she took stuff. And you had to be careful when you spoke to him—and not just to him. There were things she didn't want people to know about her; she would die if people knew about them. Yes, even if what she wanted most in the world was for people to know about her. Not those things, but for everyone, really everyone, to know her as she really and truly was.

She, Nessia, knew too much. Even about that blonde woman who came to the second house from the corner in the morning when Mrs. Golan had gone on a trip with her mother to Romania in search of their roots. Only Nessia had seen the cab stop in front of the house, and Danny Golan, who her mother thought was a good person after he had brought her two little pots of mint from his plant nursery, took the woman inside and kept all the shutters closed, just as Nessia herself did whenever she checked out or measured her special things alone in her room.

And this, too, she knew: Mati Bezalel, the third son of the Bashari family, an important army officer, comes home to visit. On Thursdays he comes home to eat the calf's-foot soup his mother makes for him, and sometimes he stays until Friday afternoon, and then you can hear the yelling that goes on in the house. Mr. Bashari, who looks like a gentle person in the street—taking small steps and always looking down as if he were looking for something—fights with him about things that Nessia does not exactly understand, and after every quarrel Bezalel leaves and slams the door behind him and his mother runs after him yelling that he should stay. "At least eat a little *hashwiya mumraqiya*. I made it especially for you. At least have something to eat," she cries out to his receding back, and Bezalel keeps walking quickly with long steps until he disappears around the corner.

You could see into the Basharis' living room from the wall around the apartment block, but the window of perfect Zahara's room faced the garden, and sometimes, when Nessia walked past with Rosie in the evening—they had a special route around Zahara's house—she could see the light in the window. On winter evenings it would filter out through the slits in the iron shutter, and in the summer you could even see Zahara herself, looking in the mirror or combing her hair or singing to herself in English. Her voice was sweet, low and warm, and Nessia though she could be famous in all of Israel like Zahava Ben or Sarit Haddad and appear on television, too. If Nessia were beautiful like perfect Zahara, she would also stand in front of the mirror and look at herself and sing. But Nessia is fat and has pimples and hair like steel wool (that's what the children said) and her voice is only good for singing off-key. Zahara does not know that Nessia sees her. In fact, she does not know she has a little, devoted fan who even collects the hair she throws away, yes, and glues it onto her little doll, the one who wears a short white dress like Zahara and even sings when you press on her stomach. The one Nessia sticks pins in where the heart would be.

If only she manages not to step on the lines, and especially now, on the eve of the holiday, maybe she will finally manage to lose weight and maybe even little breasts will begin to grow on her chest that will fit into the purple bra with the black flowers. And on top of her breasts, instead of the wide blue sweatshirt she got from her aunt Sarit, she will wear a shirt that leaves her midriff bare and tight jeans, wide from the knee down with pockets and embroidery down the side. A shirt just like that and jeans just like those were already waiting for her in her hiding place, and also red tights, which her mother had seen only once and asked: 'Where did you get those?"

"I borrowed them from Sarit for gym class," Nessia had replied.

Her mother pursed her lips and said: "For those you need a figure, don't you think? Eating all day and wearing tights just don't go together."

Nessia shrank and kept silent, and after she had folded them into a tiny package, like she had when she found them in the Mashbir department store, she put them back into the cardboard box that she hid in the shelter. There, in the shelter, where her mother never went, she also kept all her father's things—not just clothes that smelled of mothballs, but also the inhalator and the humidifier and the back brace.

Every evening, before she walked the dog, she went down to the shelter to have a look at her hiding place: A: to see that everything was all right, and B: to see that no one had moved anything. She had found the flashlight she used in the shelter at the Hikers Shop, and it too she hid in her sweatshirt. She already knew that small things like that didn't beep when you left the store. Every evening she checked her treasures: She fingered the chain she took from the boutique on Emek Refaim Street, and the underpants from the mall, and the purple bra and the midriff shirt and the tights and the tight jeans. Every evening she carefully opened the heart-shaped little bottle and breathed in the sweet perfume and every evening she touched the box of colored markers, the pencil case and the two notebooks she had taken for writing down her observation reports.

Three times a week her mother would come home late from the health clinic, because she only went to clean there in the evening, straight from Mrs. Rosenstein's house. On those days she left food for her in the morning, and every time she explained all over again how to light the stove, as if she were a little girl and not a big girl of ten and a quarter, who already knew about periods and pregnancy and all those things from sex education (and even the nurse had told all the girls that now they were already young ladies). On those days Nessia preferred to wait for her mother and not eat alone, and in the meantime she could bring things upstairs from the treasure box in the shelter.

Recently, it had stopped filling up: After she had seen on television how they caught a boy in a huge department store in America who had taken a baseball hat with a picture of Superman, and how they dragged him to the police, she got scared and didn't dare take anything from anywhere, even if she really could have found it in the dressing room after someone had left it there. It was almost boring to try on the jeans with the wide bottoms and the embroidery down the side again, and they still wouldn't close on her.

Nessia actually doesn't eat all that much, really not, and she doesn't know why she is fat. She always leaves half the meat patties, and she doesn't finish the soup, either, and she just likes to dip the bread in the gravy. A little gravy, that's all, and not more than a few slices of bread. It's just that if she doesn't eat white bread, her tummy feels empty. A kind of pit that makes her dizzy, as if she were about to fall down like a rag doll. And she also likes candy, but candy is small, not a meal. Anyway, lots of times she doesn't manage to put anything in the basket at the grocery store while Nissim is adding things up, not chocolate or wafers or anything she could eat in bed before she goes to sleep.

Mother says that this is how it is in her family—everyone is fat, and people have a fate and you have to accept it. This is written in heaven, and maybe all the other details are also written there, in heaven: that they will live in a ground-floor apartment where the sun comes in only in the summer, when it's hottest, and in winter it's dark and cold as the grave, and you have to turn the lights on and have the heat on all the time; and that they can never take a vacation or go to the beach; and that in their family, on her father's side there is diabetes and on her mother's side fat and varicose veins. Her mother says these things lots of times when they're watching *The Young and the Restless* or *Julia's Revenge*, because mixed in with her explanations of what was happening and what's going to happen, she likes to talk about what fate has in store for the two of them. Nessia remains silent and keeps her eyes on the television, and sometimes, if her mother doesn't notice, she covers her ears with her hands, but she can hear anyway.

"If they would at least let Zion out of the army," her mother says time after time, "he could help a bit with supporting us." And she also hears about Moshiko, who is in trouble with the police all the time, and about Yigal, who isn't getting married even though he's already over thirty—no wife, no children, no wonder he's in such a bad mood all the time. ("Except when Peter comes," notes Nessia, and her mother replies: "Peter's a friend, not family.") Her mother always concludes these exchanges by saying there is nothing to be done about it, boys aren't girls, they go their own way, and only girls stay with their mother. Then she sighs and says, That's how it is, that's her fate, because what has she ever done bad to anyone? Nevertheless, good people suffer and the evil flourish. Since the Bible it's been like that.

During school vacations her mother takes her to Mrs. Rosenstein's to help her with the cleaning, and there Nessia can touch thin goblets of pink crystal and the smooth, shiny bedspread and the marble panther on the buffet. Her fingers can caress the smoothness of his tensed back, and the golden frame in which there is a photograph of Mr. Rosenstein when he was still young and thin: wearing a three-piece suit and a hat with a hatband, and a mustache above his thin smile. Nessia has only seen him once, and in real life he does not look at all like the photograph: He is fat and short and he doesn't have a mustache.

Opposite this photograph is a large painting of a woman in a purple dress and a wide-brimmed black hat. She is sitting in a green velvet chair, her white arm on the arm of the chair and three gold rings with red stones tightened around her plump fingers. Mrs. Rosenstein once told her that this was her grandmother. "At least we saved this portrait from there," Mrs. Rosenstein said, and told Nessia, who didn't understand what a "portrait" was, about the beautiful house she had grown up in, with a garden that went down to the river, and how they had to leave everything suddenly in the middle of the night.

There were also books in Mrs. Rosenstein's house, lots of books in a big cupboard with glass doors. Sometimes Nessia looks at the books, and especially at the ones with pictures, and from one of them she had got the idea of the doll. Mrs. Rosenstein, who showed her the book, explained every one of the pictures to her: the chief, and the witch doctor and those dolls the blacks make when they want to harm someone. Mrs. Rosenstein gave her other books, which she could read and understand, like *Ellé Kari, the Girl from Lapland* and *Noriko San, the Girl from Japan,* for her birthday when she was in third grade, and said to her then: "This was my daughter's, and she won't need it anymore." (Mrs. Rosenstein's daughter lives in America, and when she'd come to visit with her children she would sleep in her old room again, and in the morning her curls on the pillow would look so different from her mother's straight hair.)

Nessia received Rosie from Mrs. Rosenstein, when their dog had puppies. Nessia had asked politely if the dog's name was Miss Puppydog Rosenstein, and Mrs. Rosenstein said that was rather a long name for a small puppy so Nessia asked whether it would be all right if she called the puppy Rosie for short, and Mrs. Rosenstein had laughed and said: "There, you've already given her a beautiful name. That's how you begin a relationship." Mrs. Rosenstein was always kind to her, and when

Nessia saw her looking at her with her head cocked to one side you could see that she didn't think Nessia was fat or that she smelled bad or that there wasn't a chance in the world that she would change.

"What am I going to do with a dog? Another mouth to feed!" her mother complained all the way home, but Nessia was happy. And Rosie didn't look like she was homesick, as if she too had heard Mrs. Rosenstein explaining to her mother in the kitchen that it was a good thing for two women who live alone to have a dog at home, "and especially for a girl who is a little lonely and for when you're not at home."

"Ashkenazim," huffed her mother on the way home. "They keep dogs. We don't keep animals. It's not our custom." And to Mrs. Rosenstein she said: "There's no need, really, and also I'm afraid of dogs and they dirty the house and they bring diseases."

The dog was so small that even her mother wasn't afraid of it, but when she heard that it wasn't housebroken yet and would pee and make in the house, she said: "Only if you clean up." And really only Nessia cleaned up after the dog, smacking her on the nose with a towel when it was necessary, and giving her a reward from her meatballs when she was good, and seeing that she didn't chew shoes and socks, as Mrs. Rosenstein had warned her she would. And she put Rosie to bed next to her own bed, and on the first nights she would get up to check whether she was breathing or dead. Slowly the dog grew and you could already put a collar on her and fill her dish with Dogli, and when she reached her final size she looked just like Mrs. Rosenstein's dog, although Rosie wasn't a thoroughbred poodle. If Nessia touched her and didn't hurry to wash her hands, and especially if she hugged her and kissed her, her mother would immediately yell: "Just don't come near me with all her germs. Disgusting!" But Nessia did not stop kissing and hugging her, because she simply loved Rosie. And every night before she went to sleep she would talk to Rosie, and once she even showed her the treasure box.

Now Nessia's right foot was marching along the curb and her left foot was dragging behind in the street as if she had developed a severe limp. It wasn't at all easy to stay at the edge of the sidewalk, because Rosie was pulling with all her might toward the bushes. So the two of them walked and passed the synagogue on Shimshon Street just in time to see Mr. Avital drive away in his new car, about which Yasmin had related proudly that it was the first Rover anyone had bought in Jerusalem (but she never said anything about her big sister in the institution for retarded people). When he disappeared around the corner and the two of them got close to Linda's house, she saw Zahara's oldest brother standing in front of the brown gate looking from side to side, and Rosie pulled her toward him, as if he were holding a juicy bone or a slice of salami for her. With all her might Nessia held on to the leash and waited in the yard of the synagogue, distracting the dog with clucks and caresses so that she would not reveal that they had seen him going into Linda's house, and on the eve of the holiday.

Then Rosie pulled her up Shimshon Street to Bethlehem Road, and they walked peacefully together along the street past the grocery store that hadn't yet closed and past the "Closed" sign that was hanging on the glass door of the butcher's, who never agreed to give credit. With all her might she had to pull Rosie away from there, until the smells faded, and then she started walking in front of her again in the direction of the haunted house at the corner of Bethlehem Street and Railroad Street. Now it was Rosie who was pulling, barking at the back of the house, entirely ignoring the pear tree planted in front that was shedding orange-red leaves that were all piled up against the wall around the house. It had a large gate in its center, black and always shut, and on the street in front of it stood a police car.

A policeman was leaning on it, and irritated voices were heard squawking from the communications equipment inside. What were the police doing there? If they had been standing next to her apartment block, she would have understood. But here? When she was little, her brother Moshiko told her to go past policemen as if they didn't exist, not to look at them, not to walk any faster or slower, to act absolutely normal. When he was still living at home, before he got in trouble—it wasn't his fault, but because of those drug addicts he'd made friends with—he had explained to her that the cops always picked on people, that they liked to arrest people for no reason, for nothing. "It's enough that they don't like the way someone looks," he explained, "or his friends. They don't need any more than that." And you had to choose your friends carefully—that's what he told Nessia—because friends can bring you down without a second thought: All they care about is their own ass.

But Nessia in any case had no friends: There was no one to invite her to sleep over ever, and she also never invited anyone to her house. Her mother slept in the half-room next to the living room, and Nessia's room was crowded with the desk and the bed and the wall closet. She had seen other children's homes only at class parties on Friday nights, and only when they invited everyone, but she was never one of those who stayed till the end. The girls turned up their noses when they saw her and the boys didn't see her at all. In gym class she never had a partner for exercises, until the teacher intervened and made someone be with her. And in the exercises themselves she always slowed them down or ruined them or simply gave off a bad smell—she herself didn't sense that she smelled bad, but she saw that people kept away from her or breathed through their mouths or covered their noses with their hands. (Sometimes pee-pee escaped from her at night, and if her mother had already gone to work she was too lazy to take a shower, both because there was no hot water and because she liked the stickiness and found the familiar smell pleasant.)

And in any case Nessia knew—yes, this she simply knew—that she only looked this way from the outside. But inside, deep down, in her secret life, she was beautiful and tall and thin, yes—totally thin, and one day her body was going to look just like perfect Zahara's. Because she, Zahara, was the child of her parents' old age just like Nessia, and she also had three big brothers, and Nessia's mother worked at Mrs. Rosenstein's house, and Zahara worked at Mr. Rosenstein's office, and it was obvious that these were signs of a common fate, and fate is fate, as her mother says, and no one can change what is written in the stars.

Only people who were looking from the outside, ordinary people who were always in a hurry to get somewhere, saw her eyes as small and nothing special; and the eyebrows above them as thick and joined; and her nose a red potato ("Of all things, this is what you had to inherit from your father? His nose?"). But under all this, like in the fairy tales, someone else was hiding, whose eyes were different and whose hair was different and whose body was different. This hidden person's eyes were totally green or blue as the sky, and her hair was totally smooth and her body was small and sweet, with a thin waist you could encircle with a red belt like Zahara's. No, not like Zahara's. Because Zahara's belt, which she tightens as much as possible, closes with a buckle and a hole and another hole until Zahara almost dies, like in *Snow White*. And then, maybe, if Zahara acted nice and asked forgiveness, Nessia would save her the way the dwarves saved Snow White. But first she would teach her a lesson.

Another police car blinked in front of her with a blue light, and Nessia, who knew that it was better to keep away from the police, began to pull the dog in the other direction. She pulled at the leash, with all her might, because Rosie was now insisting on chasing a black cat that crossed their path. When the policeman looked at her, she pretended she didn't see him and ran after the dog to the wall around the next house on Railroad Street.

Beyond the clipped hedge suddenly she saw two policemen standing up. "What do you say? Any chance here?" asked one of them, and knelt down again among the bushes. "You haven't given up yet, have you?" asked the other. "They would never have left it here, so close. Tell me, has your sister had her baby yet?"

Nessia meant to keep going, but at the corner of Railroad Street and Yair Street she decided to go down in the direction of the train tracks. Near the barrier the dog pulled hard again, sniffing and eager, until Nessia stopped her with a tug on the leash by one of the houses so she could tie her shoelace that had come undone. With all her weight she stood on the taut leather leash while she tied a shoelace, and opposite her, on the other side of the small gate, not far from its hinges, she saw the handbag.

It was like a handbag from a dream. She had never seen one like it, not with anyone and not in any store in the mall or anywhere else. She had once found a dressy handbag, made of beads, waiting just for her at the fair that was held once a month, but this one, so soft and gray and fine, looked like a handbag that wasn't from here. From abroad. This was a quality handbag, or as the grown-ups said, "Elegant." Between the bars of the gate she touched it with her fingers and knew that it was real leather, and she thought about Yoram Beinisch's fiancée with her five suitcases and her yellow handbag and her white hair that her mother called platinum. ("Too much peroxide," she said. "She wants to hide the roots," Mrs. Jesselson said, and blew her nose noisily. "To each his own. By us, we like blonde.") The handbag was neither too large nor too small: You could, for example, even fit a dog's leash or a lady's powder compact into it, you could hang it on your shoulder with the thin gold chain that dangled from it and you could hold it under your arm like maybe Zahara would have done.

She stretched her arm between the bars of the gate and got hold of the chain and she knew that this handbag was the beginning of the miracle. She pulled it carefully under the gate and glanced at the windows of the house and then right and then left and back at the street. A car was driving down the street, two couples were walking opposite and a thin woman stopped and set down the plastic shopping bags she was carrying and wiped her forehead with a handkerchief. A tall boy was bouncing a basketball on the sidewalk and didn't look up. The policemen—they worried her more than anyone else—weren't looking in her direction, neither the short one nor his friend, as she put the golden chain inside the handbag, folded it and stuck it under the waistband of her sweatpants.

Later, when she was alone, she would check out every compartment and pocket and find all the treasures inside it. Meanwhile, she felt the nice leather on her body, the soft touch of real leather, calfskin or kidskin or deerskin or maybe even suede, which was the skin of the rarest and most expensive kind of animal. She had once seen a similar handbag at Mrs. Rosenstein's, but bigger, and blue, and when she'd felt it her mother got alarmed and scolded: "Don't touch that. You have dirty hands and you'll leave marks. That—you couldn't buy a new one like it with a month's salary." And Nessia had shrunk back, not because of the dirt but because she realized that her mother would never have a handbag like that. And now she had one, and no one saw. She pulled the edges of her shirt down over the lump it made on her front to hide it and then she was dragged after Rosie, whose nose had scented a new smell. Nessia too was impatient: Now she had to wait until she was alone in her bed, until she heard her mother's breathing, and only then would she get up and discover what was inside.

Mother was still standing in front of the burner and stirring the soup, and its smell filled the space of the kitchen: vegetable soup and meat with bones that Peter loved. He never refused a second helping of it. Even Mother liked Peter. On every visit to Israel he would stay at Yigal's, and join him when he came to visit, and Mother would say afterward: "He's a good influence on Yigal. It's enough for Peter to come and he calms down." And he also calmed Mother, because he knew how to speak to her about everything: about how to treat her varicose veins, about how the Moroccans cooked couscous and how the Kurds fried *kubbeh* and even where it was cheaper, at the Mahaneh Yehuda market or the Bukharans' market or the Hypermarket. And when they visited together, those angry looks that Yigal would give Nessia on other occasions disappeared.

Every holiday eve, Mrs. Rosenstein let her mother leave early, so that she would have enough time to cook, and Nessia would have to help her clean the kitchen again—the sink and the countertop and the floor—but before they did that her mother wouldn't pay any attention to her. Like now, for example, as she stood at the entrance to the kitchen—"Go make some more decorations for the sukkah if you don't have anything to do," said her mother without turning around to look at her. But for Nessia, that little sukkah standing in the corner of the living room wasn't for the likes of her. It was made out of the carton from a microwave oven and it was baby stuff. Dragging her feet, she went to her room, as if she were planning to get a paper chain from there or some paper and markers, and she was careful not to reveal even her profile to her mother, in case she saw her plans (and first she argued a little, like before shower time: She always argued then, even if in the end she would wet only her face and the back of her knees, and especially the floor rag).

Rosie lay at the foot of the bed on her little carpet. She opened one eye and glanced at Nessia and closed it again and went back to sleep and growled in her dream.

First of all, even before she opened a single zipper, she found a little silver velvet wallet inside the handbag, with a bunch of shekel notes. Nessia had never seen so much money all at once. She counted it twice, to make sure: One thousand five hundred and thirty seven shekels plus change, all folded up very small in the velvet wallet. Then there was all the makeup—in a tiny golden cylinder gleamed dark red lipstick, and next to it there was a little compact of green eye shadow and gold mascara for the eyelashes and also a tiny bottle of perfume, and in a clear plastic case with a zipper there were cards and papers, and in the pocket in front there were also a bunch of keys and a comb and a pale blue paper tissue (even that was delicate and soft, so that it was a shame to use it).

How could anyone lose a handbag like that? Once, she had seen on television how they gave a reward to someone who had given back something that was lost, and for a moment she imagined how she would bring the handbag back to the well-dressed woman who had lost it—someone like Mrs. Rosenstein or Yoram Beinisch's American fiancée—and how the lady would hug her and give her a reward for being so honest. And the lady would be so impressed with her that maybe she would even ask Mother if she could borrow her daughter for a while, and raise her in her home. Why not? And she would take trips abroad with her. A woman with a handbag like this definitely traveled a lot, and she definitely had a big house like in *Beverly Hills*.

There were plastic cards inside the wallet, and even before she saw that "Visa" and "MasterCard" were written on them she knew that they were credit cards. (Her mother didn't have any—she didn't believe in them—but her brother had some.) And there was also an identity card, in a little blue plastic folder with such a blurred colored photograph that you couldn't really see the features. Only after she read the name did her hands begin to tremble. From the wrists down to the fingertips her hands shook; her eyes opened wide and she actually felt them gape open. She had never held any object that was so precious, and she had never found—really, really found—just ordinary things. And how could she not return it now? After she had read the name, explicitly, and she already knew whose it was? Yes, of all the people who could have lost it, even if she had never seen it swinging against her thigh up the street. She remembered Zahara's black handbag well, and also the jeans bag, and the brown bag with the buckles, but not this one. And on the other hand, it wasn't by chance that she had found this particular handbag and everything in it—she had really found it, and hadn't waited for some saleslady to turn away—and this was fate. And absolutely positively, if no one else had found it before her. Wasn't that another sign? It was. Zahara's identity card and the slips of paper—she could make a bonfire of them all. Of course it would burn. Yes, and the ashes, if she buried them—wouldn't they be more effective than sticking pins in a doll? Of course they would. With a decisive hand she stuck the handbag and all its contents under her mattress. After the holidays, she would decide what to do. Meanwhile, it would all stay with her.

Chapter 5

I told him so," burst out Naeema Bashari, choking between sobs, and she looked at her husband, who sat shriveled in the center of the low sofa that had been reupholstered for the last holidays. He clutched his head in his hands, as though if he let go it would fall off and break the glass surface of the coffee table, where his eyes were fixed on the shadow of his reflection. "I told him so: We have to watch over the girl, we have to . . . That she's . . . That she's too . . . too pretty . . . That she trusts everyone . . . That she cares about everyone . . ."

"You waited for two days until you contacted us," said Michael, and now, after having spent hours with them, he felt for the first time that it was possible to get on with the investigation. He said nothing explicit about it, but just nodded his head at Sergeant Yair, who was sitting on the corner of the sofa in the Basharis' living room, very close to Ezra Bashari, his fingers tight on the tiny recorder he had hidden under his thin windbreaker, as if that would improve the reception. Rays of sunlight drew a circle of pale autumnal afternoon light around the large brass bowl under the window, and when they touched the leaves of the philodendron inside it, a reddish hue mixed into the bright green. Because of the sun's rays, Tzilla Bachar blinked in the rattan armchair in the corner of the room, before she began to write down every word.

"We didn't know, we had no idea. Even when they told us to come and identify her," wailed Naeema Bashari. She stuck her fingers into her kinky gray hair, and for a moment Michael was alarmed that she was about to pull out the locks of hair she was grasping, and beat her breast as she had at the morgue, but she just took off her glasses. With her shortsighted yellowish-brown gaze she looked straight into Michael's eyes and hugged her body in her thin arms. "We thought—I don't know, she hadn't come back yet from Tel Aviv. We thought that she was still at her girlfriend's house. She'd said she might only come back just before the holiday began. We couldn't believe it. You don't think about things like that with a girl who never got in trouble, who only . . . If you had known her . . ."

Michael looked at Ezra Bashari, whose fingers were straining to hold up his hanging head, so far apart that each looked separate from the others. When they had taken off the sheet at the Forensic Institute, disclosing the mane of hair and the smashed face, Ezra Bashari had collapsed to the floor and lost consciousness. Michael had looked at Tzilla, who called in Dr. Solomon right away.

"It's our daughter," whispered Naeema Bashari, and something beyond pain, a kind of great astonishment, was evident in her whisper. She had clasped the slender ankle of the naked body with a hand tipped by wide, bluish fingernails and indicated the birthmark that marred the smooth thigh, and the wail she emitted grew sharper and lengthened into a prolonged, monotone scream that only after many long minutes was ended and shattered into its sounds. Michael shut his eyes. Steel cabinet after steel cabinet was penetrated by her cries, wall after wall. They filled the long corridor and hovered over the office floor and the lecture rooms until they came back and etched themselves on the inside of his head; like when he was a boy and had swum out into the sea and a huge wave came and blinded him.

Tzilla had whispered to Dr. Solomon: "When you're done here, give her something too," and she tugged gently at Naeema Bashari while she was still screaming and shepherded her gently out of the morgue into the long corridor and from there into the pathologist's office. A moment later Solomon came in with a hypodermic in his hand. "You have to give her something," said Tzilla.

She grasped the mother's thin arm as the pathologist muttered: "We'll give you something to calm you down, Mrs. . . . ." He looked at Tzilla with a questioning glance.

"Bashari," whispered Tzilla.

"Now, now, Mrs. Bashari," said the pathologist between her choking sobs. "This will make you feel better, for a while," and he stuck the tip of the hypodermic in her arm. After a few minutes the wails changed to sobs, which she kept up until they got her back home.

"We have to deal with Daddy dear, I very sadly fear," Dr. Solomon war-

bled, and hurried to the room to which they had taken the father. It took quite a while before they restored him to consciousness. "Where is Netanel?" he mumbled when he opened his eyes, and since then Ezra Bashari hadn't said a word.

Thus the hours passed—Yair brought them a pitcher of water and glasses, and in the ashtray the cigarette butts marked the passage of time—until it was possible to begin the initial clarification, though not yet the investigation itself. It was Yair who encouraged Naeema Bashari to talk, in the police car on their way back from the Forensic Institute to Jerusalem. Between sobs she had muttered in confusion: "She went to her girlfriend's, that's what she'd done. She'd just gone to visit a friend . . . Our flower . . . That was our Zahara . . . A flower, like her name, Zahara. There's no Zahara . . . She's gone . . ."

Michael, from his seat next to Bachar, who drove in silence, couldn't manage to hear what Sergeant Yair was asking her, and he only picked up fragments of her replies: "She was twenty-two and a half . . . Born on Shavuot . . . After three sons . . . We couldn't believe it . . . The child of our old age." Her voice grew fainter: "Until we managed . . . Until we had a bit . . . With our own ten fingers . . . By ourselves . . . With no help . . . And Zahara . . . A flower." She choked. "Again . . . I didn't watch . . . Me . . . because of me . . ."

At the entrance to Jerusalem her weeping grew louder and she beat her chest with her fists and cried out again: "I didn't watch over her. I never told anyone . . . I didn't call her brothers all those times she came in late. I didn't even worry at first. We thought she had gone to her girlfriend's in Tel Aviv. A girl she met in the army. We shouldn't have let her serve in the army. If it hadn't been for her brothers, she wouldn't have gone. A girl from an observant family has nothing to do there. What would she do there? We could have kept her at home, and would anyone have said anything? But her brothers put it into her head."

While they were still in the police car, Michael asked for the friend's name and address. "I have it written down at home," moaned Naeema Bashari then, and he repeated the request when they were sitting in the living room. "Orit . . . No, Orly. Orly Shushan. She's a journalist, an important journalist. She works at *Ma'ariv,* I think, or at *Yedioth.* I don't have her phone number," she said weakly. "Whenever I asked her, she said to me—Zahara—'What do you need it for? I'll call you.'"

"Orly Shushan," Michael repeated, and nodded.

"I know the name," muttered Tzilla, and when she went out of the room she put her mobile phone to use. Her voice out in the corridor was audible, decisive and energetic as she imposed tasks on the intelligence department.

Through the window, the front garden was visible, and from above a dentate leaf spiraled downward, this way and that, and drifted away from the fig tree from which it had detached itself. There had been a tree just like it at Michael's parents' house in the moshav, and during her last years his mother used to sit beneath it at twilight, in the lounge chair he had brought her for her seventy-first birthday ("When am I going to sit in it? Do you think I have time just to sit around? You spoil me too much," she grumbled when she got it, but happiness sparkled in her eyes). On the blue stripes of the lounge chair she stretched her skinny legs, in dark stockings, and she rested her hands in her lap. There, on the lounge chair in the shade of the fig tree, he had found her one Friday evening, her legs stretched out along the stripes but her hands dangling down by her side, with her fingers, which had turned blue, touching the ground as if she were trying to reach the row of radishes and aerate the soil there. Her head was hanging to one side, like when she dozed, and when he closed her eyes in the darkening twilight a large purple fig fell at her feet, and he said to himself, This is it. And in his increasing weakness he noticed the serenity that enveloped her broad face and dark skin, the feel of which he remembered from his childhood, and for a moment he thought he heard her voice murmuring, as she sometimes did, although maybe sarcastically, at that time of day: "Every man beneath his vine and every man beneath his fig tree."

He looked at the window. Mrs. Bashari was sitting with her back to it, and his eyes paused on the five entrances to the apartment block across the narrow street. The smooth, white marblelike façade, which was supposed to conceal the gray concrete, was a later addition to the helter-skelter construction of the 1950s, when thousands of immigrants had come all at once from North Africa, among them his own family, which had left Casablanca. When his parents arrived on the shores of Israel—this is what they told him when he grew up—his father set down his little three-year-old son, and knelt and kissed the sand. He died two years later. "Your father was a Zionist. He took it in with his mother's milk, from his great-grandfather," his mother once said to him, a short time before she died. She never spoke much about her first years in Israel, but from time to time, especially when she looked at her surroundings and touched the trunk of the fig tree she had planted during the first years, she would recall how they had driven them in the middle of the night north to a place she had never heard of, a new moshav where the hastily built cabins had not yet been inhabited. "There wasn't anything there," she said on another occasion, with a half-smile, "just two iron beds with mattresses, and there we were with six children. With his own hands your father built this house, and every day he said that it was a mitzvah to build the Land of Israel, that God had commanded it. That's why it hurt him more than it hurt me, the attitude. He couldn't believe that Jews could behave that way toward other Jews."

They had apparently added the white facing to the gray apartment blocks in the neighborhood rehabilitation program. Not only did it not make the ugliness disappear—it emphasized it. It would have been better to have left the original walls; the thought ran through his mind, astonishingly, as if all he cared about was the spoiling of the landscape. Maybe it was because of the apartment he had bought a few days ago, here in the neighborhood, two streets away. It too was in the Arab style: high ceilings, window niches, a rounded façade beyond which there was a large room that looked out onto the street. ("Remember that it's an illusion, this spaciousness," Linda the real estate agent had warned him, and she counted the square floor tiles to calculate the exact dimensions of the room. "Because of the height of the ceiling it seems to you that the room is larger than it really is.")

In the Basharis' living room, the original floor tiles were preserved, and around the pale blue mat the arabesques painted on them were visible. In the center of the mat stood a low coffee table on thin legs, and Ezra Bashari rested his arms on the glass surface. Pale heavy curtains were drawn back on either side of the large window, and on the background of the window Naeema Bashari rocked back and forth, back and forth. The rocking chair she sat in was covered in a coarse fabric and moved back and forth in the rhythm of her quiet sobs.

Tzilla returned to the room. "There's no answer yet from Netanel Bashari," she whispered to Michael. "No one is answering there and I didn't want to leave a message." Michael looked at his watch and scowled skeptically.

"What can I do?" she asked. "It will take her two hours to get here. That's what she said. She doesn't have a car and we have no one to send to bring her. She's in Rishon LeZion now, interviewing some fortune-teller, a woman who reads coffee grinds."

In the apartment block opposite them, over the railing of the balcony on the second floor, a rug with a Persian pattern was spread. A woman with her head wrapped in a colorful kerchief was thwacking it with a yellow straw carpet-beater, and when she tired she leaned on the railing and looked around. Against the stone wall beneath her slouched a fat little girl in a blue sweat suit that wasn't her size anymore. The leather leash she was holding sank into the flesh of her hands, and at the other end of the leash a small poodle struggled and pulled in the opposite direction.

"I think we have something for you," said the duty sergeant on the morning of the eve of the holiday. Early in the morning Mr. and Mrs. Bashari had come in to report their daughter's disappearance, and after he had listened to their description of her, he looked at the photograph the mother had placed before him and felt immediately—this is what he whispered to Michael on the internal phone—"This is the one you found."

In Michael's office, with trembling hands Naeema Bashari undid the folds in the faded plastic bag in which she kept her identity card and handed it to Danny Balilty, who a moment earlier, when they came in, had moved away from the door and stopped, for the moment, his harangue about apartments. Quietly, Balilty seated himself on the low steel cupboard and took the photograph she handed him: a dark girl in a white dress, with straight black hair down to her shoulders, high cheekbones, narrowed eyes and a broad smile that made dimples appear in her cheeks. Then he looked at the identity card and when he straightened up, his belly stuck out and the bottom button of his ironed pink shirt threatened to burst. Across his face spread a kind of grimace that Michael knew very well—sarcastic and victorious scorn—and his small eyes narrowed even more.

"Did you see the address?" Balilty handed the photograph and the blue identity card to Michael. Michael glanced at the card and concealed his astonishment with an equable shrug of his shoulders. "Two streets away from you," whispered Balilty. "Two streets away from where you bought!"

"Will wonders never cease," Michael said with extreme indifference, and handed the identity card back to Naeema Bashari. She wrapped the plastic bag around and around the identity card, pushed it to the bottom of her handbag and looked at them expectantly. Michael continued to examine the broadly smiling girl, considering her features beyond the smile.

"We wanted to come with our son, Netanel," said the mother. "He's a professor at the university and he understands about . . . He is more knowledgeable . . . But we couldn't find him. All our sons—we couldn't reach any of them," she explained. "My daughter-in-law . . . I phoned my daughter-in-law yesterday. She hadn't seen her, and she also said that my son, Netanel, hadn't seen Zahara for several days, but she was actually just . . . She had people there, so she wasn't paying much attention, and we . . ."

When Michael asked them to accompany him to the Forensic Institute, Ezra Bashari blanched. With slender fingers he pushed his tie aside and extracted a tiny book from the inner pocket of his jacket, and after he licked his forefinger with his tongue, he began to page through it and mutter.

"I would like my son, Netanel, to come with us," said the mother, and Michael dialed at her request, first his home and then his mobile, and finally his office at the university.

"There's no alternative," he said to Naeema Bashari. "We tried, but it's impossible to get hold of him or your daughter-in-law."

This couple resembled each other in their slenderness, their low, bent stature and their alarmed expressions ("We've never been to the police before," said Naeema Bashari when she entered the room and when she got into the car and when she got out of it), and they even resembled each other in their delicate, miniature facial features. They made him think about his mother. Their two slim bodies leaned forward and they obediently answered every question. Their frightened, serious faces, the unreserved trust they placed in the duty sergeant and Michael and even Balilty—all these reminded him of his mother sitting in offices of the municipal council and waiting there submissively for the permit to enclose the porch.

They covered the distance between Jerusalem and the Forensic Institute in Tel Aviv in silence. Ezra Bashari's mutterings and sighs and his fast leafing through the thin pages of his Psalter were also audible in the front seat. On the way back he didn't read any more Psalms.

When they returned to Jerusalem and the police car drove past the street where the apartment he had bought was, Michael glanced surreptitiously at the corner house, because he had not yet got used to the idea that he would be living there, behind the windows and the closed shutters on the second floor. Since he had left his parents' home, when he was sent at the age of twelve to the boarding school for gifted children in Jerusalem, none of the places he had lived had been home. Even the walls of his parents' house, when he went back there for the first Passover vacation, had radiated strangeness and alienation. The steel springs of his narrow childhood bed creaked when he tried to find his old place in it. The father of his ex-wife, Niva, had bought them an apartment. She, the mother of his only son, had furnished it in consultation with her parents, and there too he never felt at home. And ever since he left ("Sucker," said Balilty years later; "You could have got half of it; it was also registered in your name"), he had been living in rented apartments and saw them only as way stations.

"This is where the neighborhood begins," said Eli Bachar when they came to the intersection. The Basharis were silent in their seats. "If you take a right it's Emek Refaim and the German Colony, and if you take a left it's Bethlehem Road, the main street of Baka, and that's where we're going." Sergeant Yair was not familiar with this part of Jerusalem, and through Eli Bachar's voice flitted the tone of a tired cabdriver trying to sound authoritative.

"I've never been here before," remarked Sergeant Yair as they got out of the car, with Tzilla supporting the Basharis. "I've passed through but I've never . . . What kind of people live here?"

"What do you mean 'what kind of people'?" wondered Eli Bachar.

"What kind of people—from which community? This city is divided into neighborhoods and—"

"There's everything here," said Eli Bachar. "All kinds. There are Moroccans from the 1950s, who were evacuated from the transit camp in Talpiot. Ask him"—he indicated Michael, who had already got out of the car—"and there are even some Arabs who stayed after 1948, and there are a few Greeks who have kept their houses since then. And there are rich American and French Jews who have been coming here since 1967. There are shopkeepers from the Mahaneh Yehuda market and there are yuppies. There's everything here. University professors and criminals and lawyers. Whatever you want—you've got it here. Romanians, German Jews, Peace Now, ultra-Orthodox from Shas and also from America. Even Bulgarians."

"Why 'even'?"

"There aren't many Bulgarians in Jerusalem," explained Eli Bachar. "They went to the coastal plain, to Jaffa. But some of them do live here."

"The houses are pretty, but it's far, isn't it?"

"Far from what?" asked Eli Bachar.

"Far from downtown, from work, from the—"

"What are you talking about?" said Eli Bachar. "Do you know how much a house costs here? This is a central neighborhood, one of the most important in Jerusalem, even if it's at the edge. That's the way it is with this city." He sighed as he slammed the car door shut. "The center is dead and everything important is at the margins. Look, have a look at the shops on Emek Refaim and Bethlehem Road. There's everything here. You can never leave here for an entire year and get along without ever going downtown, even without a mall." He hastened his pace and touched Michael's arm. "Isn't that so?"

"Not now, Eli," answered Michael. "Later. We have to go in and start. They're waiting. And you—" he watched Tzilla and the Basharis as they walked slowly up the path to the house— "you're going back to the office."

"Going back to the office? Going back to the office and what? Locating the brothers?" he asked unwillingly.

"And phoning us to tell us what's happening," said Michael.

"Yes, sir," said Eli angrily. "It could take hours."

"Why are you so impatient? I thought you had a great vacation, and Tzilla says that your batteries are still full. Why are you so antsy? The moment you have them there, just let us know, bring them here, to their parents', or tell us you aren't." He looked at Eli for a moment and clapped him on the shoulder: "You know that Yair is too young to do this by himself," he added.

"There are always reasons," said Eli Bachar, "but it always turns out that I'm at the margins of the picture, and you have no idea how sick of this I am."

"Sometimes the margins are the center," said Michael. "I'm waiting to hear from you."

When they found out the Basharis' address, Michael ignored the "I told you so" expression that spread across Danny Balilty's face, and instead of telling him there was no connection between his argument about the hasty purchase and the murder victim's home, which was two streets away, he said: "So far we haven't made any progress with anything."

Balilty's extreme sensitivity to any remark that implied criticism of his effectiveness caused him to drop the matter of the apartment. "What did you expect?" he grumbled. "That I'd find her just by the one dress? It's not an exclusive model from a Paris fashion house, you know. And anyway, if you'd waited another few days, I would also have traced her for you by the dress."

Even before the final identification, when Naeema Bashari mentioned Rosenstein, the lawyer in whose office Zahara had been working ever since she got out of the army, Balilty had put everything else aside and said: "Rosenstein? I know him. Of course I know him. Is there anyone in Jerusalem who doesn't know him? He has a palace in Talbieh, doesn't he? On Marcus Street, near Sherover's villa, across from the theater"—he chuckled joylessly—"with a round façade and windows the size of a soccer field. She works for him?" And the moment Ezra Bashari lost consciousness, he called Rosenstein and informed him with no further ado of the death of Zahara Bashari.

At the other end of the line, sounds of rapid, heavy breathing could be heard. "I don't believe it," whispered the lawyer finally. "I just don't believe it. Murder? Are you sure?"

"We've completed the identification," promised Balilty. "Her parents identified her. There is no possible error."

"I don't understand . . . I don't understand this . . . Who would want to . . . Is it security-related?" Balilty remained silent and waited.

"Or sexual? In what context?"

"I'm sorry," said Balilty into the receiver. "I didn't know you were so close . . ."

"What do mean?" The lawyer's voice broke. "That lovely girl . . . A flower, she was like my daughter . . . It's been two years now . . . She was our receptionist and answered the phones . . . Everyone was crazy about her . . . There hasn't been a secretary who has stayed with us for so long . . . You don't understand . . ."

"I'm truly sorry," Balilty said, and rolled his eyes to the ceiling. He hated to be the one to break the news, and this time he was also surprised by the lawyer's emotional reaction, and regretted that he hadn't gone to inform him face-to-face, because by the time they met he would have recovered. "I'm really, really sorry, Mr. Rosenstein," he said to him again, "but I can be at your place in a little while. Just see to it that we can talk," and, wasting no time, he was on his way immediately.

Traffic police were directing drivers on the Tel Aviv–Jerusalem road into a single narrow lane, and there was a long line of cars. "Maybe you'll tell me," Balilty said to his secretary between the tasks he gave her over his mobile phone, "why they always do this in the morning? Why can't they bring a few Thais or Romanians to do it at night? Everywhere in the world they repair the roads at night, and only here . . ."

"Should I send someone to bring Netanel Bashari or should I just summon him?"

"You can't just summon him," said Balilty. "It's his sister who died like that. What's got into you? You don't tell a member of the family something like that over the phone or by summons . . . Where is he?"

"That's just it. He's roaming around somewhere, and his wife isn't home either. We looked for him at home and there was no answer. We tried the university, but it's closed and will be closed the whole week."

"Does he teach at the university?"

"He's a professor."

"Which department?"

"History. He's a professor of history, at the Russian Studies Institute. Didn't you know?"

"Russian studies?!" Balilty laughed. "A Yemenite who knows Russian?"

"How should I know? Probably he studied it. Why, don't you know Yiddish? With my own ears I've heard you speaking Yiddish with Hannah from the cafeteria, so why are—"

"A Yemenite and a professor—a killer combination," said Balilty.

"You shouldn't talk that way," scolded the secretary. "You know that on my mother's side I'm also—"

"That's why," said Balilty. "That's why I talk that way."

"Aren't you turning the siren on to get out of the traffic jam?"

"I am. When we're done. Look, this is what we'll do: Send Moshe to Bezalel with the basic information and tell him to bring Netanel Bashari. His name's Netanel, isn't it?" And without waiting for an answer, he continued: "To his parents' house."

"Okay," said the secretary, "so now we've solved the problem with him. But what are you going to do about the other brother? He's in the field now, with the army near Nablus. How do you want to—"

"Nothing easier," Balilty said, and angled the car onto the narrow margin of the road. "He has a mobile phone, doesn't he? So call him on the mobile. He's the youngest, isn't he? Bezalel?"

"Except for Zahara Bashari. She was born seven years after him," noted the secretary.

"What is he there? A company commander, isn't he? In the armored corps?"

"A deputy battalion commander, no less. So you want me to phone him? What am I going to tell him on his mobile phone? To drop everything and come because . . ."

"You'll have to tell him why on the telephone"— Balilty sighed—"or tell him something vague. We're not sending anyone specially to Nablus now. With all the mess that's going on, there aren't enough police. They're all at the Temple Mount or in Nazareth. With all those Arabs, this really isn't the time to start a new case . . . What is he, Bezalel Bashari, a major?"

"Can't a person be a Yemenite and a major?"

"He can be the chief of staff for all I care. They're babies these days, those majors. They weren't even born when we . . . How old is he?"

"Twenty-nine."

"Okay. What difference does it make? They should just bring him to where I . . . To the lawyer, not straight to his parents' house, all right?"

"All right. And there's also Eliyahu," she reminded him. "Who's going to inform Eliyahu?"

"Who's Eliyahu?" Balilty was confused.

"*Nu,* the second brother, the middle son. The one who lives in Los Angeles."

"Los Angeles?"

"I already told you that, when you phoned from Abu Kabir the second time."

"The family can tell him. If he's there, in any case it will take him two days to get here. And anyway, how much can he help us if he's been there for three years now? What's in him for us?"

"You're the one who always says you never can tell," grumbled the secretary.

"Etty, sweetie," Balilty cajoled, "do me a favor and—"

"Don't call me sweetie."

"Why? If I call you sweetie, is that sexual harassment?" Balilty giggled and breathed loudly. "It's impossible to talk anymore these days. 'Don't call me this and don't call me that,' and soon we're going to have to ask permission to breathe."

"Why don't you just turn on the siren, *nu*. Do you want us to have a debate now about what's allowed and what's not?"

"Who's talking about a debate?" The intelligence officer laughed loudly. "Debate, she says to me. Anyway, who's going to sexually harass you with that belly you're carrying?"

"Is that what you think?" Even in the midst of all the noises that filtered into the telephone Balility could hear the smile that didn't conceal the fact that she was insulted. "Do you think a pregnant woman is no longer sexy? You better believe that it turns some people on. Ask Haim if he doesn't love me this way. He's always—"

"Don't tell me. That's all I need, to hear about your sex life with another man. Etty, darling, I'm just so jealous. A husband isn't for fucking, and if he is, then you don't talk about it. And don't let it go to your head, you hear? As if you haven't fucked me enough with this pregnancy of yours, and in another two months you'll be leaving me an orphan—"

"Not two months. You wish. Less than a month."

"I don't want to think about it." Balilty sighed. "And I haven't even found a replacement . . ."

"I have."

"You have? You didn' say anything about . . ."

"I'll tell you tomorrow."

"Something good, though?"

"Some*one*, not some*thing*," scolded the secretary. "Talk nice. She doesn't know you. Her name's Sarah. She's new."

"I don't want a new girl," protested Balilty, and in the same breath he asked: "Is she good-looking at least? How old is she?"

"Haven't you turned the siren on? How do you expect me to get any work done here? She's good, I'm telling you. Better than me. Afterward, you won't want me back. You'll see."

"*You'll always have a place in my heart,*" sang Balilty. "*Forever, and ever, a place in my heart,*" and he turned on the siren in the police car and sped past the line of cars. It started to drizzle when he reached Sha'ar Hagai and the climb to Jerusalem began, but he didn't slow down and he didn't turn off the siren until he entered the underground parking lot behind King George Street.

A long silence hung in the air in the Basharis' living room, until Michael asked: "Did she have a boyfriend?"

Naeema Bashari shook her head. "No, not anyone steady," she said after some thought. "There were all kinds of . . . Everyone wanted her but she . . . She was waiting for someone . . . suitable, not Ashkenazi."

"What do you mean by not Ashkenazi?"

"Our daughter hated Ashkenazim. She hated them," Naeema Bashari said, and buried her face in her hands, through which her voice was muffled. "I don't know where . . . It's been that way . . . since her bat mitzvah, more or less. It started with the family roots project she did at school, and after that . . ." She took her hands from her face and spread them. "She's been involved with the Yemenite heritage."

"But she dated," said Michael.

"She went out, to the movies, to a café . . . But there wasn't anyone . . . you know."

"But her dates came to the house? You met them, didn't you?"

"Sometimes someone came here to fetch her, but they didn't sit . . . Boyfriends, no . . . She preferred to meet them somewhere else . . ." There was embarrassment in Naeema Bashari's voice. "She had . . . She liked her privacy," and suddenly she suppressed a sob.

"So you didn't meet anyone?" Michael asked, and heard the astonishment in his own voice.

"Maybe her brothers . . . Netanel . . . She was close to him. She didn't want us to . . . never spoke . . . maybe she spoke to Linda. Ezra, she did speak to Linda, didn't she?" She turned to her husband, but he remained in his silence. "They were sort of close, the two of them," said Naeema Bashari distractedly.

"Linda?" prompted Michael.

"Linda. She lives here, in the neighborhood, up the street." With a limp hand Naeema indicated the direction. "A good woman . . . half-Jewish, on her mother's side only, but a good person. Truly good. Sometimes girlfriends did come over, to eat, and there's also that fellow that was with her in the army. Danny? Is his name Danny?" She looked over at her husband, who didn't raise his head.

"Did she have a diary?"

"I don't know," said Naeema Bashari. "Just that little one she kept in her handbag, with all her appointments and phone numbers, and you said that her handbag . . . You said you hadn't found it."

"We'll find it," Michael said, and took a deep breath. "There's something else I have to tell you." He looked at Ezra Bashari's bent head.

"Your daughter, Zahara, she . . . ," he stammered, and made himself look Naeema Bashari straight in the eye. She removed her glasses and fixed her eyes on him. "She was in the twelfth week of pregnancy."

Through the open window, above the shiny green leaves of the philodendron, the rising and falling sound of the burglar alarm of a car parked on the street cut through the silence that fell on the room.

Ezra Bashari raised his head. "That's a lie," he whispered hoarsely. "You're lying."

Michael felt his flesh crawl on the back of his neck and his shoulders. "No, I'm really sorry, but it's the truth. The pathologist at the Forensic Institute can confirm it."

Ezra Bashari's small, full lips trembled. "It's impossible," he said in a shaky voice. "Our daughter . . . She kept herself . . . She herself told me that . . ."

Naeema Bashari rocked back and forth. She shut her eyes tight, as if trying to dam the new tears that were falling from their corners.

"I though that you could also help us with—"

For the first time since the beginning of the conversation, Ezra Bashari looked at his wife. "These are things that a mother knows," he said to Michael.

"She knows if she's told," said Naeema Bashari angrily. "If she isn't told, she doesn't know anything."

"There are things a mother knows even without being told," said Ezra Bashari. "My mother, of blessed memory, always knew such things about my sister Carmella."

"And did that make Carmella's life any better?" Naeema Bashari asked coldly, and wiped away her tears with the back of her hand. She pursed her lips.

When disaster strikes, it does not necessarily reveal the love between couples; they don't all hasten to lean on each other. There are couples for whom disaster brings to the surface all the bitter residues between them and animates all their repressed accounts. And these accounts, they had to be settled, said Michael to himself, and another voice inside him mocked his belief that these were things that could be settled.

"We have to know exactly what happened on the last day . . . the last time you saw her . . . Perhaps we can try to reconstruct . . . the places she was before she disappeared. I mean . . ." Michael cleared his throat and glanced over at Tzilla, whose crossed legs tightened as if in protection against the hostility that had been exposed. "That is . . ." Tzilla's head remained bent over the pad on which she was writing, and Sergeant Yair kept his head down and was silent. They let him ask the questions. If only Balilty had been here, he thought, because at a time like this you needed people like him, people who don't know what embarrassment is. If only it were possible to ask them separately, but it was still too early to question each of them individually. "We have to get all the information you can give us, so we can solve this. I understand Zahara was a very pretty girl . . ."

"Pretty!?" spluttered Naeema Bashari. "Pretty?! She was beautiful. A flower. You've never seen anything like her." All at once she began to cry, loudly and bitterly, and she got up and left the room.

"You probably know what your daughter's schedule was," said Michael to Ezra Bashari.

The father looked at him sharply. "She is the child of our old age, and with us it is customary . . . In our community, the mother deals with such things."

"But you certainly know, in a general way," tried Michael.

"What I know, everyone knows," the father said. "You too know that our Zahara worked for Mr. Rosenstein, the lawyer. She was saving money for her education, and everyone knows that. And she also earned a bit of pocket money, singing at celebrations. She has . . . had a special voice—very beautiful, deep. She inherited it from my mother of blessed memory. She also had a beautiful voice and she also sang at weddings, but not for money. In her day, it was considered a good deed." With a long, delicate finger Ezra Bashari touched the birthmark at the corner of his right eyebrow, and then wiped his forefinger over his eyelashes, as if trying to eradicate the vision he saw before his eyes. "Everyone also knows how active she was on behalf of the Yemenite heritage. She was planning to establish a museum at the synagogue, nearby here, and everyone knew that, too." He suppressed a sob and continued: "And sometimes, after work, Zahara . . ." He buried his head in his small hands and bent his head. "She went"—his voice faded into his hands, and Sergeant Yair fingered the recorder—"to sing, or she went out to a movie like every—"

"But the day before yesterday, when she didn't come home, did she let you know where she was going?"

"No, she didn't let us know."

"Was that typical? Had it ever happened that—"

"Never. She always let us know if she was going to be late. She knew that her mother couldn't fall asleep until she came in. She would always let us know."

"You say she always got in touch to let you know," confirmed Michael.

"I don't know details," choked Ezra Bashari. "You can't ask an independent girl of twenty-two where she is every moment, and I didn't want to annoy her . . . I wanted her to stay with us at least until her wedding and even afterward, and I've been saving money for an apartment for her since she was born . . . You can't keep asking her where she's going and with whom and when . . . The times . . . are different. . . . I only know that in the morning she went to work."

"Mr. Bashari," said Michael softly, "you know we haven't found her handbag, or a diary. Does she . . . Did she have another appointment book, with all those activities?"

"I don't know." Ezra Bashari sighed. "You probably think that I . . . that I didn't take an interest, but that's not true. What she told me, I heard. She has . . . She had . . . When she laughed, the whole house . . . the whole street . . . the whole world was full of light."

"Maybe you can recall some details? Facts?" tried Michael.

Ezra Bashari shook his head from side to side. "When she said things, I listened very carefully. But she didn't talk much about facts, what she'd done and where she'd been. Only sometimes. I know one or two of her girlfriends, I know Rosenstein the lawyer. Sometimes she would go down to Tel Aviv to go out in the evening, and then she would sleep at a girlfriend's house. Sometimes she would stay late at work. And there were always her plans to study."

"What did she want to study?"

"Singing, and abroad, in America. Her brother . . . We have a son who lives in America. He was sent there by his company here and he—"

Naeema Bashari came into the room, carrying a large envelope with exaggerated care. Her husband buried his head in his hands again, and Michael, to whom she silently held out the envelope, took colored photographs out of it and placed them in his lap.

There were twenty photographs or more: Zahara in an army uniform; Zahara in a checked shirt dangling outside her jeans; Zahara in a wet T-shirt, her head flung back and water dripping from her hair; Zahara in a long red dress—"at her older brother's wedding, eight years ago . . . She was fourteen then," said Naeema Bashari in a cold voice; Zahara in shorts, in a white bathing suit, stretched out on her side smiling at the camera, with a boy kneeling next to her.

"Who's this?" asked Michael.

Naeema Bashari polished the lenses of her glasses and brought the picture close to her eyes. "I think his name is Yossi, but I'm not sure," she said, and handed the photo to her husband.

"Not Yossi, Eitan," said the father. "Eitan Sachs, the son of Yehuda Sachs from the bank. Don't you remember that he used to take her to the beach? They went to high school together," he explained to Michael. "He isn't in touch with her anymore."

"Sachs? Ashkenazi?"

"That was when she was still in school," explained Naeema Bashari. "He didn't count as a man."

For a moment the murder was forgotten and it was as if Michael and his team were leafing through an ordinary photo album and admiring a successful daughter together with the parents. He picked out a large black-and-white photo of Zahara in a black evening dress, her smooth black hair combed in the style of an Egyptian princess and covering half her face. Her mouth was open and her two hands were clasping a microphone. "Zahara singing, at a wedding . . . ," the mother said, and choked.

Michael cleared his throat. "We'll take these pictures with us," he said. "And we'll give them back," he hastened to add when he saw the alarm in her face. "We'll also have to do a search of her room, with your permission."

"There's probably also a video from a performance of hers," interjected Sergeant Yair.

"We don't have one. Maybe in her room. Her brother Netanel has one," Naeema Bashari said, and looked anxiously at her husband, who opened his palms in front of him.

"Do whatever is necessary," he said in a cracked voice. "We won't get in your way."

Michael nodded to Tzilla. She left the room again and a moment later came back in. "They're on their way—the Criminal Identification Unit. Ten minutes, no more."

"You can get started," he said to Yair. "If Mrs. Bashari can take you to her room, you can get started."

• • •

"I'm going through everything very slowly," Sergeant Yair explained when Michael entered the room afterward. The closet was open, and its contents were already lying on the striped rug, ready to be collected by the Criminal Identification people. Sergeant Yair sat on the narrow bed and around him were strewn papers, photos, an empty little perfume flask, old diaries in colorful plastic bindings, postcards, greeting cards, notebooks, beads, hairpins, a rusty key, an earring set with red stones, brass bracelets, an inside-out cigarette package with a phone number written on it. "Do we need this?" he asked Michael, who had spread some sheet music on his knees.

"I need everything," answered Michael, and from the shelf up against the opposite wall he pulled a stack of yellow cardboard files. "Everything. Just put it in piles, and later they'll come from Criminal Identification and put it all in bags. We won't do the sorting here."

"What's in there?" asked Yair, indicating the yellow files with his head. Michael was leafing through one of them.

"A catalogue," murmured Michael as he turned the pages. "It's a catalogue of Yemenite women's clothing and jewelry."

"Take these, too," Michael said, and handed the other files to the sergeant, "but just don't start looking through them now. There are all kinds of charms and spells there."

"To cancel a spell or the Evil Eye," murmured Yair, "take the living silver called *zaibak* and the white stones found in—what's this?—the gizzard of a black rooster . . ."

"Show it to me," demanded Tzilla as she entered the room, and the sergeant handed her the cardboard file.

"Leave that alone now," scolded Michael. "What else have you found?"

"This, in the top drawer." Yair pointed at a small paper bag. "There are some pills here, and a doctor's prescription. I don't know what it is."

Michael looked at the prescription and the pills. "These are birth control pills," he said, and held the packet out to Tzilla, who examined it and nodded.

"How do you know?" she asked.

"I've seen some like that," he replied, but she was already busy with something else.

"The date is from last year," she said.

"Look at that," wondered the young sergeant. "Here we have birth control pills, and there we have how to exorcise spirits from the body and how to tell fortunes. How do they go together?"

"*Nu,* people are a complex thing," said Michael, "and when you rummage in a person's life like that, it's only surprising when there are no surprises. Write down the doctor's name; maybe he's also the doctor who took care of the pregnancy. And I want the diary from last year, with the phone numbers and all that. You'll probably find it with the rest of them," instructed Michael.

"I've already found it." Yair took a small booklet out of his pocket. "I knew it was the most important. And I also looked at the names a bit. Here's the name of that friend of hers, that journalist you mentioned, Orly Shushan, with her phone number in Tel Aviv, and also her mobile. And also her parents' phone number in Jerusalem. And there are also other people's names here, women and men and also—"

"We'll check it out in a little while," said Michael. "What's that over there, those papers in the corner of the drawer?"

Yair spread out the packet of forms on his lap. "Look," he said in astonishment. "These are mortgage forms, filled out. Where she planned to buy an apart . . . It's in her name, look. It's very strange, isn't it? Why would a girl who wants to study abroad take out a mortgage? Unless she wanted to invest, but then her parents don't . . . And there's also a letter of guarantee from a lawyer—Rosenstein and Nahir, Attorneys-at-Law. But I don't understand where this apartment is."

"Show that to me," Michael said, and held out his hand for the yellow forms. "It says here 'Railroad Street,' don't you see? It's an application for a mortgage on an apartment on Railroad Street. Yes, this is a letter from Rosenstein the lawyer saying that he guarantees the payments. Okay, Balilty is talking to him now. We'll have to summon. Try to get hold of Balilty; I want to talk to him," and as he spoke he went back to the living room holding the forms.

Naeema Bashari had never heard of any plans to purchase an apartment. Ezra Bashari demanded to see the documents.

"There's no contract," said Michael after he had looked through them. "There's no purchase contract. They don't give a mortgage without a contract. That I do know."

Ezra Bashari returned the papers to Michael with a dismissive gesture.

"I don't understand this," he said bitterly, "but there are a lot of things I don't understand, and this is the least of them."

"Do you know the apartment?"

"I know the building, from the address," said Ezra Bashari. "Sometimes I go past there on my walks. It's an Arab house. They've added two stories to it and spoiled the way it looks, and now there's some Jew living there from France. Southern France, as they say here. That is, Morocco. He made money fast and finished it fast. From jewelry, I think. Diamonds or something."

"And she never said anything to you about the apartment?"

"Not a word," Ezra Bashari replied, and lowered his eyes. "Not a word. All this is happening so suddenly. This isn't the daughter I knew. A person doesn't know his own children, his flesh and blood. What have we come to?" he muttered, and collapsed back into the sofa, burying his face in his hands.

Tzilla took the documents and put them under her arm, as Yair came into the living room and held out the mobile phone to Michael.

"You wanted Balilty," he reminded Michael, who just kept looking at the extended phone.

"I'm on my way to you," said Balilty. "With her brother and all the—"

"Netanel Bashari?"

"Not that one . . . I don't know where he is . . . ," admitted Balilty grudgingly. "The younger brother, Bezalel."

"Bring the lawyer, too," whispered Michael. He moved down the hall to the front door, and in a low voice he told Balilty about the apartment that Zahara Bashari was about to buy.

"Where is it? What's the exact address?" Balilty demanded.

"Not on the phone," warned Michael. "Come here and we'll talk."

"He definitely won't want to come with me, that Rosenstein," said Balilty. "You know how it is with lawyers. You'll have to do it officially, a summons for questioning and all that."

"Tell him that we found the mortgage papers," said Michael. "He'll definitely come, you can be sure of that."

"You want all of them there together?" said Balilty in astonishment.

"All of them," affirmed Michael, "and if there's a riot here—I want to see it."

"Have you worked out who the doctor is?" he asked Tzilla, who took a closer look at the packet of pills.

"Dr. Antar, I think. Do you want me to find out now?"

"Now, yes. Whether she was a regular patient of his, whether he knew she was pregnant. And also if he knew by whom, all that."

It was about half an hour after Michael spoke to Balilty that a black BMW stopped in front of the house. A short, elderly, thickset man wearing a dark gray suit got out. In front of the wooden gate to the yard he stopped and adjusted his blue tie, and only then did he open the gate and enter the yard. The evening light broke on the thick lenses of his glasses when he paused on the path and looked at the front door, as if gathering his courage to go in.

Michael, who saw him from inside the house, hastened out. "Attorney Rosenstein?" he asked. "I'm Chief Inspector Ohayon, the head of the investigating team."

"I've never had anything to do with crime," the lawyer said, and held out a limp hand to be shaken. "I deal with real estate and bankruptcies, always. I've never—"

"Zahara Bashari worked at your office," Michael said, and drew him into the yard.

"For two years," said the lawyer, "and I've already told that other gentleman—I didn't catch his name—that she was like a daughter to me and we all—"

"Like a daughter." Michael decided to strike immediately. "Yes, that's obvious, from the guarantee for the mortgage that you're prepared to give her."

Rosenstein blushed.

"It's strange, even if it's someone who's like a daughter," said Michael, "for a sharp lawyer like you to be prepared to make a commitment like that, isn't it?"

"What are you implying?" asked the lawyer in a stern voice. "I'm here only because I care . . . Because I wanted to tell her parents . . . You know that this is an official investigation and you have no right to—"

"Not 'official,' and we haven't read you your rights," promised Michael, "just to help us get started with something. If you were really close to Zahara Bashari, and if she was so important to you, you certainly don't object to helping solve what happened to her."

The lawyer wiped his face with a checked handkerchief and sighed. Michael thought about his former father-in-law, a Polish Jewish

Holocaust survivor who became a diamond merchant and got rich, and didn't deny his daughter anything even during the years she was Michael's wife. Yozek, who was a model grandfather to their son Yuval, also had the habit of wiping his face with a cloth handkerchief when he was tense or emotional.

"Her parents didn't know anything about the plan to buy an apartment."

"It was an excellent investment, I told her. She could pay the mortgage from the rent. She wanted to go abroad to study."

"A girl who's going abroad to study doesn't conduct a relationship like that with a man," Michael said, and looked at the wooden fence and at a young woman getting out of a taxi and rummaging in a large shoulder bag.

"What relationship?"

"The kind of relationship in which someone buys an apartment for a lady," said Michael.

"I didn't . . . I didn't buy any apartment," the lawyer said, and loosened the knot in his tie. "I have already explained to the other gentleman, that one, at my office. On the day he asked me about, I was out of town, at meetings. I have—"

"Which day was that?"

"Monday, he said. He asked about Monday, and I only got home at midnight. *After* midnight, because my wife and I were at the opera after my meetings. I don't—"

"A father-daughter relationship?" Michael, asked and looked at the petite girl who opened the gate and came into the yard. Her curls shook as she walked forward in tight green jeans that emphasized the fullness of her thighs.

"Excuse me," Michael said, and addressed the girl, who came toward him with heavy steps up the stone path, her bulging big brown eyes fixed on him. "Are you Orly Shushan?"

"And who are you?"

"Police," said Michael. "I'm from the police, and if you'll just wait a moment . . ." He turned around, opened the front door and called to Tzilla. When she came out, he whispered something in her ear, and she went up to the girl with the curly hair, who was looking her over. Her prominent eyes were focused on Tzilla, but they were expressionless.

"Look," said the lawyer apologetically. "I'm a man of seventy-two, more than twice her age—three times. I have a daughter who could be her mother. How can you think that . . . I also don't do things like that. My wife and I . . . we have a good marriage. There's nothing more stupid than an old man who gets tempted into a thing like that. And stupid I'm not. What do I have to talk about with a girl of twenty-two? Pretty, absolutely pretty, likeable, nice, intelligent. Sure, but not a woman for me. I'm already after prostate surgery . . . You people, you get, you should excuse me, stereotypical ideas. Your colleague . . ." A heavy Polish accent was suddenly audible in his speech; his lower lip, which was very thin, drooped and his expression resembled the bitter ducklike expression that would cross Michael's former father-in-law Yozek's face when something was not to his liking. "He already hinted at all kinds . . . I'm not saying that you have to go gently in an investigation like this, but believe me, you're mistaken, and this is such a banal mistake."

"And the apartment?"

"Look," said the lawyer. "I'm prepared to speak frankly with you." He looked around and moistened his lips. "The apartment was an investment. I've already got an apartment downtown, and my daughter is fixed up in the United States and she won't be coming back to Israel, and we have too much. I didn't buy it for her and I didn't take any risk. I had an interest in getting my hands on that apartment because of . . ." He paused.

"Because of?"

"Look, it's a very desirable neighborhood now. There are very few apartments in Arab houses like that on the market, and especially ones that don't need renovation. It's a real bargain, that apartment, and with times being what they are, with the situation and everything, it's the ideal time to buy real estate. Every new immigrant and every leftist who has a high opinion of himself is looking for an apartment in an Arab house. But I have enough, and I don't need anything else to declare to the tax authorities."

"I don't get it," said Michael. "It's a bargain, but you don't need it, so then what? You give a bargain like that to a junior secretary as a gift? How much are we talking about here?"

"One hundred sixty thousand dollars for eighty meters on Railroad Street, southern exposure, renovated like new, from the bailiff. The owner went bankrupt. It's a real gift, for free."

"So you just give a gift to a nice girl?"

"It really does sound stupid . . . but that's not the way it is. There was a matter of professional rivalry here. There was someone who wanted to buy it. In short, the details aren't important. It would hardly have cost me anything."

"They *are* important, the details," said Michael, "and you know that they are important. But let's assume we can postpone the names and the dates in this matter, and you tell me the main points in brief, please."

"Because of a professional disagreement—you might say competition, or rivalry. But this sounds like . . . In short, this apartment was a bargain, from the bailiff, and I didn't want another lawyer, someone with whom I have accounts to settle, to buy it. But I also didn't want to buy it myself. There are too many problems with property tax, or you might say she had power of attorney, sort of, Zahara, a shadow purchaser. It wouldn't have stayed a secret forever, of course. It's just a question of timing, and the timing—it was critical to keep it a secret."

"Critical? To that extent? Not even to tell her parents?"

"Look," the lawyer said, and touched his stubby chin, "nothing is critical, but if you go into something it becomes critical. You play it like a child who is playing in all seriousness—or you lose. I don't believe in indifference. There's tension, there has to be tension."

"And she would have taken out a mortgage?"

"Entitlement. She was entitled to a mortgage. It's more believable. Otherwise, how would she have explained she had an apartment? There's no crime here, it's just that I didn't want to let it get out, but I have no interest in hiding it in a murder investigation."

"And did you give her the rest? The down payment? Without her parents knowing? How much were you intending to give her?"

"Look, I hadn't given her anything yet. There's also a savings account at the Tefahot Mortgage Bank in her name. That was at a very early stage. I was talking to her about a hundred thousand, but there's just a memorandum of intent and we hadn't taken any formal steps yet."

"Try explaining that to her father," said Michael. "He may be as hurt by this whole apartment business as he is by any of the other things that have emerged here. And anyway, I don't need to tell you that a memorandum of intent has the same validity as a contract."

"What other things?" asked the lawyer in alarm.

"We're asking that you do a DNA test."

Rosenstein looked at him in astonishment, and behind his thick glasses his eyelids trembled, opening and closing rapidly over his small eyes. "What? What kind of test?"

"A DNA test. It's nothing, a simple blood test. You shouldn't have any problem with this, if you've told the truth about your relationship with her, and this will negate any suspicion of that sort once and for all, because . . . Of course you know . . ."

"Know what? What do I know?" Rosenstein asked in evident panic, and tugged at the ends of his tie.

"You know because of course she told you," said Michael.

"Told me what? What did she tell me?"

"She told you about her life."

"Not exactly. You couldn't say that." Rosenstein shrank and laced his fingers together. "This and that. I know that she wanted to study singing in New York. I know all about that business of hers in the past with the Yemenite Jews. She wanted me to make a contribution to a small museum . . . at a synagogue. I said that I'd think about it . . . but . . . but not personal things. Never."

"What do you consider personal things?"

"Really!" said the lawyer sharply. "Don't play innocent. You look to me like an intelligent person. You know very well what 'personal things' are."

"What's personal for one person isn't necessarily personal for another."

"Really!" said Rosenstein, and again blinked rapidly several times. "Personal things is relationships with people—with men, things like that, not with parents. I only know that she asked not to involve her parents in the purchase, because her father is a very straitlaced man and wouldn't agree to a stranger—someone not from the family, that is—giving her money. *Nu*, then he would think what you are thinking."

"But certainly someone dropped in on her at work, or at least phoned. If a person works somewhere for two whole years, you have to know something about her."

"I couldn't tell you." Rosenstein stared for a moment at an undefined point. "Look, I always . . . When I'm at the office, it's to work, and not all kinds of conversations. There's no time for such things. People are always coming in—appointments, phone calls. I don't have time to—"

"Well, you had time to talk to her about buying the apartment."

"Sometimes, when I drove her home, or if there was a special meeting, something urgent that had to be typed immediately. But I never could take the time to—"

"No men ever came to the office to meet her?"

"Not as far as I know."

"Are there other secretaries at the office?"

"Two. There are two other secretaries and there's also my partner and two interns. It's not a small office, and there is a lot of activity. You can talk to them. I'm sure that they know more about these things than I do, if at all."

"So you didn't know she was pregnant."

"Pregnant?!" The lawyer was startled, and removed his glasses. He polished the lenses, which had steamed up, with the checkered handkerchief. "She never . . . She never said a word to me. But never. No. Not a word."

"Twelve weeks. In the autopsy they found a twelve-week fetus."

"God," Rosenstein choked, and held on to the stone wall that separated the two gardens of the two-family house. "I had no idea."

"So can we talk about a DNA test?" asked Michael. "Are you willing?"

"Look, I'm a lawyer," said Rosenstein, "not somebody off the streets who does whatever they tell him to right away. You can certainly understand that yourself. You didn't really think I would agree to any such thing the moment you asked."

"No," admitted Michael. "I imagined you would need time to think about it, and maybe to consult with your colleagues about whether you should."

"Why do I even need to be in a position like this? If I tell you that on Monday, when you say she . . ."—he swallowed some air—"was murdered, why do I have to be a suspect at all if I tell you that the whole day I was at meetings in Tel Aviv and in the evening I was with my wife at the opera? Everything can be proven. They did Puccini—*Turandot*. My wife likes Puccini; I don't. People saw us at the opera. We have a subscription. Believe me that there's no monkey business here."

"On that day, when you weren't at the office, do you know whether she was at work?"

"Of course," said Rosenstein. "I spoke to her on the phone several times during the day."

"Did she sound the same as usual?"

"As usual. Happy and full of life, as always."

"Did she work as usual? A full day?"

"Even more, until five, because one of the other secretaries was on vacation for two days, and when she came back Zahara could have two days off. Because of that, we weren't worried at all, and we didn't even know she had disappeared."

"Did she usually work fewer hours?"

"Officially until three, but frequently she agreed to stay overtime, as needed."

"What exactly did she do?"

"Anything she was asked. Zahara is—was—a very intelligent girl. Officially, her job was junior secretary— answering the phones, filing, sometimes preparing materials. But because of her brains, you could give her serious things to do: to go over a file for deliberation, for example, to see if it was prepared right, to help the intern—all kinds of things. Her English was also good."

"Who are your interns?"

"There are two," hesitated the lawyer. "We considered taking another one but this hasn't yet—"

"Who are the two?"

"You can summon them," muttered Rosenstein.

"We will, of course, but who are they? Men? Women?"

"A young fellow, very bright, and a girl who is slightly older and even brighter."

"And did they have a close relationship?"

"With Zahara?"

"For example."

"I really don't know." The lawyer patted his thin hair in discomfort. "I have no idea. The atmosphere was good, at the office . . . I've always maintained a family atmosphere. There's a cake when it's someone's birthday; that's my secretary's department—Frieda, who's been working with me for thirty years. She'd know more . . . I could call her now, if you—"

"Did you notice any change in her during the past couple of months?"

"Do you mean because of the pregnancy?"

"That, and in general."

"To tell you the truth, I haven't," he answered, and screwed up his face in concentration. "I can see her face—in my imagination, that is—and I can hear her voice, and it all looks and sounds the same. But people . . . You know how it is. If someone wants to hide something, he can hide it and no one will know, especially if it's a girl. Who wants to hide something, I mean. And especially someone who's used to performing."

"Did you ever hear her sing?"

"Yes, I've heard her. I know something about singing. She had an extraordinary alto voice, with a very unusual range. I think . . . I thought she could have been a great singer, even of classical music, but she didn't have the training for that. That's already a matter of education. We took her with us several times, my wife and I, to the opera and she enjoyed it very much. If she hadn't . . . If what has happened hadn't happened, she could have had a future. She wanted to sing jazz. She had an idée fixe, to be like that English singer . . . not English, from the West Indies, who lives in England, Cleo Laine. Have you heard of her?"

"I thought she was interested in Yemenite vocal music."

Rosenstein pursed his lips skeptically. "I heard about that, but I wasn't convinced. It was just to make a living," he said dismissively. "Recently, Zahara went on a bit about those ethnic things, about how they had been done an injustice or something, but she would have got over it, with time. People get over these things."

"How do you explain what happened?" The growl of a motor was heard at the end of the street and Michael saw a car coming in the direction of the house.

"Explain what? The . . . the murder?"

Michael said nothing.

"I have no idea," said Rosenstein. "Believe me, you think you know someone, know about his life . . . For example, I knew about her involvement with Yemenite folklore and about"—he grimaced—"her hatred of Ashkenazim. Supposedly she hated Ashkenazim, but she didn't hate me, for example, or anyone else at the office, but in principle—well, *nu*, she was still at an age when principles seem to be important. What can I tell you? You think you know someone and then you always discover that there are black holes. Everyone has another life that you don't see at all."

"That's probably true about you, too."

"Me?" A bitter smile crossed the lawyer's face. "With me, it's about financial matters, like with the apartment. But I don't break the law, because it's not worth it to take the risk. A man of my age, if he's achieved what I've achieved, doesn't have much room for monkey business. And playing around with women never interested me, so you won't find me involved in anything like that. But a pretty young girl, and such a successful one—that's another story altogether."

"And you have no idea who could have killed her?"

Rosenstein shook his head. "I didn't know the people she associated with, but from what your colleague described to me about the way they found her, it was someone very, very . . . How should I put this? A psychopath. Maybe it was even"—his eyes widened in relief—"a security matter? The pregnancy one thing and the murder another? Maybe it was an Arab who abducted her without any connection to—"

At the curb, Eli Bachar slammed the door of the police Toyota and looked around angrily. He shoved the gate open, and from the end of the stone path he beckoned to Michael. "Can I talk to you for a moment?" he asked impatiently, and again beckoned to Michael so that they could exchange a few words.

Bachar's narrow green eyes were burning and his voice was shaking as he tried to whisper: "Tell me, am I an idiot, or what? Like an idiot I try to locate them, and meanwhile those brothers are already under Balilty's control. He's acting as if he were in charge here. You give him too much freedom. I get sent to locate people, and meanwhile he takes them all and I wait around like an idiot."

"What do you mean?" asked Michael in an attempt to gain a bit of time until Eli Bachar cooled down. "What do you mean by 'he takes them all'?"

"First of all, he's on his way here with the youngest brother, the officer. I've been looking for them like an . . . And I waited and waited until I found out—"

From the corner of his eye, Michael saw Rosenstein scratching his head and shifting his weight from foot to foot. "Just a second," he called out to him quickly.

"I just wanted to go in to talk with the parents," apologized the lawyer, "if it's all right with you," and the gloom with which he spoke was what made Michael look at him with interest. It might have been expected from an experienced lawyer like him that he would object to an attempt to interrogate him, that he would not be as cooperative as he had been, unless he had something to worry about. Or else maybe Zahara Bashari's death really had shaken all his professionalism, Michael noted to himself, and with an inviting gesture he indicated the front door, which was still open.

With small, quick steps Rosenstein advanced toward the house, and at the door in front of him stood the journalist, clutching the light-colored cloth bag that was hanging from her shoulder and holding in her right hand a cellular phone from which she was reading her messages. Tzilla Bachar, who had squeezed into the doorway, eluded the raised elbow and came down the path to Michael and Eli.

"Have you seen her?" asked Tzilla when she reached them. "She was never at her place, Zahara Bashari, only told her parents that she was going there but never did. That's what she says, anyway."

"Orly Shushan as an alibi for her parents," mused Michael aloud.

"Did you see how she looks?" whispered Tzilla. "Nothing special. You wouldn't look at her twice with those looks. You'd think . . . But in any case, if you think how much power she has in those reports of hers she publishes every week . . . Now she wants to write an article about this case, and especially about you," she said to Michael.

"She has a few things to do first," said Michael. "Take her with you to my office. I want to talk to her there, and tell her that first we'll have to ask her a few questions and after that we'll see."

"Are you going to give her an interview?" said Eli Bachar in astonishment. "But you never give—"

"I'm not giving her anything," Michael said, and sheltered the trembling flame of the lighter with his hand. He drew on the cigarette before he said: "Meanwhile, *she's* giving *us,* but there's no need to emphasize that. You," he clarified to Tzilla, "take her in with you. I want to talk to her in your presence, so wait with her in my office. And you," he added, turning to Eli, "summon everyone who works at Rosenstein's—two secretaries, two interns and his partner. Have them come to us. Maybe they know something."

"Do you mean that I should speak to them in the meantime?" Tzilla asked, and looked at Orly Shushan, who hadn't moved from the doorway.

"I'm relying on you," said Michael with a small smile. "You prepare the ground. She might be the last person who saw Zahara Bashari alive." As he spoke he followed the reporter's glance, which was resting on the apartment block across the street.

He too saw the awkward little girl in the blue sweat suit who was trying to pull the dog on the end of the leash away from the curb. He mused that the child had been standing there for hours, watching all the cars that stopped, and not coming near, not coming over to ask. Standing there and watching. The dog barked loudly as the Criminal Identification car pulled up, and again the girl tried to tug the dog toward the entrance to the apartment block, as if the revolving blue light were emitting dangerous radiation. The journalist was following her with her gaze. It was evident in Orly Shushan's eyes and her full, silent face that she was plotting something. Maybe she also knew that children can be wonderfully observant, thought Michael as he approached her; anyone investigating a murder case did best to talk to neighbors and especially children. It was hard to get reliable information from neighborhood gossips, he knew, although they ostensibly seemed very promising. Their prior opinions and their prejudices shaped the facts, even if they thought they'd seen something with their own eyes, and the desire to tell something sensational would cause them to make up details. But for journalists, neighborhood gossips were a treasure, because the truth wasn't as important to reporters as the scent of blood, thought Michael as he watched her. Her protruding brown eyes looked perfectly ordinary and gave no hint of her abilities, and the shape of her figure was blurred by the big checked shirt.

"Nevertheless, I'll have a word with her now," he said finally.

"Watch out for her," said Tzilla. "I've already been told that she's dangerous. Do you remember that article about the previous police chief? After that I heard that his wife wouldn't speak to him for a year or something. If she gets her teeth into something or someone, they're done for. She has a special technique, they warned me. She asks innocent questions, pretends she's a groupie, spends hours with the subject of the interview, collects gossip about him from people, writes things he never said and presents it all as if it were part of a confession. And furthermore, she gets people to talk. Remember—I've warned you."

"What do you have to warn me for?" grumbled Michael. "She's the one being interrogated this time, not me."

Tzilla tipped her head to one side and regarded him skeptically. "I told you that she wants to—"

"I don't care what she wants."

"Sometimes I wonder . . . Never mind. In any case, in your position, you can't let yourself be so naïve."

"Okay. We'll take down a transcript. You've warned me." He sighed, and went up to Orly Shushan.

"You were the last person to see Zahara Bashari alive," he said to her after introducing himself by name and rank.

"Why do you think so?" she asked in a low, quiet voice. "I haven't seen her for more than a week."

"Her mother said that she had gone to see you in Tel Aviv the night she disappeared."

"Maybe that's what Zahara told her mother, but she didn't come to my place, and we hadn't made up to meet or anything."

"So you only saw her a week ago? When exactly?"

"Last Thursday."

"Where?"

"Here, in Jerusalem."

"Did you speak to her after that?"

"Almost every day, on the phone."

"When was the last time you spoke to her?"

"A few days ago. I can't remember exactly. Maybe on Sunday." She tugged at her nose, rummaged in her large cloth bag, took out a tissue and brought it to her nose.

"You were close," noted Michael.

"Very. Like sisters," she said, and suddenly buried her face in her hands, and her words grew slower and blurred: "I can't believe it yet. I can't believe this has happened. She had so many plans. You have no idea . . ."

She turned her back to him, and her shoulders shook.

"And when you hadn't heard from her since Sunday . . ."

"I looked for her. I called her at work, and on her mobile, but I couldn't get hold of her. I didn't want to call her at home, at her parents' house, because . . ." She glanced at the inside of the house.

"Had it ever happened before that she told her parents she was going to see you when she never intended to?"

"Usually we coordinated it."

"What do you mean? That you gave her an alibi for someone? What did she have to hide?"

"You couldn't call it an alibi. It was just because of her parents, so that they wouldn't worry, if she went out somewhere that . . . so as not to get into conflicts with them. But a lot of times we really did meet in Tel Aviv, and we'd go out, and then she'd sleep over at my place. And sometimes she'd come straight after work and—"

The car that came down the narrow street squealed to a stop and made the dog bark again from the opposite sidewalk. Balilty rested his hands on the steering wheel and regarded Michael and Orly Shushan through the open car window. Next to him sat an army officer in a dusty green uniform with a black beret stuck through the epaulette of his shirt. The man got quickly out of the car, pushed the gate open and ran up the path to Michael.

"Let him go in," called Balilty as he locked the car. "He's the youngest brother. He's . . . like the father, doesn't say a word. Not a word." Balilty looked at the street. "But here comes the other one. How much do you want to bet that here comes the older brother. Look, do you see the—" Even before he could complete the sentence the gate was again flung open so it hit the fence. The man who rushed in, short of breath and very pale, moved along the path at a clumsy run. He pushed the intelligence officer out of his way and burst into the house.

Chapter 6

Netanel Bashari's hands shook as he leaned over the lighter that Michael was holding. "Forgive me," he said as he drew on the cigarette Michael had offered him. "I have to sit down." For a moment he wavered on his feet and almost fell onto the narrow bed in his sister's room. Michael sat at the desk and drew invisible lines with his finger on the Formica surface. He looked at the golden flakes sprinkled over it, and from them lifted his gaze to Netanel Bashari, who was taller than his parents and very much resembled his mother in his long, narrow face. His sharply etched, narrow lips gave his face a stern expression. Behind the thick lenses of his silver-rimmed glasses his eyes blinked ceaselessly, and when they opened they revealed the frozen gaze of a person in shock.

"If you're asking me what I'm feeling right now," he told Michael, and fixed his eyes on the window that looked out into the backyard, "I can't tell you anything. I think it's the shock. I just can't take it in—Zahara is the most vivid creature I've ever known. If you'd ask me to describe her, the first thing I'd mention would be how alive she was. You don't see vivacity like that every day. She was just so alive. I can't think of her as . . ."

He lowered his head and his shoulders trembled, and when he raised his head the lines of his face were still frozen in astonishment. "I just can't believe it," he said. "I can't believe it. At two o'clock, at two o'clock I was supposed . . . We'd made up to meet at the synagogue . . . I hadn't seen her this week . . . Who could have . . . Are you sure it has nothing to do with the security situation? How should I know? All those Palestinians are roaming around here and hating us all the time. There wasn't a person in the world who hated her . . . Who could have murdered . . . Zahara . . ."

Suddenly he straightened up and pressed his lips together. He was silent for a moment. "I promise you that if you don't find the person who has done this"—his voice resonated—"I will hunt him down myself, and I will find him, I swear."

Gradually it emerged that he had seen Zahara at the university a week earlier, after Yom Kippur. They'd had lunch together at the Mount Scopus campus. She had come to have him help her find historical documents about the Yemenites who had worked at Moshav Kinneret; that's what her business at the university had been about. A stray smile crossed Netanel's face as he quoted her argument that "if they're talking about the right of return for the Palestinians, you could also talk about the Yemenites' right of return to the settlement from which they were expelled in 1930."

She had seemed fine to him, as usual, nothing out of the ordinary. Pale? No, not at all. She looked wonderful, though a bit impassioned about the Kinneret affair, and he'd tried to calm her down. "She was thinking of setting up a small community museum for the culture and history of the Jews of Yemen, and apparently had obtained a bit of funding. That was the last thing we talked about—we argued," he said wonderingly. "Had I known that this was the last time . . . But how could I have known that? How can anyone know?"

The small tape recorder stood between them on a low, straw stool, and Michael watched one of the controls that jumped to the end of its range every time Netanel mentioned his sister, and then when he mentioned Linda. "She'll be here in a little while, Linda," he said. "Linda O'Brian. I think she was the last person to have spoken to her."

Michael gave thanks to the invisible force that had kept Balilty out of the room. He could imagine what his reaction would have been had he heard Netanel mention her.

"Linda O'Brian? The real estate broker?"

"Yes. Why? Do you know her?" Netanel Bashari suddenly straightened up again. He was tenser, and a new shade of anxiety was evident in his face.

"By chance," Michael said, and he recalled how she had turned her head away as she came up the ladder into the attic and had refrained from looking at Zahara's body. Would she have recognized the dress or the shoes then, had she looked?

"She'll be here in a moment," repeated Netanel. "She lives nearby"—

with his brown hand he indicated the corner of the street—"right across from our synagogue." He breathed strenuously. 'Everyone lives here. Bethlehem Road runs between the house where I was born and the house where I live."

Distractedly, and only after Michael had asked him twice, Netanel Bashari explained how his sister had become friends with Linda, when she was about fourteen, and told Michael how he related to his sister as if she were his daughter because of the age gap between them. "I was already not living at home anymore when she was born," said Netanel, "but because of my sense of family it was important for me to build a relationship with her. From childhood. When she was very small, I became attached to her. She's very, very intelligent, Zahara, and I was sure that she would go to university after the army. I was in favor of her going into the army to get her out of the house, out of this stagnation. I think she was very lonely with our elderly parents. There was a clear generation gap. Today my mother is a woman of sixty-nine, you have to realize, from the older generation, more like a grandmother. Because of this, Zahara . . . related to me like a father substitute. She'd always come to me with her difficulties and her problems, and also her good experiences. We thought of sending her to study in the United States, but lately she's had this obsession . . . Okay, not an obsession, but she wanted to revive Yemenite vocal music. She dug up old Yemenite songs, and she learned a lot from my mother. She got it from her. She was supposed to be singing tonight, at eight . . . I was closer to her than any of us." His voice cracked. "When I was born, Mother was eighteen, and then Eliyahu was born, and then a number of years later, almost a decade, Bezalel came, and Zahara was altogether a surprise, a miracle, a wonder, a replacement."

"A replacement for what?" asked Michael.

"A replacement for . . . for . . . Never mind. It's not relevant now."

"Everything is relevant," ruled Michael. "Believe me—everything's relevant."

"Ask my mother. I don't want to go into it."

"We will ask your mother later, but now we're asking you."

"Look," said Netanel Bashari with an effort, "my parents . . . my mother . . . comes from the family of the last chief rabbi of Yemen, and she . . . She had already lost children . . ."

"'Children?!'"

"I myself didn't know . . . I only knew that she was thirteen when she was married off to my father, who was sixteen at the time I think, no more. Zahara . . ." He took a deep breath and sighed. "Zahara went into this, not me and not my brothers. She discovered the details. Not all, but some. Enough for her . . . Enough to upset my parents' equilibrium that they'd . . . That they seemed . . ."

Michael asked, "What details?"

"Believe me," pleaded Netanel Bashari. "It has nothing to do with anything. No connection. It's something that happened more than fifty years ago. My mother's a woman of sixty-nine, and why should we dig . . . I told Zahara this too—why should we dig? I asked her, I asked her to leave it alone, but Zahara . . . If she set her mind on something—"

"With us it's different," said Michael. "Only in retrospect is it possible to know whether something is pertinent or not. And in fact, as a historian, you should realize this. You know that like . . . If you go digging around in documents, you don't always know what you are going to find. In fact, you can't even know what might turn up and sometimes you find something completely unexpected which turns out to be the most important thing of all."

"Yes." Netanel Bashari sighed, and his eyes rested on Michael for a moment. "That's true in principle, but I just don't know whether . . . Zahara found out that mother had lost one baby in Yemen, and that afterward there was something else . . . But I don't want to . . ." He straightened up in his chair and looked around and shook his head and said in a broken voice: "I can't. I can't."

"It's impossible to know now what's pertinent and what's not, and you do want us to solve the murder of your little sister," Michael reminded him.

Netanel Bashari hung down his head, and without raising his eyes he said: "There are things in our family history that I don't . . ." He straightened up and turned his head to the window and continued to speak without looking at Michael. "There are people, like those who went through the Holocaust, or from the second generation, who connect to the legend and get together once a week or I don't know how often, and talk about their childhood and their parents, and relive all . . . all the . . . And there are others who don't want to build themselves on the catastrophes of the past. They just don't want to, they just don't. Or else they can't—it depends how you define it, and I—I don't."

Michael, observing his sagging head, commented that it was strange that a historian would prefer not to delve into the past, even a painful one.

"Yes," sighed Netanel. "Zahara said the same thing. She didn't understand either." And without raising his head he explained that to be a historian doesn't mean being interested in every area of the past, and especially those areas to which one has a personal connection, because they confuse the vision. "Then you lose your objectivity," he said.

It had been many years since Michael had been at that crossroads in his life when he'd succumbed to the lures proffered by Emmanuel Shorer and joined the investigations department and abandoned the academic world and his doctoral thesis. "So would it be correct to say that this is the reason you chose to specialize in Russian history," he said questioningly, "so that you would be objective enough?"

"More or less," mumbled Netanel Bashari. "That, and a conflation of circumstances: There was a job opening, and I admired my professor very much. I had already learned Russian for my BA, and I was good at it—I could excel. I didn't feel that my ethnic origin limited me to . . ." Suddenly he sounded angry and fed up: "I hate extortionists and parasites and complainers and . . . I'm different." He took a deep breath. "Most of all I hate it when members of the Yemenite community, as they call us, or even Moroccans, or in short Mizrahis, dig around the injustices that were done to them and then want to build themselves up on them. To get ahead in life on the basis of the discrimination there was in the past."

For a moment Michael wondered whether to comment that there was a difference between advancement on the basis of discrimination and the examination of what had happened, but he let it be. Again he asked Netanel about his relationship with Zahara, and again he heard about the extraordinary closeness between them and about how there had been no tensions between them recently—that is, apart perhaps from a few insignificant differences over the meaning of "the Yemenite question."

"Insignificant?" asked Michael.

"Look," said Netanel Bashari, "she thought, and there are people who think that way, that when it comes to the Yemenites there has been a personal and collective insult to a whole community. Zahara argued, and she wasn't the only one, that the case of Uzi Meshullam was an expression of this alienation with respect to the state. As a historian, I can understand how Uzi Meshullam can be defined . . . the phenomenon of Uzi Meshullam can be defined as a stage in the maturation of the Yemenite community. That is how Zahara saw it. She argued that I, like my parents' generation that paid the price, that . . . that we, my parents and I, have a conciliatory character, and she . . . She wanted militancy and not conciliation. That's it," Netanel summed up, and pressed his lips together as if declaring that he had no intention of saying any more about it. "This really isn't a subject for now."

Nevertheless, it was possible to go into this subject more deeply and expand upon it a bit, mused Michael as he asked Netanel directly about his movements on the evening his sister was murdered. "On Tuesday, three and a half days ago," he specified.

"Tuesday? Tuesday evening? Because in the morning I was at the university, and in the evening, from seven to nine I was at the synagogue for a committee meeting. They were planning the preparations for Simhat Torah."

"And from nine?"

""From nine?" Netanel Bashari knitted his eyebrows in an effort to remember, and his breathing became rapid and loud. "I was . . . I was at Linda O'Brian's. Both of us are on the synagogue board of directors and usually after committee meetings we spend some time at her place—she lives nearby. Right opposite, on the corner of—"

A knock on the door cut him off. The door opened wide and Linda filled the entranceway, her mouth gaping open as if before a scream. "So it was Zahara? There, in the attic, was it Zahara?" she asked Michael, who regarded her agitated face. "If I had only looked, we would have known two days ago?" She sat down on the narrow bed next to Netanel and held his hand, and a wail burst from the depths of her chest. "Netanel, I didn't know. I didn't want to look there under the roof when they found her . . . It wasn't intentional, I . . ."

Netanel extracted his hand. "What difference does it make, Linda? She was dead. What difference would it have made anyway? You told me how they found her. You wouldn't have recognized her even if . . . You said they had smashed her face in . . . It is all so ironic." He buried his head in his hands.

Only Linda's sobs were heard in the room, until Netanel Bashari whispered: "It's better that you not be here now." He turned his head and without looking at her he muttered: "Hagar will probably be here soon, and the children and . . ."

Linda moved to the edge of the bed and hiccupped and went silent and did not sob any more. To Michael's question as to when she had last seen Zahara, she replied that she had seen her about a week ago—and that yes, her face looked like it always did. She had always thought that Zahara trusted her; it had to be remembered that she had always been very secretive about personal matters. "She's so secretive, it was only with me that she—not with anyone else . . ."

Michael asked Linda if Zahara had told her about the pregnancy.

To her right, on the narrow bed, Netanel froze. "It can't be," he muttered. "How could she be pregnant? She didn't have a boyfriend." Suddenly he laughed to himself. "I didn't know she . . . Did you know?" he demanded sharply of Linda, and Michael noticed the intimacy in the way he addressed her, and put it together with the way Linda had held his hand earlier (but that was not proof of anything; she had also constantly touched him, Michael, when she took him around to apartments she was showing him) and the remark about the impending arrival of "Hagar and the children."

"I had no idea," said Linda, sounding a bit insulted. "I didn't see anything different. She was . . . She popped over for lunch a week ago. She talked about apartments, about an apartment on Railroad Street, the apartment that belonged to . . . Never mind. I asked her whether . . . She didn't say anything about being pregnant . . . It couldn't be that she didn't know . . . How long?"

"Twelve weeks," said Michael.

"In her third . . . no, fourth month?!" exclaimed Linda. "She even . . . As if . . . She wasn't thinking of having an abortion?"

Michael said nothing.

"If she were intending to have an abortion, with whom would she have spoken?" insisted Netanel Bashari.

Linda shrugged her shoulders. "I thought with me, even if she didn't . . . I didn't even know that she . . ."

"You didn't know she had someone?"

"It's not my fault." Linda sobbed again. "I didn't . . . She didn't say anything to me, and only a week ago I asked whether there was someone who . . . and she laughed. You know how she laughs instead of speaking."

She looked at Netanel and suddenly covered her mouth with her hand as if she had suddenly remembered something that scared her, but Michael was already in the momentum of talking, and he said: "In all the years that you knew her—such a pretty and lively girl—didn't you know about any romantic connection with anyone in particular?"

"She . . . She . . ." Linda O'Brian looked at the two of them. "She had . . ." She hesitated. "She had . . . How can I say this? She had problems with . . . I don't want to talk about it," she said suddenly.

"We're done with discretion," said Netanel angrily. "She's dead. Do you understand?"

"Problems with her sexuality . . . I thought . . . Actually, I thought . . . She hinted that she had someone she was sort of waiting for, but she didn't say more than that. At first I thought she had a married man, and then when I saw there was no progress . . . or any signs . . . I thought that either she was a lesbian, or frigid. I thought maybe she couldn't be with a man." She spoke the last words hurriedly.

"Lesbian?!" shouted Netanel. "How could you think . . . Lesbian?! There was nothing masculine about her and . . . all that beauty, and her femininity . . ."

Linda O'Brian said nothing.

Michael leaned toward Linda. "What did you want to say before? What did you remember?"

"It wasn't anything imp . . . She . . . I . . . Lately she had a relationship . . . but not really . . . with someone who . . ."

"Who? With whom did she have a relationship?" demanded Netanel harshly.

"Not a *relationship*-relationship. I don't think it was anything romantic, she just . . . saw him a few times. He isn't for her at all, nothing serious. She just went out with . . . with Moshe Avital," whispered Linda.

The sound that came out of Netanel Bashari's mouth was somewhere between a growl and a snort: "He had something with her, too?" he asked scornfully, but his heavy breathing disclosed great anger.

"What do you mean 'too'?" answered Linda heatedly. "How many times have I told you that he's nothing to me, that he's just so . . . that it's so hard for him with the story with his daughter . . . And actually he came to me to talk about Zahara. He's very—"

Netanel interrupted her. "That man cannot take his hands off . . . He . . . Anything that moves—he just needs to see a skirt. You should see him," he said to Michael. "What a . . . He looks like a cross between Kermit the

Frog and Walter Matthau, that actor. He . . . His suits and his Rover . . . An ugly man, vain and full of himself—and he had something going with Zahara?"

"That's not how it is," said Linda quietly. "So maybe he's not a handsome man, but he's a charming man, and I feel sorry for him, and he developed a very special relationship with Zahara. Did you know he has a retarded daughter? And twice a week he goes to the institution where she—"

"What did he have with Zahara?" insisted Netanel. "That's what I want to know. I want to know if he's the one who . . . who got her pregnant, if he—"

"She didn't say anything about the pregnancy, and if he . . . I don't know. He really is a man who loves women and they . . . the women . . . they love him."

"I can't listen to this bullshit anymore." Netanel Bashari stood up. "First a lesbian and frigid and now Moshe Avital. There's a limit!" he shouted, and stuck his hands in his pockets and strode over to the window that looked out on the back garden and turned around and came back from there as if planning to walk up and down the small room.

"You'll have to come in to make an official statement and tell us everything you know," said Michael after a long moment.

"Okay," Linda said, and turned her face away from Netanel. Michael left the room.

"Like wildfire," said Sergeant Yair, looking out between the two panels of the curtain. "How long has it been since you went into the room with them? An hour? Two hours? Not longer, and now the whole world is outside here . . . Look at how many people there are, and how many reporters!"

"So what's new? It's always like that," said Tzilla. "When we get called, they come too. Either they were listening to the frequency or one of the neighbors said something. Before you go out, you should know," she said to Michael, who was about to open the front door. "The whole neighborhood is outside the house, masses of people. Just so you'll know."

"Get me all the material that's been in the newspapers over the past two or three years about the Yemenites' commissions," said Michael, who was still mulling over things he had heard from the brothers, especially Netanel.

"What?" she wondered. "What material? About what? What does that have to do with . . ."

"Sorry. I meant that whole business with the hearings and the commissions about the kidnapped babies and also about Rabbi Meshullam, the one who . . ."

"Okay. I got it. I'm not retarded. You don't have to explain to me who Rabbi Meshullam is," bridled Tzilla.

"Sorry," Michael said, and stared distractedly out the door at the front yard. It was the twilight hour before the beginning of the holiday, yet there were four mature women standing near the fence that separated the two parts of the house, almost right on top of one another and their heads bent low. One of them—in a housecoat and a faded kerchief, the one who had been beating the rug a few hours ago—was explaining something to the others in a low voice, and immediately they all stared at the door to the Basharis' house again.

"You don't say!" cried the most elderly of the woman, her back bent nearly double, her crooked fingers twisting a plastic bag from which milk or yogurt was dripping onto the stone path.

"That's exactly what I'm saying," answered the woman with the kerchief shrilly. "Just exactly what I'm saying." Her voice rose. "You know me, Mrs. Sima, that I don't lie," and all four of them looked into the neighboring yard. "You just remember what I said," the woman with the kerchief chided them, and glanced rapidly left and right, like a bird checking out its surroundings before it dives on a worm, until her eyes fell on Michael and Tzilla and Sergeant Yair, who was standing behind the other two. She stared at them a moment inquisitively and immediately made a decision.

"Excuse me, sir, excuse me," she said quickly, and hurried over to them. "Is it true what they're saying? Did they really strangle Zahara? Is it true that they broke her neck? It's a pervert or an . . . Is it true that first they . . . ?" A blush suffused the pinkish birthmark at the corner of her lips, and her light eyes darted back and forth and her voice shrank to a whisper. "Is it true that they raped her? Those Arabs who were working in the building . . ."

Michael waved his arm and hurried down the path, ignoring the scores of people who were standing on the sidewalk in front of the house, whispering and exchanging bits of information. At a glance he took in the alarmed face of a blonde woman in her sixties; her yellow hair was twisted into a bun in a way that looked familiar to him, but he couldn't remember from where. She stopped her Subaru in front of the house and got out, her left hand fingering her pearl necklace as if seeking something to hold on to there, and her right hand covering her mouth as if to hold back a scream. With slow steps, a young girl also got out of the car, and pulled the miniskirt she was wearing down over her exposed thighs. The older woman pulled her by the arm and hurried toward the gate. "What happened?" she asked in a trembling voice.

"Mrs. Beinisch," the woman in the kerchief called out loudly. "Don't ask, Mrs. Beinisch." Michael did not linger to hear what came next, but hurried over to the white Toyota that had its motor running and the blue lamp flashing on its roof. Behind the wheel sat Eli Bachar, looking around and pursing his lips. His hand dangled out the window and his fingers drummed on the white metal. And Michael, as he hastened to the door on the other side, then noticed who was coming quickly down the street: a tall, thin man in a thin jacket and a faded peaked cap, and with him the awkward little girl in the blue sweat suit. With her right hand she was tugging at the dog, until she raised her head and stared hypnotized at the flashing blue light. The man's face was wrinkled, but his blue eyes shone with a positive glint even when he squinted into the setting sun. As Eli Bachar noticed him, the expression on his face changed suddenly, and Michael tried to conciliate him for the prolonged wait.

"Hello, Eli," said the man, who stepped into the street and came up to the driver's window, and in English with a British accent said that he heard a tragedy had occurred and asked if they really, as Nessia said—he pointed to the girl—had murdered Zahara. Eli Bachar, who opened the car door and stepped out, grasped the man's arm and pulled him back onto the sidewalk. "Careful, Peter," Michael heard him say. "More people are killed in traffic accidents here than by anything else. Why are you walking in the street?"

"Nessia here," said the man, touching the girl's wiry hair as she shrank back momentarily from his touch, "tells me that they found Zahara dead. Is that so?"

"Yes," answered Eli Bachar with a severe expression. "She was murdered. Why? Did you know her?"

Apologetically, Peter said that he wasn't acquainted with everyone in the neighborhood—he knew a few faces and had heard a few stories he had heard from Yigal ("That's his boyfriend. He lives in his apartment," whispered Eli to Michael)—but he knew Zahara through his daughter, Linda. He met people mostly at the grocery store, he said, which to him was like a country club where you heard everything. Three young women, one in tight pants and a sweater and two in long dresses, also approached the car, and on the sidewalk near the house a few onlookers gathered and spoke softly. A tot with a runny nose pulled at his mother, who said something to her neighbor, and the two women stared at the police car and immediately crossed the street with the little boy.

"Excuse me," said one of the women to Eli Bachar. "We think that something needs to be said to the residents of the neighborhood. We simply want to know what has happened here, because we have small children and if, like we've heard, there's a serial murderer or a rapist wandering around here, we have to know, and it's your job to inform us. Maybe you should assemble everyone at the Community Center and tell them officially, so that there won't be this alienation between the public and the authorities."

From the expression on Eli Bachar's face, it was obvious that he was intending to say something sarcastic, but he looked at Peter and changed his mind. "We aren't able to explain anything at this time," he answered her politely. "For now, all that can be said is that a resident of the neighborhood has been murdered, and I don't know who's been talking here about serial murderers and rapists, and it's a very good idea not to fan such rumors, which only frighten people unnecessarily."

He glanced quickly at Michael, and without a smile he added: "Keeping a close eye on the children is always a good idea."

"We," said the second woman, smoothing her ponytail with her hand, "have been working very hard to make this neighborhood a pleasant place to live, to develop a community spirit and to organize all kinds of activities, both social and cultural, so as to foster a spirit of openness and acceptance of the Other. And now all of a sudden there are all kinds of rumors that there's been a murder in the political context—"

"What do mean 'political'?" asked Eli Bachar as if he didn't understand, to gain time.

"No, not political, I mean in the security context," the first woman clarified, and pulled the hem of her shirt down over a skirt that was so long it swept the ground. "People here are beginning to talk about Arabs and how they mustn't be allowed into the neighborhood," she explained, and Michael looked at her freckled face and at the ends of the long hair that flowed over her large, droopy breasts. He looked at the embroidered cloth shoulder bag with silver inlays that had lost their brightness and down to her heavy clogs and her woolen socks, and then he looked up at the sky, which was becoming gray, and asked himself whether it was going to rain soon. With half an ear he heard the other woman add to her friend's bitterness: "Because if Palestinians are involved in this, then we really wouldn't want an atmosphere of lynching to develop here. It isn't clear yet who did it, right?"

Eli Bachar nodded. "Not yet," he said with restrained aggression.

"At our house we have Palestinian workers and we're renovating now, and also because of our political outlook we're worried. I, for example, am a ceramicist by profession, and I hold a class in my studio, voluntarily, for children from the village of Oum Tubbeh. Are you familiar with it? It's the village opposite Har Homah, and the class is for children from there and children from our neighborhood, a ceramics class, and we"— she indicated her companion and the group of people across the street— "we're academics and artists and intellectuals and we have no interest in the rumor mill and the political incitement. It was exactly against this sort of thing that we founded the movement—we're a secular and non-party movement," she elucidated, "Citizens for the Other. We are for rapprochement with the Other. Probably you've heard of us, because we were fed up with Peace Now in this context and . . . Never mind. People come to our meetings from all sectors, all social classes and also from the Movement for Quality Government and—"

Eli Bachar gave Michael a long-suffering look. Michael sighed and reluctantly got out of the car and stood facing the women. "At the moment," he interrupted the speaker, "we are pursuing the initial clarification, and we are unable to . . . Perhaps later on it's a very good idea to organize a meeting. We'll consider it. Did you know Zahara Bashari?"

"Only . . . Not personally. I heard her sing once," the woman replied, and her friend, who was rolling strands of faded brown hair between her fingers, looked at her and took a long breath as if she was about to speak. But Michael had already held up his palms in a gesture of helplessness and said quietly, "That's it for now," and he waited until they turned away in demonstrable disappointment, then watched them as they crossed the street to rejoin the group of people.

"Look at those people. They have it too good in life," said Eli Bachar.

"They have no problems except uniting the neighborhood. It's too bad Balilty isn't here. He could have said: 'Those people, they're all of them leftists. You spit on them and they say "'rain,"'" he'd say, and 'I thought because of this new intifada all those leftists had realized something, but I can see that they haven't understood a damn thing.'"

The dog pulled at the leash and the girl was dragged after it to the apartment block. Next to the fence she stopped and looked at the shiny red Toyota that had just parked behind the dusty Ford. The little girl gazed at the driver with admiration and awe; he smoothed the sleeves of his blue blazer and with the fingernail of his pinky he flicked a crumb off the edge of his gray tie.

"I'd like to introduce you," Eli Bachar said, and held out a hand toward the man in the peaked cap. "This is Peter O'Brian, whom I've told you about. You remember? I told you, I met him that evening he came to talk to our discussion group. He lives in the neighborhood, up there." Eli indicated the other side of Bethlehem Street with his head.

"Oh yes, I remember you told me. Pleased to meet you," said Michael as he shook Peter O'Brian's hand. Out of the corner of his eye he examined the driver of the Toyota, who dragged his legs as if after an effort of long driving and pressed the key ring he held. The car emitted a prolonged whistle, and only when it had stopped and he'd straightened his hair with his hand did he turn his attention to the bustle and cross the street at a run and push open the iron gate to the house next door.

"Me too. Eli has told me about you," said Peter. "He wanted us to meet, right?"

"We'll get together. Yes, we'll get together. Maybe we'll take him out for a hummus," Eli said, looking at Michael expectantly.

"Delighted. When we finish with all this, then I'd be delighted," Michael muttered, and looked at the house across the street.

"Of course, of course," Peter apologized, and straightened up, then added that when he was on sabbatical, he wanted to spend three months straight here, and he would be pleased to host Michael, because cooking was one of his greatest loves and they always had guests at their place. Michael interrupted him to ask whether he had seen the murder victim recently, and Peter replied in an apologetic stammer that he'd only just arrived two days earlier and hadn't had the chance. All this time he held the little girl's hand in his right hand and looked at her dog, who was pulling on the leash.

"Will you permit me to ask you something?" said Michael to the girl in a low voice. He leaned over her until he was looking right into the yellow circles that surrounded her pupils. Her Adam's apple bobbed up and down and her lips trembled.

"Maybe you can help us. Really."

She shrugged, nodded limply and looked at him expectantly.

"Do you live here, on this street?" he asked.

She nodded and pointed to the adjacent apartment block.

"It's right across the way, so you certainly talked to Zahara on a number of occasions."

"Not so much," she said in a cloudy voice.

"But you knew her well?"

She nodded again, and with her eyes she asked Peter for confirmation.

"It's okay, Nesseleh," said Peter, encouraging her with his look and promising that "this man" wouldn't do anything bad to her; to Michael he explained that she was Yigal's little sister. "She's my mate," he said in English, and Michael nodded and recalled things that Eli had told him about the Jerusalemite electrician and his Australian boyfriend.

"Nessia, she sees things," he explained to Michael, still in English, as proudly as if he had raised her himself. "There are kids like that who see things, aren't there?"

"Of course there are," Michael replied, and turned to look at Nessia. "So you probably saw Zahara Bashari a lot?"

"Mrs. Jesselson says she's dead," said Nessia hoarsely.

"It's true, I'm very sorry to say," answered Michael, and with a grave and serious expression he said to her: "And I thought you could help us."

He saw the panic in her eyes. "I'm just asking if you saw her. Did you see her on Monday or Tuesday?"

The girl lowered her eyes and concentrated for a moment, and then she raised her head and said, "Yes. On Monday morning, when I went out with Rosie." She looked at the dog.

"Do you remember what time that was?" He looked at the pink Mickey Mouse watch that peeped out from under the sleeve of her sweatshirt.

"I don't know exactly," she said in a tone of complaint. "Early. My mother had already gone to work. Rosie wanted to go out."

"Before eight in the morning?"

The girl nodded. "Earlier," she added in a limp voice. "Maybe seven. A cab had already come for her."

"For Zahara?"

"Yes."

"Did you speak to her?"

Slowly the girl shook her head.

"She got into a cab? And that was the last time you saw her?"

The girl hesitated again. "No, no, I didn't see her after that."

"Maybe," said Michael as if he had just been struck with a wonderful new idea, "maybe you remember what she was wearing?"

The girl nodded her head, but she did not say anything and plucked at the cuff of her sweatshirt.

"Can you tell me what she was wearing?" he tried.

"The coat, it was sort of, like, blue," she hesitated. "It was pretty, with no buttons. Open, like."

"And under the coat?"

"There was something red. Maybe?" the girl said, and shivered.

"Do you remember if she had a handbag?"

He looked at her hands, which had begun to tremble.

"I didn't see," she whispered, "but there was always . . . a big black bag. A big one."

"And did you see her dress, too?"

"Pants," she said all of a sudden, decisively. "Black pants. Velvet, under the jacket. And boots. With high heels. Suede boots."

"Black pants, black boots, a blue coat and a black bag?"

"And also"—she indicated her neck—"red." Immediately she covered one hand with the other, as if to get them to stop shaking.

"And after that did you see her again?"

The girl shook her head.

"But usually you'd see her?"

The girl nodded her head.

"Every day?"

"No. Just if she went out or came home." A hint of pride crept into the girl's voice.

"Did you speak to her?"

The girl shook her head again and bit her lower lip. "No," she whispered. "She didn't . . . She . . . I . . ."

"You were shy?" suggested Michael, and out of the corner of his eye he saw Eli Bachar drumming with his fingers on the roof of the car.

The girl nodded vigorously and bit her lip again. "But I heard the way she sang," she offered.

"At a wedding?"

"No," she panicked. "In her room . . ." And suddenly she panicked even more and went silent.

"When you were standing outside?" suggested Michael. "In their yard?"

"Not in the yard, not in the yard," she promised. "Outside, from the fence . . . when I was walking Rosie."

"And the last time, on Monday morning, with the coat and the taxi?" he asked.

She nodded again and looked at him expectantly.

"Was she like she always was? Like every morning?"

"I couldn't see well," she apologized. "She . . ." Her thick eyebrows knitted together, then suddenly her broad face lit up and the freckles on her cheeks gleamed: "She was talking on her mobile phone. Yes, and her face was down, like this, and I couldn't see it well, and her hair was also covering everything."

"Tell me, Nessia," Michael said slowly, and glanced over at Peter, who was listening with his head down and his eyes narrowed—it was hard to tell what exactly he had understood of what she said—"when you took the dog for a walk, in the evening, or maybe in the morning . . . Do you take her out every evening and every morning?"

"Uh-huh."

"And you'd go past Zahara's house?"

The girl nodded and looked at him expectantly.

"So maybe sometimes you saw visitors coming to see Zahara?"

For a moment she looked across the street and her eyes opened wide, and then she shrugged her shoulders and said: "No, I didn't see anybody. Sometimes . . ." She went silent.

"Sometimes . . . ?"

"They'd come to pick her up."

"Who? Who would come?"

"They would come, with a car, and she would come out. Sometimes she also waited outside until they came."

"Who? People? One? Two? A man or a woman?"

"All kinds of people, and also a man," said Nessia after thinking for quite a while and giving Peter a panicked look.

"In a car?"

"Yes."

"An older man?"

"I don't know," said Nessia. "I didn't see his face."

"In a big car?"

She moved her head in an ambiguous way.

"Surely you know all about cars," he flattered.

"Sort of."

"Do you remember what kind of car it was?"

"Silver color," said the girl without thinking. "Not big and not small. Silver color."

"Was it a Subaru?"

"No, not a Subaru. I know Subarus. And Beetles, and Toyotas." Her eyes lingered on the red Toyota.

"I'll tell you what we'll do," said Michael after thinking a moment. "I'll give you and Peter my phone number, and if you—"

"If I remember something later, I'll phone you?" said the girl. "Like I saw on television?"

"Right. Just like on television. If you remember anything."

"It doesn't matter whether it's big or small," said the girl.

"Exactly. I see that you have a good memory for shows you see on television," Michael said, and handed her a handwritten note, and then he handed another slip of paper to Peter and looked in his eyes and moved closer to him. "She knows more," he whispered.

"Undoubtedly," Peter said in English, and looked at the child. "She knows a lot."

"And will she talk to you?" Michael glanced at the girl, who was staring at the sidewalk but obviously trying hard to hear what they were saying.

"I can only try," Peter said, still in English, then narrowed his eyes to two slits. "Children are unpredictable."

"Yes, I know," Michael said with a sigh, and explained that he didn't want to pressure her now.

Peter agreed that it was best to let her be in the meantime, and especially now, when her mother was coming, and with his eyebrows he gestured toward a woman limping down the street carrying two large plastic bags. After a few energetic tugs the dog agreed to turn around, and swiftly the girl gave one last glance up the street, and Michael saw her alarm.

• • •

"Where do you want all this?" asked the policeman who stood at the door of his office, pointing to some black plastic bags. "The Criminal Identification Unit asked where to put it."

"You brought everything here? Including the clothes?" asked Michael.

"No, they left the clothes there. You asked that they search them, so they're checking them now."

"Leave those with us," said Balilty. "We'll go through them here. That is, some of us will." He looked at Sergeant Yair. "Bring them to the small room, and start working. Let's see you build a profile."

Yair looked at Michael. "After the staff meeting?" he asked.

"I say the other way around. First a profile, then the meeting."

"And in the meantime you'll be deciding who does what, as if this were your special investigation team. Huh?" Eli Bachar said, and noisily stirred the coffee in his glass.

"Guys! Guys!" Michael called out. "We haven't even begun and you're already . . . We've organized sandwiches for you, haven't we? Just be quiet a minute, without this kindergarten stuff, and we'll decide on the order of things." He turned to Balilty: "What about the mobile phone? Have you checked it out?"

"Here." From his shirt pocket Balilty took a folded piece of paper and spread it out. "Here, take it. I have a copy. She had a lot of incoming calls, but only two outgoing calls on Monday, to the list. Don't ask how much we had to run around until . . . Never mind. If we had found the phone itself it would have been better, but you didn't find it."

"'The wicked man, what does he say? You and not I,'" quoted Eli Bachar in a mutter.

"This," said Balilty, indicating the first number on the list, "is Moshe Avital's phone number. He called her twice. Here's the time, in the next column. And there are other incoming calls: Netanel Bashari phoned her, and her parents, Linda O'Brian, her boss, Rosenstein, her friend the reporter. See? There's a whole column here . . . The whole world phoned her, but there are only two outgoing calls, and they're both to the Tel Aviv Hilton."

"The Hilton is a big hotel," muttered Eli Bachar.

"She called the hotel switchboard," said Balilty. "I've already looked into it: On that day the hotel was full. There were five conventions there, three of high-tech companies, one of travel agents and one of the

Vintners Association. Not to mention ordinary guests."

"So we don't know who she was looking for," summed up Eli Bachar, "and we'll never know."

"That woman is waiting for you outside," said Balilty to Michael, and as he opened his sandwich he pulled out of it thin, nearly transparent slices of yellow cheese with holes. "I promised her an answer as to when you could talk to her, so she shouldn't just wait around. Why isn't there feta? There goes my diet. They give me yellow cheese, on white bread. If my doctor knew about this—"

"There wasn't any feta. I asked, but they were out of it, and they don't have pita," explained Yair.

"Big deal—she's just a journalist," Eli Bachar said, and sprinkled some salt on his sandwich. "Since when do we tell people how long they'll have to wait?"

Balilty shook a long, sharp finger at him: "Don't you start looking down on journalists," he warned. "Just don't you spoil my relationship with them. Half of my informers are journalists . . . I, in any case, need a few more things from her. What should I tell her? How long will this meeting last?"

"I don't know . . . An hour, two hours," said Michael distractedly.

"An hour and a half, final price," summed up Balilty. "I'm sending her to the Turk around the corner so she can eat something in the meantime, okay?"

"There's no Turk," Sergeant Yair pointed out. "Today's a holiday. He's closed. You think I went all the way to Emek Refaim just for the fun of it? It's lucky that the café there is open, otherwise you wouldn't even have yellow cheese."

"What a life," grumbled Balilty. "The Sabbath isn't the Sabbath and a holiday isn't a holiday. No wonder this country looks the way it does."

No one answered him, and he left the room and came back after a moment. "The hag left. Are they organizing a funeral? Who's going to the funeral the day after tomorrow?" He looked around. "The day after tomorrow at eleven. Who's going?"

"I can go," said Tzilla, "if you organize the bag for me."

"Is that a problem? Bring it and we'll organize it. This one? The black one? Should we buckle it for you?" asked Eli Bachar, and without waiting for a reply he took the bag and left the room with it.

"It's not good to have a husband and wife on the same special investigation team," said Balilty into the air of the room. "And who's going to take care of the children? Don't they have a mother and father? Today's a holiday. You don't have to work together."

No one replied to the remark, which had become a regular part of the routine of the special investigation team they had just put together. "Ask the Turk if it isn't a holiday today," said Balilty.

Tzilla spread out the worksheet and Michael lit a cigarette and and set it down on the lid of the instant coffee tin before he dictated to Tzilla the list of people to be questioned, whom he divided among them.

"Give me that lawyer Deri again, and I also want Moshe Avital," said Michael.

"Deri?" asked Eli Bachar as he came back into the room and handed the bag to Tzilla. "Which Deri? A relative of the sainted Aryeh Deri?" To Tzilla he said: "They're fixing the buckle for you. You'll have to be careful with it. It's a supersensitive camera. Something brand-new, the latest word."

"He means Deri Aharon, the lawyer who wanted to buy the apartment from the bailiff, the one Rosenstein wanted and that Zahara Bashari was . . . ," explained Tzilla. "And I also asked Einat to come work with us," she said to Michael.

"Einat's good. She has brains," said Yair, "and she's also a pleasant person, because when I worked with her—"

"We know, we know," said Balilty. "You already told us last time, with the Danino couple. Don't you remember? In the end you're going to marry her from wanting to work with her so much. And then what? Sabbaths and holidays, and the children with no mother and father."

"What are you warning me about? She's really nice," Yair said placidly, and turned to Michael: "She can work with me on the material, okay? If we go through the things tonight, then first thing in the morning, even before the funeral . . ."

The muddy sediment was revealed at the bottom of the glass as Michael sipped the last bit of coffee. "I just want to see everything before you write up the report about it, still in the sorting stage."

Yair nodded and pushed aside the bottle of mineral water and the grapefruit juice and the empty coffee cups. When Michael began to assign tasks, all the tensions were forgotten, and even Eli Bachar didn't look bitter when he was told that he had been allotted the two Bashari brothers. "Right after the funeral," stipulated Michael. "While they're sitting shiva. We can't wait. And also the parents, at the same time, each of them individually. And now I want us to have a look at the neighbors' statements. Yair, you spoke to—what's their name?"

"The ones who live on the other side? Beinisch. I spoke to the wife, Clara Beinisch, and with her husband, Efraim Beinisch, but not with their son, Yoram Beinisch. He wasn't home. I'll talk to him later." He looked at his watch. "I arranged with him for an hour from now, there."

"Beinisch is from Hungary, no?" clarified Balilty. "Last year at Passover we were in Budapest, three days in Prague and two in Budapest. Incredible goulash, and everything's dirt cheap."

"There aren't good relations between them," said the sergeant. "Those two families—a world war, but that's how it is when people live in two-family houses. Either they're like one big family or they are the worst enemies. I know this from the moshav, because—"

"They're asking you when they last saw her," interrupted Balilty, "so what are you bullshitting about?"

"It could be connected," protested Yair.

Michael sighed audibly.

"Okay, I'll stick to the facts at this stage," conceded Yair. "The mother saw her for the last time on Saturday evening, the father hasn't seen her for a week or more and the son, Yoram, already told me on the phone that he had seen her a long time ago, he didn't remember when. He usually comes home late and doesn't see anything."

"That is to say—there's nothing," noted Balilty with satisfaction.

"They weren't in the mood for me," explained Yair, "because the son's fiancée had come from America, and there's . . . It's a big deal for them. He's an only child."

"What are they warring about?" asked Michael.

"That's already part of the neighborhood history, and nobody knows by now. Some people say that it started as soon as the Beinisch family moved in and took over the parking, and some say that Naeema Bashari put a curse on Clara right when they moved in, and some . . . They called the police twice, but it didn't end."

"In every neighborhood there are feuds between neighbors. It doesn't end in murder," remarked Eli Bachar.

"No?!" Tzilla leaped up. "What are you talking about?! Almost every day there's nearly a murder here, and it's just luck that—"

"Nearly isn't the same thing," said Eli Bachar.

"I—the grocery store, the man in the grocery store saw her on Thursday morning, early, right when he opened, at six-thirty. She bought milk, bread and—I don't understand why—sanitary napkins."

"He remembered all that? A week later?" wondered Michael. "It's a very busy grocery store. I can't see how—"

"First of all, she didn't pay for it but signed for it, and Mr. Bashari doesn't like to take things on credit, so the grocer writes down exactly what they take, and in addition to that she ordered a bottle of wine from him. I've got it written down here, and in addition to that he said that if Zahara Bashari comes to the grocery store first thing in the morning he knows that he's going to have a good day. Every entrance of hers is an event. He remembers what she was wearing and everything—"

"What? What was she wearing?"

"Wide black trousers and a black sweater," replied Eli Bachar.

"Why did she buy sanitary napkins?" Michael asked Tzilla.

"Maybe she was spotting. Maybe her mother . . . checked the supply of napkins so she was acting . . . was pretending that everything was all right . . . that she had her period," said Tzilla thoughtfully. "And maybe"—she suddenly sat up straight in her chair—"she was intending to end the pregnancy. I spoke to the gynecologist who signed the prescription for the pills. She had been his patient until about a year ago, and since then he hasn't seen her. He said that she had been taking birth control pills since she was eighteen, and that even the first time she came to him she had been having full sexual relations. He can't understand how she got pregnant, unless she stopped taking the pills. And he can't understand that, either, because she was terribly afraid of getting pregnant. He remembers her very well," explained Tzilla. "Apparently she really was something, that Zahara."

"We saw that in the video, too," said Balilty.

"From the age of eighteen? Full sexual relations? With whom?" demanded Michael.

"How should I know?" protested Balilty.

"Baka, the area of Bethlehem Road—how many secrets can you keep there?"

"Okay, I understand," said Balilty in an insulted tone. "So it'll take another day. Today's already a holiday. No one is going to—"

"I want an answer to that simple question: Who was she sleeping with at the age of eighteen, and who got her pregnant? A girl whom everyone in the neighborhood knew—it's not unattainable information."

"At our moshav," said Yair pensively, "there was this woman, like a nun. No one—her house was closed, she didn't speak to anyone. And this is a moshav. Everyone knows everything, worse than a kibbutz, and all of a sudden she was pregnant, and no one dared to ask her. And she had a son and no one knew who the father was, and not even—"

"Not again!" protested Balilty. "What is this, *Peyton Place?*"

"I'm not saying it's the same," said Yair without looking at Balilty. "It's not always that way, but if a woman wants to—she can hide things, especially if it's a onetime thing."

"What are you talking about, a onetime thing? What are you talking about?" fumed Balilty. "Birth control pills since the age of eighteen!"

"Who remembers what she did when she was eighteen? Maybe since then she didn't—"

"And her mother doesn't know anything about it," murmured Tzilla.

"Okay, okay." Balilty flung his arms up toward the ceiling. "I give up. It doesn't matter. Let's suppose you're right. Let's say there was a onetime thing and suddenly she's pregnant—who did she go to the attic with? Huh? Forget the history. We're talking about now. Do you intend to find out who the sonofabitch was, or not?"

Sergeant Yair looked at Balilty and said nothing.

"Right. Now he's not saying anything," said the intelligence officer triumphantly. "Shuts up like a . . ." He looked at Yair and smiled slyly. "Like a gecko."

Chapter 7

There was just a baking pan left in the sink from all the cooking for the holiday, and now that she had completed all her other chores, Nessia was scrubbing it hard until it gleamed. Out the kitchen window to her right, it was not yet completely dark, but the apartment was already cold and she shivered as she examined the square enamel baking pan with bits of food that would have been stuck to it forever if she waited until after dinner. This pan, it was better to clean it really well, or otherwise her mother would dig it out of the cupboard and show her every spot. Again she scrubbed the last of the spots with steel wool, and then she rinsed off the crud that was clinging to the steel wool, and she dried the pan with the dish towel lengthwise and widthwise, until she could see her face reflected in it, round and blurred. She put the rubber stopper in the drain and sprayed bleach into it, and with Scotch-Brite she scrubbed the bottom of the sink and rinsed it twice, and when she shut the faucet she heard the whoosh of water being poured from the bucket—her mother had washed the floor in the bedroom—and wondered whether she would have a bit of time now to herself, before her mother gave her another chore. Through the window, in the dimness of the emptied street, she could still see one police car parked in front of the Basharis' house. They won't be sitting in the sukkah tonight, she thought, and she wiped her hands on the sides of her pants and headed with the stealthy steps of a cat toward the front door.

"Where are you going? Haven't you showered yet?" Her mother's voice sounded muffled. Maybe she had bent down and was cleaning under the bed. Even at that moment, when she was busy with the bucket and the rag, she heard every sound in the front of the apartment. Nessia had already opened the door, and when Rosie stood up and wagged her tail, she sat her back down quietly and said to the wall of the corridor: "I need some more decorations for the sukkah."

"Leave that sukkah alone now. It's always the sukkah. Have you finished the kitchen? And you still have to take your shower," she heard her mother shout as she closed the door behind her and slipped down to the shelter. In its depths, among the treasures that had accumulated in the cardboard carton, she also kept the set of colors that she had found in the stationery store downtown. She still didn't dare use them, because every time she touched the box she remembered how risky it had been to get them out of there, in front of the guard who stood at the door and didn't take his eyes off her; only when he had been distracted for a moment had she stuck the box into her sweatpants. She was very scared then, when she walked out of the store and as she ran down the street in the direction of the bus stop, ignoring the irritation on the inside of her thighs the way she hid the sores that had developed there from her mother. Not for a moment did she look back. Now she intended to take out the gold felt pen and color the leaves that Peter had cut out for her that morning, to stick onto the blankets that formed the walls of the sukkah. All year long the naked skeleton of the sukkah stood there, and only on Sukkot was it wrapped in old blankets and white sheets that had yellowed with time.

She also intended to take another peek into the gray handbag. Nessia was not stupid: If they murdered Zahara, they would be looking for the handbag, and they could even come to search their shelter, so she had to find a new place to hide all her treasures, and especially the gray handbag. She knew that she should give it to the police, or at least to the tall man—he wasn't wearing a uniform, but he was also a policeman, the commander of them all—who spoke especially to her, her, out of everyone else, and asked her to help him. It was strange that such an important man, of whom everyone asked permission, nevertheless had such sad eyes and hardly smiled at all; he looked to her like someone from a movie, and so was she, for a moment, when he told her to contact him if she remembered anything. Thanks to him, in her own eyes she was tall and slender like a movie star, someone who acted in *Walker* or even *Beverly Hills,* but she couldn't part with the purse. It was too beautiful, and she would never have another one like it, or in any case until the spell came true.

On television, she had once seen how thieves take the money and throw away the wallet. Maybe she could do the opposite. Take the wallet and throw away—no, not throw away, give back—the money; but she also didn't want to part from the money. She kept all the bills in a plastic bag inside her underpants, because never in her life would she have so much money again. And she also didn't want to part from the little lipstick, or from the bottle of perfume and the mascara and all the other things, which were hers now. And what good would it do them if she gave them back? What they needed was the papers, the notes and the little diary and the identity card and the plastic cards, and anyway they were of no use to her. So it would be enough to give them back, and she should just do it quickly, before they come around to search in the shelter.

But how could she give them back? They would ask her where all the things came from and they would even think that she was the one who had stolen them, and this time she really hadn't stolen, she had found. How could she give the tall, sad man the papers, without him knowing that they came from her? A wave of heat flashed through her belly as she thought about this. And the scary notes she found there, with all those words she didn't understand, what would they do with them? Again her belly fluttered. It can wait in the meantime, maybe until after dinner, when she goes out with Rosie for a short walk. This is what she decided as she pushed open the heavy iron door and stood in the doorway. But if they come here, she said to herself, and they look hard, in any case she would be in big trouble.

Just as she was about to enter the thick darkness inside the shelter, she heard the door of their apartment opening and her mother's voice, high and shrill: "Nessia, Nessia, where are you?" And something in this shout, which she hadn't expected at all, caused her to leave the door of the shelter and rush up the stairs and stand breathless in front of her mother and say only: "I went to look for . . ." But her mother only wanted her to shower and get dressed in her holiday clothes before Yigal and Peter came. Afterward, Nessia consoled herself, after dinner and after Mother falls asleep, she would be able to sneak down to the shelter again and make sure that no one had touched the gray handbag. And the leaves that she wanted to color with the gold felt pen, they could also wait until tomorrow. After all, the holiday lasted for a whole week.

And at that very moment, shortly after the holiday began, after the building at the Russian Compound had quieted down a bit and from the window on the second floor the light cast by the streetlamp was etched on the asphalt beneath it—at that very moment Michael Ohayon was drumming his fingers on his desk, because the investigation wasn't making any progress and he hadn't been able to extract anything from his interlocutor. Orly Shushan's protruding brown eyes were fixed on him as before, full of expression; had he been asked to define that expression Michael would have hesitated between strained persistence and admiration. There were moments when it was possible to think she was mocking him. In any case, she looked away from him because of the exaggerated unhappiness she was demonstrating as she reminded him how she had tried to interview him for a profile right at the beginning of her career as a journalist and how he had rebuffed her outright then. He himself remembered neither the attempts nor the rebuff, and now as she sat there opposite him in the investigation—Tzilla had refused to leave him alone with "that journalist everyone knows is a barracuda"— Michael interrupted the flow of her speech and turned on the tape recorder. Tzilla sat opposite the corner of the desk, the yellow pad in front of her and her hand poised to write.

In reply to his question, Orly Shushan recounted her first, "fateful" meeting with Zahara Bashari. It was evident that this was not the first time she had told this story; how, when she had been an education officer in the career army at the girls' boot camp and was walking past the showers, she had suddenly heard that deep, dark, exciting voice from the gut singing that passage from the Song of Songs, "My love is gone down to his garden, to the beds of spices," and how she had stood there, enchanted by the voice and by the song that she hadn't heard since she was a girl, and how, after a moment, she had gone into the showers and among the girls from the A Platoon she had seen "this girl, drying her hair on an army towel and without moving and without any mannerisms, still half-wet and with all the girls standing there and listening to her, from inside the showers or on those benches they stand on to get dressed, and that was a picture it is impossible to forget." Orly Shushan peeked at the yellow writing pad as Tzilla turned a page that had been filled. "And immediately I summoned her to my office and—how shall I put this?" She looked around as if searching for words it was obvious she was going to find and that had served her not once and not twice but many times when she had told this story. "I fell completely in love with her."

When Orly Shushan left the army she knew she would not return to her parents' home in the Kiryat Menachem neighborhood of Jerusalem

("They, my parents, are from a different generation. They came here from Morocco, at the beginning of the 1950s, and straightaway they were sent to a public housing project in Kiryat Menachem.") And there, in the small apartment ("five children and the parents in two and a half rooms"), is where she spent her childhood. "I'm the child of their old age, like Zahara and like you," she hastened to add, and her eyes fixed on Michael and opened wide and bulged even more. "Because of this I so much wanted to write about you. I felt . . . I felt that perhaps there was a kindred spirit here. I wanted . . . I wanted to show how even from there, from children of immigrants from North Africa, stars can emerge—"

Tzilla quietly cleared her throat, but Michael was in no need of her warning; a wave of disgust rose in him because of the counterfeit shared fate she was forcing on him, and he didn't say a single word in response, but insisted on continuing his questions about the nature of her relationship with Zahara. With that same devoted look, Orly Shushan talked instead about her path as a reporter—first writing for a local newspaper, and very quickly ("It's unbelievable how quickly. After four months they called me in and made me the offer") for a national newspaper, and how at such a young age she had become a star journalist because of the profiles she succeeded in writing, and how meanwhile Zahara had completed her military service, but did not move to Tel Aviv as she had dreamed.

"I did. I have an apartment on Melchett Street. I had enough of this choking Jerusalem. I wouldn't come back here for any price."

"Why not?" injected Michael.

"Isn't it obvious? Everyone is fleeing this city . . ."

"No," he corrected, "not everyone. Why didn't Zahara move to Tel Aviv as she had dreamed?"

"Oh, that. For all kinds of reasons. First of all she didn't have the money, and she also knew that it would break her parents, and she found a job right away in Jerusalem. Anyway, she also has Linda here, who helped her, a good friend of her oldest brother, and also . . ." She began and stopped.

"Also what?" insisted Michael.

"It was like . . . like she wanted to move to Tel Aviv like everyone else, but there was something that kept her here, something . . . something that . . . I don't know, but right away I understood that all the talk about Tel Aviv was just talk, not serious."

"A man maybe?"

"You mean someone specific in Jerusalem? No. I'd know, wouldn't I? Because I knew about everything she had going and . . ."

"But you didn't know who she was seeing?"

"That's just the thing." She breathed deeply. "I didn't. That is, she wasn't seeing people. She didn't want to. I thought that she . . . and I also asked her, 'What's with you?' I said to her, 'Do you just want to sit around like this and be an old maid?'"

"And what did she say?"

"She? She didn't answer. She laughed. At first I thought she had something going either with someone who was married or something else, I don't know what. In any case, she had some secret."

He spent some time on the standard questions: What exactly happened the last time they met, what had Zahara been wearing and did she look as usual; whether there was anyone who hated Zahara ("Zahara? It's obvious you didn't know her. She was so incredible, an in-CRED-ible person. Anyone who saw her just had to love her. There's no one who didn't!"); and whether she had any idea who could have caused Zahara to go of her own free will to that attic, among the water tanks.

"Of her own free will? Are you sure? Didn't they murder her first and then bring her up there?"

Michael shook his head and said that she had gone up the ladder of her own free will. An expression of disbelief appeared on the reporter's face, and she said: "I think that she never went all the way with anyone . . . I thought that she was a virgin. People came on to her all the time and she . . . nothing."

"Are you sure? That there wasn't anyone?"

"I've already told you."

"She'd definitely been with at least one man," said Michael in a matter-of-fact way as he followed the body that tensed and the eyes that narrowed. "This emerged without a doubt from the pathological examination."

"Listen," said the journalist in an annoyed tone of voice. "You can see that I don't know anything about this, and I also don't believe it. I don't care about a 'pathological examination,' I simply don't believe it. Zahara told me everything. I knew about everyone who tried to come on to her. There were so many. Believe me, there's nothing that—"

"Start counting," said Michael.

"Counting? Counting what?"

"Counting everyone who came on to her. Name them."

"No." She shook her head. "Not like that. I didn't always know who . . . Sometimes at a café, sometimes at a pub, in the ticket line for a movie, once near the video store. Who didn't? The guy from the video store and the pizza delivery boy—no one could remain indifferent to that beauty of hers, but I'm telling you, she didn't go out with anyone, anyone! It was as if . . . Now that you're asking, I think that she acted like someone, like . . . as though she was being faithful to someone, but I had no idea! I hadn't the slightest idea what was going on in her head!"

"Being faithful?"

"Yes. As if . . . How can I put it? As if she had . . . as though she was waiting for someone who was a prisoner."

Tzilla, who raised her head from the yellow writing pad, looked at Orly inquiringly. Her long silver earrings tinkled delicately as she shook her head and said quietly: "A week or two ago in the weekend magazine you interviewed the wife of that officer who's being held prisoner by the Hezbollah, didn't you?"

"Yes, three weeks ago, but what's that got to do with it?"

"It has to do with your associations, about faithfulness and all that," explained Tzilla.

"No, no," Michael hastened to say. "I'm quite interested in that. Do you really have no idea what gave that impression, that she was being faithful to someone?"

Orly Shushan shook her head. "Maybe it'll come to me later on."

"I'll tell you why I'm asking," he said as if he were stating a well-known fact. "Because of the pregnancy."

There was no doubt about the shock and the astonishment in Orly Shushan's face.

"Pregnancy? What do you mean, pregnancy? What pregnancy? *Zahara's* pregnancy?!"

"Twelve weeks, the beginning of the fourth month," Michael specified, and he did not take his eyes off her face.

The reporter's thin lips trembled, and from the depths of her throat burst a sound like the beginning of a sob, raw weeping, suppressed. But it had no continuation.

"Zahara? Zahara was pregnant?!" She definitely looked insulted.

"We saw it in the pathological examination."

"Could I have some water?" she asked in a broken voice, and pointed to the bottle of mineral water. Tzilla put the yellow pad in her lap and poured water into the foam cup she pulled from the carton at her feet.

"Didn't you know?" asked Michael, leaning forward as she was gulping the water. Her hand shook and she steadied it with her other hand and shook her head.

"Is it certain?" she whispered.

"Twelve weeks."

Anger joined insult in her eyes as she said: "I can't understand how she didn't tell me. We were so close. I thought we were . . . And it turns out that . . . In other things, I was the only one she trusted."

"Other things?" Michael tensed. "What other things?"

"She'd come to me with the whole family story, and I really helped her . . ."

"What family story?"

"You see," said Orly Shushan, and a trace of satisfaction crept into her tone of voice. "You don't know everything."

"There's no doubt that we don't know everything. Very little, in fact. And really, you, and maybe only you, can help us, especially with your skills," Michael said, and avoided looking at Tzilla, so as not to see the disgust that was probably crossing her face upon hearing this gross flattery. But Orly Shushan swallowed the bait. ("It's because of his eyes," Tzilla said later at the special investigation team staff meeting over the tape recorder that was playing the reporter's voice. "Before that, he looked at her with that look of his, you know what I mean, and then he was silent and struck," and Balilty laughed aloud and said: "Do we know? For years I've been trying to learn that look, but he won't teach it to me. How does he get them to believe even that kind of bullshit?")

"Zahara told me that there was a secret in her family, that something happened and they don't talk about it. I wouldn't have told you without her permission," she said, and lowered her head, "but because of the murder, because Zahara was murdered, and because of this story about the pregnancy . . . I can't keep it all to myself anymore. And anyway, in the end I would have written an article about it, and I'm still going to do that. With a full profile of Zahara. I'm telling you now, so you won't say I didn't tell you."

"But not until we solve this case," warned Tzilla, and Michael gave her a scathing look (and at the staff meeting afterward he commented that she was liable to have cut off the reporter's monologue) and he was relieved when Orly Shushan ignored the warning and went on to say: "A whole series of articles, not just one or two. But that's later. Zahara, because of my profession, which she thought I was very good at, wanted me to help her find out, because all the talk with her mother hadn't got her anyplace. Zahara told me that every week or two her mother would simply disappear. Without saying anything, she'd just make extra food and leave it in the pots on the stove and disappear for a whole day. Several years ago, Zahara asked her where she went, but didn't get an answer. Not only that, but every time she asked, her mother would get angry, so annoyed that Zahara couldn't ask her anymore.

"A few months ago Zahara told me about those disappearances and asked me to help her find out what was going on. I told her that there was nothing simpler, there wasn't even any need for a private detective or anything. Her mother doesn't know me all that well, because I'd only been to their house maybe two or three times, and even if she did recognize me, it wouldn't be a problem to say that I was there in connection with my work. So one day Zahara called me and said, this is it, she's getting ready. I hopped into a cab and waited by their house, and followed her to the central bus station, and saw her get on a bus to Rosh Ha'ayin." Orly Shushan paused for a moment. "I said to myself that this has something to do with Yemenites, because Rosh Ha'ayin—how should I put it?—Rosh Ha'ayin is associated with Yemenites."

Michael nodded affirmatively, and because she did not continue, he went on to say: "Definitely."

She followed Zahara's mother to Rosh Ha'ayin and saw her go into Rabbi Kappah's house. There was no way she could go into the house, and to stand outside the windows was also impossible, but from the cab at the street corner she could follow quite well the other people who went into the house, and afterward ("It wasn't as hard as people think") she found out through the grocery store and the neighbors about a weekly meeting of a group of men and women who had immigrated to Israel in 1949 from Yemen through the transit camp in Aden to the immigrant camp at Ein Shemer. "At the time I did not know what they did or what they spoke about. One might have thought it was a kind of regular reunion, but I continued to investigate until I came up with what was happening there."

Michael waited in silence. A minute went by, and then another.

"I'm thinking about whether to say any more," Orly Shushan said suddenly, and leaned back. "This is first-rate journalistic material and I wouldn't want it to get out without . . . I think that perhaps I need permission from my editor, unless . . . unless . . ."

Michael, who knew that she was waiting for him to urge her on, waited in silence.

"Can we sign an exclusivity agreement now?"

"Meaning?" Michael inquired, and laid his hand near the edge of the table, close to Tzilla, whose body was already tense. "Exclusivity regarding what, exactly?"

Then the journalist gestured toward the tape recorder and Michael, after deliberating a moment, pushed the button and the tape stopped. In a very low voice Orly Shushan explained that she was asking for exclusive rights to publish the story if she gave it to them, and she stipulated another condition: Michael's commitment to be interviewed by her. "An exclusive interview," she clarified, and her eyes again took on that sealed look they contained when they'd met in the Basharis' yard.

Tzilla gaped, but one look from Michael silenced her ("I've never heard such nerve," she grumbled afterward at the staff meeting. "They think they're the kings of the world, those journalists").

"I fear that there's a misunderstanding here," Michael said, and enlisted for this statement and his ensuing statements the courtesy and caution he kept for situations in which evident anger is not efficacious. "We're in a police investigation now, not volunteer work."

"I beg your pardon," said the journalist in a tone similar to his, so that it was possible to think that she was mocking him again, but her eyes revealed neither mockery nor irony. "You didn't summon me here with an official order and I am not being questioned officially or under caution. You told me to come and I did."

"That's not exactly so," elucidated Michael. "Everyone who is connected to the case is called in for questioning, and in your case we dispensed with the formal processes, because we formed the impression that you were a good friend who was interested in helping with the investigation, but . . ."

"But what?" demanded Orly Shushan, and as he remained silent she asked: "Do you mean to say that I'm here as a murder suspect?"" and this time in her question there was a tone not only of mockery, but of anger.

"You might say," said Michael with forced indifference. "You might very well say."

"Pardon me?" she said in astonishment. "Me?! How could you . . . On what basis? I hadn't seen Zahara for more than a week."

"That's what you say," Michael said, and lit a cigarette.

"Well, do you want me to bring proofs? How can a person prove that . . . I can only tell you what I did during the hours when Zahara . . . This is totally impossible!"

And at that moment Michael tossed the burning cigarette into the paper cup, and after listening for a moment to the sizzling in the residue of the coffee, he leaned across the desk and said that the time had come for her to talk, and talk to the point, and especially in light of the phone conversation she had with Zahara on the day of her death and in light of the fact of the bad quarrel she had with Zahara the last time they met.

At once the face opposite him went pale, and now fear was evident in the prominent brown eyes. "How do you know about that? Did Zahara tell her brother or Linda?"

Michael did not reply. He had already turned the tape recorder back on, and with his head he signaled her to keep talking. ("Of course he didn't answer her," explained Tzilla to the assembled staff, who listened to the silence that had been recorded on the tape. "What would he tell her? He couldn't tell her that he was playing poker, or that he had deduced one thing from another, so he left her hanging, and from that moment she was completely in his hands.")

Orly Shushan insisted on calling the quarrel a "disagreement." She repeated the word "disagreement" two or three times, and once she used "differences of opinion" and spoke about Zahara's fiery temperament ("When she was really angry, nothing stopped her"), and also about Zahara's refusal not to let the story out "at this stage." In the end, Zahara would have given in, and it was only natural that she, Orly, as a journalist, would see the social potential of the private family story, as it was kind of a metaphor for the terrible injustice that had been done in this country to the immigrants from the Arab countries. And not only that, there was the fact that a large picture of Zahara, in the center of the spread, with her beautiful face, and a few words about her musical talent, would advance her cause. But under no circumstances did Zahara want a public outcry without getting her parents' agreement, and she hadn't even told her older brother Netanel—or at least that is what the journalist thought—about what she had discovered.

"And I," she said bitterly, "I'd already done all the work—do you know what kind of investigation went into this?" She sat up straight in her chair, and with a severe expression announced: "But I'm not revealing my sources to you, no matter what. I don't reveal my sources."

He maintained his silence.

"Zahara's mother came from a good family—she's the daughter of the last chief rabbi in Yemen," said Orly Shushan, "and because of that they made a good match for her, with Zahara's father, who was a promising young religious scholar. The mother was thirteen, and the father a bit older. They had a baby son who died right after he was born. Imagine, a girl of fourteen has a baby and he dies. Can you imagine such a thing?"

As she looked at him expectantly, Michael nodded.

"So then, imagine something even worse. Imagine that this girl, Naeema Bashari, gives birth again in the transit camp in Aden, on the way to Israel, and she gets to the immigrant camp at Ein Shemer, with a two-month-old baby girl . . ."

"Zahara?" asked Michael.

"Zahara. Big Zahara."

"Did she die too?"

"No, apparently not," Orly Shushan said, and crossed her legs. "She was taken away—that's what happened to her. We're talking about 1949. Do you know what happened in that year?"

Michael said nothing, but had an expectant look on his face.

"And not only in '49. Until 1954 they could take immigrants' children—not just Yemenites, but also Romanians—and give them up for adoption and just tell the parents they died. Haven't you read about this in the newspapers?"

"I've read about it," confirmed Michael in the tone of an obedient but helpless pupil, "but I didn't make the connection, because I haven't investigated the . . . But you, you've investigated."

"In 1953 alone, in a single year, more than a hundred fifty children were given up for adoption without the knowledge of their parents. I won't give you the sources, but I am prepared to tell you that before I got onto the matter of Big Zahara I had already spoken with a woman from the Women's International Zionist Organization from England, a very old and sick woman who had adopted a girl in 1953. They even let her take the child out of Israel. Can you imagine? But the facts, of course, are known: Between 1944 and 1949, two thousand Yemenite children disappeared! After they got sick and were sent to hospitals, they simply vanished. The parents who came to look for them were told that the children had died, but there were no death certificates, no graves and no nothing. Why do you think Rabbi Meshullam and his followers went on their rampage?"

Michael said nothing. He did not mention the well-known "Sarah Levine" trial, in which it was revealed from a DNA test that a woman who believed with all her heart that she was the daughter of one of the Yemenite women whose children were stolen for adoption was not really her daughter.

"In any case, I've checked and I've got proof: Naeema Bashari had a daughter, and two months later this daughter was taken from her."

"But you haven't spoken to Naeema Bashari about this? Or to her husband, Zahara's father?" Michael half inquired, half stated.

"No. Zahara didn't agree," Orly Shushan said, and bit her lower lip. "She wasn't willing to let me do that. I didn't want to endanger my relationship with her at this stage. I knew I would be able to convince her, and that was what the disagreement was about the last time we met."

"And you talked about this when you were with her on the day she was murdered," said Michael in the same tone as before.

"No, of course not," said Orly Shushan, aghast. "How could I? I was . . . If only I had been with her . . . She wouldn't . . . Nothing would have happened . . . I waited for her and she didn't show up."

"When was she supposed to have come?"

"At eight. We'd arranged for eight o'clock."

"And you didn't look for her after she didn't show up?"

"No, I was afraid that she . . . I was afraid that she had told her parents that she was at my place, and was somewhere else."

"Where were you on Monday?"

"I've told you. I told the first guy . . . the one with the belly, the one called Balilty. I told him everything I did on Monday—from the swim at the Gordon swimming pool, through the coffee meeting and the meeting at the newspaper and lunch with—"

"You didn't leave Tel Aviv?"

"I was waiting for Zahara. From eight in the evening I was waiting for her at home. People phoned me at home. There are people who talked to me. Are you asking . . . Really, why should I . . . And anyway, how would I have carried her up to the attic there? On my shoulders?"

"But you talked to her on the mobile that day," Michael reminded her.

"Yes, I spoke to her. I phoned her to confirm our appointment, and she said she'd be at my place at eight. That's what she said."

"Do you know of anyone she was planning to meet at the Hilton?"

"At the Hilton? Hilton Tel Aviv or Hilton Jerusalem?"

"Tel Aviv. Did she mention anything about that to you?"

"Nothing," said Orly, astonished and insulted. "I didn't know she even knew anyone who frequents the Hilton."

"Did you ever hear the name Moshe Avital from her?"

"Avital?" A furrow appeared between her eyebrows. "Avital . . . I think she mentioned that name. I think it's someone . . . someone who's friendly with Linda? Could that be it?"

"Tell me"—he leaned forward again—"did you know that she was planning to buy an apartment?"

"An apartment?!" She snorted. "Zahara? What apartment? Don't you know that she lived with her parents? And was planning to go abroad to study, next year. She was just saving for the trip and—"

The door opened wide, and Balilty's large body blocked the opening, almost completely hiding the person who was standing behind him. "Listen to this," he chortled, and leaned forward a bit and made a flowery gesture with his hand, as if trying to imitate the servant of a French noble, who had got his hands on some sensational news that couldn't hurt. In the middle of his ceremonious bow he caught the piercing look that Tzilla shot at him and immediately stood up straight and retracted his hand. At the sight of Orly Shushan he went silent and changed the expression on his face, and cleared his throat loudly to signal Michael to step out of the room.

Michael, who realized that if he did not respond immediately Balilty would say whatever he had to say in front of the journalist, hurried out of the room. His face wore the expression of "What now?" but in the corridor he took a pack of cigarettes from his pocket, pulled one out and let the intelligence officer light it.

"I've got two things," said Balilty festively.

Michael held up his forefinger as if to start counting.

"I've spoken to Deri."

"Aryeh Deri?" said Michael in astonishment. "What's he got to do with—"

"No, with the other buyer's lawyer."

"What other buyer?"

"Someone who wanted to buy the apartment on Railroad Street, the apartment Rosenstein wanted Zahara to have."

"*Nu?*"

"And it's really true," said Balilty with a disappointed expression on his face. "He wanted the apartment and Rosenstein beat him to it because of some technicality, and is going to get it, so at least about this he wasn't lying. And Mr. Avital, the owner of the apartment, is on his way here. He didn't even argue."

Michael regarded him in silence.

"So that's it," Balilty, summed up and turned as if to leave.

"Danny," said Michael.

Balilty turned around and looked at him, the amused glint back in his eyes. "Yes? What?" he asked.

"Are you playing Columbo now?" asked Michael.

"Huh? Huh? What have I said?"

"It's what you haven't said. You intended to leave and come back right away. In a minute you would have gone off and forgotten to tell me the main thing."

"Ah, yes." Balilty smiled broadly. "You tell me if it's the main thing or no." He nodded his head in the direction of the end of the corridor. "She's waiting for you in the small room. I didn't want to let her wander around here so that everyone could see her and—"

"No, I can see that until you see me fall flat on my face in amazement, we won't have any peace around here." Michael smiled. "Perhaps you would be so kind as to tell us who's waiting?"

"Come and see," Balilty said, and headed, slowly, toward his room, demonstratively straightening his back. Michael, bemused, trailed after him.

The small room, which was usually a repository for files on current cases, office equipment, coffee, sugar, long life milk and cartons of disposable cups and bottled mineral water, was at the end of the corridor. Their footsteps echoed in the nearly empty space. From the first floor, sounds of laughter could be heard, and the fluorescent lights cast a musty, sallow and depressing hue on the floor tiles and the walls.

On the only chair in the room, next to the steel desk under which the cardboard boxes were stored, sat Ada Levi-Efrati, with her legs crossed— the old office lamp that lit the room cast shadows on her face and her body—and now she looked up at him with her small, pale face, which was illuminated by an embarrassed smile.

Balilty hung around near the door. "So now that I've done my good deed for the day, and now that she's forgiven me," he said with satisfaction. "What do you know? She didn't want to talk to me, but she had no alternative, because they didn't let her go up to the second floor, and you don't have a mobile phone and you don't answer your pager, so she spoke to me even though I'm a rotten fascist, and we made up. Have we made up?" he said, turning toward her, and she lowered her head in silence.

"Okay, there's no need to get so excited," he said sarcastically. "Justice is relative, and I just want you to know that this contractor, your Arab, is a Jew-hating anti-Semite. Only a blind person couldn't see that. If someone would strike out at you or if you were in danger, do you think he would save you?"

Ada Efrati did not answer.

"Okay, forget it." Balilty sighed. "The main thing is that we've made up and you've seen that I'm not just a shit. Have fun." He smiled, and left.

"Just a minute." Michael went out after him.

"Listen," said the intelligence officer with a serious expression and leaning against the wall. "I'll continue with her—with that journalist. We haven't got anything to do so I'm asking you, let me continue with her. I also know this job; do me a favor. We'll also work it out with Avital, believe me. There are things we can manage without you. Inside in that room"—he pointed to the door—"sits a woman, a pretty woman, a quality woman, waiting for you. When I asked her about that, she said to me: 'Personal.' And I know you, and I've already seen the way you were looking at her there, in that house where we found the body. Do you get me?"

Michael said nothing.

"Hasn't the time come for you to get over that other story?" begged Balilty. "Do me a favor, me and everybody, take today—that is, what's left of it—that is, tonight, and have a holiday meal like a human being and all that. As a favor, a personal favor to me and to Tzilla and to Eli Bachar and to all of us. What do you say?"

The excited, expectant expression on Danny Balilty's face touched Michael's heart, and he smiled.

"What do you say? As a personal favor, even though she thinks I'm a shit. I have no problem with that," pleaded Balilty.

"What can I say? I can say that Matty will kill me, because of me she'll be sitting all alone in the sukkah," answered Michael.

"Matty, if I tell her why, if I tell her that you're with someone, and someone so classy, and one you've already had . . . Never mind. If I tell her that, Matty will be in seventh heaven and she won't kill anyone, not even me. And anyway, what do you think? All the children and my sister-in-law and also . . ."

Michael turned up his palms in a gesture of surrender, and Balilty clapped him on the shoulder and turned to leave with a whistle of joy.

"Wait a second," Michael called after him.

"What now?" asked Balilty suspiciously, as if expecting Michael to change his mind.

"When you go over Tzilla's notes, you'll see that she says there, Miss Orly Shushan, something about Zahara keeping faith with someone. Spend some time on that point—I didn't get it."

"Tell me something, buddy. Are you gaining time, or what? Is this the first time I've questioned anybody? What's got into you?" He pointed to the door. "There's a woman waiting for you."

"And what about you? Are you playing Zorba the Greek?" Michael said, and went back into the little room.

Chapter 8

Will wonders never cease," Michael Ohayon whispered at five-twenty in the morning to Ada, whose face was very close to his as he caressed her smooth, tawny arm. Her cheekbones were even more prominent in the yellowish glow of the reading lamp, its shade tilted, and a faint halo surrounded her narrow face. A sly half-smile crossed her full lips and stole into her brown eyes, which narrowed to look at him exactly as they had done years ago, as she stood at the foot of the ladder in the work camp. In amazement he touched the crease etched between her eyebrows and the fine down above her upper lip: Thirty years later it seemed as though they had come with utter naturalness from that grapefruit grove to this bed, to the small bedroom in a ground-floor apartment in an apartment house in the western part of the city. He was amazed by the intimacy he had felt in the small room at the Russian Compound and all the way to the car and from there to her place, an intimacy that did not evaporate even upon entering her apartment and facing the visitors who were waiting there, and even more amazing was the naturalness with which he sat down to the holiday dinner with her daughter and her son and their partners, and with her sister, whom he was meeting for the first time.

He himself was also amazing. For years, women he loved and men to whom he was close had accused him of being closed, of a tense alertness and a lack of spontaneity in intimate relationships, but throughout the holiday dinner he felt easygoing and serene, as if he had come home, even during the course of this ritual that the years of his marriage, as well as the years that followed it, had taught him to loathe. And also amazing was the natural way members of the family related to him, as if they had known him for a long time, and as if it was nothing extraordinary to have him dining with them at their table.

"After all, you were my mother's first kiss," said her daughter, giggling; with her cropped hair and her gray eyes, she looked like a blonde but exact copy of Ada. With this she had solved the nagging question of what they knew about him, and he did not correct her or mention the existence of that boyfriend who had held him back, and who had certainly kissed her more than once before he had.

"You were the Don Juan of your grade," her sister said with a small smile, and shyly looked sideways. "Most probably you don't remember me—I was two years below you and kind of a little mouse, scared of my own shadow. I never stopped crying at night, out of homesickness, and it took me half a year before I could manage to fall asleep in the dormitory." Almost apologetically, Michael admitted that indeed he did not remember.

"Not exactly Don Juan," corrected Ada with the half-smile that almost always accompanied her observation of him. "There were no proofs— you never saw him in action and he didn't go from one girl to the next. None of the girls in our grade reported any personal experience. There were stories. The girls were crazy about him, but he—he was unattainable. They said you had a story with an older woman. Is it true? Did you have a story with an older woman?" she asked, turning to look at him.

He blushed and cleared his throat, grimacing in negation. Although Becky Pomerantz, the mother of his good friend and classmate, had died several years ago, it never occurred to him, at the table or at all, to tell anyone about the musical education or about the seduction. He lit a cigarette to cover his silence and was again amazed at his serenity, which even the half-mocking conversation did not ruffle. It was the excited serenity of someone who did not need to choke off expectation lest he be defeated; and paradoxically, the more this expectation was prolonged, the sweeter it became. He even knew for certain that this woman—who even beneath the dark hair threaded with gray still preserved the image of his youth—would allow him to touch his image and her image of long ago. He did not understand whence this certainty came, and uncharacteristically he did not force himself to understand its reasons. No "what ifs" and "how shoulds" pecked at him.

The first time they'd sat together, in the café on Jaffa Street, after Ada had lashed out at Balilty, he'd already felt how pleasant it was to sit with her and talk with her. Even though he knew that Solomon the pathologist was waiting for him, as was Sergeant Yair, whom he had left to wait for him at the office without a word of explanation, he had not hesitated at all—after she had calmed down a bit about the matter of the contractor and Balilty, and it was possible to talk to her about a different subject—to ask about her life.

Thus he heard how she had made an early marriage to a man who was fifteen years older than her ("My father died, and my mother was dependent on me . . . In any case, I was the oldest, and my sister was still in the army and my little brother—he was really little—and it was natural that I would fall in love, or think I had fallen in love . . . In any case, Jedediah . . . he loved me so much, and I thought . . ."), and how she had gone abroad with him, sent by the geological firm that employed him, to drill for oil in South America, where her two children were born. She also told him about her husband's long illness and his death, and very little about how she began to do photography ("At first, stills, just pictures of the children, and then with a film camera, and courses and . . . Don't ask"), and how in the end, after three years of study in Paris, she had become a director of documentary films, and how she had gone from place to place on behalf of the Dutch film company that employed her ("It was awfully hard with the children. They weren't babies anymore, but . . ."). She spread her palms out to her sides and with her whole mouth she smiled a full, helpless smile, before she looked into his eyes and asked: "And you?"

They hadn't really talked about meeting again in the future, because when he glanced at his pager he found three messages from Sergeant Yair and one from Dr. Solomon, and he had to hurry to his office. But the very next day, at his initiative, they met at a café again and talked for hours, about him and about her, and finally, inevitably and very cautiously, about the two of them. And then, and not just once, the subject came up again that had come up at their first meeting: Why hadn't he tried to find her since then (to which he replied with a question that ticked her off: Why hadn't she tried to find him?). Once she mentioned the summer work camp, but she hung back when he asked why she had left school, and he let it be.

At this meeting he held her hand in his and stroked her fingers, and told her that he would like to get to know her again, "But for real, slowly, like it should be."

And she laughed and asked in a low voice: "Slowly? Why slowly? We have a head start, don't we?"

"How should I know?" Michael muttered, and leaned over her hand. "People change—and then, we didn't really know each other in depth," and she, not laughing anymore, said that the taste of his kisses and his touch had been with her all these years, and that the body is never wrong, and that people who know each other through their bodies know each other best.

"I'm not sure," said Michael. "I used to think that, but now I'm not at all sure. Maybe it's a necessary but not a sufficient condition." When he walked her to her car, she laid a hand on his cheek and looked at him. The tenderness in her gaze sent a shiver through him and he knew then that they would meet again, once he was done with this case, "which will get into high gear in another day or two, I hope, after we identify the body," and that maybe they would talk on the phone during the days he was up to his neck in the investigation. And therefore he had been very surprised to see her that evening waiting for him in the little room at the Russian Compound, but he was also very glad about it and without wavering much had accepted her offer and got into her car and driven home with her for the holiday dinner.

As if they had spoken about it in the car on the way to her house, he also stayed after all the other guests had left, and from a rectangular living room almost empty of furniture, where she had set the table, he followed her into a small kitchen and leaned on the windowsill there, looking at the line of dark hair cropped along the nape of her long, slender neck, at her narrow back, and at the swiftness with which her hands moved with the plates, from which she threw the leftovers into the bin before she put them in the sink. He watched himself in astonishment as he stood close behind her until his lips rubbed against the nape of her neck, and after she turned around—against her lips, as if he had really known her for a long time. And when she, a head shorter than him, lifted her face to him, he paused at the sight of the smile that lit up her soft, brown eyes, which revealed joy in their depths, and alarm and passion.

"Even your smell is the same," she now whispered hoarsely as he slowly moved his fingers from her face and her hair to her deep, soft waistline—she was lying on her side. "Then too you had the smell of tobacco and—how shall I say it?—a clear smell of starch and unscented soap, and even then you were smoking. I remember how we, the girls, would go to see you in the smokers' hiding place, even before the summer work camp."

"But you had a boyfriend then," Michael reminded her, and he himself was amused by the tone of complaint that had come out of his mouth.

"I did," she confirmed, "but I wanted you. The fact is that he took off right afterward."

"I had no idea," murmured Michael. "You didn't show me any signs, nothing. I thought you weren't interested in me at all." Nevertheless, the memory of the "boyfriend" who was talked about then had pecked at him; he had been older than them, a soldier, maybe even an officer.

"Okay," she said, and stretched out on her back. "It's because you didn't want to. And I'm shy."

"I? I didn't want to? I'm telling you that you didn't show any signs. How could I know whether you wanted to or not?" He couldn't really remember afterwards whether he had wanted her or not, but now, as he lay beside her and stroked her skin, it was obvious to him that he had, and it was only that talk about the boyfriend that had put him off.

"What self-indulgence," she murmured, and looked at him with a smile. "Just self-indulgent pride."

A few seconds went by before he understood what she meant by "self-indulgence."

"You mean I'm not allowed to be shy?"

"No, you don't understand." She straightened up and plumped the large pillow and supported her back on it in a half-sitting position. "Me—no way, no."

The sweet torpor that spread through his limbs slowed down his thought. With an effort he said: "You mean?"

"I did all kinds of foolish things, but thwarted love—no. Not that."

"How did we get to 'thwarted love'?" he wondered truthfully.

Her hand sliced through the air above him as she said decisively: "I wasn't crazy enough to fall in love with someone everyone knew had an older, experienced woman, and who didn't show he was interested."

He was required to protest, at least formally, but he felt so good with her face so close to his, and only because she was looking at him now expectantly did he give in and say: "But you left school right after the camp, and you had a boyfriend, and there was no sign that you—"

"That has nothing to do with it," she said decidedly.

And again, as in a half-dream, even though more than anything he wanted to curl up in the silence, he found himself answering her heatedly, as if they were two children arguing: "No? Nothing to do with it? Was I supposed to fall in love with you and go after you even if you had a boyf—"

"Enough with that Boaz," said Ada angrily. "He's no excuse. If you had fallen in love with me or really wanted me, you wouldn't have cared whether or not I had a boyfriend."

Like her, he tucked a pillow behind his back and sat up, because suddenly the discussion had become serious, and in fact, he now realized, it had become a discussion of the difference between women's expectations and men's. "Do you mean to say," he said cautiously and probingly, "that I was supposed to look for you and chase after you then, to conquer you and convince you?"

"Of course."

There is no such thing as a liberated woman, Michael Ohayon said to himself, and there is no equality between the sexes. Even women don't really want it, that equality they're all talking about, and in fact they want defined roles, and there is nothing that would make them happier than to find out that they had dazzled the man. Or in other words—that they had magic control over him. But he didn't want to use the word "control" now and preferred to talk about her passivity: "So I should have found you and woken you up from your coma with respect to me, or what?" he asked.

"There wasn't any coma," answered Ada, half-insulted. "I was just reacting to the fact that I picked up that I wasn't on your mind. There weren't any other vibes."

Michael lit a cigarette and placed the porcelain ashtray on his covered knees.

"So what you're saying is that it's the guy's role to initiate and to run after the girl and court her and convince her and all that, right?"

"Of course it's the guy's role." Ada threw him a challenging look. For a moment he didn't know whether she was being serious or teasing, having a bit of fun, and the dim light cast yellow shadows in her eyes when she said with great feeling: "What did you want? For me to run after you? You never tried again after the work camp. Every evening at the camp, a whole week. And after that—nothing."

Even though Michael could not recall that it had happened "every evening," he didn't want to pursue the argument there. Instead he remembered how he had asked about her when they went back to school at the beginning of twelfth grade, and how it turned out that she had left the boarding school. "You weren't there anymore," he said defensively. "After that you weren't . . ." Suddenly it occurred to him to ask what he hadn't asked at their previous meetings. "Why did you leave school?"

Ada lowered her eyes. "My father was dying then," she said quickly, as if it was hard for her to speak. "My mother needed . . . She couldn't manage alone and I had to . . . I completed my matriculation exams afterward, before I . . . before I married Jedediah, and before we went to Peru. Why didn't you look for me?"

"I thought you had a boyfriend, that you weren't interested," he repeated, because he felt that this was what she really wanted to talk about and if they had this dialogue, he would also understand other things.

Ada beat her hand on the down quilt, and he touched her arm to calm her down, but she still said angrily: "Who told you? Just on the basis of rumors? I never told you anything about him, and maybe I would have left him for you, if only you had looked for me. It's very simple—you didn't love me and you didn't want to bother."

Michael laughed inwardly. This conversation, with its circles and repetitions, amused him, but there was great seriousness in its depths. "And you?" he challenged her. "If you wanted me so badly, why didn't you look for me?"

Like a little girl who is reminding someone of the rules of the game, Ada postulated: "It doesn't work that way. I'm a girl, right? The guy has to chase around the whole world until he finds the girl, doesn't he?"

Now he answered her in total seriousness. "I can't understand this. I can't understand how an independent woman, a woman who has looked after a sick husband for years and all the household chores, a woman who has raised two wonderful children almost on her own, who has found herself professionally—how could she . . ." He sighed.

She laid a hand on his cheek. "Are you having a hard time?" she said, laughing.

"I'm asking myself," he mused aloud, "whether it's a result of the way you were brought up, or of Hollywood movies with all kinds of Humphrey Bogarts gazing slit-eyed at women in high heels with a seam up the back of their stockings, before they toss aside their fedoras and sweep them up in their arms. To see them in a silk slip."

"Satin," she corrected.

"Satin?"

"The slip. That's the sort of thing I do know."

"In any case, black."

"Okay, black. Pink is also a possibility."

He really did want to understand, once and for all, and with Ada it seemed as though he could get a real answer—what was at the basis of all those rules of the game that women had so often flung at him during the course of his life, saying that he wasn't fulfilling his designated role. "I just want you to tell me where you got this fantastic theory about who has to make the first move," he insisted.

"It's not fantastic. That's just the way it is. And it's that way for everyone—my mother and Humphrey Bogart and Ingrid Bergman and Lauren Bacall. That's my generation. That's how it is in my generation. They tell me that nowadays young girls know how to make the first move. I've heard from all kinds of girls and young women, even my daughter, that now a girl can go up to a boy and ask him out . . . really start with him. They also aren't getting married at the age of twenty and they aren't in any hurry. But me—if someone doesn't want me, don't bother. And you—it's undeniable. You didn't want me." She said these last words very decidedly, as if she would brook no argument. And for that very reason he found himself arguing.

"Who called whom now?" he asked, childishly.

"Okay, so you phoned me first," she admitted limply, and as if submissively.

"And who really extended himself," he continued in the singsong he had learned from Solomon, "and in the middle of working on a complicated murder case found the time to meet you twice—in twenty-four hours? At his initiative. Who?"

"Okay. You—I admit. I thought it was to talk and close information gaps. For that," she said in an unconvincing tone, with a kind of coyness that amused him again. He laughed aloud, but at the same time he was angry.

"Is that what you call it?" he demanded. "An 'information gap'? Is that what it was? Do you think we could have been here now like this"—he waved his arm above their bodies and pulled at the blanket, which fell away—"without having spoken beforehand? Without knowing something about our lives . . ."

"There are stories," she mumbled into his shoulder.

"What stories?" he insisted, and removed her face from his shoulders to look into her eyes, which were half-shut.

"That two people," said Ada dreamily, "without exchanging a single word, who . . . who want each other so badly that . . . without a lot of pre-liminaries and clarifications, even without knowing each other at all . . . are suddenly overwhelmed by wild passion and find themselves together in bed."

Michael laughed again, but this time it wasn't happy laughter. He was suddenly alarmed lest she was expecting some sort of detached adven-ture with him. He himself heard the aggressiveness in his tone, but he was not prepared to allow any misunderstanding on the matter: "A one-night stand? Is that what you wanted?" he demanded angrily. Even though he knew that she hadn't wanted that, he needed to hear it explic-itly: "In any case, those people aren't me."

She was insulted. "Never in my life," said Ada heatedly, "have I heard that someone seriously tells someone else that he . . . sort of wants her, but not right away, that she should wait a month or two because he's busy in the near future, that now they have to wait until he . . . until he hasn't got other things on his mind. I was sure that it was just talk, that you didn't know how to get out of it or something."

Michael was not sorry that he had been cautious in their two previous conversations. He also didn't really understand why she was insulted, because he felt that the delay was a sign of the seriousness of his inten-tions and the possibility that they would be together. He didn't want to begin another relationship with a woman when his mind was on some-thing else. Had it not been for the eve of the holiday and had she not shown up like that at the Russian Compound, he would really have pre-ferred to have waited until he could give her his full attention. "First of all, you see that we did not wait a month or two. And apart from that, look at us now— is this just talk?! I wanted it more than you, and that's a fact. And anyway, you were the one who didn't want this."

Now there was a switch, and she immediately retorted: "But who waited for whom for over an hour? And on the eve of a holiday? And stuck in that cubbyhole at the Russian Compound and in addition to everything else asking favors of that fascist bastard, whatsisname, Balilty?"

"What can I do?" protested Michael. "I'm in the middle of investigating a murder! And I was afraid that I wouldn't be able to concentrate on anything else."

"There are always reasons." Her fingers, which were fluttering gently on his chest, rose into the air and brushed away the perfect smoke ring he had sent to hover between them. "Reasons are no excuse."

She had no way of knowing his work habits, he told himself, and it was necessary to explain to her explicitly: "I know myself. I already know that when I'm at work I sink into it entirely and there's nothing other than work . . . and anyway, that's the way it is."

"And what about me?" she charged. "Don't I work? Aren't *I* in the middle of a huge project and . . . ? I told you, I saw . . . It seemed to me like you were listening . . ."

"'It seemed to you'?! Are you saying that I was just *pretending* to listen?"

"Sorry. I *know* you were listening."

"So what's going on? Are you being coquettish? Do you think this is charming?"

"I think," she said in a conciliatory tone, "that it's because I was insulted, because after I tell you that next week I have to go to Brussels and Amsterdam and meet with all the organizations that are funding the film, you keep on telling me about your work as if it were an act of God or something."

"Tell me"—he shrugged—"what are we talking about here? Who wants this more?"

"No. Yes. That too," said Ada, confused, "but also all those thirty years. Look what a waste. In another minute we die. We could have . . ."

Michael sighed. "Those thirty years" had been the main topic that had engaged them in the two meetings that had preceded this evening. From the first moments there had been an argument between them. Ada never stopped thinking about the missed opportunity, and because of it she had asked him several times about women in his past and the reasons he was living alone. Nevertheless, he was willing to talk about this again. "You're the one who believes in fate," he said to her. "The fact is that we couldn't."

"Because of you." She pinched his thigh.

"So I'm to understand that I'm to blame for everything?" he said half-questioningly, and kissed the palm of her hand.

She folded her fingers over his touch and passed her other hand over his face and his forehead and raked through his hair. "Only you."

From within her hand he breathed as he recited again: "Because I didn't look for you and I didn't chase you and I didn't stand in the doorway and toss my fedora?"

With utter seriousness and without a hint of blame she replied: "Because you didn't even think about me."

And that, thought Michael, was unfortunately the absolute truth, although not precisely accurate. He hadn't thought about her in the way she meant, not in the sense of "what if"—not about her body the way it is today and not about that face of hers that he could hold like this in his two hands and that was looking at him now—but she had been part of his hoard of memories. And from time to time he would remember her, for example in the spring when the citrus blossomed, or when he thought about women he had kissed. Now, looking straight into her face, which was raised to him, he heard himself saying: "Who says? Who says I didn't think about you?"

"Even worse," said Ada dismissively. "You thought and you didn't do a thing about it. Shame on you."

Without thinking, Michael said: "I'm a passive person."

First she laughed—and her laughter, which reverberated in the room, warm and deep and full of gaiety, instantly melted his uncertainty about whether she had understood what he had said. And then she thought a moment and said, "Yes, in fact that could be true, even with all your stories about women. I remember how you got married. She wanted to, and you got married."

"How do you know?" he wondered.

"I was told. There was someone who told me," Ada said, and twisted her lower lip, a gesture that reinforced the childish expression that on the face of another woman her age might have been ridiculous, but was suited to that small face, the tilted nose and even the crease between her eyebrows. "I looked into it. And anyway, I also understood from what you told me yesterday. Sometimes I also understand what isn't said explicitly."

Instead of asking who had told her, he pulled her toward him. "Do you want me to compensate you now for all the time that you supposedly took an interest in me and I supposedly didn't take an interest in you?"

"That too. But right now I want you to explain to me how come . . . how come it's so . . ."

"Good?"

"That too. Yes. Good. That I can understand, maybe. But how come it's so . . . so right. 'Right.' That's the word."

"Trust," he said without thinking, and he wondered at the word that had escaped him unexamined. "And don't ask me to explain," he added, "because I don't have any explanations, I just feel it, from you to me and from me to you."

"Trust," she echoed, insulted. "What is this, friendship? Labor relations? And what about passion? And what about . . . falling in love?"

"It's the same thing," said Michael quickly. "As far as I'm concerned, at least, and as far as you're concerned." He hoped that she had understood what he meant. He hoped that he had succeeded in saying succinctly something about how each of them had been through all kinds of experiences and had been burnt, and how both of them were now in a place where there was no longer any need for games of love and falling in love, and how because they had known each other when they were young, and had touched each other even before they knew what life was about and the circuitous paths each of them would follow—how because of all this, intimacy like this could exist between them, which wasn't possible between strangers.

"The same thing?" asked Ada in astonishment and protest. "Trust and falling in love are the same thing?! Not at all. Those are two completely opposite things. When you fall in love there's . . . It's sex, it's a war, there's no trust. When you fall in love you're afraid the whole time, and now I'm . . . I'm not . . . not afraid—in any case, not of that. I know you won't do anything bad to me, and there won't be games, so is this falling in love?"

"I don't know. If you call falling in love what happened between that man with the black fedora and the woman in the black slip, then maybe there it's a contradiction because they . . . they were looking for something altogether different . . ."

"Yes?" she asked argumentatively, almost threateningly. "Explain to me what they're looking for?"

"Them?" dismissed Michael, and with utter frankness and without a moment's hesitation he revealed to her the thoughts that he had formulated over the years he had known women: "They're looking for the kind of excitement that . . . Technicolor excitement. They don't have any real interest at all in each other. They are falling in love with the story, with what is happening to them. With the reflection of themselves in the other. They have no real interest except in the excitement, in the war, in winning, in keeping the other person in their pocket."

"Whereas we?" She lay on her side, and her dark eyes widened expectantly.

"Whereas we . . ." For a moment he found it hard to speak. If she didn't get what he was going to say to her now, maybe she wasn't who he thought she was, who he wanted her to be. "We really see each other. We've found, both you and I, something else, from the beautiful side of ourselves. The side that hasn't been spoiled yet. I've found it in you and you've found it in me."

Though he had upset her, he was relieved when she said, half-insulted: "I haven't even told you yet . . . I haven't even told you yet that I . . . We aren't talking about love here at all. You don't even want to know . . . You aren't asking whether I . . ."

"What needs to be asked here?" The small face resting on his chest rose and fell with his breathing. "I saw you and I heard you. Look at us. Is there anything to ask here? I know that you love me, I simply know it. And you also know it."

"I . . . I don't, I don't know anything if I'm not told," she said, and moved her head from his hands.

"You do. You most definitely do," he said to her, and did not wonder at his own certainty anymore. He added: "You just don't want to give up the backdrop, the piano from *Casablanca* and the slips, but that's all nonsense."

She buried her head in his arm and murmured: "If that's nonsense, why don't you just give it to me?"

"No way. I can't stand those things."

"Can't stand them?!" she exclaimed. "But all those years, I know about all kinds of . . . And I'm sure there were . . . flowers and candles and slips and everything . . . and that there were married women, on the side, hotels and all that. So what was all that?"

"There were," said Michael, swallowing his saliva with effort. There was no point in the whole thing if he didn't tell her the whole truth: "But I want it this way, like now, with friendship. That's what I've always really wanted."

"And is this at all possible . . . Trust?" she asked hesitantly.

"Trust and understanding and partnership and . . . Okay, love. Is that what you want to hear?"

"So where was this all those thirty years?"

"Oho. So you want to begin at the beginning again?" He rolled his eyes demonstratively. "Can't people get any sleep around here?"

"Usually by six in the morning no one is sleeping," she teased him, "but I'll give you a break if . . ."

From the small armchair in the corner of the bedroom, where he had put his clothes, came a sharp beep that was not muffled by the fabric.

"What's that?" Ada asked, and sat up.

"That? That's a beeper."

"They're calling you? Before six o'clock in the morning? On a holiday?"

"The world is now demanding its pound of flesh—I'm in the middle of a case," he said, and was already pulling on his blue jeans and looking at his beeper. "I have to make a phone call."

"'Urgent'?" said Balilty. "Of course it's urgent. Do you think I would bother you if it wasn't? Never mind. In short, two things. A: There's a new lead, but it can wait a minute, and B: The girl has disappeared."

"What girl?" asked Michael. He held the telephone receiver pressed between his shoulder and his ear as he picked his white shirt up off the carpet near the legs of the armchair and pulled out the sleeves.

"I've been roaming around here tonight, going over things, after I raked over that Avital," continued Balilty in a rush, as if he hadn't heard the question, "and about half an hour ago I came into the building and who do I see next to the policeman on duty? Your boy."

"Who?" asked Michael in alarm. "Yuval? At the building?"

"No, of course not Yuval. I'm talking about your farmer, the brilliant Sergeant Yair. He's standing next to the duty officer and they're talking about roses. At four-thirty in the morning they're talking to me about roses and diseases of geraniums. Did you know that there is a terrible blight now of—what do you call it, boy?" Balilty went silent for a moment. Through the receiver came a muted voice in the background, and then the intelligence officer said: "That's it. Pelargonium line pattern virus. Did you know that? I didn't know either. In short, they're talking about geranium viruses, and I'm standing there listening because Matty has a collection of flowerpots with geraniums and I thought maybe I'll learn something here and . . . Never mind. In short, and who comes in? The girl's mother with her big brother and his boyfriend, his boyfriend-

boyfriend, his significant other, a couple yet, and the boyfriend, his name is Peter O'Brian, an Australian, introduces himself and—"

"Danny," warned Michael, "when are going to get to the point?"

"I'm telling you, no?" protested Balilty. "You're always yelling that the details are important, and now all of a sudden you're . . . . Never mind. Did you have fun?"

Michael cleared his throat.

"All right, *nu.* I realize you're not alone. In any case this Peter is telling us that the girl has disappeared."

"What girl?"

"The girl. *Nu,* Eli Bachar told me that you spoke to her on the sidewalk near the car, that you gave her your phone number. That little girl yesterday . . . Was it yesterday?"

"Yes, I remember. Where is she?"

"That's what I'm telling you—she's disappeared, and only because we happened to be standing by the duty officer and they came to report it immediately, I realized that it could be connected, and I wasn't the only one who realized, our Buddha also realized and even said so to the duty officer. A bit phlegmatic, but he said so even though Drori is telling me now that there's no connection."

"Is Drori there?" Michael injected a note of amazement into his voice and wondered what the district commander was doing at night at the Russian Compound. "Now? At six A.M. on a holiday?"

"It's because of the situation. I also didn't believe it at first. I see him coming out of a room, at four A.M. on a holiday! Imagine! I say to him—Drori, what's with you? You've gone and become a district commander and you're working day and night, and he says to me: 'Haven't you heard? There have been disturbances in Beit Safafa, Jews throwing bottles at Arabs.' And he also asked me where you were, like that in the same breath: 'Where's Chief Superintendent Ohayon at a time like this? I want the head of the investigations division to be here day and night when there are disturbances.' Don't worry," added Balilty silkily. "We covered for you. Tell me, don't you listen to the news? You needn't bother—you won't hear it on the radio. They're not talking about it on the radio. In any case Drori said—"

"And the girl?" asked Michael.

"Drori says that it could be security-linked. He himself—imagine—stands there and asks this mother who doesn't stop crying whether the girl had any friends from Beit Safafa and right away she yells at him—her daughter have Arab friends? Do you think she messes with Arabs?" Balilty lowered his voice and commented dramatically, "In fact, there is a connection here to Arabs, but it's not for the telephone," and in his regular voice he added: "So Drori says to her, Baka is close to Beit Safafa."

"When did she disappear?" asked Michael.

"Come on in, talk to Eli. He'll give you the details."

"Where is he?" he heard Eli Bachar asking as Balilty handed him the phone. "Take it. Talk to him," replied Balilty, and other voices were heard in the background. "Where are you?" asked Eli, and as Michael did not reply he said to him: "Okay, never mind. Do you remember Peter O'Brian, that Australian I introduced you to yesterday, across from the Basharis' house? And there was a girl with him? She's his boyfriend's little sister. Nessia, she's called."

"What boyfriend?"

"*Nu*, I told you at the time. You said you remembered. The electrician, Yigal Hayoun, and she's the little girl on the street you asked about Zahara . . ."

"Yes. *Nu?*"

"So a quarter of an hour ago they showed up here, without even phoning. Yair and Balilty called me. We didn't want to disturb you if it wasn't really necessary. Her mother came with this Peter O'Brian and his pal Yigal, and they told us the girl was gone. She hadn't even slept in her bed. Vanished. Yair was sure that there's a connection." His voice dropped to a whisper. "Don't let Balilty tell you it was his idea. It was Yair's idea. Right then he said so. What? Do you think the girl just went out to walk the dog and didn't come back? Since last night? I saw that you left the car here. Do you want me to—"

"No, no. I'll be right there," Michael muttered, and looked questioningly at Ada, who was already standing by the bed and tying the sash of her blue bathrobe with a swift motion. He hung up the phone.

"What girl?" asked Ada. "Has something happened to a girl? Is it connected to . . ."

"A girl of ten and a half from the building across the street from the house. She's disappeared," Michael said, and headed for the bathroom. Ada followed him, her bare feet pattering on the floor tiles.

"Across from which house? My house? That I bought?" she asked with evident anxiety.

"No, across the street from the Basharis' house. Since last night. She went out for a walk with her dog and didn't come back," said Michael as he washed his face. He wouldn't have time to shave, he thought as he rubbed his chin. To his right he saw her face in the mirror as well.

"Another one." She spread her fingers. "First that girl, Zahara, and now a child . . ."

"She's disappeared. Children sometimes . . . Maybe she quarreled with her mother . . . Maybe she went to friends. I don't know any details and it's not at all certain that there's any connection between the two cases," but even he heard the hollow echo in what he had just said.

"Do you think that you'll find her in an attic too?"

"I don't think so, and I told you—maybe it isn't even connected."

Ada sat down on the edge of the bathtub. What he said hadn't reassured her. Through the opening in her bathrobe she saw how she was breathing hard. "I have to give back that house," she said. "I shouldn't have bought it."

Michael set down the towel and kneeled in front of her. "What are you talking about?! What does that have to do with anything?"

"I don't know." Her eyes were half shut. "People—they shouldn't jump into things that are beyond what they deserve, beyond what's written in their fate."

He had already glimpsed this side of her, when she had spoken about the hand of fate, but nevertheless he was taken aback by the palpable presence of superstitions in a person like her. "Written where?" he asked quickly.

"I shouldn't have done it," mourned Ada as if she had not heard his question. "That house . . . I don't deserve it, it's not my fate. For years I've been looking at that house and knowing that it's not for people like me. That it's too beautiful, has too much presence, too much character, it's too expensive. It's not for me. It's too much . . . And now, it's a fact."

"What's a fact?" He sat down beside her on the edge of the bathtub and wrapped his arm around her, and when his hand touched her thin shoulder and her delicate collarbone he tried to hush the voice inside him that urged him to hurry up.

"It's a fact that the moment it's mine, even before I've moved in," she said as a bit of a wail crept into her voice, "first of all there's the corpse and then there's a child who . . . And why did I have to decide to build on the roof? To break through the floor and pour a new floor and put in walls and insulation—it's beyond the budget that I . . . You know I can't afford things like that and to mortgage my whole life like that at my age . . . And in the attic . . . I never should have touched the attic. It's all because of greed. The house was greed, and the attic even more so."

"You could see it the other way around," said Michael.

"How? What other way around?"

He saw the face of four-year-old Yuval, standing devastated in front of the cage of hamsters they had been charged with feeding on a Saturday when the kindergarten was closed. "They're dead, Daddy. They're dead. I was sleeping and they . . . they were dying. I killed them. Ora the kindergarten teacher will be angry at me. Is my teacher gonna kill me?" Ada's eyes hung on him like Yuval's eyes, anxious and waiting for salvation that they didn't believe in anymore.

"You know very well," said Michael, "that Zahara Bashari wasn't murdered because you bought a house. You are perfectly aware that if she hadn't been murdered in that house, it would have happened somewhere else. Whoever killed her didn't know that it was you who had bought the house."

"But he used that opening we made in the roof," wailed Ada. "If only I hadn't started with the roof . . ."

"Do you really think that because you made an opening in the roof . . . And anyway, there already was an opening to it, from outside the apartment, but never mind. Do you think that because of that they killed Zahara Bashari?"

"I don't know what to think anymore," she said in a strangled voice, holding back her tears.

"Do you think," he said musingly, "that you've revived the myth about something evil hiding in the attic, like in a Gothic novel? Is that what you think?"

"All I know is that I shouldn't have gone so . . . so far with . . ."

"With what? With the desire to have a house you would love? What is it, this house? You'd think you've bought a palace. It's pretty, but there's no need to exaggerate. It's not even a house. It's an apartment within a house . . . And anyway, if we're talking seriously—can we talk seriously?"

She nodded and pulled her nose.

"Look, I'm not saying that the myth of the attic is nonsense. People think . . . not think . . . believe that under the ground, in the cellar, in shelters, behind the walls, in invisible places—that there's chaos hiding, and if they open the cellar or the shelter or, worst of all, the attic, they will discover a dead body. Have you understood so far?"

"But this doesn't comfort me. It's a *fact* that I opened the attic and a body was discovered, no?"

"Okay," said Michael. "It's already been discovered. Get it? There's nothing to be afraid of anymore. The body has been found, and there isn't another one there. And you don't have a cellar. There isn't any other ghost that's hiding there. Yes or no?"

She kept silent and smiled limply. "It's very nice that you're reassuring me like this but it's not really what—"

"So let's make it even simpler. Even simplistic," he said tolerantly. "From a different angle: If you hadn't started with the roof, he would have murdered her downstairs, or in some other house. And anyway, if you hadn't bought the house and touched the attic, and if you hadn't come to check before the renovations, we wouldn't have found Zahara Bashari. And if we hadn't found her there, you and I wouldn't have met after all those years and—"

"You see?!" she cried. "Everything here is chance! There's nothing here that's intentional. This whole encounter has been chance."

"On the contrary," said Michael, and instead of reminding her of what she herself had said about the hand of fate that had brought them together, he said: "It's all the exact opposite of chance. You deserve this house, because you wanted it so badly. It will also suit you, and you are going to enjoy it very much. A person has to live in a place that he loves, so he'll have a home, in the deep sense of the word. You bought the house because you decided to do something that you wanted, and a person who dares to do what he really wants—it also opens up other things to him, all kinds of things, that you wanted before and had already given up."

"I forgot." She hung her head. "You don't believe in chance. Even when you were seventeen, you didn't believe in it. You needed to . . ." She looked at him and stopped talking.

"What did I need?" Just because she had calmed down and had said those things with relative serenity, he was curious to know what she had intended.

"To go on to a Ph.D. in history," said Ada. "To be a historian. For someone who doesn't believe in chance that's exactly . . . What are you working in the police force for? How can you live like that? Every time with all that blood and the horrible things. Well, I suppose you get used to it."

"You don't get used to it," said Michael. "Who said you get used to it? On the contrary, you become more and more vulnerable to it. You yourself told me how life becomes more and more complicated. Didn't you tell me that people don't become immune to the evil they see all around?"

"Did I say that? When?"

"The night before last, in the café across from the post office. Before we left."

"How can you remember?"

"I was there. When I'm really somewhere, I don't forget a thing. You, you'd remember too if you weren't so upset because of . . . because of the corpse and because of Balilty and the contractor and all that. But the fact that I do remember makes everything more disturbing. In work like this you witness evil and wickedness every day, and all the perversions of the human race. Especially if you have a memory, you find yourself wondering most of the time which is more common—evil or wickedness."

"So why don't you get out of it?" she asked him again, and this question he was not prepared to answer now.

"And how would I have met you?" Now he too smiled. "If I'd left the force a week ago, we wouldn't have met this way."

"That means that the house I bought, that I'd dreamed about all my life and also"—her arm encircled them both in the air—"this story, about us . . . both of them are like . . . stepping on corpses. Both of them. Both of them, and forgive the histrionics, are . . . covered in blood."

"Tell me," he said, annoyed, "did you kill someone to get to that house? Did I kill someone to get to you?"

"You . . . Don't pretend that you don't understand! It's no trick to be rational about superstitions."

"You're the one who said that." He rose from the edge of the bathtub, looked at his watch and moved toward the door.

"What did I say?" she asked in a small voice. She too stood up.

"Superstitions. You said it." And he reminded her that he was in a hurry.

"I'll take you," she hastened to say, "and that way we'll have a few more minutes together." She moved closer to him. "In another minute, you'll say something like 'Women!' Don't bother. Do you think that I don't know that I'm being superstitious?"

He gently removed her hands from his shoulders, and in the silence he could hear the water trickling from the faucet of the sink, until he shut it. "Are you going to put something on or are you going to take me there in your bathrobe? I just want you to know that both the house and the two of us are a reward . . . Yes, a reward for us being, when you get right down to it, within our limitations, not such bad people."

The drive, which on a normal morning would have taken half an hour or more, took only ten minutes. They drove in silence. Because it was a holiday and early in the morning, the streets were empty and silent, but the holiday atmosphere had been spoiled and he automatically turned on the radio, to hear about the previous night's shootings—"shooting incidents," they said—and where people had been killed. Ever since the "pogrom" (which, to the distress of Balilty, who called him a traitor, is what Michael insisted on calling that Yom Kippur eve in Nazareth when Israeli Arabs were shot as a Jewish mob surged on them), he had listened with increasing anxiety to the news and had not let himself be distracted even when he had to get ready for work.

He felt almost weightless, as if during the night he had shed his skin. This wasn't only because of the lovemaking, during which he'd allowed himself to revel in Ada, whose boyish body he had not actually known, though he felt as if he had known it all those years, every touch affording him both the pleasure of surprise and the pleasure of confirming what he seemed to have already known. He turned off the radio and regarded her profile, her pursed lips and the tiny creases at the corner of her mouth, the fine down above her upper lip and the tilted nose, and he was filled with joy. That face, with its severe and inward expression, tugged at his heart.

He had to summon up a different mode of being to get back to work and to the chubby little girl in the blue sweat suit and the dog, apparently a poodle, that had disappeared along with her. Nessia, that's what the girl was called; even then he had felt that she knew more than she was saying, and apparently he had been right. And what she knew had hurt her. But he hadn't thought about that in time. If at the time he had thought that she knew more, why hadn't he seen to protecting her? Why hadn't he sent a policeman there, or got her out of there? True, it's impossible to protect everyone who might know something, but if the girl had really disappeared for reasons related to the case, then clearly it had to do with someone in the immediate environment, from the neighborhood or even from the street, someone from the inside—but what that "inside" was, he did not know.

And between the girl and Zahara's smashed-in face there had been Ada and the honey scent and her tawny skin and her brown eyes that narrowed as if suspiciously, and her full, heavy breasts, so different from the budding breasts back then, and surprising on her thin, boyish body. All that might have strengthened someone who was deep in a murder investigation, but nevertheless, at the turn near Terra Sancta, he panicked at the thought that he might not be able to keep things separate. He feared that the total release he had allowed himself this time, unlike his usual pattern on the first night with a woman and even many nights thereafter, was tantamount to sloughing off all the demands of his profession.

Ada took her hand off the gear stick and laid it on his arm. Through the open window he inhaled the cool, fresh air—it was already daylight and the blue sky hinted at a bright, clear sunny day—and he had a passing glimpse of the walls of the Old City that were suddenly visible beyond Independence Park once the Sheraton Plaza Hotel no longer blocked the view of them. The walls were pale blue in the early light, and splendid, and he mused on this city and how full sunlight would illuminate and reveal its misery: branches left over from roofing sukkahs tossed away on the sidewalks, empty beer bottles, crushed beverage cans, cigarette butts, old newspapers and the piles of garbage heaped up along King George Street and the Jaffa Road. Two Filipinos lounged on the steps of the bank at Zion Square.

"Disgusting," Ada muttered, and stopped at the traffic light.

"What? Those Filipinos?"

"No. What Filipinos? They're just unfortunate—they don't have anywhere to go on their day off. What's disgusting is this city, with all its filth. It's all coming out now, and not just the garbage. Anyone who stays here—and, what's more, buys a house—is crazy."

"Here we are. You can drop me off here." He indicated the lottery booth at the corner of Queen Heleni Street. "I can walk from here, and that way you'll be able to keep on going straight and get back to bed."

"I'm dropping you off where I want, if at all," muttered Ada as she turned into the street, "and I'm not going back to any bed. I'll also go to work, in solidarity, and you're going to phone me and tell me exactly what happened to the little girl. Look at that dome," she said, pointing at the Russian church and its towers, gleaming in the sun. "If you want a bit of beauty around here, you have to look upward, toward the sky, and not at the streets."

"And for that very reason," he said as the car stopped in the Russian Compound, "it's better to build on the roof as well. So you can look up."

"It's just that there was a corpse there," she reminded him again as he was about to open the car door.

"And because we found her," said Michael patiently, "we got a reward. I did, anyway. And you did too, I think."

"So you're saying," she called after him as he swung his legs out of the car, "that we're living on her dead body?"

"Or the other way around," he answered as he walked around the car and stood at her open window and caressed her arm. "Despite her dead body. And despite the fact that we'll be that way too, in the end. Despite the dead."

Chapter 9

S igns of the disturbance were already evident at the junction of Emek Refaim Street and Bethlehem Road. Two police cars blocked the intersection, and two policemen stopped every vehicle for inspection. It was only eight o'clock on the morning of a holiday, and there was already a long line of cars stretched beyond the roadblock. One of the policemen signaled to Michael's car to stop. Balilty, who was still deep in his report on the questioning of the journalist that night and the difficulty he had in finding Moshe Avital, stuck his head out the window, intending to scold him, but the policeman had already hurried over to the car and said excitedly to Michael: "They're waiting for you, sir, on Yiftah Street," and respectfully he also turned to Balilty and said: "Sergeant Ben Yair asked me to tell you that you were right. They found something in that house there, just like you thought."

"The little girl? Did they find the girl?" asked Balilty.

"No, not the girl," said the policeman, "but they've found someone else: an Arab, I've understood—I don't know the details. They just told me to tell you that they're waiting for you to get there."

So as not to disclose his anger at Balilty, Michael said nothing and kept a poker face. Only after they had driven away from the policeman did Balilty say to him apprehensively: "I didn't get a chance to tell you, but over there, behind the house on Bethlehem Street, on Mordechai Hayehudi Street, there's an abandoned house. It used to be Labor Party offices. Do you know it?"

Michael waited for him to continue.

"So last night, in the middle of questioning Orly Shushan, I suddenly had this feeling . . . like a psychic attack. You know what I mean?" And without waiting for an answer he went on talking, thus making things easier for Michael, who had not yet decided how he was going to deal with this intelligence officer who was acting as though he was in charge of the case. "It was like I saw a picture, really like a dream. I seemed to see that little girl curled up there. Nothing like this has ever happened to me before; I'm not one of those psychics. You know what I mean?"

"Of course I know what you mean," replied Michael coldly. "You saw a picture. And did you hear voices?"

Balilty ignored the sarcasm. "I sent two people out there. What was there to lose? Just to be on the safe side," he added in English. "Now did you hear what he just said?"

Michael stopped on Bethlehem Road before the turn into Yiftah Street. He pulled the hand brake and did not turn off the motor, but let it run a while longer until Balilty grew impatient. "Okay, there were too many things to bring you up to date on," said Balilty. "I just didn't get around to telling you. Don't tell me you're angry at me."

"It's not a question of anger," replied Michael severely. "We're organizing the search in a methodical way and then you go and do something in an arbitrary way at your own initiative, and behind the backs of Eli Bachar and Yair, and they're responsible for the search. You know that Eli is very sensitive about these things, and I don't need to explain to you that splitting authority just impedes the work. I'm not the one you should have reported to, but Eli Bachar and Yair, before you sent people out. And you should have left this for them to decide, so that they don't send people to that house to search."

"All right, I'm sorry," said Balilty with unwonted humility and gloom. "I just had this feeling about this house. It's been standing there for years, half crumbling, and I thought . . . *Nu,* I had a feeling."

"I'm not making light of your feelings," said Michael coldly, "but you're ignoring *other* people's feelings, and it poisons the atmosphere."

"Don't worry, I'll fix it. I'll make it up to them," promised Balilty, but before Michael could manage to tell him that not everything can be fixed, he added, "Don't turn into the street. It's probably all jammed up there," and pointed to an empty spot on the sidewalk between a truck and a utility pole at the corner of Bethlehem Road and Yiftah Street.

They got out of the car and Balilty ran forward down Yiftah Street. From the corner, Michael saw how the intelligence officer stopped next to one of the police cars that filled the small street and leaned over the driver's window. When Balilty got there, he straightened up and let the policeman who was driving get out of the car and point to his booty in the backseat—a dark, skinny young fellow sitting hunched over. "We found him there. He says his name is Jalal ibn Mansour, sir, and that he's from East Jerusalem and he has an Israeli identity card. Look," the policeman said, and proffered the blue plastic cardholder.

Balilty grabbed the identity card. "A forgery," he whispered to Michael, and handed him the ID card. "Forged papers. If he's from Jerusalem, I'm from the moon. What do you want to bet that he doesn't have a residence permit?"

"He slept in the backyard, at 8 Mordechai Hayehudi. There's a kind of stone hut there. Maybe it was once a shed," said the policeman to Michael. "In front there's the house. It's impossible to get into it because there's this huge tree there that blocks the entry. The door has an iron bar across it, with a serious lock. He probably crawled in through the window, he's so thin. Not into the house, to the hut nearby. There aren't any Romanian workers there like you said, sir," he said, turning to Balilty. "The neighbors told me that for several months now the house has been shut tight and the Romanians had been kicked out because they used to sit on the front porch and—"

"Clear out a minute," said Balilty to the policeman who was sitting at the wheel. "We'll question him here."

"Where? In the car, sir?"

Michael crossed his arms and shook his head. He leaned into the back window and looked at the youngster, who shrank even more under his gaze. "Come on out," Michael said to him, and the young man moved his body toward the back door, as if making an effort.

"Where are you going to talk to him?" muttered Balilty, who was standing behind Michael. "Are you going to take him in for questioning now? Maybe you should leave him and go to the Basharis. You wanted to talk to them about the business of the—"

"There's no need for an interrogation room to find out his name and address and what he was doing there," said Michael sternly, "and as long as I have anything to say about it, I'm not leaving you alone with any Palestinian." Balilty kept his mouth shut.

The youngster stuck out his long legs and extricated his body. He was wearing dark and dusty gabardine trousers, a plaid flannel shirt and a short leather jacket. He gave off the sour, musty odor of someone who had slept all night in his clothes, and his face was covered with a dark two- or three-day stubble. But all these details—the odor, the stubble, the wrinkled clothes—could not disguise his good looks. Michael took in the long, slender face, the naked fear and the defeat in the deep, dark eyes. "How long were you there for?" he asked in Hebrew, and the youngster gave him a frightened look and said: "Me? Since Monday—three days, from Monday."

"Why?" asked Michael. "What were you doing there?"

"I was sleeping there," whispered the lad.

"People are looking," warned Balilty. "We can't just stand here." Out of the corner of his eye, Michael saw Peter O'Brian and Yigal Hayoun, Nessia's elder brother, running up the street. Peter waved his arms at them. "Please," said Balilty to Michael with evident frustration, "in a minute Bachar and your farm boy will come along and there'll be a scene here. Instead of constructive questioning, we'll be spending the time conciliating everyone."

"Okay, come, take him over there," said Michael, indicating the top of the street. "We'll sit for a minute over there, in my car," he explained to Balilty.

"Too late," said the intelligence officer, with an anger in which a bit of "I told you so" was evident, as Yigal Hayoun and Peter O'Brian approached and signaled them to stop.

"Jalal," called Yigal Hayoun, and laid his arms on the shoulders of the youngster, who lowered his glance. "I've been looking for you since yesterday. Where did you disappear to?"

Jalal shrugged helplessly.

"This is Jalal ibn Mansour," said Yigal Hayoun. "He's . . . ," Yigal began, and looked aside. "He works with me. He's my employee, a qualified assistant electrician. I've been teaching him the trade for two years. He's all right."

"We found him in the abandoned house on Mordechai Hayehudi. There's a shed there that he lives in. If he's all right and an employee of yours, then why was he hiding?" Balilty demanded to know, and his glance moved from Jalal's tortured and anxious face to the round, flushed face of Yigal Hayoun. The intelligence officer's small, light eyes narrowed in suspicion and perplexity.

Yigal Hayoun opened his mouth in order to say something, but Balilty did not let up: "Are you together?" he asked, and without waiting for an answer he added: "So how come you didn't know where he was? And why is he roaming around here without a permit? If he's with you, then you're also in trouble for covering up and collaboration and employing an individual who doesn't have a permit to reside within the Green Line."

"What are you talking about?" protested Yigal Hayoun. "He has an identity card. He's an Israeli citizen. He lives in East Jerusalem."

"Is this what you're referring to?" Balilty asked, and indicated the blue plastic cardholder in Michael's hand. "This is a fourth-rate forgery. Look how they stuck on the picture. Look, can you see the stamp? Is it touching the photograph?"

"I'm telling you that I know him," protested Yigal Hayoun. "I'll vouch for him."

"Didn't I tell you that there was a connection between the disappearance of this girl and Arabs? Did I or didn't I?" whispered Balilty into Michael's ear.

"I know him too," intervened Peter. "Jalal is absolutely excellent," he hastened to add, "and he hasn't done anything wrong. This has nothing to do with . . . ," he said, and waved his hands in the direction of the dozens of police, neighbors, civil defense volunteers and young people from the Scouts who had already clustered in front of the apartment block.

"Can we go in for a moment to see my mother and sort this whole thing out?" asked Yigal Hayoun, and with his head he indicated the entrance to the apartment block.

Balilty looked doubtfully at Michael. "We'll go in," decided Michael. "We'll finish this up."

In the front yard of the large apartment block stood the neighbor from the second floor, and in her hand she held a stool with a woven straw seat that she set down among the rampant weeds. "Sit, sit, Esther. If you don't want to go inside, sit here a while," she chirped in a loud, squeaky soprano voice as she sat Nessia's mother down on the stool with a push on her shoulders, and even more loudly, as if to call attention to the kindness of her heart, she said: "Sit, sit a while. Give your feet a rest."

Esther Hayoun sat obediently on the straw stool, and with half-closed eyes continued to look at the policemen who filled the yards and the entrances to the building. Between her dark fingers, crooked from years of using cleaning materials and wringing out rags, she now rolled the soft stalks of dew-dampened wild sorrel she'd plucked out of the earth. "They haven't found her," Michael heard her say to her son as they approached. "They haven't found her."

"They'll find her, Mother," Yigal Hayoun promised, and ran his hand over the stubble of his beard and his thinning hair. "You'll see. They'll find her."

Inside the apartment, in the tiny hall, stood three policemen. One of them ushered Michael toward the girl's room. "The dog handler is there with his dog now. They're letting it smell all her things." Michael peeked inside. All the doors of the large wardrobe were open, and its contents— starched white sheets several decades old, faded towels, shoes and winter clothes—had been taken out and strewn on and beside the bed. They had removed the mattress and leaned it against the wall, and a brown rubber sheet was folded at the foot of the bed.

"Here," Balilty said, and indicated the little niche that served as the mother's bedroom. "Can we go in there?" One of the policemen nodded his head "Why not?" and Balilty went in, followed by Michael, Jalal, Peter and Yigal.

"There isn't room here for five," said Yigal. "We won't have a breath of air like this. You can wait outside, Peter." And Peter, whose face went purple, obeyed without a word.

Balilty shut the door and motioned to Yigal and Jalal to sit down on the double bed. Michael leaned against the wall and breathed in the oppressive air, heavy with smells of mildew and perspiration. Breathing was an effort.

"This document is a forgery," said Michael after a moment of silence, "and you," he added, turning to Jalal, "were in an abandoned house and not at the address that's listed here. Here it says you live in East Jerusalem, at 15 Haroun Al Rashid Street. Why do you need to sleep in an abandoned house on Mordechai Hayehudi Street in Baka?"

Jalal said nothing. Michael, who was standing so he saw the young man's profile, looked at its fine lines, the delicate curve of the nose, the lips and the bristles around them that emphasized their fullness. He looked to be in his early twenties, younger than his son, and when he turned his face toward Michael, Jalal's eyes were moist with tears. He lowered his dark, long-lashed eyelids and examined his dusty shoes. "I . . . ," said Jalal, and looked pleadingly at Yigal Hayoun.

"Look, friends," said Yigal Hayoun—he pinched his bulbous nose and crossed his arms on his little potbelly—"the facts are simple. Jalal works with me and lives with me but now, because of Peter . . . When Peter comes to visit, there's no room for him at my place, quite simply. And we haven't had time to make any other arrangements for him."

"Why doesn't he go to 15 Haroun Al Rashid?" hectored Balilty. "He has a home, he has an address."

"That's where his family lives—his parents and his brothers and his sisters. It's not comfortable there. It's crowded. He doesn't have his own place," argued Yigal Hayoun.

"Look," said Balilty, "I don't want to go into your personal affairs now, but this identity card is forged, and if you don't say here and now where he's really from—"

"From Ramallah," the young man cried, and burst into tears. "I'm from Ramallah."

"Okeydokey," drawled Balilty with forced serenity, "so now we know. From Ramallah, without a residence permit. How long has he been in Jerusalem without a residence permit?"

"Nothing, maybe a few months . . . Maybe three months," ventured Yigal Hayoun.

"Two years," Jalal said, and lapsed into sobs. "Two years. Really. No more. I'm telling you the truth now, but I haven't done anything. I swear I haven't done anything. Just a bit of work with Yigal."

"You sent him to the abandoned house because Peter came and there wasn't room for both of them. Is that right?" Michael asked Yigal Hayoun.

"Look," whispered Yigal, "it's not the way it seems. For ten years now Peter and I have been together and not together. Jalal knows. I don't have any secrets from him, or from Peter, either. You saw that he knows Jalal, but he doesn't know exactly what . . . how . . . that Jalal and I . . . Peter is a wonderful, generous person, but how can I say this? I don't feel good about it. It's not my apartment but Peter's, and he lets me use it, like, to live there when he's not here, and if I have Jalal there, how does that look? Do you understand what I'm saying?"

"So every time Peter comes, Jalal moves to the Labor Party's abandoned house?"

"No. That's not how it is," said Jalal. "Sometimes I go to my mother's, but now there wasn't . . ." He looked around helplessly.

"Does 'now' mean since the murder, since Nessia disappeared?" asked Michael.

"No. That has nothing to do with it," pleaded Jalal. "With the whole mess of the intifada, it's hard to get out of Ramallah. There are road-blocks, and they check."

"Let me explain," said Yigal. "Up until a while ago, there were Romanian workers living in the house on Mordechai Hayehudi Street. We got to know them when we did some electrical work at a building they were also working on. They'd been there in that house for about ten years, in four large rooms. It isn't a house . . . it's a ruin, if you know what I mean. It only looks like a house from the outside but inside everything is rotten and there isn't even any electricity. But sometimes they would make room for Jalal. We were friendly with them, really great guys. They were also here with-out papers," he said enthusiastically, as if that would somehow make things easier for Jalal. "Illegals, so to speak. And nice, really good people. In the summer they would sit on the porch and listen to music and drink beer. We would go drink with them sometimes and when we needed to, they would let Jalal live with them. Do you see what I mean?" he asked Michael, who gave no sign of understanding.

"They kicked the Romanians out. They kicked them out . . . oh, maybe two months ago," explained Yigal Hayoun. "This contractor came along. They'd sold him the house. He hasn't done anything there yet. He just shut the front door with an iron bar, and he also blocked the back entrance. You can't get in from in front because the entrance is boarded up, and you can't break in, either. And the windows have old-fashioned grilles on them. But in the yard there's a little structure that belongs to the neighbor who bought up the land around the house, and now the contractor is fighting with him to get rid of it. He dumped piles of sand there with a bulldozer—you know how contractors can be. He—"

"Who's the contractor?" asked Balilty.

"A guy called Asheri. I worked with him once. I nearly killed myself running after him for my money."

"Asheri? A guy of about thirty-five, the glamour-boy type, with an Alfa Romeo sports car? The one who built the penthouse on Queen Esther Street?"

"Do you know him?" asked Yigal Hayoun in astonishment.

"Of course I know him!" Balilty cried, and turned to Michael. "He's a Mafioso, that guy. You get it? There's this house for preservation—you're not allowed to touch it, you can't change a thing and you're not even allowed to renovate it on the outside—and then he comes along and builds a new structure on the roof, on top of a building that's designated for preservation, without a permit and without anything and no one says a word. Why?"

"Tell me, are you in the real estate business?" asked Yigal Hayoun respectfully.

Balilty ignored the question. "It's all corruption. He pays the municipality not to interfere with him building wherever he wants, and do you think anyone tells him no? Wherever—"

"Now," interrupted Yigal Hayoun, "there's an intifada going on, and he doesn't have a residence permit. That is, he does have one but he's afraid that they'll find out about . . . Never mind. In any case, he can't move around freely in East Jerusalem or in Ramallah. And if he goes off to Ramallah, he can't come back. We said—let him be there, in the little house, for a day or to, until everything blows over."

"And Peter?" asked Michael.

"Peter doesn't know anything. He didn't even know that Jalal was there. Peter knows Jalal, and if I would ask him he would agree to let Jalal live with us . . . but I didn't want to break his heart," said Yigal Hayoun, "even if Peter and I are no longer . . . no longer . . ."

"No longer a couple, so to speak?" said Balilty with gleeful smugness that was evident beneath his matter-of-fact tone.

"More or less," said Yigal Hayoun.

"But you and Jalal are a couple?" continued Balilty.

"Danny," warned Michael, "this really isn't the issue now. The issue is murder and the disappearance of a young girl. Did you know Zahara Bashari?" he asked Jalal.

"He did some work with me on the electricity at their house," volunteered Yigal Hayoun before Jalal could get a word in. "I told them, he's working with me, and I do all the electrical work in the neighborhood—repairs, everything. You can ask anyone. Everyone knows me."

"So you knew her," said Michael to Jalal. "You did know Zahara?"

"No, I didn't really know her. I just saw her once and she never even spoke to me," Jalal said, and wiped his brow.

"And Nessia? When did you last see Nessia?"

"Yesterday morning, at the grocery store," said Jalal. "I even said hello to her."

"What are you thinking?" burst out Yigal Hayoun. "Do you think that Jalal would do anything to my little sister? Do you think he would break my heart and my mother's heart?"

"Are you close to your little sister?" asked Michael, as if casually.

"What do you mean?" said Yigal Hayoun. "She's my sister, isn't she? She's family, and blood is thicker than water, isn't it?"

Michael said nothing, and Balilty continued to gaze at the two men sitting on the bed side by side.

"Are you trying to insinuate something?" Yigal Hayoun demanded, and rose from the bed to a semistanding position. "Do you think that Jalal would do anything to her and I'd cover for him?"

"Sit down, sit down. Don't get excited," scolded Balilty. "Nobody's insinuating anything. We're just checking. Do you have a problem with that?"

"And Peter?" asked Michael.

"What about Peter?" asked Yigal. "Are you trying to say that Peter would do anything to her?"

"I saw him talking to her," explained Michael. "He had a special relationship with her, didn't he?"

Yigal Hayoun blushed. "Do you think that Peter messes around with young girls?" he asked in disgust. "What do you think, that he's some kind of pervert who messes around with little girls as if . . . like . . . You people don't understand Peter," he said bitterly. "He's just a good soul. He felt sorry for Nessia and he would always talk about how lonely she is and all that, and because of that he paid attention to her. Do you think that everyone who gives a little girl a bit of attention is automatically a pervert?"

"Maybe you'll explain to us what happened with her yesterday?" asked Michael.

"Who? Nessia? I already told *him*, when we were at the police station"—he indicated Balilty. "I told him, we had our holiday dinner, Peter and I and my mother and Nessia, and that's it. My two brothers weren't there. They . . . Never mind. It's not important."

"Your brother Moshe has a criminal record," noted Balilty. "We have quite a file on him."

"Because they got him in trouble. Moshiko has a heart of gold, and if he got in trouble, it wasn't his fault. Okay, it has nothing to do with it," blurted Yigal Hayoun. "I'm answering him about something else now, right?" Michael nodded in confirmation. "We had our holiday dinner with couscous and all the things that Peter likes, and Nessia decorated the sukkah before that, and afterward Peter and I left and there wasn't anything until my mother called at five in the morning and told me about Nessia being missing."

"Did anything happen during the evening? Anything unusual? Was she in any kind of special mood, your sister?"

"Nothing. Nothing happened. Everything was as usual. Nessia never talks a lot. Sometimes you might think that she's deaf or something. Okay, so she's a girl who's kind of . . . well, lonely. She hasn't got any friends or anything. But she was like she always is."

"Maybe she'd quarreled with your mother?" Balilty suggested distractedly, and glanced at Jalal, who had crossed his legs tightly and was sitting with his face buried in his hands as if he wanted to disappear.

"She hadn't quarreled or anything," replied Yigal Hayoun angrily. "It was the eve of a holiday. Why should she quarrel?"

"You really aren't that close to your sister," stated Michael. "You don't know very much about her."

"Okay, so I haven't been living at home since she was born and we aren't very close," said Yigal Hayoun in embarrassment. "She's a little girl. What is there to know? Peter, now he speaks to her a bit. She had something going with him."

"And did you speak to her?" Michael asked Jalal.

Jalal relaxed his lips into a kind of ironic smile, but there was still the same alarm in his eyes. "Me?" he said in astonishment. "Not me. She didn't come to the house and outside she also . . . If I happened to run into her, we'd say hello and that's all."

"And apart from at the grocery store, you didn't see her?"

"I didn't see her. Really I didn't," pleaded Jalal. "I was just waiting there at the house so that there wouldn't be all that tr . . . so that the police wouldn't catch me . . . ," he whispered, and wiped his cheeks with both hands.

"Okeydokey," Balilty said, and gave Michael a questioning look.

"We're going to transfer you to the Russian Compound now," Michael said, and Jalal hung his head as if accepting judgment.

"But he has nothing to do with it!" cried Yigal Hayoun. "He hasn't done a thing. Nothing. Believe me. He isn't involved with anyone and just wants to live in peace, to work, to stay alive, to live. Don't you understand? Why can't you turn a blind eye?"

"I understand very well," said Michael quietly, covering up for the distress he felt, "but even you understand that we cannot ignore . . . that we can't pretend that we don't know that he's a Palestinian from the territories who doesn't have a residence permit within the Green Line."

"And definitely not now, with all these riots," added Balilty, "because how could we let someone go who's broken the law like that? Now if you had at least . . . at least some essential information about Nessia or in connection with the murder of Zahara Bashari . . ."

Balilty dropped his eyelids like an oriental merchant who has begun the process of haggling over the price of a carpet and is waiting for the counteroffer. Jalal shook his head in negation. "I wish I did know something," he whispered, "I wish I did. I'd give anything not to go to jail now. Anything."

"He can't even make things up," pleaded Yigal. "Look at him—straight as a ruler. He can't make something up just so you'll leave him alone. He'll get two years for this. They'll give him two years for falsifying documents and interfering with due process and who knows what. And especially now, with all those disturbances, and then they'll send him back to Ramallah and nothing will make any difference."

"I'm sorry," Michael Ohayon said, and meant it. "There isn't any way we can avoid this." Even Balilty didn't look particularly happy. It was obvious that Jalal had touched his heart too, whether by his frankness and submissiveness or by his beauty, which was impossible to ignore.

"I can't go with him, because of Nessia," said Yigal Hayoun in a broken voice as they stood beside the paddy wagon. He lowered his voice to a whisper when he spoke to Michael: "Could you put a word in so that they don't rip him to shreds? So that they won't . . . At least so he won't suffer so much. He's pretty delicate."

"It'll be all right,"' Balilty said, and whispered something to the policeman in the driver's seat. Before he slammed the door of the paddy wagon he leaned over to Jalal and said to him: "With recommendations to the court, it's possible to get a lower sentence—sometimes even a year off. Isn't that so, Ohayon?" Michael nodded weakly and then watched as the paddy wagon moved off down the street.

"They won't give him even a month off," said Balilty as the vehicle disappeared around the corner. "These guys always get two years. What can I tell you? He looks okay, but who doesn't look okay? Their biggest murderers look okay, and they also talk okay, until they blow up a busful of children."

"And what about us? How are things looking with us?" Michael asked, and brought his attention back from the street to the yard. Esther Hayoun was still sitting there on the straw-seated stool, staring vacantly into space and surrounded by a circle of neighbor women. From beyond the wall floated the voice of the woman from the second floor: "Don't you remember that Arab from Baka? For three years he was murdering people here. What? Don't you remember how much blood there was? With a knife he slaughtered them, one after the other, with no mercy. The memorial plaques are still there, over on Yair Street, where they put them on the thirtieth day after the killing. God forbid we should find the girl like that."

"Enough, Janina. Don't talk," begged another woman. "You don't want to bring the Evil Eye. With God's help they'll find Nessia and everything will be fine. The police will find her."

"It's such a beautiful day. A perfect day for a picnic," grumbled Balilty, and out of the corner of his eye Michael noted the authoritativeness with which Yair was instructing the policemen. He divided them into groups and then looked at the map Eli Bachar had drawn for him and watched as they entered the yards in front of the houses. Up the street, the tracking dog pulled at the leash held by the police dog handler, a clumsy man in a checked flannel shirt and running shoes, and down the street Eli Bachar led a group of five uniformed policemen toward Yael Street.

"I don't understand why you're putting that baby boy, who barely knows the city, in charge of the search teams," grumbled Balilty, "and especially when there's such a shortage of manpower. I mean, it's going to take hours until we manage to recruit more volunteers from the Scouts, and while that's going on the girl could already be buried in Beit Safafa. Why on earth did you put him at—"

"I need you here," replied Michael. "It's you that I need here, and I can dispense with him at the moment." Predictably, Balilty immediately changed his tone and his complaining was replaced by the story of his conversation with the district commander. "Didn't I tell you about Drori?" scoffed Balilty. "What Drori said to me? 'I don't understand why the head of the investigations division is fussing over a murder case when I've got riots like that going on at the Patt junction.' 'Sir,' I say to him, 'a saint can't just drop good works in the middle,' so he says to me: 'You can tell Ohayon that I am not pleased. Convey to him for me that right now I need the head of the investigations department of the Jerusalem District to deal with the general situation and not with a single murder case,' and then he asks me whether we are even aware of what's happening at the Patt junction and how Jews have rampaged in Beit Safafa with bottles and stones and broken windows there and stopped Arabs' cars and made them get out and all that. 'Yes, we are aware, sir,' I say to him. 'Of course we're aware, and this whole case that we're dealing with, of a body that was found in a house that is about to be renovated where Arabs were roaming around, could also be connected to the situation. But of course,' I say to him, 'of course they're attacking Arabs' houses in Beit Safafa, if they've started to shoot at Jewish houses and rape and slaughter our women and kidnap our little girls. Are we going to sit back and do nothing?' I talk to him and talk to him and he— what does he give me in the end? Forty-seven policemen and another ten from the Missing Persons Unit and this dog handler, Motti, who hasn't woken up yet and . . ."

Michael listened distractedly and looked at the Beinisches' son, who was standing by the fence between his parents' home and the Basharis' wearing a white undershirt and shorts. He took a quick peek at the street and examined the muscles in his arm and displayed indifference to everything that was going on all around him until he suddenly shivered as though he felt Michael's gaze from across the street. Then he hugged himself with his bare arms and hurried back into the house, where the blinds were drawn.

"I suggest we split up now," said Michael without taking his eyes off the house. "You wanted to talk to Rosenstein about the apartment, so go talk to him. As for me, I'm going in to see the Basharis about that matter that Orly Shushan talked about."

"Don't you need me there? At the Basharis'?" asked Balilty suspiciously.

"I could have used you there," said Michael, weighing his words carefully and avoiding anything that could lead to insult or stubbornness, "but you've already started with the lawyer, and we haven't got the manpower to work in pairs. Do you feel," he asked cunningly, "that you won't manage with Rosenstein on your own? Maybe you're afraid that such an established and experienced lawyer won't cooperate with you?"

"Me?" Balilty laughed. "Who does that Rosenstein think he is? When you get right down to it, he's just a lawyer, and an anxious one at that, and, believe you me, he has good reason to be."

"So you won't be needing me?" asked Michael.

"No, of course not," said Balilty. "I'm off to Talbieh to his house, and I even phoned before we left to tell him that. I'm on the mobile if you need anything. You'll be keeping your beeper on, won't you?" Michael ignored the warning tone of the question and tapped the pocket of his jeans in reply. "There's also the kid, Nessia, and we're in the middle of a case and you can't turn it off. And furthermore," he added with a smile, "maybe the lady will be looking for you."

"Sit down, sit down," Netanel Bashari said to Michael from the sofa, where he was sitting next to his father. "You can take the armchair, or that tall chair there, and we don't need to sit on the floor, either, because the holiday overrides mourning observances."

Michael sat down on the only wooden chair in the room and cautiously fingered the small recording device he had tucked into the pocket of his windbreaker. He folded up the windbreaker and laid it across his knees and then looked at Naeema Bashari, who was rocking back and forth in the rocking chair, staring at the floor and biting her lower lip. In her hands she held a half-full glass of water.

On the sofa, between his two sons, who hadn't shaved because of the mourning and whose faces were covered with dark bristles, sat Ezra Bashari, holding a small Psalter.

"I . . . hmmm . . . I . . ." Michael cleared his throat and looked from the father to the mother to her sons. "I've come here to hear about . . . How shall I put it? In short, to hear about Big Zahara."

Naeema Bashari tensed and looked at him in suspicious alarm. Ezra Bashari coughed and touched the white stubble that had sprouted on his face.

"If possible," said Michael to Netanel courteously but authoritatively, "I would like to talk to your parents only, please."

"Why does he need them alone?" asked Bezalel Bashari, as he straightened the fold in his khaki shirt. He had not yet changed out of his uniform.

"Go, go," said Naeema Bashari suddenly to her sons. "It's better that way. Go and come back later." And as they showed no signs of leaving the room she added, "I'm not going to talk about this in your presence, Bezalel, and your father won't either."

"I want to understand what this has to do with it," Bezalel Bashari said, and crossed his arms on his chest. He stuck his legs out straight in front of him and dug his heels into the floor.

"Didn't you hear what he asked?" his father burst out. "Didn't you hear that the gentleman wants to talk to us alone, and didn't you hear your mother?"

Bezalel Bashari shrank. He opened his mouth to speak but his elder brother looked at him and over his father's head touched his shoulder. "Forget it, Bezalel. Forget it. Later you'll understand. What's the hurry? The main thing is that it might help find the . . . I don't know how it can help, but . . ." He rose and signaled to his brother and waited by the door until Bezalel Bashari stood up, stretching his small body and protruding his chest. "What are you?" he asked Michael. "Are you Yemenite?"

"No," Michael said, and managed in time to hold back the word "unfortunately," which might have sounded ironic. "I'm not Yemenite, but I came here at the age of three from Morocco," he hastened to explain as though this could justify his existence.

"Okay, you're not an Ashkenazi, so in general, in principle, you can understand what all this is about," Bezalel Bashari muttered, and moved toward the door, which his brother held open for him. "At least they didn't send some pompous Ashkenazi," Michael heard him saying outside the door a moment before it was closed, and also Netanel's restraining murmur: "Cut that out now, Bezalel. Do me a favor. You're talking like . . . ," but Michael missed the end of the sentence.

Very quietly, in short sentences, Michael told the couple what he had heard from Orly Shushan and explained the need to get to the bottom of the issue that had concerned Zahara before her death. "And especially something as loaded as this," he said, and apologized for having to add to their pain by "reopening an old wound."

Naeema Bashari snorted and pursed her lips. "What's old here?" she growled. "If you've lost a child, it doesn't matter how many years have gone by. It's not a wound that ever heals. It's always there."

"But I understand that you don't . . . don't talk about . . . haven't ever agreed to talk about this with your children," said Michael, "and when Zahara wanted to know something about it, you got angry at her."

"That has nothing to do with it," said the mother dismissively. "That was because I wanted them not to have our pain. I wanted them to grow up free, without hatred. I can't understand"—she sighed—"why Zahara went into all these things, which were none of her business at all. Her life could have been . . . better than ours . . . if only she hadn't . . ." Suddenly she burst out crying, and as she sobbed she muttered vague phrases about "fate" and "blows," and also mentioned Job and cried: "Why? Why did she have to meddle in that?"

"Maybe because there are children who can't stand it when there are secrets in the family without figuring them out," said Michael patiently. "Maybe, in fact, it was because she didn't have a way into the whole affair, and maybe she wanted to get closer to you."

"No," she said decidedly. "Maybe it was because of her pregnancy. Maybe it was . . . the thought of . . ."

"I still can't believe it," muttered Ezra Bashari, "and I can't see how a story from fifty years ago, our own personal business, could l have anything to do with . . . That little girl from across the street—do you think that's also connected?"

Michael spread out his fingers and said that it wasn't yet possible to know whether there was any connection between Zahara's death and Nessia's disappearance, but the more he knew about the lives of the victims . . .

"Fine, so he's explained why," said Naeema Bashari to her husband, and then to Michael: "Do you want to hear? Then I'll tell you. I'll tell you a story you won't believe. You won't believe that things like this happened here."

Michael wove his fingers together and touched the pocket of his windbreaker, where—he hoped—the tape recorder was running.

"In 1949 we were in the transit camp near Aden when I gave birth to a baby girl," said Naeema Bashari. "I was just a child myself. I'd already had another baby, who died, and I didn't understand anything yet. I just knew that I had a living baby, and such a pretty one, with blue eyes."

"She did have blue eyes," confirmed Ezra Bashari. "All our children were born with blue eyes. We didn't know they could change later, because both of us were children ourselves."

"Her eyes wouldn't have turned brown. They were a blue that doesn't change," insisted Naeema Bashari. Michael nodded as if in agreement and she continued: "They took us to a new immigrants' camp at Kibbutz Ein Shemer. We were there for a week, maybe, and they put our baby in the communal infants' house. They gave them medical examinations and all that, but they brought them back afterward. Every day they brought them back for nursing. And all of a sudden—one day they didn't bring her back. The baby. She disappeared." Naeema Bashari swallowed her saliva with an effort, and spoke again. "She was two months old. We called her Zahara, and she disappeared. One morning they told me that they'd taken her to the hospital. The evening before I had nursed her and she was perfectly healthy—a mother knows whether her baby is well or sick. And I'm telling you: She was well. And in the morning—they took her to the hospital. I went, I asked, they didn't say anything. Not which hospital and not what she had."

"Later we heard that there was a polio epidemic. Everyone was very scared. If a child had a fever they were afraid that . . . ," added her husband.

"She didn't have a fever," said Naeema Bashari angrily. "I'm telling you—she didn't have anything, and the polio . . . Back then there wasn't . . . Only afterward . . . But what did I know? They sent me back and forth and I felt . . . Right away I felt that I would never see my daughter again." She bit her lips and went silent.

Michael waited.

"A few days later, maybe a day or two—don't think I've forgotten how much time went by; even then if you had asked how much time went by I wouldn't have known, because the whole I time I'm wandering around like a madwoman, crying and screaming, and they give me a pill and say, 'She'll recover, she'll recover,' and me—what do I want? To see my baby. A mother can't stand it if they take her baby away from her just like that . . . And Jews yet . . . ." She wiped away the tears that flowed from her eyes. "Suddenly, after a day or two, Ezra says to me, 'They're calling us over the public address system.' There was a public address system at the transit camp," she explained, "where they made all the announce-ments—if someone had arrived, if they wanted someone at the office, things like that—I hear the public address system. Ezra and I were stand-ing there listening, and over the loudspeaker they announce: 'Zahara Bashari has died . . .'"

"Over the loudspeaker?" said Michael in astonishment.

"I couldn't believe it," said Naeema Bashari quietly. "I *didn't* believe it. I ran to them. I said where is she, I screamed that they should show her to me dead, that they should show me a body, a grave, something. But what could I do? They didn't let me see any grave."

"Every day we asked, and every day they didn't answer, but we didn't give up. Four or five days later," continued Ezra Bashari, since his wife had gone silent, "they called us urgently into a small room next to the main office. Both of us went."

"They gave me a bundle," said Naeema Bashari, "a package inside a little crate. They said, 'Here is your baby, dead, but don't open it. Don't open the bundle.' That's exactly what the nurse said. I look inside the crate—inside the bundle, with rags—and the nurse says to me, 'See, Naeema? The baby is dead, but don't open the bundle.'"

"We were children. Maybe we didn't understand what was going on," said Ezra Bashari, "but we wanted to open it, because what if it was some other baby?"

"I thought they could even have put a cat in there, so I started to open it," his wife said in a choking voice, and laid her hand on her chest. "I've never talked about this before. I didn't even tell the rabbi all the details," she said to Michael. "This is hard for me."

"It's a very hard story," Michael confirmed in a weak voice. The shock had paralyzed his brain.

"They said don't open it but I opened it," related Naeema Bashari in an expressionless voice. "I stood there in that little room, and I unrolled rag after rag. I had to see, do you understand me? Ezra was waiting outside. They didn't let us come in together."

"She said, the nurse, 'Let her be alone in her sorrow,'" interjected Ezra Bashari. "To this day I hear her voice ringing in my ears: 'alone in her sorrow'! To leave her there alone . . .'"

"I've never forgiven him," said Naeema Bashari. "I've never forgiven him that he did what they told him . . ."

Ezra Bashari shrugged powerlessly and buried his face in his hands.

"I stood there alone unrolling rag after rag," she continued after a moment of silence, "and I got to the last rag. That's where I got to."

Michael waited for her to continue.

"There was no baby. Just rags."

"Really?!" asked Michael, and not because he had any doubt, but because the story was horrible.

"Yes, really!" cried Naeema Bashari. "Of course really. What do think, that I could make up a thing like that? You would have thought that they would have at least put some other dead child in there. What did they think? That I was retarded? When I was standing there holding those rags I said, Well, good, at least the baby is alive, and all we have to do is find her."

"When she came out of that room," intervened Ezra Bashari, "at first she didn't say a word. Then she said, 'They have to show us the grave.' I went to them and demanded that they show us the grave, so we would have where to go to say kaddish, something. Even our patriarch Jacob, I said to them, when they showed him the coat of many colors, asked to see the grave. They said—impossible. Naeema said, 'Why is it impossible?' and they said, 'Because we buried five babies in a common grave.' That's what they said, as if they couldn't show us a common grave.

"It was impossible to catch them. Even today I don't know who they were. There was the camp manager and there was a nurse, but their names? So how were we going to look for the baby? We are shut up in an immigrants' camp, no one understands our Hebrew, what were we? Children. And my parents . . . They were already completely shattered. Nobody could help us."

There was silence. Only the chirping of the blackbirds broke it. And this chirping, just because it was pretty and joyful, struck a false note in the room, and perhaps in order to blur it Ezra Bashari went on and said: "Then they transferred us to the transit camp in Jerusalem, in Talpiot. We were maybe the only Yemenites there, everyone else went to Rosh Ha'ayin. But we—we were sent to Talpiot. And afterward to this house, which they gave us because it was abandoned. In 1949, at the end of the year. All of a sudden they brought us here, they gave us a house, and afterward I thought it was so as to keep us quiet, so that we wouldn't come with complaints."

"All those years we never spoke about this to anyone," said Naeema Bashari. "We only began to talk about it years later. First I told my brother, and he spoke to Rabbi Halevi in Bnei Brak, and then I started to go to meetings in Rosh Ha'ayin. All of us who had babies taken from us would meet there, once every two weeks, sometimes once a month, and talk and talk. And Zahara—she sensed it. She noticed that I was disappearing without saying anything and she wanted to know why. It's been quite a while since she . . . Some time ago she started to ask and . . . I got angry at her because I didn't want her to . . . And in the end . . ."

"But Bezalel also started up with this," noted Ezra Bashari. "He also couldn't leave it alone. The moment he sensed something—he fell on it, and we . . . I quarreled with him about it . . ." His voice was scratchy with misery and regret. "Especially a while ago, when he brought our immigration certificate, and the baby's . . . And when I saw it, it went to my . . . I didn't want him to . . ."

"The baby's immigration certificate?" asked Michael in a broken voice. "There's an immigration certificate?"

"Yes. It says there"—Ezra Bashari snorted bitterly—"Zohar, male, died in Ein Shemer, and the date—March 13, 1949. They couldn't even write the name properly, 'Zohar' instead of 'Zahara.' From that alone you can see the scorn."

"But he didn't find a death certificate then," his wife reminded him. "He said there wasn't a death certificate."

"Instead of a death certificate they pulled an entry from the computer that ID card number so and so—the baby had an ID number—left the country in 1963. Can you understand that?"

"No, I can't understand it," said Michael.

"My son Netanel," explained Ezra Bashari, "looked into it and found that in that year they did a census, and whoever left the country was spit out by the computer. That's the only explanation he found for that. There is no other. That was the year they did a big cover-up of all the cases, before anyone began to yell."

"But in the end it didn't help," said Naeema Bashari bitterly. "It didn't help because these deeds come out from underground, and if it also has anything to do with Zahara's . . ." She shrugged and went silent.

"Justice will win out," said Ezra Bashari.

"Did she talk about this with her brothers?" asked Michael.

"I don't know," said Naeema Bashari. "We don't talk about it at home, just that one time when Bezalel came with the certificates and the paper from the computer . . . And his father was so angry that he never . . ."

"You have to talk to him yourselves," said her husband. "You can ask the boys, and Yermiyahu, too, our second son. He'll be arriving tonight."

"Perhaps now I could . . ." Michael hesitated, and vaguely indicated the door.

"Perhaps. Why not?" said Ezra Bashari. "They'll talk to you."

But the moment he rose from the chair, carefully holding the windbreaker with the tape recorder hidden in it, his beeper went off and in the message on the screen he saw that Balilty was looking for him. "Call. Urgent," the message said.

Chapter 10

They shouldn't have agreed to let Michael's office at the Russian Compound become the search headquarters, at least not as long as Moshe Avital is sitting there in the corridor on the wooden bench and sighing every time she opens the door or steps out. This room is too central, and phone calls keep coming in that have nothing to do with the search, and everyone thinks they can come in and shoot the breeze. On the other hand, it is no longer possible to ignore Moshe Avital's soft brown eyes hanging on her face as if she and only she could help him, and those lips of his, that droop like a small child's, when she says to him: "Not yet." Or: "There's nothing to be done in the meantime. You'll have to wait a bit longer, until Chief Superintendent Ohayon returns." Or: "Those are the instructions I received. I can't let you leave." He looks like an ugly duckling in that soft yellow sweater, and with his short legs. There's no question about it: Handsome he isn't. They could kill her but she couldn't understand how he had acquired the reputation of a Don Juan, with that peculiar face of his, and with his pointy skull, top and bottom, and with that non-chin of his. But then, he is fixing his eyes on her as if she were a good fairy or something, as if she were the only person in the world who interested him, and somehow it is working on her, even if she knows that that's the way he talks to every woman. It's a fact that she isn't yelling at him.

The door to Michael's office is wide open and from the corridor she hears the transmitter beeping and the telephone ringing and she rushes in to answer in time, and so it happens that Moshe Avital is hanging around at the door, waiting, and he hears Yair on the loudspeaker. "We're done with Yiftah Street. Eli is going down to Yael Street and we're splitting up."

"Roger," she says, and with the green felt pen she draws an arrow in the direction of Yael Street on the enlarged map of Baka that is spread out on the desk, and she has the red felt pen handy to draw the second arrow that will show the route of Yair's group. And the whole time she can feel Moshe Avital's moist brown eyes hanging on her, waiting, and she can't even close the door in his face now, while with the one hand she's holding the telephone receiver and with the other holding the felt pen over the map.

Yair says: "Yiftah is done. We knocked on the doors of all the apartments and we've spoken to almost all the neighbors, with everyone who was at home. We went from building to building and we were in all the shelters and the shops and the gardens and the boiler rooms and the attics and everyplace you can think of, and there's nothing."

"Roger," says Tzilla into the speaker, and into the telephone receiver she says quickly: "I don't have time now, Balilty. Go wait for him outside the Basharis', or come wait for him here," and she hangs up.

"You should see the scenes that are going on with that dog here," Yair tells her on the background of noises and static over the receiver.

"What dog?" she asks, and waggles her hand at Moshe Avital to leave the room, but he apparently thinks she just means the open door, and comes into the room and shuts the door.

"Storm, the tracking dog. He didn't want to leave the watchamacallits', the Beinisches', yard. He dug there like crazy, and we thought . . . But there was nothing. And he also latched on to Yoram Beinisch, the son, jumped on him and almost devoured him." Moshe Avital is sitting in front of her. He has moved the chair away from the desk and is looking at her with those eyes and she can't even, simply can't, tell him to scram.

"*Nu?*" she says into the transmitter. She hasn't got a lot of patience right now for this slowness of Yair's.

"Nothing," says Yair. "The dog handler says that judging from Storm's behavior you might think the little girl was everywhere. Are you leaving the transmitter open all the time?"

"Yes, of course. What do you think?" she answers, and looks at Moshe Avital. And nevertheless she presses the red button and leaves her finger on it, and the transmitter goes silent. "You'll have to wait outside," she says to Moshe Avital in the most authoritative tone she can muster, but even when he sees how pressured she is, he isn't moved at all and he gets up very slowly, and again says to her: "What do you care? You have my mobile phone number. Why shouldn't I go out in the meantime until he comes back? I'm not running away anywhere."

And she still can't be strict and brutal with him. At most she says to him:

"Where would you go, anyway? Everything is closed because of the holiday," and also: "Wait. He'll be here soon, but wait outside. Do me a favor." And she looks at him as he very slowly goes out of the room, as if meaning to annoy, or perhaps he's waiting for her to change her mind, and he doesn't even close the door all the way, but she has to take her finger off the red button and she can't possibly run to close the door properly right now.

Once again the room is filled with noises and squeaks, and on the background of them comes the voice of Einat, who is searching with Yair and yells into the wireless, "Tzilla, Tzilla, Einat here. Can you hear me? Over."

"Roger, roger. Over," she replies, and hears the tiredness in her voice, and it's only a little after ten in the morning, and that nudnik Avital has been waiting since six, ever since Balilty left him, and really, how long can she—

"We're at the Greek's house on the corner of Othniel and Bethlehem. Over."

"I've written it down," she replies, and just then her mobile phone rings. "You don't need to draw my route," Eli says to her on the mobile. "I'm on the wireless with Aliza, and she's sitting there at the switchboard, and she has a map so it won't be too much for you . . ."

"Have you spoken to your mother?" she asks him, and sets aside the red felt pen.

"Yes. The children are fine—only *I'm* falling off my feet," says her husband without even asking how she is. "Aliza will bring you my reports upstairs to you, if there's anything, and then you can collate everything."

The conversation ends or is cut off, but she doesn't have time now to call back, because over the transmitter Yair's voice is heard again. "This house," he says to her. "It's a palace, not a house. There's Jerusalem stone here. Unbelievable how beautiful it is!" He doesn't even say "Over" to her and she restrains herself from telling him that he has no cause to get all excited about Jerusalem neighborhoods right now, because he's not on any holiday walk, and she also doesn't remind him that there probably aren't things like that in Tel Aviv, or at his moshav, but only says: "The corner of Othniel and Bethlehem? Over."

"It's locked," she hears a muffled voice in the background saying. "They've locked everything up, and the windows are boarded."

"Einat here. We are proceeding toward Shimshon Street. There's a *mikveh* there. We're going in. Over."

Tzilla marks the structure on Shimshon Street with a star, and for a moment a picture flashes before her eyes of a small body lying at the bottom of the murky greenish water of a ritual bath. She shudders. If only she had been smart enough to have brought some coffee with her at least, to this office in which she is now shut up like some kind of prisoner.

Someone is knocking gently on the door, and before she manages to say "Yes," the door opens slowly, and who is standing there if not Moshe Avital with his yellow sweater. Now he looks like a soft yellow frog, but in his two hands he is holding paper cups, and he extends one of them to her, and steam is coming out of it and the room fills with the smell of coffee. "It's from the machine downstairs in the street," he explains to her surprised look—she does not even know what surprises her more: the coffee and the soft pretzel they sell in the Old City, or Moshe Avital's nerve—and on the desk, taking care not to touch the map of the neighborhood, he untwists a strip of newspaper. "There's hyssop and sesame and salt for the soft pretzel. Hyssop without sand, absolutely clean.

"*Nu*, drink," he urges her with a small smile, and his deep big eyes don't stop gazing into hers. "Why wait when it's hot?"

What can she do? The coffee really is hot, and just what she needs. She drinks and pulls off a piece of the soft pretzel, splits it in half with her fingers and sprinkles some hyssop mixture on it. Now she can't throw him out. How can she throw out someone who has brought her coffee and a soft pretzel? She manages to say, limply: "Thanks, but you left the building."

"It was just for a moment," he answers her, and smiles—he has big white teeth, but not straight and even, and the edge of his front tooth is broken a bit, like Matan's. Matan broke his in a game of hide-and-seek. Where did Moshe Avital's get broken? Who was he chasing? And in his cheek, in a straight line under his right eye, there's a small dimple that is only now visible, when he grins.

"Einat here. There's nothing in the *mikveh* on Shimshon Street. Over." And again there are noises in the background, and with a bit of the soft pretzel stuck in her teeth and the green felt pen in her hand, she bears down hard to mark a thick X and takes the soft pretzel out of her mouth and says: "Noted. Over."

"Get a load of this orchard," she hears Yair's voice. "Will you just look at those figs. A jungle of figs, and so neglected!" It's a good thing Balilty isn't here yet. He would have said something nasty had he heard those comments of Yair's. "An abandoned storage shed," says a voice she doesn't know, and loud barking is also heard.

"Is Mr. Balilty also supposed to be coming here?" Moshe Avital asks her, and she nods affirmatively. What is she going to tell him with her mouth full of soft pretzel and hyssop that he has brought her, with coffee that is too sweet? "So maybe he'll get here first, before Ohayon," Moshe Avital murmurs, and extends to her an open packet of Marlboros, from which one cigarette protrudes.

"No, thanks, I don't smoke," she says, and he lights one for himself. Without asking if it's all right.

"You must wait outside." Since when has she been so namby-pamby?

"It's not good to be so tense. It's bad for your health, and you such a pretty young woman. You have to watch your health."

Nothing like this has ever happened to her. That man is sitting there— as if he were some friend of the family, an old friend who is giving her advice, and she . . . What's happening to her? Maybe it's the exhaustion.

"We're going up to Gideon Street. Over," says Yair's voice, and in the background she hears a man's voice saying in strange English, "There's a playground in the middle," and then there are squeaks and barks and a few cries of annoyance. "A basketball field. Empty. Just a few kids. Over," says Yair into the wireless.

"Tell them to look in the shelters of the housing projects over there," Moshe Avital says suddenly, and instead of telling him to get out of here and not meddle in her business, she asks: "Why?"

"Those are big housing projects there," he says, and his French accent grows more pronounced. "There are a lot of people, and no one pays attention."

"*Mikveh* on Gideon Street. Locked. We're breaking in now. Over," says Yair.

"Have you gone into the shelters in the projects? Over," she says, putting down the soft pretzel and marking with the green felt pen.

"They're looking there now, with the dog. I can't understand why there are so many *mikvehs* here."

"Sweetie," a woman's voice says to him, Einat's maybe, "where do you think you are? This is Jerusalem here, haven't you noticed?"

Moshe Avital wipes his lips with a paper napkin and smiles. He isn't even pretending not to hear. He's simply eavesdropping on the conversation.

"But I thought this was a secular neighborhood," says Yair. "And it was more becoming to you before, forgive me for saying so, with your hair like that . . . Ooof, too bad I said so. I shouldn't have said anything."

Now Tzilla is certain that the voice is Einat's. And something in the way she and Yair are talking to each other makes her feel uncomfortable. "What? It isn't secular here?" she hears Yair asking.

"There are no secular neighborhoods in Jerusalem. How can anyone be secular when the religious have so much power? Never mind the municipality—even the mayor is in their back pocket. Without that, he wouldn't get elected." Where do they think they are?! Why are they talking like that to her in the office? And Moshe Avital smiles with all those teeth and the dimple below his right eye.

"So what is this, like in Mea She'arim?" asks Yair, and Tzilla suddenly interrupts and says into the transmitter: "A *mikveh* or a synagogue. Or both. Get used to it. That's the way it is here. Have you opened the *mikveh*? Over."

Moshe Avital laughs and the transmitter goes silent until Yair's hesitant voice is heard. "Do you have someone there with you?" he asks.

And then there is a long silence, as if they had turned it off until again there are noises, among them the "Einat here," which is beginning to get on her nerves like the chatter of the broadcasters on the Army Radio tunes and traffic report show at seven in the morning. "Proceeding toward Bethlehem Street in the direction of Boaz Street. Over."

Maybe to show that she is in the know, she now says: "So search at the British Council, too. It's right there. Over."

"I have it marked. Don't worry, Tzilla," says Yair. "And also the park with the fountain . . ." The cough that reverberates over the speaker cuts off the sentence. And Moshe Avital shrinks back. You would think that germs come over the radio waves.

"And there's a way down in this yard to a storeroom and a cistern. Yigal Hayoun wants to talk to you. Over."

"Put him on," Tzilla says, and looks at Moshe Avital's hand lighting a cigarette he is holding between his third and fourth fingers. A ray of light coming in from the window behind her illuminates the gold ring he is wearing.

"There's a way down here to a storeroom and a cistern," says a strange new voice. "When we were kids we used to throw stones down there and wait to hear them hit the bottom. The water is really deep here."

"Not only that," interrupts Einat's voice. "There's an underground chamber here the size of the whole house and that's where the opening to the cistern begins. Over."

Tzilla holds the green felt pen—the cistern and the underground chamber are not indicated on the map they prepared for her—and marks two points on the route. "So what's the problem?" she asks as she marks. "Are you going down there or not? Over."

"We need a flashlight. Do you have one?" She hears Yair's voice on the background of loud barking. "Wow!" gushes Yair after a few moments. "Will you look at that? The water is black and there are patches of mildew on the walls that look like . . . Look how beautiful it is, with all those kinds of mold—isn't it? Just like an ancient cave with paintings."

"Eeek!" She hears a yelp and Moshe Avital tenses in his chair, and from the speaker comes Einat's hysterical squawk. "What are those things?"

"That's nothing, just naked snails. They don't do anything." Beyond the map and the sounds of the voices, Tzilla can picture them exactly—fat and slimy, sticking to the wall and glistening—and she is nauseated. In a moment she's going to throw up the pretzel.

"She's not here. Tell her that she's not here." She thinks that the voice is the voice of Yigal Hayoun, and this voice is the one that is suddenly shouting into the system: "No one could have dragged her here without anyone noticing. Nessia is not a skinny child."

Squeaks and squeals fill the room at the Russian Compound before Yair says: "Returning to Bethlehem Road. Over."

"Where on Bethlehem? Over." Tzilla fills her mouth with a piece of the soft pretzel, and as Einat speaks she marks an arrow on the main street of the neighborhood in a southerly direction. She also marks a spot next to the first greengrocer and another one next to the second greengrocer, and a curving arrow into the yard behind the shops. "What?" she clarifies with Einat. "What did you say? The greenhouse? Where is there a greenhouse? Over."

"It's not a greenhouse," says Moshe Avital as if he had been asked. "It was a place where they had potted plants . . . What do they call it? A plant nursery? But now there's nothing there."

Anger gives her courage. "Do me a favor and wait outside, like I asked you," she says to him, and moves aside the cup of coffee and the soft pretzel and the hyssop mixture. "You can't be here now."

"Am I in the way? Sorry. I just want to help," he says, not in the least insulted, and saunters out of the room.

After that things take on a rhythm that is soothing in a way, if you disregard what it is all about. She almost forgets that they are looking for the little girl who has disappeared, because she is so busy concentrating on marking the map: the thin arrow along the narrow lane between Bethlehem and Mordechai Hayehudi, to the house that used to belong to the Labor Party.

"There are signs that someone was here," insists an unfamiliar voice.

"This is still here from the Romanian workers. No one's been in here with those boards blocking the entrance," answers someone else.

"Do you have a synagogue there at the end of Mordechai Hayehudi?" asks Yair. "Over."

"I have a star here," she replies, "a kind of Star of David. There's a synagogue on the map at the end of Mordechai Hayehudi, but it's a dead-end street."

"What difference does it make if it's a dead-end street? Over." To this question she has no answer.

Again she hears blurred voices, talking about a grape arbor, and somebody mentions a kiosk. At that moment the door opens noisily and Balilty is standing there. "I stopped off at home. I've brought you . . ." He is panting as if he has run the whole way. "Matty sent this for you, a little chicken soup and some rice with okra and meat." And as he speaks he sets a large plastic bag down at her feet and unties the knot to show her a tower of square plastic containers. The smell of food fills the room, and Balilty nods in the direction of the corridor. "He's wrung out, that Avital, huh?"

"So you take him," says Tzilla. "Just get him off my back. All morning he's been driving me crazy."

"I can't," says Balilty with a sigh and a miserable face. "I've already done my bit with him. My job was to find out about the apartment and the alibi—*nu*, eat something, Matty put in a fork and a soup spoon. Look, take it out while it's still hot, it'll get cold, no?" And without waiting for an answer he takes the top square container out of the bag and opens it, and the smell of chicken soup that comes to her nostrils reminds her how hungry she is.

"And does he have one?" she asks, carefully bringing the spoon from the container to her mouth.

"What? Ah, an alibi. Not really. You couldn't say he has much of an alibi. A lot of talk, that's what he has."

"He's been sitting here since six o'clock in the morning," Tzilla says, and drops the spoon on the desk and brings the corner of the plastic container to her mouth and sips the soup from it.

"Tell me," says Balilty, looking out the window, "what do they see in that ugly thing? You women drive me crazy—even you. How did he get his hooks into you, too?"

"No one has got his hooks into anybody," she corrects him, and moves on to the second plastic container. "Tell Matty that since my mother died I haven't had chicken soup like this. Tell her, you hear? Don't forget."

Balilty turns away from the window. "Taste the okra. No one cooks okra like that. He met with Zahara Bashari on the day she died. Imagine."

"When?" asks Tzilla in astonishment. "In the morning or in the evening?"

"He says in the afternoon, but go know," says Balilty, helping himself to a piece of okra out of the plastic container. "He said that they had lunch together at a grilled meat place. The restaurant owner, a guy named Itzik, in Mahaneh Yehuda, still has to be asked. I know him, Itzik. I haven't got—"

"So let him go home already and call him in later," demands Tzilla. "Are you afraid he's going to run away somewhere?"

"What's the matter with you?" Balilty settles into a chair, crossing one leg over a knee in a proprietary way as if he were about to colonize the office, and at the corners of his mouth there is the beginning of a smirk, after which would normally come some annoying, smart-ass remark. But the loudspeaker squelches him.

"There's nothing in the synagogue," says Yair. "They're coming out of the grape arbor. There's an old kiosk here, on Yehuda Street, where it meets Mordechai Hayehudi. We'll check it out. Over."

"Okay, I've marked it. Over," Tzilla says, and hangs back because of Balilty, who is leaning over the desk.

"Hey, kid, there's no point in looking in that kiosk. It's been closed for thirty years. It's a battered old kiosk from the time of the British and no one ever goes there. Over." The communications system goes silent. They can't even hear the barking anymore. Tzilla calls into the speaker a few times, then looks at it helplessly.

"I'm sending Avital home to wait," says Balilty. "I'll take the responsibility. And I'll talk to the boss, and he'll talk to him there already. Where is he?"

"Who? Where's who?" Tzilla asks, and doesn't take her eyes off the speaker. What is she going to do if it chooses this moment to go on the blink?

"Do me a favor, sweetie. Eat something before you go completely nuts. Have you tasted the rice? Our commander, where is he? Still at the Basharis'?"

"Call him on the beeper. How should I know? What's going on with this communications system? Isn't it working?"

And as if in answer to her question the speaker squeaks and groans. "Tzilla, Tzilla, can you hear me? Over."

Later, Yair said that had it not been for the rose, he would not have lingered there, even if the dog had insisted and kept on barking. And, stricken by the innocence of the blueness of her eyes, it was to Einat that he admitted that what had drawn him to the abandoned kiosk was the rose that for the first time in his life he saw blooming in the fall. "For people like me, who have spent so much time growing roses in hothouses," he told her in embarrassment, "this strain of Old Rose is a particularly precious strain . . . It's like a rare stamp for collectors, and everywhere in the world it blooms in the spring, once a year, and here it is, suddenly blooming in the fall."

Because of that rose blooming in front of the entrance to the kiosk, which was mostly covered by other flowers blooming out of season, he approached and also saw the broken branches of the bush blocking the entrance. He stood in front of the rosebush and closely examined the blossoms, luxuriant in dusty pink petals, and Einat followed him. "How lovely," she whispered breathily. "It's like the flowers that were embroidered on cushions in my grandmother's house. Do you know what I mean?"

"This," murmured Peter, who suddenly stood behind them, "is *centifolia*, in my opinion. Right?

"I think it's *rosa gallica*," Yair said hesitantly, "but maybe it's *centifolia*, as you say. We should look it up. In any case, it's a very old bush, probably from when the British were here. Look how it covers everything," he said, and bent over the stalks as the dog came up to him and whined.

"What is it, Storm?" asked the dog handler, and to Yair he said: "Something here is really making him nervous. More than before."

And only then, when the dog's breathing was close to his neck, did Yair notice the heap of damp, loose soil near the roots of the rosebush. He scattered it with the toe of his shoe. The dog leaped to the spot and dug with his paws.

"There's something here," said the dog handler again, "but we don't have anything to dig with."

The tracking dog wouldn't let the heap of dirt alone. He stuck his moist muzzle into it, scratched in the dirt and didn't stop whining.

"Get me a shovel," called Yair to the uniformed policemen. A long moment went by before one of them came running up with a large shovel in his hand. Yair began to dig in the heap of dirt, feeling the softness of the soil. "Hold him now," he ordered the dog handler. "He's getting in the way," and at that moment, the body was revealed. First they saw the black and white fur, and then the crushed skull.

"Oh my God," cried Peter. "It's Rosie, Nessia's dog."

Chapter 11

I feel sorry for them," said Balilty, leaning on the stone wall, "especially for his wife. A nice woman, really. Apple tart like that I haven't eaten for years . . . The crust . . . it melts in your mouth, definitely with butter . . . She put a whole packet of butter in there, I'm telling you."

"Did you talk to him about the apartment in the presence of his wife?" Michael rested against the stone wall of the apartment, next to Balilty, who was waiting for him there when he'd come out of the Basharis' house.

"Of course in his wife's presence. It's in their house, isn't it?" Balilty twisted his full lower lip. "On purpose I spoke to him in her presence, so as to see if she knew."

"*Nu,* and did she know?" Michael asked, and examined the end of his burning cigarette.

"Zilch," Balilty said in amazement, and blew his nose into a paper tissue. "She didn't know a thing. I told you, I feel sorry for her. A person buys an apartment, or almost buys one. You could say 'buys,' no? For a twenty-two-year-old girl, and he doesn't say a word to his wife . . . He's lost his marbles, that Rosenstein, if you ask me. It happens to elderly men. They lose their marbles."

"Did you tell him that you'd checked with the other lawyer? Whatsisname—"

"Deri. Attorney-at-law Deri. Yes." Balilty hesitated, and plucked two yellowish flowers from the jasmine bush that grew by the wall. With half an ear, Michael heard the voices of the searchers. "Look," said Balilty. "I started out slowly, from the business of the apartment in general . . . I saw that he would rather his wife wasn't in the room, and when she went out to the kitchen he tried to say something, but I pretended I was a complete idiot, and I mentioned the little girl and the search, and just then his wife came back and said how awful it was, Esther's girl; you know that she"— Balilty gestured with his back at Esther Hayoun, who was still sitting on the rush stool in the front yard, surrounded by a congregation of neighborhood women—"that she's their cleaning lady? And furthermore, she's also the mother of your real estate agent's father's boyfriend."

"I didn't know that she worked at the Rosensteins'," Michael said, and enumerated to himself all the coincidences and relationships that had been revealed in the events since Zahara's body was found in the apartment Ada had bought. Against the backdrop of Balilty's voice he tried to negate the significance of these relationships, but he immediately took himself to task: Wasn't he the one who had said earlier that there's no such thing as coincidence, and that these links have significance? And all of a sudden, just like that, he's changing his mind? Maybe the meaning isn't evident only because the full picture hasn't yet been disclosed.

"So make a note of it," said Balilty, obviously pleased with himself. "Esther Hayoun, the mother of the boyfriend and the mother of the girl who's disappeared, is also the Rosensteins' cleaning lady and has been working for them for twenty-seven years. She's like a member of the family there, because Mrs. Rosenstein is such a nice lady her cleaning lady is like family and she knows their daughter very well and the grandchildren and everything and I've already tried to ask her about them but it's better that you ask. To you she'll speak, but not to me."

Michael shrugged. "Do you need something from me?" he asked Balilty.

"Me?" said the intelligence officer. "Nothing. I don't need . . . Why? Why do you ask?"

"Because you've started to flatter me," said Michael.

"I wasn't being complimentary," cried Balilty, who until now had spoken in a low voice and kept looking around to make sure that no one was nearby. "I'm serious. There are people who talk to me, and there are those who don't. She," he said, indicating Esther Hayoun, "you can see on her face—she's the type who doesn't trust anyone but she knows that you're, like, the commander and you . . . Believe me, to you she'll speak."

"Okay," said Michael. "We'll check it out in a moment. Let's get back to the matter at hand."

"So where were we? Ah. She brings in the coffee, his wife," Balilty continued, and licked his lower lip, "and I'm there drinking it—also excellent, in old-fashioned cups, thin porcelain with a handle, from a good set, you can tell, with whipped cream and that tart—and I'm looking around: What a house they have! A palace! And in good taste, I'm telling you, classy, everything in its place and clean as . . . Persian carpets and oil paintings and statues and all kinds of . . . And the mister is tense, v-e-r-y tense! His hand on the cup is shaking like in the movies, like someone just before they catch him, and he looks at his wife . . . And me? I'm drinking the coffee and eating the cake as if there was nothing going on, and talking about the apartment on Railroad Street, as if it was just an apartment, and I see that his wife doesn't know a thing. I tell him that we checked, and the apartment was really, just like he says, up for sale, but not from the bailiff and all that. And Avital, the owner? The so-called French jewelry merchant, even though they say that he's apparently in difficulties—I wish I had his difficulties. Bankrupt shmankrupt. He was simply selling, but the apartment really was a bargain. 'But nevertheless a real bargain,' I say to him, Rosenstein, as if his wife wasn't there at all. 'You don't have to buy every bargain. We weren't convinced,' I say to him, 'that some rivalry with another lawyer is a serious reason to register an apartment in Zahara's name.' And his wife, she doesn't say a word, not a word, just looks at him like that"—Balilty tilted his head to demonstrate—"and she's listening like that without speaking and her hand isn't shaking or anything, completely calm. A woman like that, she's old now, but you can see that she was beautiful. In the style of Grace Kelly. Do you remember Grace Kelly? No? Some kind of princess, aristocratic?"

Michael nodded distractedly and listened to the voices of the searchers, who had spread out through the whole neighborhood. They'd been searching for hours and hadn't found anything. In the distance, to his right, he could hear vague cries. Maybe they were calling the girl's name.

"But there's something else," Balilty said, and took a toothpick out of his shirt pocket and probed his teeth. "I'm looking around," he continued in a whisper, and threw down the toothpick and rubbed his hands together, "and there's a piece of marble on top of the radiator, a kind of shelf, and there are photographs on the shelf. I go up to the photographs, so then Mrs. Rosenstein says to me, 'This is our daughter, and this is her husband and here are our grandchildren' and all that but I am looking and there are pictures of her, of that daughter, when she was a little girl, and pictures of her as a teenager and also from the wedding and from now and . . ."

Michael tensed.

"You say to yourself," said Balilty, "How did two elegant Poles like that, with everything tip-top, suddenly have a kid that looks like that? And the grandchildren are exactly the same. The mother is blonde and even has blue eyes, and Mister Rosenstein looks one hundred percent Ashkenazi, so how did they have a kid like that?"

"What? What are you saying?" said Michael, startled. Perhaps because of the thought that had crossed his mind a moment ago about the points of connection among the people that had to do with this case, he was now attacked by a sense of foreboding, as before a disaster.

"What I'm saying," said Balilty in sudden seriousness, "is that Rosenstein's daughter—we have to check whether she's adopted or something, because this is no biological child of an old Polish couple. Do you see what I'm saying?"

"But you didn't speak to them about that?" asked Michael, trying to reconstruct the details of the conversation with the Basharis.

"About that—no," acknowledged Balilty. "You're the only one I'm telling this, but first thing tomorrow morning I'm checking at the Interior Ministry . . ."

"How old is she, Rosenstein's daughter?" asked Michael.

"She's forty-nine," said Balilty. "I asked. I even asked where she was born. In Haifa, they said, she was born in Haifa. I don't know why I asked," he said pensively. "I had a feeling . . . a kind of strange feeling . . ."

"So what else came up in the matter of the apartment?" Michael wanted to put off for now the stage at which the pieces of the picture would come together.

"At a certain moment," said Balilty with the satisfaction of a story-teller who has succeeded in capturing his listeners, "I turn directly to the missus and I ask her straight out, like brutally, whether she knows that her husband bought an apartment for Zahara Bashari."

"And did she answer you?"

"Yes." Balilty sighed. "She's looking at me with those blue eyes of hers and she says to me, 'Of course I know.' And I'm telling you, she didn't know a thing. And very coolly she answers me that she knew. Without any hysteria. What a woman! I would give anything to be that fly there, and see what she said to him after I left. If only they would invent some camera you could attach to a fly . . ."

"How did she explain it?" asked Michael, and at the same time the story of the baby at the Ein Shemer immigrant camp buzzed in his brain.

"My words exactly!" Balilty cried, and looked about in alarm and low-ered his voice. "That's what I asked her. 'Mrs. Rosenstein,' I said to her, 'how do you explain it that your husband bought it and all that?' And she, she smiles at me, but her eyes aren't smiling, just her lips, and she asks me if I want another piece of cake. That's what she talks to me about, and after that she says to me, 'If my husband decided that, then it's right.' And I look at him and I see on his face that he's wiped out, without hiding it, but I don't know what he's wiped out *from*. It was like from her knowing something he didn't want her to know . . . but not like he'd been caught red-handed, not like he was scared, but more like . . . like he was sorry, like he wanted to spare her something. Do you under-stand what I'm saying?"

"More or less," Michael said pensively. "What do you think he wanted to spare her?"

"I don't know, but it's something that has to do with Zahara Bashari, and not something conventional, if you know what I mean. Even if there was an affair there, if he lost his marbles, it wasn't—"

"Do you think that Zahara Bashari blackmailed Rosenstein? Is that what you're telling me?"

"That's it." The intelligence officer beamed. "That's exactly what I'm saying. Do you think so too? I say: She blackmailed him, but not in a romantic context."

"But about what, you don't exactly know," mused Michael, and for a moment he wondered whether there was anything to the hypothesis that crossed his mind.

Not yet," said Balilty, "but give me another day or two and I'll tell you exactly what, and that's apart from the business about the apartment. Because you see," he said lowering his voice, "it isn't reasonable that a man of that type, a sharp lawyer and all that, would give an apartment to a girl like Zahara out of the blue. And seriously now, I don't really believe that he got her pregnant—for years now that man hasn't . . . How should I put it? His prick's in his pocket, if you know what I mean. You know what I mean?"

"I know what you mean," said Michael.

"And the whole time," Balilty said, and looked over into the front yard, "this whole time I have the feeling that she"—he again indicated Esther Hayoun with his eyebrows—"knows things. Why don't you speak to her?" he pleaded. "Now, I mean. Exploit the momentum. I tried in the morning . . . Now she's muzzy from the sedative they gave her before, that's why she's so quiet now. If you would have seen her before . . . at six in the morning, the way she was screaming then, but to talk—she didn't say much, only when I asked her, after it turned out that she works for them. I asked her about Rosenstein's daughter, and she went pale as . . . pale as . . ." Balilty looked for the words. "Terribly pale, all the blood drained out of her face, I'm telling you, it's not only what I said. Only because of the holiday I can't get into the computer at the office, but tomorrow, first thing in the morning—"

"It's the intermediate days of Sukkot and the Interior Ministry is closed. What are you going to do? Call in the director-general to turn it on?"

"Don't you worry," scoffed Balilty. "I have connections. My connections will go into the computer for me tomorrow, and then we'll see exactly—I'll have to pay for it, it's going to cost me," he muttered as he pulled his nose. "It's this woman who once . . . Meanwhile, she's lost her looks, heaven help us, but what a bombshell she was, and now she's going to want to . . . I can't do it, I simply can't do it . . . But maybe I'll get out of it just with a lunch. Maybe at the Tel Aviv port, or some Romanian grill. That's how it goes—once she loved to make love and now she loves to eat. We aren't getting any younger . . ." He looked up at the sky. "It's after lunchtime," he said mournfully. "Aren't you dying of hunger? Coffee, at least?" he asked worriedly. "Yems are actually all right about things like that—not like the Persians." He looked for another moment at the Basharis' house, at the wide-open wooden gate and the tightly closed blinds, and went on to say: "I have their daughter's birth date, the Rosensteins'."

"So at this opportunity," Michael said, and pulled Balilty close to him, "when you're going into the Interior Ministry anyway, get out the details on Zahara Bashari."

"What details?!" wondered Balilty. "We have all the data. Why on earth—"

"No," clarified Michael, and now he himself looked right and left to make sure no one was listening to them, "not that Zahara Bashari. There's another one. That other Zahara Bashari, the first one," and in a few sentences he told the intelligence officer what he had heard from the Basharis. "She was also born in '49, in a transit camp in Aden, and they told me that there's a death certificate for her, but I want to see a copy . . ."

"You don't say!" marveled Balilty when Michael finished talking. "How can it be that . . . that there's exactly a connection like this between . . . Do you think they took that other Zahara Bashari for . . .? I don't believe it," and suddenly in a burst of renewed energy he urged again: "You have to talk to her, before anything else, listen to me," and he nodded his head in the direction of Esther Hayoun. "Catch her while she's alone—now's the time. Her son, Yigal Hayoun, the queer? He went to look for the girl with his boyfriend, with Yair's group; I hope they don't go and drop him off on the street . . . Anyway, everyone's gone off to eat," he said with a gloomy look. "You can smell the food, from all the houses . . . Whoever isn't searching is eating now. It's already after three," and in another burst of enthusiasm he hastened to say: "Catch her *now.* The mother. Don't wait, before the Romanian neighbor woman comes back with her new round of lemonade." Balilty stopped talking, and his nostrils expanded and his head turned toward one of the apartments above them. "Even though I stopped off at home and grabbed something, I'm still hungry." He stuck out his nose and sniffed again.

"Tell me," he said after some thought. "If they kidnapped their baby, the Basharis, and gave it up for adoption, they didn't testify about this to the commission that investigated the kidnapping of the Yemenite children?"

"No," said Michael. "They put it off. There was . . . They tried . . . Naeema Bashari tried . . . At first she thought not to go into it but afterward I think they intended . . ."

"But you asked Tzilla to get you the transcript from the commission, no?" said Balilty after a moment of silence.

"I haven't had a chance to go over it," Michael said, and he heard the embarrassment and apology in his own voice.

"But I, last night, when you were busy, I did have time," Balilty said with a wink. "She's already got part of the transcript, and I started to read it, not only because you'd asked but also because I had . . . Even before, I already told you that I had a feeling that it's not so simple with this Rosenstein, that there's something there . . . Did I say so or not?" And without waiting for a reply he went on: "There are terrible stories there! You just can't believe it's true, I'm telling you, you just can't believe it. But you, you'd better go talk to her." Michael shook himself and looked over at Esther Hayoun. "That one, for twenty-seven years she's been working there, for Mrs. Rosenstein. I asked her when she came about the little girl, and right away she says to me: 'Every day, except for Saturdays and holidays.' Twenty-seven years, imagine. Six days a week. I sensed . . . I'm telling you, that one knows everything that needs to be known. But the problem is, even though she was muzzy, she didn't want to talk to me. She knows something, but she doesn't want to. Loyal to her boss and so on, but you'll be able to get something out of her. You—that's your field. Everyone's good at something. I'm good at intelligence, that's why I'm in intelligence. You're good at questioning. You should have been a psychologist. Did you ever think about studying psychology at the university instead of law?" He twisted his lips into an angry expression and licked first his upper lip and then his lower. "You just went back to university without thinking about it, but you should have taken psychology from the beginning. What have you gotten out of your degree? So today you're a lawyer. Really now—a beginning lawyer, how much money can he make? A psychologist—yes, now you're going to need a lot of money, because of that house you bought as though you . . ."

Again Michael looked at Esther Hayoun, her dark, crooked fingers distractedly plucking fresh wild sorrel stalks and rolling them between her hands, knotting them together and unraveling them as if untangling yarn. Like a flock of hens the neighbor women scattered away from her, each to her own affairs, and suddenly she was left alone. He approached and stood beside her, casting a shadow on her with his body, and then he knelt low very close to her bandaged legs, smelling the smell of chlorine bleach and perspiration that rose from her, and in front of his eyes were the faded blue flowers on the fabric of her black dress.

She lifted small eyes to him, squinting because of the sun.

"Mrs. Hayoun," he said quietly, "perhaps we can go inside and talk a bit. I want you to tell me more about Nessia."

Without saying a word, she leaned on his arm and rose from the rush stool. Very slowly, with tiny steps, she walked in front of him to the apartment, the door of which was wide open. Her legs carried her heavy body with an effort. The hair on her frizzy head was untidy, and the locks escaping from the hairpins looked like an omen of chaos.

"This is her room," she said in a cracked voice, pointing to the room near the front door. It was gloomy in the apartment, the gloom exacerbated by the dark gray floor tiles. Faded flowered sheets were spread on the couch in the living room.

"They've already checked there, in her room. They made a mess of everything," she said, tapping her heavy thigh with her hand. "They took out all her clothes for that dog of theirs to smell. Do you want to check there too?" she asked, and held the door so it wouldn't close. Again he glanced at the narrow bed, and at the exposed mattress, and at the rubber sheet, and at the white sheets that had been pulled off it—you didn't need to be a psychologist to understand that the girl wet her bed and that her life wasn't easy—and at the squashed pillow in the corner of the bed. The contents of the closet were scattered at the foot of the bed and an emptied schoolbag lay between the heap of clothing and the pile of books and notebooks and the writing implements that had been dumped out of a pencil case. "I don't know what this is," said Esther Hayoun, as she bent down with an effort and picked up a purple brassiere. "This . . . She probably took it from someone for a Purim costume. She still doesn't have . . . She still doesn't need . . . ," and she hobbled up quite close to him, clutching the collar of his windbreaker with both her hands, and then she encircled his arms with her chapped fingers. "You're a good boy," she whispered, and brought her forehead close to him. "I know. Not like . . . not like those policemen who make trouble for my son and because of them he doesn't come near the house now, not like . . . your colleague there"—her head indicated the front yard. "He's Kurdish, judging by his name, and Kurds I don't trust, but you, you have a good face. You'll bring me back my little girl."

Gently Michael removed the chapped hands from his arms and held them for a moment.

"I can't go out and look for her because of my legs," Nessia's mother said in a bitter, desperate voice, and dropped her hands to her sides, "because of the veins."

"In work like yours, it's the most difficult thing, the legs," Michael said, and led her out of the girl's room into the small living room. She pulled off the sheet that was protecting the sofa and indicated that he should sit down. "It's because of the dog," she said, and fingered the sheet a bit. "It leaves hair all over everything, and where is that dog now? What kind of dog doesn't guard? From the beginning I knew it wasn't worth anything."

Michael asked for how long they'd had the dog.

"Three years, almost," said Esther Hayoun after thinking a moment. "From when it was this big," she added, moving her hands a small distance apart.

"It's hard to keep a dog in such a small apartment," said Michael, just to keep the conversation going.

"That dog," Esther Hayoun said, and narrowed her thin, ruined lips in disgust. "If it wasn't from Mrs. Rosenstein, I would never in my life have even taken it."

"Did Mrs. Rosenstein give you the dog?" He again marveled at how simple remarks that were only intended to fill a silence suddenly opened something up.

"She's a good woman, poor thing," said Esther Hayoun in the way people speak about a helpless child. "It's from their dog. It had puppies, maybe ten. Three of them died and one of them she gave to Nessia. A good woman, Mrs. Rosenstein, but not . . . not practical . . . She didn't think about. . . . What do we need a dog for in such a small apartment? And it doesn't even guard anything. Yesterday she just took it down to go around the block and come back, and she didn't come back. I waited for maybe an hour and she didn't come back, and two hours later she still wasn't back. I waited some more. What could I do? And the television was on and I fell asleep. And it was one o'clock at night when I saw she hadn't come back and I phoned my son. He lives down the street here but there was only the answering machine. So I left a message. I couldn't think of anything else to do. I said, 'Yigal, I don't know what's happened to the child. I'm worried that she hasn't come home yet.' I didn't want to go to his place. I was afraid that if I left the house and Nessia came back . . . So I waited. What could I do then? He heard the message maybe two hours later. At three o'clock at night he came here with Peter. Do you know who Peter is? He's a professor. He knows everything, so we looked around a bit and we called her name. We called her name everywhere, even though it was night, and finally we went to the police. As soon as it got light we went to the police. I didn't want to have a dog but I thought, A girl with a dog, what could happen to her? Only it's a toy dog and all it does is make noise. How did she let them do this to her? How? Tell me." She suddenly encircled his arm. "You're a good boy—tell me. Is she still alive, my daughter?"

Slowly and authoritatively, carefully choosing every word, he said to her: "I believe that she is alive," and he stroked the hand that was grasping his arm.

"How many plagues of Egypt there are in our street . . . Yesterday Zahara, and today my Nessia . . . Zahara is also the child of her parents' old age after three brothers . . . If only with her it isn't like with Zahara, may she rest in peace, that she isn't . . . ."

"We are not certain that there is any connection between the cases," said Michael, formulating a cautious statement he could stick by.

"I don't know what to think anymore . . . ," said Esther Hayoun hoarsely. "With all those Arabs roaming around the neighborhood, I said to Yigal . . . He has an Arab worker, a good boy, but an Arab. For some time I've been saying to him—"

"Nessia, she doesn't have a lot of friends?" asked Michael.

"No," said Esther Hayoun, massaging her swollen knees. "My sons, when they were little, there were always . . . The house was always . . . Friends, kids from the neighborhood, school, but Nessia, she . . ."

"She's shy?" suggested Michael after a few seconds.

"Yes, shy," agreed Esther Hayoun, and after a moment she squinted at him and sighed again. "And also, what can I tell you, she doesn't . . . She's alone a lot . . . I work all day and there are days when I . . . A girl needs to have her mother at home, with a hot meal and everything, but I . . . Every day I work . . ."

"She's probably very attached to the dog," said Michael, who was looking for a way to get back to talking about the Rosensteins.

"It eats from her plate and sleeps with her in her bed," said Esther Hayoun, grimacing in disgust.

"But Nessia loves her, and a lonely little girl like you describe, it's important that she . . . Does she also like Mrs. Rosenstein?"

"There isn't a person in the world who doesn't like Mrs. Rosenstein," said Esther Hayoun decidedly. "Mrs. Rosenstein is the most . . . What can I tell you? . . . She puts her whole heart into . . . anyone who . . . How much she's helped me!"

"Is the whole family there like that? Mr. Rosenstein too?"

"With him I don't speak so much, he's at work all day."

"And their daughter?"

"Tali. She's also very nice. Very, very nice."

"But isn't she living abroad?" asked Michael, as if he didn't exactly know.

"Of course abroad. She lives in the United States and she has a house—a palace. I saw pictures of it," said Esther Hayoun with evident pride. "Ever since she got married . . . Her husband is also a big businessman . . . For twenty years now . . . more than twenty years . . . There isn't a year she doesn't come, at the holidays and in the summer, and they also go there, every Passover and at Christmas. Only this year she didn't come, because they didn't let her."

"Who didn't let her?"

"Her parents. They were afraid because of the situation, and with the grandchildren . . ."

"Is she their only daughter?"

Esther Hayoun nodded and sighed. "Mrs. Rosenstein couldn't have any more," she whispered, as if sharing a secret. "And even this one with a lot of difficulty, we shouldn't know from such problems. And Mrs. Rosenstein just loves children! That's how it is." She sighed. "Everyone has their own problems."

"But didn't you know her when the girl was a baby?" Michael said, and wondered whether he was getting close to where the door would close. He was still disturbed by the daughter's appearance as described by Balilty.

"How could I have known her when she was a baby?" said Esther Hayoun dismissively. "I've seen *pictures* of her as a baby. Mrs. Rosenstein, when she's missing Tali, invites me to look at the albums with her. There's an album for every year of her life. They took so many pictures of that girl, bless her." And she turned aside and spat, "Tfoo-tfoo," to keep away evil spirits.

"Are there also pictures of Mrs. Rosenstein when she was a young woman?"

"Not from before they came here, only from afterward. She was so beautiful!"

"Are there, say, any pictures from the pregnancy?"

"Why are you asking that?" she suddenly demanded, and angrily she said: "There aren't any pictures from Haifa, just from Jerusalem. They were all lost in a flood in their apartment, and after that they moved to Jerusalem, and of all their mementos—nothing was left."

For a moment, a silence hung in the air between them.

"Does this have anything to do with my Nessia?" she said, suddenly waking up. She tilted her face toward him, knotted her eyebrows, looked at him with yellow suspicion and said: "Because if it doesn't, why are you asking?"

"There's no resemblance," admitted Michael, "between the daughter and the parents, don't you see?"

"So what if there's no resemblance," she dismissed angrily. "That does-n't mean anything. When I first knew her, Tali was a big girl, after the army, and at first I worried that she wouldn't get married . . . She's not so . . . She doesn't resemble her mother . . . And now, look how she's fixed up."

"Her mother is a beautiful woman," commented Michael.

"Mrs. Rosenstein? Like . . . like a queen, and if you could have seen her when she was younger, she had such blonde hair. Golden. Golden."

"And the daughter, Tali, doesn't resemble her father, either?" tried Michael.

"Tell me," said Esther Hayoun, narrowing her eyes suspiciously, "What's on your mind? What are you looking for? Is this connected to Nessia or not?"

"We don't know yet," he admitted, "but maybe it's connected to the sad affair of Zahara Bashari."

"How? How is it connected?" demanded Esther Hayoun.

"I'm just trying to find out whether Tali is their biological daughter," replied Michael dully, as if apologetically.

"What are you talking about?!" she cried. "If you could see the way she loves them—so what if she doesn't resemble them? Nessia also doesn't resemble . . . Nessia doesn't resemble her father at all, or me. Everyone . . ." Her voice broke.

He was afraid she was going to burst into tears, but her suspicious, narrow eyes hung on him resentfully. "Why aren't you searching for her, for my Nessia?" she said accusingly. "Why are you bothering with all that? It's a waste of time. It's all probably because of him." With her head, she indicated the door as if Balilty were on the other side of it. "He's making things up. Doesn't everyone have enough troubles without all that?"

"Mrs. Hayoun," said Michael after he took two deep breaths, "I'll tell you the truth, but you will have to keep it a secret—can I trust you?"

She nodded without saying a word and pursed her lips. She clasped her gnarled hands under her heavy bosom in a demonstrative gesture of knowing that there was no point to what she was about to hear.

"We suspect that the . . . that Nessia's disappearance really does have something to do with the case of Zahara Bashari," he said slowly, and watched her face turn white.

"I knew it," moaned Esther Hayoun. "I knew it right from the first. Right from the first I knew it. Are you telling me that she . . . that she's also like Zahara?"

"No, no, no," said Michael quickly. "I'm sure she's not. I hope . . . I'm sure we'll find her alive and unharmed, but we thought that maybe Zahara Bashari's murder is somehow connected to a Yemenite baby who disappeared fifty-two years ago, a baby girl who was . . . who we think was maybe . . ." At the sight of her eyes, which were glued to him, he hastened to reassure her and said: "Mr. and Mrs. Rosenstein didn't know about Nessia. They haven't done anything, heaven forbid," he said as he saw her eyes open wider in fear and her lips tremble. "Understand," he pleaded, and laid his hand on her arm, "we don't want to hurt them or do them any harm. All we want to know is whether it has any connection to the fact that Zahara Bashari was murdered and also to Nessia's disappearance."

"You," said Ester Hayoun, sitting straight up and removing his hand from her arm. "I'll tell you what—you find Nessia for me and then I'll tell you what I know. If you don't find her for me, I'm not saying a word."

"Mrs. Hayoun," he said authoritatively, "I promise you—" The beeper in his shirt pocket went off. He looked at the display and at the words written there: "Urgent. Call Tzilla."

"What? What's that? What did they say?" asked Esther Hayoun in a trembling voice. "Have they found her? Show me what's written there," she said, and grabbed the beeper out of his hand. "Who is Tzilla?" she demanded, and the hand holding the beeper waggled at him in a threatening gesture. "What does this mean?"

"Mrs. Hayoun," Michael said soothingly and held out his hand to retrieve the beeper delicately. "If you'll take me to the telephone—you do have a telephone here, don't you?" he said calmly and soothingly, as if talking to a frightened child. "If you'll let me phone Tzilla—she's the policewoman who's coordinating all the information about the search—we'll be the wiser."

Silently she laid the beeper in his palm and tilted her head in the direction of the bookcase at the far end of the room. A pale blue telephone stood there on a white lace doily next to an old black-and-white picture of a bride and a groom. Even in the bridal gown and despite the glamorous aura with which the photograph tried to endow her, she still looked— Michael continued to dial Tzilla—like a woman who had a hard life. It looked as though the smile had been forced on her by the photographer, and was directed at him, rather than at the skinny, delicate-featured man who stood beside her.

Chapter 12

T hey got there before the ambulance. Michael supported Esther
Hayoun to the opening of the abandoned kiosk. From the moment
they left the apartment until they reached his car, and again on Yehuda
Street, when he stopped in front of the kiosk and they both got out of the
car, she leaned on his arm with all her weight and her rapid, heavy breathing was interrupted by voiceless sighs and mutters of "God help us, God
help us." Around the small stone structure there was already a crowd of
dozens of people. A police car was parked on the narrow sidewalk and next
to it the Criminal Identification lab vehicle, and up the street was another
police vehicle and the dog handlers, heading for Hebron Road. For a
moment, Esther Hayoun stood fixed to the spot, leaning on his arm and
looking around her at the people who made way for them, until her gaze
fell on Balilty and her mutterings and sighs increased at the sound of his
orders to clear the area. He was standing on the sidewalk in front of the
kiosk, waving his hands in all directions and with his body reserving the
parking spot for the ambulance that was on its way there.

Only right in front of the green iron door did Esther Hayoun drop
Michael's arm and suddenly stand up straight. With long, rapid steps she
walked right into the dimly lit structure, snapping on her way a large
branch that hung down from the old rosebush. A lovely shower of petals
fell on the threshold before Michael followed her into the moldy rectangular space, where there were smells of vomit and mildew and urine.

The flashlight he had borrowed from the Criminal Identification man
faintly illuminated the room, into which the rays of autumn light could
not penetrate, even after they had broken the locks on the rusty green
iron shutters. In its wavering beam he picked out knots of cobwebs,
patches of mold, peeling whitewash, shreds of yellowed newspapers,

rags, a large rusty tin can and the desiccated cadaver of a cat. Esther Hayoun shoved Sergeant Yair aside and bent over the body sprawled there on its back, ignoring her son, who stood close to her and said: "She's just fainted, mother, but she's alive. She'll be all right." Michael watched her as she laid her head on the chest of the girl, who was lying there with her legs spread and her arms close to her body, her head to one side and her eyes shut. With surprising gentleness the mother ran her rough-skinned fingers over her daughter's cheek, as if to redraw the map of freckles on the grayish skin. Lines of filth ran from Nessia's closed eyes down to her mouth, the tracks of tears that indicated something of what she had endured. With wavelike, gentle movements Esther Hayoun palpated her daughter's arms and legs and caressed them. And Michael was astonished at the sight of this delicacy, the existence of which he had not imagined.

Behind him, Sergeant Yair drew Yigal Hayoun back and said sternly to Peter, who stood to his left: "You too. Don't touch. Leave this to the Criminal Identification Unit. They haven't finished checking here yet, and anyway, you mustn't touch anything." When Michael turned around he saw Peter pulling his hand back from the tangle of rope that had been thrown into a corner of the room among the spiderwebs and dried excrement.

Slowly Esther Hayoun felt the girl's swollen elbows and then leaned over and put her lips to the red cracks that had been cut there by the ropes. Kneeling, she examined the signs of the knots on her ankles, feeling the scratches and carefully touching the deep cut on the top side of the right foot, from which descended a thin thread of dried blood. And quietly, as if afraid to wake her up, she said: "Nessia, honey, Nessia, sweetie, it's Mommy, Mommy's talking to you."

Nessia did not respond, and from the entrance Yigal Hayoun called, "She can't hear you, Mother. She's unconscious," and he hastened over and knelt beside her, but her whispers had already turned to shouts.

"Nessia, Nessia," and Esther Hayoun did not stop until her eyes took in the large, damp patch on the front of the blue sweatpants. She pulled them down with a swift movement and leaned her head over and felt the crotch she had exposed. Michael heard her sigh as she looked at the palm of her hand and said, as if to herself, "There's no blood," and as if they weren't there she pulled down the underpants and spread the girl's legs and looked carefully between the thighs. After a long moment, she rose from her knees with an effort, supported by her son, stood on her feet, wobbled a moment until she steadied and with an amazement in which there was something of a relief she said: "He didn't do it to her, like he did to Zahara."

As if apologetically, the Criminal Identification man approached the girl and looked warily at Esther Hayoun, who stepped back a bit. He knelt down, carefully felt the girl's skull and lingered a bit on a big bump on her forehead, examined her swollen neck and looked at the signs that had been etched there, drew her swollen, pudgy hand toward him and with a sharp instrument scraped under the bitten nails. Then, from the leather case he had brought with him, he took out a rectangular glass slide and carefully smeared it with the tip of the instrument.

"Is the doctor on the way?" whispered the Criminal Identification man. "I need him to take some tissue for me here," he explained to Sergeant Yair, indicating the cut in her neck. He beckoned to the second Criminal Identification man, and when he approached and started taking pictures with his camera, Michael shaded his eyes, and beneath his hand he saw Esther Hayoun squeezing her eyes shut every time the flash went off.

"He's already arrived, the doctor," said Sergeant Yair. "They're parking the ambulance now," and he pushed the door wide open with his foot, preparing the way for the doctor and the laden stretcher they would be taking out of here.

"We better wait outside," said Michael to Yigal Hayoun, whose mother had frozen to the spot next to her daughter. "The doctor will examine her first here, before they take her to the ambulance," he added. And as if to confirm what he said, at that moment the doctor entered, a plump, dwarfish man who was short of breath. He patted the fair hair that was carefully brushed like a little cap covering his round skull and, still panting, he blurted: "Please leave the room."

Esther Hayoun looked at him and didn't move even when he looked directly at her. "I'm the mother," she challenged him, but he had already knelt down next to Nessia, bringing his stethoscope to her chest.

"Go outside, lady. You'll have to wait outside a minute," he ordered her impatiently, and she, as if considering whether to leave, was pulled out after her son, who tugged at her arm and supported her as they left.

Michael followed them out and stood next to Sergeant Yair and Sergeant Einat, who was rolling a rose petal between her fingers. "How he crushed the dog," she said, looking at the black plastic bag the Criminal Identification people had set down next to the fence.

"Do you want a pathological examination or should we take it straight to the lab?" one of them asked Michael from there, and he shrugged and looked questioningly at Sergeant Yair.

Yair hung his head as if scrutinizing his feet, and after a moment he looked up and said, "I think . . . ," but did not complete the sentence.

Out of nowhere, Balilty appeared as if waiting for him to hesitate, and interjected: "It's a waste of time. It's pretty clear how this dog died. He didn't poison it," said the intelligence officer. "He smashed its head in, slashed it and—"

"So straight to the lab?" asked the Criminal Identification officer impatiently, and Sergeant Yair nodded.

"Good for you, boy," said Balilty without looking at Yair, rubbing his hands together. "I didn't believe we would find her alive, and so fast, today! Had we found her in another day or two . . . Really, good for you. Did you tell him?" he asked Michael. "Did you praise him?" And without waiting for an answer he continued: "If he didn't tell you, then I'm telling you: Good for you, really. If we hadn't found her today, she wouldn't have been alive. It's certain that there's hemorrhaging inside the skull. He banged her head on the floor, the maniac. For sure there's a crack in the skull, and that's the big danger," he explained with satisfaction. "How did you get here?" he asked with a cunning but seemingly innocent look: "Probably the dog . . . because of the girl's dog, no? The dog didn't leave the place, because of that—"

"The dog barked a lot of times before then," Einat hastened to say. "It was Yair's idea. He—"

"It's because of the rose," Yair apologized, and turned to look at the door and the bush that was creeping along it. "No, not what you're thinking. I just saw that there was a broken branch here, as if someone had . . . It's all rusted, it's been shut for years, and suddenly you see a branch and you can tell someone broke it not long ago. It hasn't even dried out."

Balilty sighed and rolled his eyes. "So in the end farming does us some good, eh, Ohayon? They who sow in sorrow—," and because Michael clenched his jaw and remained silent, the intelligence officer looked at the young sergeant again and said: "There's one thing I don't understand. What were you doing looking at this bush at all? Pink like an old woman's underpants."

"Not so," said Yair assertively. "You won't find this color anywhere. It's impossible to imitate it."

"Balls," dismissed Balilty gleefully. "Believe me, this is panty pink."

Michael shaded the cigarette lighter, and for a moment, in the light of the flame that flickered on his hand, he saw the curve of Ada's thighs and the smoothness of her shoulders and her neck and her eyes. A shudder ran down his spine.

From the entrance to the kiosk emerged the two medics, bearing the stretcher to which the girl was strapped, and the door slammed behind them.

"You get into the ambulance and go with them," Michael ordered Einat, "and stay in the picture the whole time. The moment there's a medical opinion you let me know, and also the moment she wakes up you inform me."

"Don't you want me to go with her?" asked Yair.

"You stay here now," said Michael. "Until she wakes up, we still have work to do."

"*If* she does," said Balilty skeptically. "It's not at all certain that she's going to wake up so fast. And even if she does regain consciousness, do you think she's going to talk? How often have I seen that they don't remember a thing, from the shock? You can't count on it."

"I want a full medical report," said Michael to Einat. "After they bring her in, you get a copy of the intake form from them and you tell them to fax it to us, and you don't leave her alone for a minute. You're at her bedside the whole time, so that the moment she wakes up—"

He was interrupted by the doctor, who paused next to him and watched the two medics as they cleared a way for themselves through the people who had crowded around and put the stretcher into the ambulance. "Well," said the doctor, "there are both fractures in the skull and internal hemorrhaging. We still don't know how many internal injuries there are. And she's also dehydrated. I gave her an infusion of fluids."

"So she's still unconscious?" confirmed Michael.

"She won't be conscious for a while yet," said the doctor. "She won't come to so quickly. It could take days. And I don't know about her spine. We had to tie her to the stretcher, with a board underneath. It was quite a business to move her."

Yigal Hayoun supported his mother, who climbed heavily into the ambulance behind the stretcher. "I'll come with the car in a little while. I'll go get it," he called after her, and Michael saw Peter go up to him hesitantly. His long shadow looked sad and desperate.

Balilty also followed them with his eyes, but Michael was grateful that he didn't say anything and only waggled his head at them. He leaned his back against the utility pole, crossed his arms and gave a big yawn. "I'm wiped out," Balilty informed everyone around. "If I don't snooze for an hour or two, you'll also need a stretcher for me. I'm going home. Nothing's going to run away. There isn't anything big now, is there?"

"Yes, you go rest," said Michael, "and we'll get something to eat."

"Where are you going to eat?" said Balilty, suddenly waking up. "You aren't going to the Old City now, with all the mess, are you? Don't even go to Abu Ghosh now. Where are you going to eat? Have you got anything at home?"

"Give me your phone a minute," requested Michael, and Balilty handed him the mobile telephone with a challenging look.

"How do you do this?" asked Michael, looking at the phone.

"Tell me the number and I'll dial," said Balilty, with a sly gleam in his eye.

"Don't bother," insisted Michael in embarrassment he couldn't conceal. "Just tell me if I need to dial 02 first."

"If it's in Jerusalem," said Balilty nastily. "Is it in Jerusalem? Because if it's to a mobile phone, then you need the phone company's code and not an area code . . . Who ever heard of a head of an investigations division who doesn't have a mobile phone? It's against the law, and if it's not against the law, then there ought to be a law about it. A person in the twenty-first century who hasn't learned to use a mobile phone! And he even thinks this is admirable. That's what kills me," he grumbled as Michael dialed. "Hit SEND," said Balilty. "SEND, SEND, push the green." And Michael, who moved aside and turned away from them, whispered into the small phone and on his back felt Balilty's curiosity burning as he strained to catch every word.

In a whisper and briefly, he told Ada how they had found the girl alive: how they had thought of the *mikveh* on Shimshon Street and the underground cistern, how they had searched the crumbling Labor Party house, how they had gone down into all the shelters in the housing projects and how in the end they had found her in the abandoned kiosk on the corner of Mordechai Hayehudi and Yehuda.

"Kiosk?" she wondered. "Where is there a kiosk there?" and after he explained to her exactly she said only: "Never mind. The main thing is that she's okay and the main thing is that they aren't in the attic again. There's a limit to how rational a person can . . . Can you hear me?"

"I'm not alone," warned Michael. "I . . . There are people here."

"So this evening? Will you come this evening?"

"But maybe late," he said to her.

They took Balilty back to his car, which was parked on the narrow sidewalk on Yiftah Street. In front of the entrance to the apartment block Eli Bachar was waiting for them. "Good for you," he said as he slipped into the car after Balilty got out.

"It was just by chance," apologized Yair, and Balilty regarded them for another moment with a considering look, like a child whose mother's call to come home had interrupted his game.

"That's the way it is in our line of work anyway," said Eli Bachar without any bitterness.

"Listen a minute," said Yair. "There's something else . . . Before we . . . I'm also dying of hunger, but maybe before we go back, would you mind if for just a minute . . . It's just that, before, I heard the woman upstairs saying that the girl went into the shelter a lot, so maybe we ought to . . . And there's also another thing, but maybe it's nothing."

Michael took his hand off the steering wheel, pulled the hand brake and turned around to look at Yair's face.

"When I found her, when we first went in? There was a smell there . . . In addition to everything else, in addition to the stink, there was kind of a faint smell coming from her, but I can't really . . . It was something I'd already smelled, but can't remember, like a perfume or aftershave."

"Like what? Paco Rabanne, or Hugo Boss? A woman's perfume or a man's?" asked Eli Bachar.

"How should I know? No, not a woman's perfume, something kind of bitter, sharp, with a hint of lemon, something that not too long ago . . . But I can't remember. Maybe a deodorant or . . . Is there perfume for hair?"

"After she was lying there for twelve hours?" said Eli Bachar doubtfully. "Maybe it was something from the Criminal Identification people, or the people who—"

"No," insisted Yair. "It was from her skin, from her face. I bent down to see if she was breathing and I smelled it. But I don't know what it is."

"Take your time. It's one of those things you remember suddenly, even in the middle of the night," Michael reassured him. "Do you want to go into the shelter now or not?"

"We were already there, at the beginning of the search," Yair said, and looked out the window, and a moment later he opened the car door and stood next to it, looking at the other side of the street. Michael followed Yair's gaze to the carport, at the edge of which Yoram Beinisch was standing in shorts and a white T-shirt and stylish sunglasses and spraying water from a rubber hose onto the roof of the red Toyota. A large puddle spread around his bare feet and a muffled bass rhythm came from the open radio in the car.

Michael looked for another minute and got out of the car. Eli Bachar glanced at his watch and sighed.

"What?" asked Michael.

"That car was perfectly clean. I think he even washed it yesterday," Yair muttered, and shook his head in perplexity. "Is that what he does with his life? Wash his car all the time?"

"There are people like that," said Michael pensively. "Obsessive. They have to . . . Especially a brand-new car like that one."

"When the dog was in the Basharis' yard, on the other side, not under the Basharis' window, on the other side, the Beinisches' side, he went especially crazy there, next to that Judas tree over there, and I would . . . I think . . ."

Michael leaned on the car window and looked at Eli Bachar, who wiped his brow and grumbled: "Okay. I get it. I'll tell Tzilla that we've been delayed. She'll have to sit there again with that Moshe Avital, who's been waiting for two hours."

"So come on," said Michael patiently. "If you want to talk to him, let's go."

Perhaps because of the radio and the rush of the running water—Yoram Beinisch's foot was tapping in the puddle to the rhythm of the bass—he didn't notice them until they were standing very close to him. Michael cleared his throat. Yoram Beinisch turned around startled and dropped the rubber hose, and the water flowed along the concrete surface of the carport.

"Excuse me a minute," said Yair. "I just wanted to ask you something."

Yoram Beinisch looked at him and said: "Ah, it's you. What do you want? . . . You've already—"

"Maybe you should turn the water off," said Yair. "It's a pity to waste the water. And you know that you're not allowed to . . . It's against the law to use a hose to wash a car. There's quite a high fine."

"Okay, all right, all right. I'm turning it off. Jesus, you'd think that you were paying the water bill," Yoram Beinisch grumbled, and with a slight limp hurried into the covered parking space. When he returned Michael noticed a large red patch on his ankle, close to the bone. "We have a plague of pigeons," he explained. "If you park under that tree, the whole roof of the car gets covered in it. If you leave it on the roof of the car the . . . their shit, it leaves stains that don't come off. It finishes the paint job."

"Do they get into the carport? The pigeons?" inquired Yair, and Michael, who stayed back on the sidewalk, intertwined his fingers in tolerant expectation, as if he weren't really interested in what was going on.

"No, but the car was parked outside and—"

"Why was it parked outside if you have your own carport?" Yair asked with an innocent look, and leaned over the back wheel.

Yoram Beinisch removed the narrow sunglasses, and his blue eyes were revealed as he carefully examined the sergeant's face. His right eye was red, and there was a scratch under it. He set the glasses down on the roof of the car, wiped his hands on the side of his shorts once, and then again, and stuck them in his pockets.

"What are you looking for there?" he demanded, and came up close to the back wheel, but Yair had already straightened up, and he too stuck his hands in his pockets.

"Why wasn't there space?" asked Yair. "Your parents must have taken up all the space, and when you got back you couldn't get in, is that right?"

"Yes, there's barely '*space*'"—he used the English word—"for two."

"You made the carport out of garden space," noted Yair critically.

"Yes, there's still enough garden space on the sides and in back," said Yoram Beinisch, "and if you'll excuse me now"—he glanced at Michael—"I've already turned off the water, no? So you haven't got . . . Because I'm busy. So it would be better if '*you guys*'"—again, the English expression—"told me if there's something you want from me, because if not, I have to . . ." His voice faded, and his eyes darted from Yair to Michael. Neither of them said a word.

"They told me you found the girl," said Yoram Beinisch, "*alive and well*, and that nothing happened to her."

"It would be a bit of an exaggeration to say that nothing happened to her," commented Yair. "They gave her a terrible beating."

"I meant that she is alive and she'll be all right. That's what I heard them say. The woman across the way"—he nodded in the direction of the apartment block—"came to tell my mother. I heard that she's unconscious. Is that true?"

"Where were you last night?" asked Michael.

Yoram Beinisch's upper lip twitched when he replied: "What, what? What do you mean?"

"Quite simply," said Michael, his eyes resting again on the wounded ankle, "where were you last night?"

"Why are you asking?" bridled Yoram Beinisch.

"Because you came home late," said Michael calmly, as if the fact of this explanation justified the question.

"*Who says so?*" demanded Yoram Beinisch. "Who says I even went out?"

"So you didn't go out?" asked Michael. "Were you at home all evening?"

"I don't understand what business it is of yours," Yoram growled, and took the sunglasses off the roof of the car. "Do I need to account to you for anything?" With a sharp gesture, he slammed the car door.

"Excuse me a minute," the sergeant said, and walked around the car and opened the front door on the right-hand side.

Yoram Beinisch leaped forward, made a fist and pounded on the roof of the car. "What are you doing? You can't just . . . How . . . It's my private car . . ."

"That's just the thing," said Yair as he leaned over the floor of the car. "Just because this is your car." He pulled his head out and stood up straight. "And you also have to come with us now."

"What?" said Yoram Beinisch in astonishment. "What for? *What the hell* . . . What do you want from me?"

"You heard him," said Michael without looking at the sergeant. "You have to come with us for questioning. We have to ask you a few questions."

"So ask!" Yoram Beinisch raised his voice. "*Be my guest,* who's stopping you from asking? Why should I . . ." His eyes again darted from one of them to the other and finally rested on Eli Bachar, who had slammed the door of the police car on the other side of the street. "Listen," he said angrily, and it wasn't clear to which of the two of them he was speaking, "do you think that I'm some sort of illiterate who doesn't know which end is up? I don't have to go anywhere with you. What do you think I am? Some Arab you can hassle like this? I'm not going anywhere with you. *No way.*" He stuck the earpiece of his glasses into his shirt, put his hands in his shorts and glared at Michael.

"You say you didn't leave the house yesterday?" asked Michael as if he had not heard the protest.

"I went out, I didn't go out—*it's none of your business.* What business is it of yours? I have no intention of answering you about anything if you don't explain to me why. If you would have told me what it is you want, I might have volunteered to help you of my own free will. Didn't I answer him yesterday when he came to ask me about . . ." He indicated with his head the yard next door, and then Yair. "But like this?!"

"We need the Criminal Identification people here," said Sergeant Yair to Eli Bachar, who was standing at the edge of the carport. "They need to check out this car."

"What's that? What's that?" demanded Yoram Beinisch. "Can you just go ahead and search private property without a . . . Just like that?"

"You're not cooperating," explained Michael, "and there are some things we have to know."

Yoram Beinisch laid his hand on the roof of the car and leaned on the driver's door as if bodily defending his property against vandals. "What do you need to know?"

"First of all, where were you yesterday evening and last night?"

"At home. I told you, I didn't go out."

"Did anyone else take the car? Did you give it to someone, maybe a friend or a neighbor?"

"The car was parked here, all night," said Yoram Beinisch, and directed his gaze at the bit of the street before the carport. "*All night long.* It was blocking my parents' car. Under the tree, all night, and I've only just brought it in now, to wash it. The hose doesn't reach . . ."

"Did you clean it inside, too?" interrupted Sergeant Yair as his eyes quickly scanned the area of the carport. "With a vacuum cleaner?"

"'Inside'?" Yoram Beinisch repeated the word as if he did not understand what it meant. "Why should I clean inside? I told you, the pigeons crapped on the roof and I—"

Eli Bachar, who was standing behind the car, felt around with his fingers for a moment, and then the trunk opened. He looked inside. "But there's a handheld vacuum in the trunk," he said, picking up the appliance, "and it's still hot."

"So, what does that mean?" burst out Yoram Beinisch. "Why are you rummaging around without permission? So it's hot, from the sun. I don't—"

"From the sun? How?" asked Yair. "How can it be hot from the sun when there's shade here, and it isn't all that hot today? You'll excuse me a minute," he said, and took the vacuum from Eli Bachar. "We're taking this with us." And he mildly explained to Yoram Beinisch that the Criminal Identification lab would check its contents.

"You can't take anything from here that doesn't belong to you!" shouted Yoram Beinisch. *"What the hell!* What are you picking on me for? If you . . ." He shook with fury. "If you don't give that back to me right now and get out of here, I'm calling now. I'm calling a lawyer right now." He put his hands on his hips and glared at them, his stance reminiscent of that of a third-rate actor rehearsing his part in a western.

"Please," Yair said, and spread his arms out wide. "We have to talk to your parents anyway, to confirm that you didn't leave the house yesterday, so if you have no objection we'll go inside with you now, and you'll call your lawyer."

"You can't go into the house now," blurted Yoram Beinisch. "You can't just . . . Only my father's home now, and he's resting. My mother has gone out, and even when she comes back, she's not feeling so well, and we have company—my fiancée is here—and you can't just . . . You've already spoken to me," he protested to Yair. "Didn't you ask me about the whole—"

"Look," said Michael, "you're wasting everybody's time. You don't want to come with us for questioning now, so cooperate here. Do you want us to talk to you in the street or in the house? Because we're not just going to let you go. Do you understand me?"

"Okay, so come on in," agreed Yoram Beinisch after thinking it over. "It's better than going with you. And in the end, I have nothing to hide. We'll get it over with quickly and that's it. Just be quiet, because my father is resting now."

"We can start out like this and then we'll see," Sergeant Yair said, and looked at Michael.

"Go ahead in," said Michael to Yoram Beinisch. "We're coming."

For a moment he looked suspiciously at them and at the car. "Why aren't you coming in with me?"

"Tell me," said Michael, "what happened to your eye?"

"It was scratched in the garden," said Yoram Beinisch without missing a beat. "I got a branch in my eye when I was showing my fiancée the garden. You can ask her if you don't believe me," he added with a defiant smile, "only she's not here right now."

"Should I lock the car?" Eli Bachar asked Michael. "It'll take a while, won't it?"

"Lock it, lock it," Michael said, and for a moment he felt dizzy with hunger. "And you go on in," he ordered Yoram Beinisch. "What are you waiting for? All of a sudden you don't want to leave us alone?"

He followed Yoram Beinisch's slow steps. He was dragging his foot in a slight limp as he walked past the hose and turned toward the front door. "Now tell me, what's this about? What did you find?" he asked Yair.

"Here, this is the thing," the sergeant replied, and put his hand in his pocket and spread it out. In the center of his callused palm was a rose petal, which was wrinkled and brown around the edges. "And I'm sure that there are a few more of these around, or ones like them, or pieces of them, something that the Criminal Identification Unit can find," he added confidently.

"Tell me, are you sure that going by one petal it's possible . . . possible to identify a whole bush?" Michael said doubtfully, and looked at Yair's palm.

"No," said Yair. "The truth is that's it's not one hundred percent." From his other pocket he drew out a flower, and he put the petal beside it. "You see? It looks the same, but I picked the flower today and the petal . . . Maybe it's been there since yesterday . . . It's no longer exactly the same shade," he said sorrowfully, "not enough to prove anything. Maybe the Criminal Identification Unit or a big expert could. I'm not a big expert on roses at all, but first of all—the color, it's a rare variety these days. They don't have roses like this here in the garden. I've been in this garden here already. They have simple modern roses. He told me, that Australian, Peter, that Baka is a neighborhood of roses, but that's irrelevant, and there's no rose like this here. And this petal isn't from a week ago, I told you. It's at most from yesterday night, and the color we'll have to check, but there's nothing like it." He looked down and shuffled his toe before he said in a whisper: "I myself have seen you use less than this to get someone to loosen his tongue."

"You mean to say that you really do want to call in the Criminal Identification Unit?" asked Eli Bachar, who was standing behind them. "I thought it was a trick."

"No, it's not a trick. I want them to check the contents of the vacuum cleaner and the inside of this car, because I'm ready to bet that he—"

The door of the house opened. Yoram Beinisch stood there sticking his arm into the long sleeve of a blue shirt. He did up the buttons slowly, folded the sleeves back to under his elbows and patted his cheeks. He had changed from shorts into long pants.

"So we'll bring in the Criminal Identification vehicle," summed up Eli Bachar.

"How are you going to bring it?" whispered Michael. "Without his agreement we can only do it with a court order and we don't have time now to—"

"You two go ahead inside," said Eli Bachar, "and I'll see to all the rest."

"And then afterward it won't be acceptable in court," said Michael, "so what will we have gained?"

"How did our friend from intelligence put it? You want it to be acceptable in court? No problem, I'll make it acceptable for you," promised Eli Bachar, and his greenish face gleamed with evident relish. "You go inside and leave this to me, okay?"

"Hold on, wait a minute," said Michael. "If you're already going back to the office, do me a favor and get started with Moshe Avital. He's been waiting for me since six in the morning and I can't see how—"

"No problem," Eli replied, and smiled broadly. "Anything else? I wouldn't want you remembering after I've already left."

Yoram Beinisch moved aside a little when they entered the house and continued to watch Eli Bachar, who was still standing next to the Toyota. Perhaps for this reason he didn't notice that the sergeant's nostrils flared as he entered the house. Yair paused for a moment and sniffed the air, and then he signaled to Michael with his eyes and said, "That's it. That's the smell," and Michael inhaled deeply the faint lemony bitterness mixed with musk.

Yoram Beinisch shut the door and walked in front of them into the living room. With his hand he indicated the white leather sofa, and both of them sat down on it across from him as he sank down into the leather love seat. He moved aside a tall, spiky vase and rearranged the carnations that were threatening to fall out. He coolly put his feet up on the thick green glass coffee table. The leather shoes he was wearing looked new, and it looked to Michael as though the left sole was thicker than the right. And while Yair was looking around and gazing in astonishment at the large oil painting on the wall, nothing but one red streak on a white background, and beyond it the huge television set, Michael tried to tell whether the wounded ankle had been bandaged. There was no ashtray visible in the chilly, pale and polished room, and Michael wove his fingers together and in a low voice asked Yoram Beinisch what happened to his ankle. Yair looked at it, as Yoram hastened to remove his feet from the plate glass.

"Nothing," he said with seeming innocence. "Maybe I got a knock from the sprinkler or the fence. It's nothing."

"It looks like something serious to me," said Michael, "and I noticed that you're really limping. Apparently it hurts."

His eyes never left Yoram Beinisch, who looked away and moved aside two colorful volumes of a journal in German and a ball of knitting with needles stuck in it. "Show me a minute," said Michael in a friendly way that did not allow for refusal. "Show me that injury a minute. I know something about these things, and maybe a doctor needs to see you."

"No, what for?" protested Yoram Beinisch. "It's nothing, really . . . I didn't even feel—"

"Show me, show me," urged Michael, and he had already risen from the leather sofa and moved over to where Yoram Beinisch was wriggling uncomfortably in the matching leather love seat. "Allow me. I don't want to hurt you," said Michael. "Could you take your sock off for a minute?"

Yoram Beinisch looked at him helplessly. Michael knew very well that the affable tone he was using and his frank interest in the welfare of the person he was talking to made it impossible to refuse. Yoram Beinisch rolled down the sweat sock, and then Yair got up and came over to them.

"This, it looks like . . . Did someone bite you?" asked Yair with an assumed naiveté. "There are tooth marks here. You haven't got a dog, have you?"

"It's nothing," Yoram Beinisch said quickly, and hurried to cover up his foot again. "It hardly hurts anymore. It's been a few days now."

"How many days?" inquired Michael, who was still standing by the leather love seat as Yair regarded a large black-and-white photograph hanging over the television set. Inside the thin, gilded frame was a little boy, with his front teeth missing and his expression very solemn, clasping a medal in both his hands. "Is this you?" Yair asked, and moved closer to the picture.

"Yes, at the age of six," said Yoram Beinisch. He seemed relieved that he didn't have to answer Michael's questions for the moment. "I won a medal in an arithmetic competition, first place among three schools," he explained with a smile. "They thought I was . . . that I had a talent for math, my parents . . ." He waved lazily at the picture. "They like to reminisce," he said, and grinned, revealing small, white front teeth.

"How many days ago?" Michael repeated the question with demonstrable politeness.

"I can't remember exactly. Two or three," replied Yoram Beinisch.

"How come," wondered Yair without taking his eyes off the picture, "when I spoke to you yesterday or the day before—when was it?—there was nothing wrong with your foot, and you weren't limping?"

Yoram Beinisch looked as though he had lost his confidence and was angry at himself for having fallen into a trap. "So I don't remember," he said crossly. "I told you—it's nothing. Yesterday and the day before it didn't hurt."

"Excuse me," said Yair, "but there seem to be tooth marks there, and that's not nothing and a doctor should see it because you might need a tetanus shot."

"Or even a rabies shot," added Michael in a tone of fatherly concern.

"Where's the third one? Your colleague?" asked Yoram Beinisch with obvious irritation. "How long does it take him to lock your car?"

"This girl, Nessia," said Michael from behind the love seat, "did you know her?"

"The little girl?" wondered Yoram Beinisch. "No, why should I? I've just seen her around. She was out in the street all the time, with her dog . . ."

"Have you ever spoken to her?" asked Michael.

"No, never," said Yoram Beinisch with slight disgust, and he angrily added: "But maybe you'll go ahead and tell me what you're looking for. There wasn't a moment's quiet here all day and my mother, she has . . . She isn't feeling so well. First the police and then that journalist that didn't give us—"

"What journalist?" demanded Michael sharply.

"I can't remember her name," said Yoram Beinisch, and his eyes turned to the door to the room. "That girl . . . Not very impressive . . . Not one you'd remember, wearing jeans and a big shirt, with curls, like . . ." He touched his yellow hair, which was darkened by dampness.

"Orly Shushan," said Yair.

"Could be." Yoram Beinisch grimaced. "I think that's what she's called."

"Zahara Bashari's best friend," noted Yair.

"What do I know?" muttered Yoram Beinisch. "She drove us crazy."

"What did she want to know?" asked Michael.

"Whether I knew . . ." With his head he gestured toward the outside wall of the living room and the house it concealed, as if he didn't want to mention Zahara's name.

"Whether you knew Zahara Bashari?" asked Michael.

Yoram Beinisch nodded.

"And did you know her?" Michael asked, and crossed his arms.

"I already told *him,*" said Yoram Beinisch, nodding at Yair. "She wanted to know whether we played together when we were little, and whether I noticed how beautiful she was, and how come a fellow like me and a girl like her didn't—"

"I asked you something," interrupted Michael.

Yoram Beinisch sighed irately. "I already told *him.* *Yesterday* I told him. Don't you two speak to each other? I never spoke a word to her. Her mother and my mother . . . Our parents . . ." He tapped the sides of his trousers as if he had nothing more to say.

"But when you were little you played together," Yair stated, and turned and sat down at the edge of the sofa, near the love seat.

Yoram Beinisch paled. "I don't remember anything like that," he said in a shaky voice. "My mother would have killed me. I don't think I even . . . I was bigger than her. I wasn't interested in babies."

From the hall came the sound of heavy footsteps, and after a moment Yoram Beinisch's father stood at the entrance to the living room, smoothing thin strands of whitish-red hair over his skull. "Who? Who played together?" he asked, and felt his cheek as if smoothing out wrinkles after deep sleep.

"Nothing. It's nothing, Daddy," said his son dismissively.

"Are you from the police?" Efraim Beinisch asked Michael. "Wasn't it you I spoke to on the day they found Zahara Bashari?"

"Yes," confirmed Michael, "and you told me that Yoram hadn't left the house last Monday, in the evening. You said he was home by six and didn't go out."

"Right. That's the way it was," said Efraim Beinisch. "So what is it now?"

"It's because of the little girl," explained his son.

"As a matter of fact, what's happened to her?" inquired Efraim Beinisch.

"They found her. She's alive," said Yoram Beinisch quickly.

"Thank God," said the father. "Really, these children, until they grow up you could lose your mind. What happened? Did she run away from home?"

Yair looked at him in surprise. "Run away from home? Someone kidnapped her and beat her nearly to death."

"What are you saying?!" said Efraim Beinisch in alarm. "Who kidnapped her? You don't know?" He clicked his tongue. "They don't let you live in peace and quiet here. But how can we help you now?"

"We have a few questions for your son," said Michael pleasantly. "We've found the girl, but she's unconscious. She can't tell us anything."

Efraim Beinisch's face clouded. "We can't help you," he said hesitantly, and looked at his son. "We've been busy. My son's fiancée arrived here from the United States a few days ago, and she's not just some . . ." Again he looked at his son, and this time his glance was wary. "She's a very special girl, a princess. Isn't she, Yoram?"

"Let them be, Daddy. It doesn't interest them," said his son impatiently. "Aren't you making yourself some coffee?"

Michael looked hard at the face of the father, whose smile faded, and for a moment it seemed as though he was looking at his son fearfully. Then he said: "Yes. Yes, can I make some for you?"

"No thanks," said Yoram Beinisch. "We've already had."

"And the journalist, she didn't ask about the little girl, about Nessia?" asked Michael, and Efraim Beinisch, who was still within earshot, stopped near the doorway and paused there a moment before he moved off and left the room.

"About the little girl? Sure she asked about the girl, but what could I tell her? I don't know that little girl. I don't know anyone here. We're not . . . Our family isn't . . . We don't have relations with . . ." His hand described an arc that indicated the street.

For a moment Michael was sorry that Balilty had left. "We know for certain that you knew Zahara Bashari quite well," he said suddenly, adopting one of Balilty's traps for his own use.

"That's not true," protested Yoram Beinisch loudly, and as if he had scared himself he immediately dropped his voice to a whisper. "I'm telling you, our parents aren't on speaking . . . I've never spoken to her in my life . . . My mother, if I would even speak to"—again his arm indicated the other side of the wall—"anyone from that family, and especially their daughter, she would simply have killed me." He looked at Yair and said: "It's not that I'm afraid of my mother, but I don't want to break her heart. I'm her only child, and that family has ruined her life."

"There are kids who are, hmmm, curious, and if they get hold of someone or something, they won't let go," said Michael as if musing to himself.

"What are you talking about?" asked Yoram Beinisch, and he stuck his fingers into the space between the cushions on the love seat.

"That little girl, Nessia. It could be said that she was a nosy child, a little spy, right?" said Michael in a tone of casual complicity.

"*How should I know?*" protested Yoram Beinisch.

"You've lived in the United States," said Michael.

"Half a year, in New York, when I was sent there by the company," Yoram Beinisch explained in the tone of one who knows his own worth, and brought his hand back to his side. "I'm in high-tech, and my fiancée . . . my girlfriend, she's also from New York. She arrived here a few days ago. We're getting married in December. She's also in high-tech, that's how we met, but she doesn't really need to work because her family—" The front door slammed and he stopped talking and stood up with a start. "Is that your colleague?" he asked, annoyed, but it was his mother who stood in the doorway. Dressed in a pale, straight skirt and a greenish silk blouse, she stood there, a thin jacket draped over her shoulders and her hair gathered in a bun, and even though her neck was bare she fingered an invisible string of beads around it.

"What's this, Yoram?" she asked in alarm. "Are you home? Because your car isn't . . . I thought you'd gone out."

"The car isn't in the carport?" he asked in a panic. He ran to the front door and rushed outside and after a moment came back. "The car isn't there!" he shouted, and looked at Michael accusingly.

"Maybe you forgot to lock it?" suggested Sergeant Yair kindly, and Michael saw how Clara Beinisch's eyes, blue like her son's, were examining the two of them, and how her hand was climbing from her neck to the mole beside her small nose. In suspicious alarm, she looked at Michael's face.

"Where's my car?" demanded Yoram Beinisch loudly and squeakily.

"I told you," explained Yair pleasantly. He turned to Clara Beinisch and said to her: "He came inside with us a little while ago and forgot to lock it."

"They've taken it. They've taken my car. The police have stolen my car!" complained Yoram Beinisch to his mother, his face red.

The pretty, severe face of Clara Beinisch changed its expression from alarm to anger. "It's been two days that you haven't been giving us a moment's rest," she protested. "You come and go, make a mess here, and now you're taking Yoram's car away? It's a brand-new car. He got it from his job . . ."

"They'll find it, for sure," consoled Yair, "and if not, there's the insurance or—"

"Insurance?!" screamed Yoram Beinisch. "You've stolen my car—it's obvious!"

"Mrs. Beinisch," said Michael patiently, "perhaps you'll tell me where your son was last night?"

Clara Beinisch ran her hand over her big bun of hair, felt her neck and looked at her son. "Why don't you ask him yourselves?" she wondered. "Why should you ask me? Here he is. Ask him."

Her son opened his mouth to say something, but Sergeant Yair's hand was already moving toward him quickly and grasped his arm: "You keep quiet now, you hear?"

"What's going on here? How can you talk that way?" said Clara Beinisch in astonishment. "He was at home."

"All evening?"

"All evening. Of course all evening," she said, and her voice rose too. "What kind of . . . We were tired from the trip. In the morning we took Michelle to her relatives at the kibbutz and in the evening we watched television, his father and I and him, and then we went to sleep."

"Michelle is the fiancée?"

"Yoram and Michelle are getting married in December," said Clara Beinisch proudly. "The wedding will be in New York."

"When did you go to bed?" Michael asked, and saw how Yoram Beinisch's eyes narrowed.

"I don't see why you . . . At about ten," and Clara Beinisch's Hungarian accent became more pronounced the more she spoke. "We always eat early and go to bed early. There wasn't anything to watch on television, nothing," she said. "There are a million channels and nothing to see. I also wasn't feeling so well."

"Did Yoram also go to bed at ten?" inquired Michael.

"Yoram's a big boy," his mother said, and looked warily at her son. "You don't tell a man of twenty-three when to go to bed. Maybe he stayed up to watch a video or something."

"But he didn't leave the house," affirmed Michael.

"He didn't go out," promised the mother.

"Mrs. Beinisch," said Michael, indicating the armchair, "perhaps you'll sit down a minute." He waited until she straightened the hem of her narrow skirt and arranged her light jacket on the back of the armchair and sat down, her legs angled to one side. "Do you sleep well at night?" he asked.

She looked at her son as if considering what to say, but his face was frozen and his fists clenched.

"Not all that well," she finally said. "I haven't been feeling so well . . ."

"So you take sleeping pills?"

"Not every day," she said cautiously. "Only sometimes—once every two days, one pill." She fingered her neck, and suddenly she added in alarm, "But with a doctor. A doctor gives it to me. A very good pill, Bondormine. You sleep well and also when you wake up . . . it has no side effects."

"And your husband?"

"He too. He also doesn't sleep well, so it's been several years now that we . . . Two or three times a week, not every night . . . We also had a few problems at work. My husband's an accountant," she explained importantly, "and I work for him as his secretary, so . . . we work together."

"So then," said Michael comfortably, "if Yoram goes out after you've gone to sleep with a pill, he could leave the house and you wouldn't even know?"

"Yes, maybe," hesitated Clara Beinisch, and she hastened to add: "But then he tells us in the morning. Yoram tells us everyth—and he's also very tired. High-tech is twelve, fourteen hours a day, all week long. They give benefits but—" Suddenly she went silent. "Why are you asking me all these things?" she rebelled. "What has he done, Yoram? Yoram is a wonderful boy, he never—"

"Mrs. Beinisch," said Michael, "look at this please," and in a single motion he went up to her son and raised his foot and peeled off the sock. "Come and look at this ankle close up."

She got up slowly, approached her son, leaned over and examined the ankle. "What's this, Yoram? What's happened to your foot here?" she asked in alarm, and laid her hand on the bruised spot. Yoram Beinisch shrank back, but controlled himself quickly.

"It's nothing," he said. "It's from a few days ago and it's already—"

"A few days ago?!" said his mother in astonishment. "Yesterday there was nothing wrong there. I didn't see a thing." She turned toward Michael. "I see everything about my son, even if he wants to hide something so I shouldn't worry, but right away I see," she explained with a half-smile. "And I didn't see that, and as a matter of fact I had a good look at his feet yesterday because—"

"Enough, Mother. Stop it," said her son quietly. "You don't realize what they're doing. They've taken my car away and we need a lawyer."

"A lawyer?" she said in alarm. "Why a lawyer? What have you done?"

"I haven't done anything," said her son in despair, "but they're saying I have."

"What?" Clara Beinisch stood up. "What?" Her eyes slashed Michael. "What do you want from him?"

"We have reason to think that he is connected to the disappearance of Nessia Hayoun," replied Michael calmly.

"Nessia Hayoun is that fat little girl who disappeared, from the building across the street," said her son.

Clara Beinisch let out a scornful snort. "You must be out of your . . . mistaken. What does my son have to do with the little girl from across the street?" she asked Michael. "We don't have anything to do with anybody. We don't even know the neighbors here on the street. What does he have to do with this girl?"

"They found her," said her son, "this afternoon, near Yehuda Street."

"And she's alive?" asked his mother.

"Alive. Completely alive," said Sergeant Yair, "and the indications that we have are that your son—"

"Nonsense!" dismissed Clara Beinisch, and she added in a scolding tone: "Can't you hear what I'm saying? My son, Yoram, would never hurt a fly, even when he was little. Baby birds, a little kitten—he brought everything home, and once when he had a rabbit and the rabbit died, do you know how much he cried? Our son is an angel, everyone knows that. Do you know what job offers he's received? They're always making him offers from other places. Everyone just wants to have him. Do you know how much Michelle's parents love him? And they aren't just anybody, they're a family with very high status. Her mother's family goes back to the American Revolution, they came from England, and her father is also three generations in America. It's a family with status and everything, and how they love Yoram! You're talking nonsense. Just nonsense."

"Perhaps after tests, if he comes with us, it will turn out to be nonsense," agreed Michael.

"What tests?" she asked suspiciously, and clasped her hand to her neck.

"Various procedures," replied Michael.

"I'm not going to the police," said Yoram Beinisch. "And you have no right to take me against my will. Only a judge can—"

"What judge, Yoram?" said his mother in alarm. "There's no need for a judge. You haven't done anything."

"We won't take you if you don't agree," said Michael, looking at him with hard eyes. "We will take you with us with your full agreement, and any lawyer you consult will tell you that it is better to—"

"But why?" pleaded Clara Beinisch. "Explain to me what he has done. I'm telling you that he hasn't—"

"That bite on his ankle from last night is enough, isn't it?" said Yair. "It could be from the little girl's dog. Whoever kidnapped the girl slaughtered her dog."

Clara Beinisch trembled. "This is nonsense you're talking," she repeated tremulously, "but I don't understand about these things. Let his father come in. He understands these things, because of his clients. I've already heard that the income tax people can . . . Where's Daddy, Yoram? Still sleeping?"

"We're talking here about kidnapping and attempted murder, and not income tax," said Michael.

"What murder?" demanded Clara Beinisch in astonishment. "You said that this girl is alive, no?"

"The murder of Zahara Bashari, the daughter of your neighbors on the other side," explained Sergeant Yair.

In the doorway of the living room stood Efraim Beinisch, a cup of coffee in his hand. "What's going on here?" he asked, and set the cup down on a shelf near the entrance to the room. "What's going on, Clara?"

"But you've already spoken to us about that," said Clara Beinisch without looking at her husband. "I told you yesterday already: I don't wish a disaster like that even on my worst enemy, not even that family, but I have nothing to say about those people. They're simply primitive, Asiatics. And all these years"—her voice broke now—"all these years I've hoped that they would understand and would . . . And my son, Yoram, I can say this to his face, even as a child he was as good as . . . Really, so good, and he tried to patch things up and he asked . . ." She lowered her head. "I told him then and I'm telling you now: You can't change people. They don't change. And it's not by chance that with them in particular, there in particular—"

"Just a minute, Mrs. Beinisch. I want to understand," said Sergeant Yair. "What are you saying? Are you saying that the whole family . . . that the neighbors themselves are to blame for Zahara Bashari's murder? Is that what you're saying?"

"Clara, Clara, calm down," her husband said, and moved close to her. "She's not very well," he explained to Michael with a worried look.

"I'll tell you what I'm saying," said Clara Beinisch. She shook her husband's hand off her arm and sat down. "You're a young fellow, and maybe you don't understand these things yet, but there are families in which it's impossible that things . . . in which . . . It isn't in every family that someone gets murdered . . . But in our neighborhood, on our street . . . not all the families . . . Sometimes there are . . . It's a matter of blood . . . There's good blood and bad blood . . . and the blacks . . ."

"Mother," her son warned, and looked warily at Michael, "I've told you a thousand times not to talk like that."

"Don't you tell me. They understand what I'm saying." A crease appeared between her plucked eyebrows. "Here in this country there are a lot of Asiatics and they—how can I put it?—they're people who . . ." Her gaze moved from Michael's face to Yair. "Where are your parents from?"

The sergeant smiled and said they were born in this country. "Third generation, from Metulla and Rosh Pina," he said proudly.

"Never mind." Clara Beinisch sighed and shook her head. "You're too young to understand. Because in this street there a lot of Levantines—"

"Mother!" interrupted her son warningly.

"So what should I say? People from the eastern communities? Okay, so because of the people from the eastern communities, the level of this neighborhood and the street and . . . this whole country . . . You listen to what I'm saying to you. It's not the standard we thought . . . we were used to . . ."

Michael regarded her with interest. After a moment of silence he said: "Without any connection to good blood and bad blood, Mrs. Beinisch, we will have to summon Yoram in for questioning, as well as you and your husband. This can be done with a lawyer or without one. Which do you prefer?"

Clara Beinisch looked at her son and at her husband. "We will wait until we speak to a lawyer," she said finally, and laid her hand on her son's arm. "We have a cousin who's a lawyer, and he understands about these things. You can wait or you can go. You won't take a boy from a good home in for questioning by force. We aren't people like that . . ."

"Can you phone him now?" asked Michael.

"Of course we can," she declared. "He's family, isn't he?"

"So is it possible to phone him and ask him to come here?"

"It's possible," she said and got up and headed for the corridor.

"No, Mrs. Beinisch," said Michael, "you won't have any private conversations with him now. Just tell him to come here."

"But the phone is out there," she said angrily and suspiciously, and pointed to the corridor. "There's one in the hall and there's one in the kitchen."

"So if you don't mind . . ." Michael said, and got up and followed her out, and behind him came Efraim Beinisch.

Chapter 13

I want to tell you a little story," said Emmanuel Shorer, holding the narrow glass in front of his face and trying to catch the waiter's eye. "Whenever you don't need anything they're all over you and asking if everything's okay, and when you do need something—it's just then that they don't see you," he said with a laugh, and beckoned. The proprietor, who looked at them from behind the counter, hastened over to them.

"More grappa?" he asked, and Shorer nodded yes. "And the lady, too?" asked the proprietor. His thick beard jiggled as he spoke.

"Just coffee for me," replied Ada with a smile.

"For me, too," Michael said, and rubbed the back of his neck, which had been bothering him for the past few hours.

"Look at this place," said Shorer, gazing at this surroundings. "Twelve o'clock at night and it's completely dead. Two months ago you'd come in here after midnight and there wouldn't be a place to sit. Never mind *two* months ago, a month ago even. They won't last much longer with this intifada."

"The city's completely dead," agreed Ada. "It's never happened to me before that I got here at ten o'clock, and during the intermediate days of the holiday, and there was room. And by the window yet."

"You have to know that Emmanuel Shorer has connections," said Michael, "and there's not a restaurant in Jerusalem that doesn't—"

"I got here before him," said Ada. "Imagine, I got a table by the window without connections and without anything." Her smile somewhat blurred the tension he had seen in her eyes when he arrived at the restaurant an hour late and found Shorer sitting across from her, plunging a knife into a huge steak and looking at Ada as if expecting her to answer a question he had asked. He beckoned to Michael, who stood in the doorway looking at the two of them, but Ada had not yet noticed him, and her lips trembled in the attempt to answer Shorer's question. But from where he was standing, Michael had already discerned a film of disappointment on his close friend's face and understood that his appearance had truncated a kind of test that Shorer had been giving Ada. Michael had no doubt that she was glad to see him when she turned toward him, and even though she said lightly, "There's nothing left that your friend doesn't know about me—had you come half an hour later we would have gotten to age three," her voice sounded a bit tense. Now, when they were on dessert, he thought that she was more relaxed than she had been, and she even looked at Shorer from time to time with a smile, but her look was guarded, as if before an invasion.

"There are places that I don't care if they shut down, like those restaurants in Baka and the German Colony, glatt kosher or vegetarian for American tourists with yarmulkes," grumbled Shorer, "but this place . . . I feel bad about it. I also feel bad about . . . Do you remember Meir's restaurant in the building with the curse on it in the market?"

"Closed," Michael said, and pushed his plate aside, wondering how it had emptied so quickly. "Two years ago."

"Too bad," said Shorer. "Meir also knew what to do with a piece of meat. When we were young," he explained to Ada, "a few years ago, we would sit there after we'd solved something, but now we don't deserve it, because from what I'm hearing we haven't exactly solved anything, hah?" And at the sight of Michael's expression he hastened to say: "But you've made progress, you've made good progress. You've got three suspects now, and every one of them is a story in and of itself. You never know from where salvation will come. That's really something, that story with Avital, really something. Maybe total bluff, hah?" The last question was directed to Ada.

"Are you asking me?" She blushed. "I . . . I don't have any problem with a story like that. I definitely believe that a young girl would tell intimate things like that to an older man who gives her . . . who gives her sympathy, just because he's a stranger."

"No," corrected Shorer, "it's not because of the sympathy and the strangeness. It's first of all because he saw her. You might say he caught her red-handed."

"If you see a girl in the lobby of a hotel in Netanya does that mean you've 'caught her red-handed'?" insisted Ada.

"Apparently Zahara Bashari didn't have a criminal mind," said Shorer with a smile. "There are people who . . . automatically have a guilty conscience. She thought that anyone who knows her and recognizes her in a hotel in Netanya would immediately know what she was doing there, and with whom."

"If that's the case," argued Ada, "then why did she sit there in the lobby and tell him? After all, she wasn't alone."

"Ask *him*," Shorer said, and looked at Michael. "Why did she tell him there in the hotel lobby?"

Michael shrugged. He and Eli Bachar had already dissected that today, and they would dissect it again tomorrow. "According to him, she *was* in fact there alone. The person who was supposed to have come hadn't arrived and she . . . She already had a room there at the hotel, so she told him. He says. She didn't talk about herself at all, but supposedly about a good friend of hers, and she was very vague about the man's status. According to Avital, he wasn't exactly married, the man, but he had all kinds of commitments, and he didn't know anything about the pregnancy. Don't forget, all that we have is Avital's story, and insofar as we know now, he was the last person to have met Zahara on the day of the murder."

"But he has an alibi for the cardinal hours," noted Shorer. "Maybe you don't *like* his alibi much, but he has one."

"What was it Balilty said? That he should have the same number of years left to live as the number of alibis like that he's heard," said Michael. "Men who refuse to give details in order to protect a woman's reputation? We must have had at least a hundred. Going by that, you'd think that everyone, all the time, is just having some *affair* with a married woman."

"But in the end he did give you the details," Shorer said, and drank down the last drop of grappa. "And the lady confirmed it. And he's prepared—and I see this as the main thing—to take a DNA test without any lawyers or anything. And despite all this, you're turning up your nose, as if the matter weren't closed. You said that he's a sympathetic person?"

"A real charmer, almost a professional. One of those people who know how to talk to anyone in the world. Women are crazy about him," agreed Michael.

Shorer smiled and muttered under his thick mustache: *"It takes one to know one."*

Michael ignored the remark. "And he doesn't have an easy life, either, with that daughter of his, but never mind that. You wanted to tell me a little story," he reminded Shorer.

"No, not just you. Both of you," corrected Shorer. "It has to do with the case, but it's . . . She can also do something with it. Maybe you'll even make a documentary film about the Yemenite children?"

"I'm not sure that the Dutch are going to be interested in that," said Ada to Shorer in an intimate tone, and for a moment her voice sounded as though they had known each other for years. He tried to recall if he had ever seen Shorer acting so affectionately with other women he had introduced to him, but just then the proprietor put a thin-necked bottle of grappa on the table, and with it three glasses.

"I only asked for one," said Shorer in surprise.

"After you taste it, you'll want more, and they will too," promised the proprietor. "We'll discuss it after you taste it."

"Do you come here a lot?" asked Ada, and Shorer shrugged abashedly.

"Sometimes, when there's something to celebrate." He regarded Michael with satisfaction and poured from the bottle into the three glasses. "And we will now drink to your beautiful choice." Michael obediently raised the glass and said nothing.

"He's blushing," Shorer said, laughing. "Look at him—he's blushing!" he cried, and knocked with his glass on the table before he drank. "Extraordinary," he confirmed. "This proprietor, I knew we could count on him, no?"

Michael drank and nodded his head in confirmation. A young waitress with an exposed waist and red eyelids set the coffee cups on the table, and before Shorer could take another sip Michael reminded him: "You promised a story."

The waitress left and Shorer, who gazed for another moment after her exposed, receding waist, began to speak: "When I was about seven years old . . . Let me think a minute . . . Seven or eight, I think . . . It was in '49, so I was seven," he said wonderingly. He looked at Ada and said: "I'm already quite an old Jew, not like you two."

"Really antique," she murmured.

"Don't laugh," he said to her, and pulled the ends of his white mustache. "We're from different generations, he and I"—he indicated Michael with his glass—"and that's why he has respect for me, right?"

Michael smiled and nodded with exaggerated obedience. "Yes, sir," he murmured, and asked himself whether he could dare to define the easy sense of serenity he had been feeling for this whole past hour—especially from the moment he had come in and seen the two of them deep in lively conversation, and heard Ada laugh—as happiness.

"In any case, I was apparently seven years old. I remember it as if it were today. We were already living in Jerusalem, in a house near the Mandelbaum Gate, a small house, just two rooms, but below it there was a . . . kind of a one-room apartment. Not a basement, a semibasement, with windows right above the ground, and my mother didn't want to rent it out. There were always new immigrants who had just arrived then, so she'd let them live there for a while until they got fixed up. At that time there were already all kinds of Holocaust refugees in the country, every one of them with a story no one wanted to hear. I can remember them. Some of them lived downstairs. First there was this young fellow, alone, I think he was from Sudan. He had very dark skin and he would bring me transparent marbles from the printing press where he worked. He was a print worker and his fingernails were always black . . . And then a family lived there with a fat little girl, about my age, but she didn't speak to me, the girl, and to this day I don't know why. And finally, in '49, a couple came. And about them I remember that my mother told me they came from 'there'—that's how they spoke in those days. They didn't say 'refugees' or 'Holocaust,'" he explained to Ada, who was looking at him hypnotized, as though she was hearing something completely new. "In any case, I remember how she told me, my mother, to behave nicely with them and not to play near the apartment downstairs. And I liked to play right under the stairs, and not just me, all the kids in the neighborhood . . . Then there were really neighborhoods, with children who played together, and not like now when I see how my daughter drives her little boy to his friends' houses and to after-school classes like in America . . ."

He emptied the glass in a single gulp and poured himself another, looking at them questioningly. Michael covered the glass in front of him with his hand and Ada shook her head. "I remember I was afraid of them," Shorer said, and examined the bottle. "They were . . . like rabbits . . . All the time they would look at you like who knew what you were going to do to them. Apparently they were quite a young couple, but they looked old to me, very old and also . . . they were so pale and white, as if they'd been dipped in flour. . . In those days they didn't tell us things much. They never said anything explicit—you know how it is. . . . But there were words in the air: Auschwitz, Buchenwald, ghetto, 'Hitler may his name be eradicated' and then they'd spit, 'there,' bunker, Mengele. Mengele was the scariest name, because after you heard them say 'They were with Mengele,' there would be a silence. And sometimes when they said 'Mengele' I would hear my mother sigh. Groan, really. We, the children, would spy on our parents, listen to them talk without them knowing, so as to understand something, to put together some story, and something would remain of it—after all, with the help of their imagination children fill in the missing details. 'There' was a kind of place, a different place."

He smiled a sad and pensive smile. "And I would hear my mother saying about them, that couple, how awful it was that they were so sad and lonely, and my father would say that eventually they'd have children and a family. He was always optimistic, except during his last years, and my mother would say to him, 'Not a chance. What are you talking about? She was with Mengele. She doesn't have anything inside.' To this day I remember those words: 'She doesn't have anything inside.' I had nightmares because of them. I thought . . . I imagined that she had nothing under her skin, not that I knew what there was supposed to be there in the belly . . ." Shorer paused and looked at his glass and tilted it and then swirled it.

"That's really how it is. That's the way children's imaginations work," said Ada to break the silence, and Shorer set the glass down and nodded.

"Okay, *nu*, give me a cigarette," he said to Michael. "Just one, after the meal . . . ," he apologized, and leaned over the lighter. "At least not like you, one after the other," he grumbled. "Don't you have any influence on him?" Ada smiled and fingered the lapel of her blouse as if to rub out an invisible stain.

"In any case they didn't have children. They lived downstairs for a long time. I was in first or second grade and they were still in the apartment downstairs, and from time to time there were arguments between my mother and her sister. She wanted her to take rent from them, but my mother would on no account agree. Every time she would say to my aunt, 'Kindness to living things. It's out of the question.' And one day . . . One day a child appeared there. I remember that I came home from school, and there was a little boy there, a baby, but he could already walk and talk a little. A skinny baby with big blue eyes, and a kind of crest, like a rooster, a sort of blond curl in front. Legs like matchsticks, I remember. And I asked my mother whether he was their baby and she said, 'They're taking care of him for a while, until he can go back home.' You were just born then," he said, looking at Ada, "or in any case, he was just born but wasn't in this country yet and you, too, if I know my arithmetic."

"She's younger," said Michael. "She was born in 1950."

"Really a baby, then," Shorer said, laughing. "So you don't know, but in the winter of 1950 there were terrible floods in Tel Aviv and the north. Everything was flooded, and the immigrant transit camps were also flooded, and they had to evacuate them. Jerusalem wasn't under siege anymore, but there was the austerity regime and rationing, and it was impossible to get any normal food—that is, if you didn't go to the black market. And because of the flooding, they sent the children from the immigrant camps away. They evacuated all the families from there and some of the children were separated from their parents. Places had to be found for them. They sent them to all kinds of foster homes to take care of them in the meantime and this little boy, this baby, and to this day I don't know how or why, Moishele he was called, ended up with this couple. Damned if I know what their name was. I've forgotten completely and there's no one left to ask . . . She was a good woman, my mother, there's no doubt about that. I remember she would bring them the eggs that her sister would get for us, everything half and half, half for us and half for them. They took care of the child. We heard laughter from inside that apartment downstairs, and we didn't have to be so quiet anymore and we could play hide-and-seek again around the house with the children from the neighborhood the way we could before they came. The woman would smile at me, and I remember how she would hold that baby. It was like . . . like everything had come right.

"But then, before Purim—I remember that it was before Purim because my mother was sitting at the sewing machine making a pirate costume for me. Back then Purim was a big deal and they didn't buy ready-made Purim costumes but made them from scratch. There was a competition at school, with prizes for the best costumes. Never mind— even you can remember things like that. And my father came in, pale and shaking, and looked at me for a moment, and sent me out to fetch something, I don't remember what, from the grocery store maybe. They would always send me out like that when they wanted to talk. I knew right away that it was an excuse to get rid of me, so I stayed and hid behind the door but I didn't take in much. They spoke Yiddish so I wouldn't understand, and I only remember the word 'Canada' and then the noise of a chair falling. I went inside as if nothing had happened and no one asked me where the things from the grocery were. They had completely forgotten about it. My mother, she was a woman as soft as . . . as butter." Shorer mused for a moment. "She was a woman who never raised her voice to anyone, and all her short life she just wanted people to have a good life. But really good. Not like in that Beinisch family, where it's all just on the surface. She was a wonderful woman, really. She'd help anyone with no thought of return, and she really didn't care where people came from—that is, to which community they belonged. My mother, of blessed memory, she was a saint. Suddenly I see her standing there, standing there by the sewing machine and saying, 'Absolutely not. On no account, a promise is a promise . . .' 'But who's going to stop them?' my father asked her, as if there was no chance. He was also a good person," Shorer hastened to add, "but with less . . . He didn't have the strength my mother had. He also worked hard, but she . . . she was something special, also in that gentleness of hers . . . ," Shorer said, and wiped his eyes on the cloth napkin. For a moment Michael was alarmed. When people who are closed and restrained by nature suddenly allow themselves to get so sentimental, he thought, who knows where it will lead, even here, in a French restaurant under soft yellow light, late at night, during the intermediate days of the Sukkot holiday.

But Shorer just sighed and turned to Ada. "Ask him. A person can become an orphan at any age, and you're still young and you don't know, but the older you get the more you miss your dead parents, or your childhood . . . In the end it looks like the most important thing in life. But never mind, I'm rambling. She stood there, my mother, and said to him: 'A promise is a promise. A deposit is a deposit,' and she left the room and I followed her out, and I can still remember my father shouting after her: 'Masha, Masha,' but she didn't stop. She went downstairs, and I followed her like a shadow but she didn't even notice me. And she knocked on the door and without waiting for even a moment she flung it open. There was just one room in the downstairs apartment, where they slept and ate and everything, there was the kitchen in one corner and the shower in another corner, everything together, and that was also a miracle. There was an outhouse in the yard, shared by both families, and my father's big plan was to build an indoor lavatory, but that's already the subject of another story. Those were wonderful years," Shorer said sadly, and smoothed his mustache with his hand. "We were poor and life was hard, but we had so many hopes and anyway we didn't know any rich people. In the whole neighborhood there was maybe one car and even that was an old commercial van, but when everyone's poor, it's tolerable. In any case, she opened the door to the downstairs apartment, and she sees this couple, who hardly ever spoke or anything, standing there, and next to them are two of those brown suitcases that people used to have, bound with ropes and straps, and another bundle, and the woman is holding the baby. And the woman sees my mother standing in the doorway and starts to cry, and I mean really cry, hysterically. And she goes down on her knees, literally on her knees, with the baby in her arms, and she says all kinds of things to my mother in Yiddish, and my mother, who really was a softhearted person, she puts her two arms out, like this." Shorer stretched his arms straight out as if pushing aside two sides of a doorframe. "She stands there in the doorway and doesn't let them pass. And she doesn't say a word and just shakes her head. And the man, the husband, looks at his wife and lifts her from the floor and he's crying too. Like two children they were crying, only in adult voices, like I've never heard. And the woman grabs my mother by the apron and pulls her hand to her lips, to kiss, and keeps on crying all the time. My mother pats her head for a moment, like you pat a child, but then she immediately puts her hands back on the doorframe and says quietly: '*Das kind bleibt dooh.*' I remember those words even though I didn't understand them then, because she said them again and again. Only when I was older did I ask what that meant, and they told me, 'The child stays here.' And finally the woman put the baby into my mother's arms. And she and her husband went out into the night, like thieves, and disappeared from our lives. Later I heard they had gone to Canada, and they had a small business there, and in the meantime both of them have died. They died too."

"And the little boy? The baby?" asked Ada.

"He went back to his parents. The next morning they came to get him," said Shorer, "but I'm telling you this story because people . . . There were terrible things then, conflicts that I don't understand how . . . My mother never spoke about that couple, but afterward they rented out the downstairs apartment to some student, and then they did the big renovation and enlarged the house, so that the toilet was inside and the room downstairs became my parents' bedroom. They gave me the good room upstairs. That is, not just me, but also my little sister and my little brother. Nobody thought of a room for each child back then."

"And the couple? Did they have another child?" asked Ada.

"I told you, they left the country. They went to Canada," said Shorer tiredly. "When I was older, I once asked my mother. She never brought them up herself but she told me that they'd gone to Canada and started a small business there, a grocery store or something. I can't remember what. But that was a long time ago, and in the meantime he got sick and died and she also died later."

"And they didn't have another child?" insisted Ada.

"No," said Shorer. "I asked, and my mother said; 'No, there were no children. By the time they'd adjusted to the new reality in Canada, without any help and alone, they weren't of the right age anymore.' And why am I telling you all this?" he said to Michael. "So that you'll understand that I have some sympathy for this couple, attorney Rosenstein and his wife, and so that you should know that things like that happened then. It's not that they just went and kidnapped Yemenite babies to make servants of them. These were people who couldn't have children of their own and they . . . I'm not saying it was a good thing to do, or that it was legitimate, but in all the messy chaos that there was in this country then and all that . . . Nothing surprises me, so I'm not saying—"

"But now they're suspected of murder," Michael reminded him. "I explained to you all the . . . We think that this whole business about the apartment for Zahara was hush money. We really do think that she had threatened him, and that afterward he decided to . . . If not himself, then he sent someone . . . although the pregnancy isn't . . . This doesn't explain the pregnancy. But maybe the two things aren't connected. And apart from that, I don't understand. Do you really think it's forgivable to take a child from a family only because you're miserable because you don't have any children? Do you really think that there's any justification for such things? What's got into you?"

"I don't know," admitted Shorer. "Maybe because I drank all that wine and the grappa, or because I see that at long last you . . ."—he nodded at Ada—"and because we're getting old and I'm about to retire. All these things make you sentimental. And I'm telling you this, even though you're maybe the most sentimental creature I've ever met, really"— Shorer giggled a moment—"but nevertheless I feel that you don't have enough pity on them. And also because you don't have enough evidence that they or he initiated the murder of the Bashari girl. But I haven't even seen them and . . ." He paused and beckoned to the waitress to bring the bill.

Ada looked at Michael, and he spread his hands and said: "Forget it. He'll just say that it's his turn. I know this scenario."

"It really is my turn," said Shorer. "Last time we ate at the Tel Aviv port you paid. And anyway"—he looked at Ada, "you've given me pleasure." He rested his eyes on her for another moment, but when he turned to Michael his face grew a bit grave: "It's only a pity that . . . How's the boy?"

Michael almost began to report on how Sergeant Yair was, but then he realized that Shorer meant his son, Yuval. "Fine. He's in great shape—studying a lot, working, things like that."

"He's already become a man," Shorer said, and looked distractedly at the bill the waitress had put in front of him and at the ring in her navel, "especially since he's been living with that girl. What's her name?" he asked. "Ayala?"

"Ofra." Michael smiled. "You're in the right direction. Both names mean Bambi."

"And you? Why are you smoking? At your age you should stop," Shorer muttered, and put a credit card down on the bill. "Look, I stopped and I'm still alive. It's all a matter of willpower. Don't you want to live?"

Michael smiled and said nothing.

"*Nu*, okay," muttered Shorer. "You can't do everything at once, buy a home for the first time in the middle of your life and also all of a sudden, at long last—" He looked at Ada and grinned under his thick mustache. "It's late, but not too late," he said, and stroked her hand. "I, if you'll excuse me, am a good judge of people. And my only complaint after I've gotten to know you a bit is, Where have you been all these years?"

"Oh, that," said Ada with a smile, and she pushed back her chair before she rose. "You should ask him that, not me."

"She says I didn't want her," explained Michael. Now the three of them were standing by the table.

"It isn't that he didn't want you," Shorer said, and looked at the banknotes he put on the table next to the signed credit slip. "He wanted you, but he just didn't know that he did."

"She says that it's the same thing," explained Michael, and Shorer looked at Ada for another moment and smiled.

"She's right," said Shorer on the way to the parking lot, "and you should listen to what she's telling you." They stopped next to the big, dusty Toyota. "You really should," Shorer said to Michael and kissed Ada's cheek. "And now get some sleep before you swoop down on the lawyer and that Beinisch. Nothing's going to run away; the dead are already dead and you've already saved the little girl."

Chapter 14

I
t happened every time he had to face grown men who were obviously strangers to weeping—men whose faces crack and whose entire stance suddenly collapses. The sound of the continuing sniffles and sobs and the way attorney Rosenstein was blowing his nose made him feel embarrassment and pity.

"Can't you stop it?" asked the lawyer as he wept. "Or take out a restraining order?" His wrinkled hand dropped and tapped on the large pages that lay on the desk between them. "Doesn't it interfere with the process of investigation, to publish it like this?"

Michael looked at the upside-down headlines and listened to the lawyer's plaints and arguments. When Rosenstein mentioned the state of his wife's health and cursed journalists and especially "those girls who make trash out of everything, everything, a person's life and also his death, like . . . like . . . What's that animal called, like a coyote but not a coyote . . ."

"Hyena," said Michael finally, responding to the lawyer's eyes.

"That's it, a hyena. They eat carcasses, or that bird . . . the buzzard, like a buzzard . . . ," Rosenstein cried, and threatened that he himself, legally or physically, if necessary, would stop the publication of Orly Shushan's article that was about to appear in the special holiday supplement for Simhat Torah. "How did you let her do this?!" he protested hoarsely. "How can you allow a thing like this?"

Michael leaned back in his chair and lit a cigarette. Only when Rosenstein's eyes hung on him in expectation of an answer did he stretch his hands out in front of himself resignedly and say that there was no information in the article that would interfere with the investigation, and that it wasn't concern for the process of investigation that was shocking the lawyer but rather the mention of his private life and its revelation to the public eye. "And I can understand your pain. A person feels very bad when his life is exposed to the public like that," he said to him, and puffed on the cigarette, "but with pain you can't stop the world from going round. And, in a democratic state, a journalist or anyone else is allowed to publish an article about a young, talented and pretty girl who was murdered in such a horrible way."

"And are they also allowed to write about all the families she has some connection with?!" protested the lawyer.

Michael shrugged and said: "Why not, if it's relevant."

"And this is just the first article in a series!" Rosenstein cried, and buried his head in his hands. "Who knows what will come afterward? She's planning three more!"

"It says here," observed Michael, turning the page toward him, "in the note at the end, that in the next articles there will be details about the hearing committee on the Yemenite children and . . . here, what they call 'shocking revelations about the disappearances of the children and one story of rescue.' This already goes quite a distance from your story."

"All our lives we've tried to protect Tali and keep her away from the . . . ," Rosenstein mourned, and blew his nose loudly on a plaid handkerchief he took out of the pocket of his gray jacket. Michael examined for a moment the worn sleeves of the pale blue shirt he had distractedly put on that morning, and reflected that the lawyer's three-piece suit of pale gray fabric with fine silvery threads in the weave had not provided its owner the defense to which he was accustomed. This cloth and the soft black matte leather from which his shoes were made were signs of the luxuries in which a wealthy older man indulged. And all these items ("props," Sergeant Yair had called them this morning, as he sniffed his wrist where various after-shaves had been sprayed one after the other and presented to his nose as if in an identification lineup) were aimed at providing defense against the mess and muddle the world would put in his way, but he never expected a mess like this; impotent and defenseless he faced Orly Shushan's article, which revealed the lie with which he had protected his wife and his daughter. Balility had been especially irritated by his shoes, which in fact emphasized the smallness of his feet in comparison to his rounded potbelly ("I don't feel sorry for him, just his wife," Balilty had grumbled several times).

Against the background of the lawyer's voice, who was now emotionally saying that his entire intention had been to "protect her from exactly things like this," Michael again marveled at the competence of Balilty, who refused to say exactly how the article had come into his hands or to attribute any importance to this. "I have connections with someone who has access to the computer at the newspaper and . . . Never mind. What do you care where I get things for you? Don't ask me about my sources. That's what the journalists say, isn't it?" Balilty said this as he was handing out a copy of the newspaper article to each of the members of the special investigation team, and when he got to Tzilla he asked: "She hasn't woken up yet, the girl?"

Tzilla nodded her head, which was leaning over the article, and muttered: "What a slut. Would you believe it? Look what it says about you here. Did you see it?"

"I saw it," confirmed Michael, "and I've also seen that there's nothing that can be done about it. There's no point in even applying to the court." Opposite them, Yair was still sniffing the scent in one of the flasks that Alon from the Criminal Identification Unit had lined up along the office desk.

"Have you got any Paco Rabanne?" Balilty asked Alon. "It's the only aftershave that I . . . And not just me, my wife, too. The only one! The ultimate aftershave! Try it yourself," he said scornfully to Yair, and winked at Alon, "and you'll see how women throw themselves at your feet. You can even ask *him*—he has a doctorate in chemistry."

"Where did she get all this from? Who told her about the women? Who gave her the story about your ex-wife and about . . . even that business with Nita . . . and the story about her brother? Who told her?" asked Tzilla, and she looked at the other members of the special investigation team, expecting them to be as shocked as she was.

"What do you want?" said Balilty. "What were you expecting? He didn't give her what she wanted and she's getting back at him. As someone a woman made eyes to and he ignored it, believe me he's gotten off cheaply. I know what I'm talking about from experience—the revenge of a woman scorned is the worst. Everyone knows that."

The lawyer continued his lugubrious plaint about the lightness with which some people ruin a person's life, and Michael thought about Eli Bachar's strange silence at that moment when everyone was reading the article, and how he had lowered his eyes and avoided meeting Michael's eyes or anyone else's, and how he had left the room with a copy of the article and disappeared for quite a while.

"We aren't the way you think we are," Rosenstein said, and folded the plaid handkerchief, "and what's so awful is that not only is Zahara dead, but my wife, whom I've tried to spare . . . Zahara . . . I don't know. She was examined a few years ago about this business of the family history, I don't know why, but I think it's connected with a boy, maybe an Ashkenazi boy who humiliated her . . ."

Michael tensed. "So after all you do know something about a man in Zahara Bashari's life."

"No, no, no. That's a misunderstanding," the lawyer hastened to say. "If I knew anything, believe me I would have told you. And you did ask everyone—no one knew, but I mean that people, if you look into it, and they have some ideology that they fight for—it always has something to do with something that happened to them personally. That's what I think. That's what I've learned over the years and now that I've seen this"—he pointed to the newsprint pages spread out on the desk between them—"it's really . . ."

Michael glanced again at the upside-down headline of the article. "In any case," added the lawyer, "when she came here to work, Zahara, she was already completely into the ethnic thing and she never stopped going on about it, but up until a few months ago I never heard the story about her sister, the one who . . ." He paused, examined the sleeve of his suit jacket and pulled a loose silver gray thread at the cuff.

"And really, it's about time," said Michael, "that you explain to me how exactly you found out the whole story, and how the purchase of the apartment came about."

The lawyer sat bolt upright in his chair. "It's not like she writes here," he said in disgust, and pushed aside the pages of the article. "It has nothing to do with the pregnancy, and I never slept with Zahara, even when . . . It just wasn't in the cards, and I have no idea how she got to the information about our Tali because—"

"I asked you how you found out about Big Zahara, and what the apartment has to do with it," Michael reminded him.

"A few months ago," said Rosenstein, averting his glance, "in May, I think, one afternoon when we were alone at the office, she came into my room and closed the door behind her, and I didn't understand what she wanted. And she asked me whether I had a few minutes and I said yes, I have all the time in the world for her, and when I looked at her face I saw right away that nothing good was going to come of this. But it never occurred to me that it had anything to do with us. I thought it had to do with her, with her life or her plans. I thought . . . Do you want to know the truth?"

Michael nodded. "The whole truth and nothing but the truth."

"I thought she was coming to tell me that she was leaving . . . that she'd found something else . . . If only that had been the case . . . ," Rosenstein said, and paused.

"But that wasn't the case," remarked Michael without taking his eyes off him, and the lawyer nodded and lowered his face and sighed.

Without looking at Michael he said quickly: "Straight to the point, with no prologue, she said that she'd checked out our family's whole past, including the fact that my wife had been . . . that my wife couldn't have children. Tali wasn't our natural daughter. Those were Zahara's exact words, 'not your natural daughter,' and then I started to perspire and deny it, but she cut me off like a knife and said, 'There's no point. I have all the details and I also know that the baby whom that friend of yours brought you from the hospital is my big sister, and I can prove it.'"

"Of course it was a shock to hear all that," commented Michael, because the lawyer had raised his head and was looking at him expectantly.

"'Shock'? 'Shock' is an understatement!" said Rosenstein, who had apparently heard sympathy in Michael's words. "I mean, we didn't know anything at all about the baby they brought us. We didn't want to know—not who her parents were and not what had happened to her . . . And out of the blue Zahara tells me that I got her when she was two months old, that she was brought by the nurse who worked in the immigrants' camp at Ein Shemer . . . She knew every detail. I have no idea how she found out, and believe me . . ."—he tugged at his large nose—"we didn't even know where they had brought us the baby from. All that I wanted was for my wife to . . . I also wanted children but my wife, she . . . she would cry at night, and I saw that if I didn't get her a baby then . . . And nowadays you can get babies from Brazil or from . . . But then you couldn't buy a child like that, and I had connections. That nurse, she was from my city. I had smuggled her little brother out of the ghetto and I . . . Never mind. I got him through and I got him to the partisans, and his sister . . . She was . . . She felt, as they say, eternally indebted and she brought Tali right after I had spoken to her. I only mentioned it to her once, in a café in Haifa. I asked . . . I didn't even ask her, I told her about it and just a month later she brought the baby with no questions asked and no papers. And so one day I could come home and put a baby in my wife's arms and that saved her life, I'm telling you. It was a matter of life or death. We didn't know, we didn't want to know. You don't think about the parents, it's impossible—"

"Even today," said Michael, "you're still ignoring the fact that so you—let's say your wife, but also you—could be happy, you were willing to ruin the lives of other people, and you don't even . . . ," and he surprised himself with the anger that rang in his voice.

Rosenstein tilted his head and examined Michael. "What is it you want? For me to be sorry? For me to have regrets? For me to ask for forgiveness?"

Michael was silent.

"Tell me," said Rosenstein quietly. "It says here"—he tapped the article—"you have a child. It says you do. A son, right? Yours? Natural?"

Michael nodded.

"So how could you understand?" argued the lawyer, taking off his glasses and polishing them on the end of his silk tie. Without them, his expression looked blunt and impenetrable. "And anyway, how can a man in your position be so . . . so naïve?"

"Naïve?" wondered Michael.

"Don't you know that if you want to live, you always live at the expense of somebody else?"

"No. It might come as a surprise to you, but I don't know that," said Michael. "That is, I've heard of extreme situations—people eat each other on a desert island, and during my lifetime I've met some murderers and liars and villains, things like that, but this 'always' of yours I don't really know." And after a moment's thought he added: "And I have grave doubts as to whether your view of the world is correct. In any case, it's not really an axiom," he said dryly.

"What are you talking about?!" the lawyer exclaimed, and put his glasses back on. "You're an intelligent individual. I don't need this *paskustva*, this filth"—he indicated the pages of the newspaper article—"to know that you're an intelligent individual and—forgive me, maybe this isn't going to sound good, but it's the truth—you act like . . . like a European."

"What do mean?" asked Michael, stifling an ironic smile.

"I must say . . . I . . . It came as a surprise to me when I read here that you came to this country from Morocco," said Rosenstein. "I even thought it was a mistake, because you don't behave like a Moroccan." He looked at Michael with cunning satisfaction, as if certain that he had said things his interlocutor wanted to hear.

"Really?" said Michael coldly. Now he also chided himself for the feeling of insult that had surprised him. "How exactly does a Moroccan behave?"

Rosenstein hesitated. "More like . . . How can I put it? . . .Like someone who comes from a position of inferiority, sort of . . . more wildly . . ."

"And a European?" asked Michael. "How does a European behave? He makes use of the head nurse? For example?"

The lawyer was silent for a moment, but immediately gathered his wits and said quietly: "Look, for a long time I'd been talking to you like a lawyer to a police officer, but for hours now . . . I've realized that you're not . . . that I can talk to you straight from the heart, and believe me, I haven't got anything against oriental Jews, Moroccans or Yemenites or . . . whatever. But if we're really talking, just like there are jokes about Poles . . . there's no need to be bitter if there are also . . . The Moroccans, all the oriental Jews cry about how we discriminated against them—you might think that we ourselves were living in paradise. It was the oriental Jews who lived peacefully in their diaspora and we . . ."

Michael expected the obvious mention of the Holocaust, but the lawyer leaned over and pulled Orly Shushan's article toward him and pointed with his finger to the middle of the page. "She writes here," he said heatedly, "that you were married to a Polish girl—by the way, I think I knew her father. He was a well-known lawyer, a bailiff, if I'm not mistaken, one of the first in the country, right? That is to say, an Ashkenazi woman, and it also says here that you are known, that a known attribute of yours, is that you prefer Ashkenazi women, so I understand that you . . . All right, never mind. I see that you're getting angry."

"Let's go back for a moment to the matter of living at the expense of someone else," said Michael. "I want to understand this exactly. Because according to what you say, it's not just a matter of extreme circumstances, and not a matter of ethical questions in the philosophical sense, but you're talking in a practical, everyday sense. And going by what you say it's also permissible, as you see it, to murder, say, a young girl who threatens your domestic harmony, or your wife's health or your only daughter's happiness or . . . These are sufficient reasons to—"

"Don't talk nonsense," interrupted the lawyer. "What I mean is that . . . It's like . . ." His face suddenly lit up. "Have you read *Altneuland*?"

"*Altneuland*?" Michael was astonished. "Herzl's book?"

"Yes, Yes. It was years ago . . . I noticed that he . . . Why do you think he didn't mention the Arabs at all? He dreams about the state and he describes it . . . describes Palestine . . . as if there are no Arabs. Why?" Behind the lenses of his glasses his small eyes, which didn't expect an answer, sparkled and took pleasure in the possibility of explaining. "Because if he had taken them into account, he would have really had to have taken them into account. Do you see what I mean?"

Michael did not reply.

"And then maybe there would never have been a Jewish state, right? Because if a person wants to live," Rosenstein summed up, "then how can I put it? If you're doing something big, taking a big step in life . . . at the crucial moments of life you can't take into account . . . Believe me . . . I've seen it, I was there . . . and I'm not talking about the Germans, that's obvious and well-known. It's trivial to say that the Germans were monsters . . . I'm talking about what the Jews did to each other in order to stay alive and these . . . these are people who . . . you can't judge . . ." A desperate, pleading note entered his voice. "Like Herzl couldn't think about the Arabs, I can't . . . That is to say, the Yemenites . . ." His voice grew stronger, and fervently he added: "You yourself said: In your work you see it all the time . . ."

"What I see," said Michael, "is that there's always a choice. This is what I believe, and I have proof. Not everyone is prepared to eat another person in order to survive on a raft or a desert island. You have to take into account that there are some people who would prefer to be eaten."

The lawyer examined his fingers. "In all my life, I've never met many people like that," he said finally. "Very few cases . . . On one hand . . . Maybe my wife, if she knew how the child came to us . . . But the fact is," he said triumphantly, "she never asked how. She held the baby tight in her arms and didn't ask a thing. And Tali, she didn't even look like . . . She had blue eyes and fair skin, but afterward . . . And believe me, Lydia Abramov, that nurse, was a good woman. She didn't—"

"She's no longer alive," noted Michael. "She died eight years ago, in Petach Tikva."

"She had Parkinson's," said the lawyer matter-of-factly. "No one needed to kill her."

"It's interesting that you're bringing up the subject at your own initiative," remarked Michael.

"I was being sarcastic," explained Rosenstein apologetically, "before you start investigating whether I also murdered her in order to shut her up, the way you say I—"

"She testified about the Yemenite children before she died," noted Michael, "and her testimony—there was no remorse in it. All she said was, 'We did the best we could in the conditions that prevailed.' I remember her exact words. She just explained how because of the panic about the polio epidemic every baby who had a high fever was hospitalized immediately, and at the commission of inquiry she had the feeling that they had done the right thing. And I also noticed how she described there the way the Yemenite parents didn't come to look for their children for weeks . . . 'As if they didn't care,' she said. She didn't know details . . . couldn't remember . . . And she also claimed that there were lots of children who disappeared, all kinds, who were hospitalized and never went back to their parents. Ashkenazi children too. From Romania, from the whole world, not just Yemenite children. There was . . . There was a story there about some woman, a millionaire from WIZO in England, who came to Israel and got a child from Romanian parents and took her back with her to England. This particular story Lydia Abramov remembered very well."

"We didn't know anything," insisted the lawyer. "We didn't know she was a Yemenite baby. Had I known from the beginning, maybe . . ." He stopped.

"Yes? Maybe what?" demanded Michael.

"Maybe we would never have taken her, because . . . Don't jump as though I were some racist. I have nothing against Yemenites, I'm simply a practical person and I didn't want people to know . . . It's . . . She doesn't look like she's her mother's daughter. Had I known in advance, maybe I . . ." He drew the chair closer to the desk and leaned forward, as if about to share a secret. "You must understand, we didn't tell Tali that she was adopted. We didn't say a thing to anyone. We moved to Jerusalem and we closed everything down in Haifa. Maybe someone suspected, and once she even asked, Tali, but I said, 'No. Of course not.' I've been told that there's an age when children think they are adopted, and I was afraid . . . I was afraid that someone had said something to her—this is a small country where everyone knows everyone else." He turned his face away and brought his forefinger to his eye, pushing it under a lens of his glasses.

"Let's get back to Zahara," said Michael as if making a suggestion. "So she came into your office and . . . ? Did she say, for example, where she had obtained the information?"

"I have no idea how she found out," answered Rosenstein bitterly. "She came in and threw a cardboard file down on the desk, with copies from the Interior Ministry of a death certificate and a birth certificate and she said that her sister was . . . that Tali was . . . born . . . and I looked at the birth certificate. It said Zahara's parents' baby girl was born in . . . April? And we got Tali in January, and I say to her, 'Zahara, Tali was born in January,' and she says, 'You can't prove it. Everyone there faked things. Look, it says "Zohar" in the certificate and not "Zahara," so why shouldn't they be wrong about the dates?' And I said, 'Zahara, sweetie, there's a difference between a two-month-old baby and a five-month-old baby,' but that didn't convince her. 'No, there are all kinds of babies,' that's what she said, 'and you got her from the immigrants' camp at Ein Shemer, and isn't it true that she had blue eyes?'"

Michael supported his chin on his hand and in a very low voice asked the lawyer what he thought Zahara wanted. Justice? Revenge?

"I really don't know," answered the lawyer miserably. "I even asked her. I said, 'Zahara, what will you do with this information after fifty years? You'll just ruin everyone's life and what good will it do you if . . .' But she was like a person with an idée fixe, and she kept saying 'to bring the truth to light, to reveal the truth. You won't go on living here quietly with grandchildren and all the . . . when my parents are broken like that . . .'"

"And then?" asked Michael. "Do you really think that people who are . . . who like you say, are in the grip of an idée fixe, people like that—did you really think that it's possible to silence them by buying them an apartment?"

"I don't know," admitted Rosenstein. "In a situation like that, you can only try . . . There's no one who can't be bought. Don't look at me like that. You weren't born yesterday. It's just a matter of the right price, the price that suits the person. I thought that she wouldn't be able . . . that she would owe me . . . What interested me," he said emotionally, "was that Tali and my wife hear nothing about this. I didn't know . . ." He indicated the newspaper article with his head. "I didn't know Zahara had spoken to anyone, and with . . . with a journalist, yet. And I thought that if she owed me a favor—it wasn't exactly extortion what she did; she didn't say, 'If you do this and that I won't talk'—and I, I have experience with people. I knew she wanted to study and I knew she didn't have an apartment of her own and that she wanted to move out of her parents' house, and I thought . . ." He swallowed. "Only I didn't know she was pregnant. That would have changed the whole picture . . . Had I known . . . I couldn't tell you what I would have done . . . All I cared about was that my wife and Tali wouldn't hear what she had to say."

"But after the confrontation with Zahara there was no escaping it," said Michael. "Then you knew that they would hear."

"Not Tali," said Rosenstein in alarm. "I thought that just my wife, and she . . . My wife knows somewhere . . . We . . . People always know more than they think they know. In fact she knew."

"The safest or the most effective way, and in fact, the only way," said Michael pleasantly, "to silence a person with an idée fixe that threatens your life is to silence him entirely, isn't it?"

Rosenstein drummed his hands on the desk in despair. "You've checked out our story," he said with exhaustion. "You saw that we were at the opera, like I said. How—"

"More than that," Michael said, and leaned forward, resting his elbows on the desk. "We compared your DNA to the fetal DNA, and there's no match."

"You compared the DNA?!" exclaimed Rosenstein. "How could you do that without . . . I didn't even give blood and—"

"It doesn't take all that much time," said Michael, "and as a lawyer I'd have thought you knew that blood isn't necessary for a DNA test. I'm surprised that you—"

"I've told you a thousand times, from the beginning: I've never dealt with criminal cases. I don't touch that dirt. How did you do that test?"

"We have our methods," said Michael. He wasn't going to say a thing about the strands of hair Balilty had brought from the Rosensteins' house. "So we know that the baby isn't yours. But as a lawyer I don't need to tell you," said Michael, "that people of a certain standing don't need to do jobs like that with their own hands . . ."

"Against that," said the lawyer, his fingers gripping the edge of the metal desk as if he were hanging on for dear life, "against an argument like that I have nothing to say, except that she wrote there"—he nodded at the pages of the newspaper—"that Zahara went to a place where . . . Of her own free will, and she wasn't a girl who went with every . . ." He leaned back in the wooden chair and his eyes wandered for a moment, until he suddenly sat straight up and cried: "It's that fellow, Baleeti. Isn't that what he's called? He went to the bathroom, roamed around the house. Is he the one?"

Michael said nothing.

"If you think I'm a Mafioso who pays a hired gun, then I don't have . . . I'm telling you, please, think whatever you want. Now that my wife knows

I have nothing to lose . . . I'm prepared to . . . what's that?" he asked in alarm. "Did you hear that? What was that?"

"I think it was a sonic boom," said Michael reassuringly. "It didn't sound like an explosion."

"No," said Rosenstein. "What was that scream? There was a woman's scream."

"I didn't hear any scream," said Michael.

"You didn't hear that?!" Rosenstein looked at him suspiciously. "A woman's scream . . . as if they were cutting her throat . . . How could you not hear it?"

"Maybe because I'm concentrating on what you're telling me," Michael replied, and touched the drawer where the tape recorder was whirring.

"Do you beat people here when you question them?" asked Rosenstein, and his fingers clenched.

Michael dropped his hands to his sides and said: "*Nu*, you see how we beat and torture people here."

Rosenstein looked at him confused. "But there was a scream, a woman's scream," he insisted. "I'm not used to dealing with criminal matters," he said warningly.

Michael said nothing.

"Are we done?" asked Rosenstein. "Is that it for now?"

"Just one more little thing," said Michael.

"What? What thing?" said Rosenstein in alarm.

"That the apartment wasn't from the bailiff, and Moshe Avital wasn't about to go bankrupt."

Rosenstein hung his head. Almost inaudibly he said: "Okay, that's nothing. So you've realized that I wanted to buy it. So I gave . . . I gave a few details that . . ."

"What interests us is how you got something for such a bargain price," said Michael.

"Ah," said Rosenstein. He raised his head, and his face took on a cunning look. "That has to do with a completely different matter. That concerns Mr. Avital himself."

"Yes, but how does it concern him?" asked Michael impatiently. The lawyer was annoying him now.

"He knew that it involved Zahara and he made a special price for her," declared the lawyer. "Such things happen."

"Why did he 'make her a special price'?" insisted Michael.

"That," said Rosenstein with a look of satisfaction on his face, "you will have to ask him."

"But no doubt you have some suppositions?" said Michael coldly.

"Suppositions, suppositions. They won't stand up in court. Of course I have some. So do you. Zahara was a very pretty girl. And that's all I have to say about it. Are we done?"

"We're done for today," said Michael thoughtfully.

"And if it turns out that I'm not . . . What difference does it make?" said Rosenstein. "Nothing makes any difference anymore. From the moment my wife sees the newspaper . . . and if she doesn't see the newspaper, then someone is sure to . . ." He stopped and looked out the window over Michael's shoulder. "We have to be thankful for the years we had," he muttered gloomily. "Even so, it was a miracle, and whatever happens, happens. I did my bit, the best I—"

And at that moment Balilty burst into the room, and ignored the lawyer and the slamming door. "I need you," he said to Michael, breathing hard, and he lowered his voice to a whisper. "I need you right now, because things have gotten utterly and totally out of control . . ."

"So there was a scream!" There was victory in Rosenstein's voice. "A woman screamed there in the room. I wasn't just hearing voices, you see?"

Michael pushed back his chair. "Wait here a moment," he said to Rosenstein, and called a number on the internal phone. "Someone will be here right away to arrange with you what comes next. We also need to speak to your wife."

"Does it have to be today?" said the lawyer in alarm.

"Why not?" asked Tzilla, who suddenly appeared in the doorway. "In any case she'll know everything the day after tomorrow."

"But I wanted . . . ," called Rosenstein after Michael, who had already risen from his chair and was on his way out of the room. "I wanted to talk to you about the restraining order."

Balilty stopped and turned around. He gave the lawyer a piercing look. "Mr. Rosenstein," he said to him, "the less noise you make, the less attention it will get. That's how it works, and you know this from experience. Listen to me—drop it." He patted his arm. "Be a fatalist, like your wife. She's waiting for you there." He waved his arm in the direction of the end of the corridor. "There's a girl there with her."

The lawyer paled, and he grasped the desk. "Was it she who screamed?" he whispered. "Was it she? What have you done to her?"

Balilty tilted his head. "Mr. Rosenstein," he said to him solemnly. "Your wife—I would not let them lay a finger on her . . . and she's just fine, better than you, I would think. We didn't tell her anything new. She knew everything. And you took so much trouble," he added, and Michael was astonished to hear the pity in his voice. "You could have saved yourself all the trouble had you taken your wife's good sense into account. She's already phoned your daughter. What your wife wants now"—Balilty laid his hand on the lawyer's shoulder—"is a DNA test for your Tali, to see whether she's the Basharis' or not. That's what she wants."

He pulled Michael quickly along the corridor, then all of a sudden he stopped and turned back. "I have something to tell Tzilla," he muttered, and went back to the office and opened the door and called Tzilla out.

Next to the door, Balilty said something to her. Michael, who had begun to walk toward them, could not see her expression well, although he did manage to hear her say, "That's an absolutely crazy idea," before she went back into the office.

In half an hour," Balilty called to her. "In another half hour," and he pulled Michael and ran down the steps with him to the bottom floor. There he stopped by one of the doors and opened it wide. "You wanted Chief Superintendent Michael Ohayon? So here he is, in person."

Michael looked at the red patches on Clara Beinisch's neck and at the beads of perspiration that were glittering on her son's forehead. The front of the mother's blouse was wet and water was dripping down her arms. Her legs were stuck straight out in front of her, and her brown pumps were lying under the chair. With her right hand she fingered the large, pale birthmark on her cheek. "The lady fainted here," whispered Balilty to Michael, "and it was lucky that our dear sergeant was a medic in the army, because he knew enough to raise her feet and open her blouse."

"The moment she heard about the search at their place, she began to hyperventilate. She got dizzy and she almost . . ." Sergeant Yair pointed to the floor, to show that she had almost collapsed there.

"It's against the law," said Clara Beinisch faintly. "You're not allowed to come into our home without permission or without . . ."

"Without a search warrant," her son finished, and wiped his hands on the sides of his trousers. "You got us out of the house so you could search, like you stole my car in order to—"

"Why are you holding them in the same room?" asked Michael. He looked at Yoram Beinisch, who pressed his pinkish lips together and sat up straight in his chair. "Why aren't you holding them separately? And where is Mr. Beinisch?"

"She wasn't prepared to . . . ," said Sergeant Yair. "She fought it tooth and nail . . . It was impossible. And the father is upstairs. Talking to Alon and Yaffa, because there are questions that the Criminal Identification Unit . . ."

Michael sat down in Balilty's chair behind the black iron desk, and the intelligence officer, who leaned his shoulder against the closed door, returned his gaze.

"It's very simple," said Balilty. "The hysteria began the moment we told her about the Ralph Lauren. We brought his bottle from the house. It's the same smell Yair identified. We told her and then she began to scream."

"It's not an aftershave that . . . A lot of people use it," said Yoram Beinisch suddenly. "It doesn't prove anything."

"By itself, it's no proof," replied Sergeant Yair. "I've already told you that by itself it's no proof, but there are—"

"What? What else do you have?" asked Clara Beinisch.

"There are indications that . . ." Yair looked at Michael, and Michael nodded to him. "There are also indications in the contents of the material from the car," he said cautiously.

Yoram Beinisch crossed his arms and narrowed his eyes. "What do you say?" he muttered sarcastically. "Did you find a fingerprint there or something?"

"No," said Michael. "What we found was material that has enabled us to compare your genetics with Zahara Bashari's fetus. It will take a day or two, and everything will be perfectly clear."

"That nonsense again!" shouted Clara Beinisch. "My son never . . . he never even touched her!"

"That's not what we heard from her brother," said Michael. "Her brother Netanel. Do you remember what he did to you when he caught you in the shed with Zahara?"

Clara Beinisch sprang up, as if the anger had imbued her with strength, and moved to the desk and banged her hands on the iron desktop and shouted: "We don't need to be here! I told you—he was at home. He didn't leave the house!"

Yair pulled her back to the wooden chair, sat her down there and stood behind her. Michael did not take his eyes off Yoram Beinisch. "Do you remember that occurrence?" he said to him. "There are things you never forget, especially when they catch you naked and pull you out of a crate by force. Do you remember anything like that?"

"There was never any such thing," said Yoram Beinisch coldly.

"That's not what her brother told us," insisted Michael. "We heard exactly how you played as children, despite all the prohibitions."

"Maybe," Yoram Beinisch said, and examined the tips of his fingernails. "But not everyone remembers everything from his childhood. I don't remember anything like that. And definitely as far back as I can remember, I never spoke to her at all."

"But you saw her," interjected Balilty.

"Okay," said Yoram Beinisch scornfully. "I'm not blind. How could I not see her? She lived on the other side of the fence. Sometimes in the morning . . ."

"A pretty girl," commented Balilty.

"I didn't look," Yoram Beinisch said, and turned his eyes to the window and looked out at the parking lot and the rows of police vehicles that were parked there. "Not my taste, in any case," he added after a while.

"That's not what you thought when you were little," said Balilty.

"I don't remember," replied Yoram Beinisch after a long moment. "I don't know what you're talking about. Also about that little girl you said to me . . . and I never in my life spoke to her, the sticky pest. Underfoot all the time, coming into the yard all the time. I almost caught her once but she ran away. On purpose her dog would pee on the wheels of my car. On purpose."

"When you were little," said Michael, "you played . . . doctor and patient in the hiding place? Mother and father?"

Yoram Beinisch shrugged. "I've already heard that. I told you: I don't remember and I don't believe it. Her brother invented that story to incriminate me, because they hate us."

"They want our house, that's what they want," Clara Beinisch said, and clasped her hands. "It's all because they want all the land and—"

"They informed on us to the income tax," cried Yoram Beinisch, "so is it any wonder that he's telling you things like that about me? They did everything to—"

Balilty stuck his hand into the inside pocket of his windbreaker and took out an opaque plastic envelope. He put the envelope on the table in front of Michael. "Ask him about this," he said, and went back to stand by the wall, where he put his hands in his pockets and leaned on the windowsill with a sealed expression.

"Here we have"—Michael opened the envelope as he spoke—"this item." He set down on the table a large, pale pecan nut with holes on either end attached to a thin chain. Under the fluorescent lamp that illuminated the room it was hard to tell whether Yoram Beinisch's face paled. He sat absolutely still.

"Do you recognize this?" asked Michael. "There's a hole here, as you know, and this hole is sealed with wax. This was in a leather pouch, and inside" . . . He shook the nut, and a faint sound emerged from it. "Tell us what is inside."

Yoram Beinisch shrugged. "I don't know," he said with exaggerated indifference. "What am I, a magician? Why should I have any idea?"

"Because," said Michael pleasantly, "we found this in the glove compartment of your car—which, by the way, was found last night—and we checked to see if there was any damage . . ."

"How lovely that you are so concerned about the *well-being* of the citizens of this country," said Yoram Beinisch scornfully, "and all by yourselves you found the car you stole. Last time they stole my car, you never found it and the police, when I came to file a complaint, laughed in my face."

"This, as you see, is attached to a chain," said Michael Ohayon, "and do you know why?"

Yoram Beinisch raised his eyes from the pecan and tilted his head a bit. "No, I don't know *but I know you are going to tell me,* because you're a nice person, aren't you?"

"You know that this is an amulet. And it's connected," said Michael as he drew a rolled-up slip of paper out of the envelope, "to what's written here. Do you want to tell us, or shall I read it to you?"

Yoram Beinisch put his hands on his knees. "My fiancée has been waiting for me at home for hours and she doesn't know where we are. My mother isn't feeling well," he protested, "and you've been keeping us here for hours, without a doctor or anything. If anything happens to her, it'll be your responsibility."

Michael spread the small scroll out in front of him and read aloud: "To cancel a spell or the Evil Eye, take the living silver called *zaibak,* and the white stones found in the gizzard of a black rooster, male to male and female to female, add a pinch of salt and put everything into a pierced nut. Seal the hole with wax and then wrap the nut in leather and hang it around the neck of the person in need and he will be saved, so that neither the Evil Eye nor a spell shall rule him."

Yoram Beinisch snorted, but the snort was truncated when his mother said: "What is this? I don't understand what this is, Yoram. Is this thing yours? Are you dabbling in magic? *Oy*, I feel terrible," she whispered, and laid her hand on her chest. "I feel so terrible."

Yair poured some water from the bottle at her feet and handed her the cup, but her hand was shaking so hard she couldn't hold it. Without hesitating, the sergeant brought the cup to her lips, and with his left hand he tilted her head back. "Drink, Mrs. Beinisch. It's from the anxiety. You get dehydrated. It's common."

He moistened her lips, and then she said: "I'm not afraid that Yoram did something wrong. I'm just afraid that you're going to believe those people, who want to eliminate us."

"You don't understand. They hate us only because we're Ashkenazim," said her son. "From the moment my parents came they hated us. They hated us because my parents are white and speak Hungarian."

"Not only that," said his mother, who had raised her head as if she had been filled with new strength. "Also because they want the land."

"If we were Yemenites, it wouldn't bother them so much, the land," said her son. They're envious and that's all. They're envious of everything. They . . . The envy eats them up, because we're advanced and they're primitives, and they know this very well. It's very good that they know that we are better than they are. Even with their son the professor, who built that synagogue. Do you think he isn't primitive? It all comes from the home, from the mother's milk."

"Is he also envious?" inquired Balilty. "Does he also wish you ill?"

"Of course," declared Clara Beinisch. "Because of his parents, nothing will do him any good—bad blood. All those blacks shouldn't have been let in. They're like the Arabs. Worse."

"So let's get back to the little girl," said Michael.

"The girl," said Yoram Beinisch. "She . . . You . . . He," he said, pointing to Yair. "He says that she's unconscious, so wait till she comes to and her. Ask her if I ever touched her . . ."

"We certainly will ask her, buddy, you can be sure of that," said Balilty. He looked at his watch and examined his fingers with interest. "But not everything needs to be asked. There are things that are plain to the eye—for example, that note inside this nut. This explains it." He moved over to the desk and pointed to the scroll. "We didn't have to break the shell. It's all written down there, and it's in your car. How do you explain that?"

"Somebody put it there," said Yoram Beinisch. "Maybe even you," he said to Balilty. "How should I know? I don't do black magic."

"This isn't black magic," said Michael. "It's a Yemenite amulet and it was in your car. There are two possibilities—either you got it out of the little girl somehow, or . . ."

A tense silence hung in the room. Clara Beinisch felt the locks of her hair, which was disheveled, and then touched the wet front of her blouse, her fingers curling around its edge. "Or? Or what?" she burst out, as if unable to bear the silence.

"Or Zahara Bashari made it especially for him," Balilty explained to her. "She wanted to exorcise the spell that you cast on him, that's what we think."

"You should be ashamed of yourself, a grown man talking such nonsense! I'm his mother," Clara Beinisch cried, and half rose from her chair. But her trembling legs brought her back down.

"Yes," agreed Balilty, "and that's just the point—he couldn't be with Zahara because his mother didn't let him."

"It's obvious you don't know anything," dismissed Clara Beinisch with a flap of her hand." Don't you know he has a fiancée? A wonderful girl whose parents—"

"Yes, yes, yes," said Balilty as if bored. "We're well aware that you love this fiancée, Michelle Pierce. We also know that her parents are well-to-do and all the rest, but he," Balilty said, and put his small hand on Yoram Beinisch's shoulder, from which Yoram Beinisch immediately shook it off, "didn't want Michelle. Do you know who he wanted, Mrs. Beinisch? He wanted his neighbor. Not Nessia. He wanted the Yemenite beauty, the black girl, the girl next door on the other side of the fence. She's the one he wanted. At first, at least. It was with her and not with his fiancée that he met at the Cliff Hotel."

Yoram Beinisch's eyes widened in obvious fear. "What's the Cliff Hotel?" he whispered.

"*Nu*, that hotel in Netanya, as you know very well, where the two of you would meet," said Balilty indifferently. "Out of town, far from Mommy's eyes."

"Are you out of your mind?" said Yoram Beinisch angrily. "I wanted her?! Zahara Bashari? Why should I want her? And anyway, if I wanted her so much in your opinion, why would I kill her?"

"That's exactly what we're waiting for you to explain to us," said Balilty. "That and the matter of the little girl, Nessia."

"I never touched that little girl," replied Yoram Beinisch, and a disgusted expression spread over his face. *"I wouldn't touch her with a ten-foot pole."*

"And that treasure that was buried under the tree in your part of the garden?" said Yair. "Was that a coincidence?"

"Of course it was coincidence," shouted Yoram Beinisch. "It's that little girl, who was always wandering around the yard under the windows and she . . . It's things she collected. Am I to blame for that, too?"

"There are indications in the car that you were there, at the place . . . at that kiosk," said Sergeant Yair, "and that the dog was in your car. You put the dog in your car, and that was a big mistake . . ."

"Who says?!" demanded Yoram Beinisch. "Where did you get that from?"

"We found all kinds of other slips of paper there too, like this one," said Michael, "and I just wanted to know if you'd ever seen them. Do you understand what's written in them? Give me that envelope, please," he said to Balilty, "the one with the photocopies."

"It's there in the drawer, where you're sitting," said the intelligence officer.

Michael moved back and opened the drawer, in which another recorder was spinning in addition to the one that was in plain sight on the desk. From the depths of the drawer he extracted a large envelope and took a number of pages out of it. "We have here a number of photocopies of the slips of paper we found," he explained, "and I want you to look at them and see if you can identify anything."

"After all this," exploded Yoram Beinisch, "you still want me to help you? In another minute you'll ask me to . . ." Deep anger flamed in his pale eyes.

"Here," Michael said, handing him one of the pages. "It says here: 'To find favor in the eyes of kings and ministers: Write the name 'Gotel' and put it under your tongue.' You've probably heard that from Zahara, right?"

"Tell me," said Yoram Beinisch, with aggressive tiredness. "Is this going to go on forever? Because I don't have to be here and listen to all this talk of yours. I haven't done anything and you don't have any proof. This is all . . . It's all a collection of circumstances, the aftershave and the slips of paper and this thing"—he pointed to the nut—"that you planted in my car and . . . We're going home, Mother." He rose from his chair, went up to her and held her arm. "They can't hold us here forever. They don't have . . . Let them arrest us if they want to, but like this? Absolutely not. I'm not—"

Clara Beinisch rose from her chair and looked around hesitatingly. Balilty, who had gone back to lean on the wall by the door, looked at the handle and as if in answer to his look it moved and the door opened. In the doorway stood Tzilla, signaling something with her fingers.

"What's happening?" Michael asked, and saw with some discomfort the smile that was spreading over Balilty's face.

"The girl has woken up," proclaimed Tzilla, and Michael, who was afraid no one would believe her because of the forced way she'd just spoken, was surprised to see Yoram Beinisch stop in his tracks. His mother, whose arm he was holding, stopped with him on the way to the door, and both of them looked at Tzilla.

"*Nu*, has she said anything?" asked Yoram Beinisch indifferently.

Tzilla looked hesitantly at Balilty, who now had his hand on the door handle. He blinked as if he had been dazzled by a sudden flash of light.

"You can speak freely," Balilty said to Tzilla. "You can tell the whole truth, because we have no secrets here, right, friends?"

Clara Beinisch looked at him with obvious disgust. Balilty's problem, mused Michael, is that sometimes his tricks cross the line, and sometimes, like now, it turns out that they are totally unnecessary. One look at Yoram Beinisch's face showed that he wouldn't fall into this trap.

"Has she said anything?" asked Yoram Beinisch again.

"She's talking now. She's just begun," answered Tzilla.

"You can go anywhere you want," said Balilty to the mother and her son, "but it won't pay. It won't help. The girl has regained consciousness, and now she's going to talk and no one is going to silence her."

Chapter 15

W
ell, what is there to say?" Ada said, and tossed aside the photo-copied pages of the reporter's article. "It's simply disgusting, filth. I don't want . . . How did she get her hands on all those details?" she asked in a throttled voice. "There's a summary of your biography here, with all the stories about . . . those things. Everything. How did she know about all that? Did you speak to her?"

"Not a word," Michael said, and pushed aside the glass of wine that was in front of him. "I didn't speak to her and I am not going to speak to her."

"So how did she know?" Ada blew gently on the dancing flame of the fat orange candle that illuminated the sitting area, which hinted at the way she had intended they spend the evening, and after the candle went out and smoked a bit, she moved the bottle of wine she had bought specially.

"It's true what they say, that filth sticks to whoever touches it." The prolonged expectation of his coming and the late hour at which he finally arrived were what had caused the slight unhappiness in her voice. He examined her face again and made an effort to decipher her expression. The crease between the high arches of her eyebrows had grown deeper and the fine wrinkles at the corners of her mouth gave her small face a bitter look, and this made him anxious.

When he'd told her about Orly Shushan after the encounter at the Basharis' house and had jokingly mentioned the journalist's wish to interview him, and the phrase "twin souls" she had used then, Ada had pressed her pretty lips together in the same way, and commented that the few times she had been compelled to be interviewed by journalists—"In order to sell, you have to do that sometimes," she explained, "and even if it's a film for the BBC the producer needs you to do this, and you yourself, if you want anyone to know about it"—the experience had often left her with a heavy sense of discomfort or in total embarrassment. "Not because of the exposure, because what have you got to hide," she said, and her lips parted the tiniest bit, "but because of the vulgarity and sensationalism of all the things that get attention today. Sometimes," she said when he first told her about Orly Shushan, "you can't believe what you're hearing. One day a while ago I had a phone call from some television producer. They're doing a program on 'how to be a successful blonde,' she tells me, and they want me to be on it."

"Were you blonde?" asked Michael.

"No, of course not. For years now I've been like this," she said, and raked her fingers through her hair from forehead to nape, "and that's what I told her. I said, 'But I'm not even a blonde,' and do you know what she answered?"

Michael shook his head slowly. He did not know what the producer had said to her and he did not know what the moral of the story was supposed to be. "Without missing a beat she said to me: 'Okay. I got it. So now we know you're not a blonde, but you can represent the non-blonde who has always dreamed of being a blonde, or something.' See what I mean? And then my cameraman gave me a long lecture and bawled me out for being such a drag and taking myself too seriously, because I didn't agree. There's a limit."

He then confirmed with a nod that he had understood.

Now, he watched her as she crushed the candlewick between two fingers and stifled the last of its smoke.

"Do you want me to leave?" Michael asked miserably, and stretched his arm out to the hassock to gather the pages that had been put down there. He crushed them into a ball, and in a theatrical movement that even he found repulsive, he threw the ball to the corner of the room and missed the mouth of the large ceramic vase that stood there. "I'm sorry that she dragged you into all this," he said, and lowered his eyes, "but if you want me to—I'll leave right now."

"Don't talk nonsense." Ada laid her hand on his cheek. "I'll get over it. It's just froth, filth. It'll pass. It's just newsprint—tomorrow someone will wrap fish with it in the market. But there is something that does interest me, and I insist on talking about it," she said pensively.

"What? What interests you?" asked Michael, and since he was relieved to see that he wasn't the one she was angry at, and grateful that she wasn't fed up with him, he leaned over her and caressed her fingers.

"How is it that if you didn't speak to her . . . Don't you think it's strange that she found out all those details about you in such a short time? What kind of detective are you if you're not thinking about this?"

"Do you know how many strange things happened today?" said Michael evasively, and still he tried not to think about this thing that had been bothering him since that morning.

"Yes, I've understood that," Ada said, and glanced at her watch. "A person goes out at six in the morning and comes back at two o'clock the next morning. It's understandable. But even so, didn't you have even a minute to ask yourself how she could have got all that information?"

"I don't want to think about it," said Michael vaguely, weighing his words so as not to disclose the suspicion her remarks had aroused. "I don't want to, but I . . . All day long I tried not to think about it, and I was so busy that it . . . Why aren't you asking about Moshe Avital? He didn't even object. He cooperated like a good boy, and that, in fact, is what's strange. I find it strange that someone gives a blood sample for a DNA test, willingly and with no fear, and he doesn't even have an alibi for the time the little girl disappeared, and he even knows the girl. I know types like that—types who cooperate willingly and tell you everything they know, supposedly, and afterward it turns out . . . Why aren't you asking about the test, about the DNA? It's more interesting, believe me, the way from a bloodstain or a hair or anything that has a human cell they can . . . They dissolve the membrane of the cell, and through a technique of cutting and duplication . . . In America they have a DNA database, like a fingerprint database, but here there's no money—"

"Fine," interrupted Ada. "In my opinion you have no choice. But I'm not pressuring you. At your own pace." For a moment a slight smile crossed her face, but it immediately faded. "Presumably it's someone close to you who talked, right?"

"I don't want to talk about it now," replied Michael. "We'll think about it later. Tomorrow, after tomorrow. Now I want . . ."

"Now you want to get some sleep? To shower and go to sleep?" said Ada, looking at him with her dark brown eyes. "Is that what you want?"

"To shower and lose consciousness," Michael said, and with an effort extricated his body from the cushions of the small sofa into which he had sunk.

Ada held out her hand to him, and he grasped it in order to rise. "*Nu*," she said, "it's a good thing she can't see you now, that journalist. You would ruin all the glamour she arranged for you."

• • •

Under the stream of hot water he directed at his back, his speculation from the morning disturbed him again, and he leaned his shoulder against the white ceramic tiles and listened to the running water. Among the events of the day that flowed together with the water—the embarrassment of the woman who was called in to confirm Avital's alibi for the murder and the lilting French in which he spoke to his wife on the telephone; the uncontrollable trembling in Efraim Beinisch's leg when he didn't manage to walk to the door after he heard that his wife and son had left; Balilty's clouded face after he had reprimanded him for his tricks in the matter of the little girl—among all these lingered Tzilla's face and her expression at the sight of the cardboard box. It had been removed from the shelter of the building where the Hayoun family lived, and Tzilla looked at its contents and ran her fingers over every one of the objects, as if memorizing their texture. "Look at the treasures that this Nessia collected. It kills me, all these things," she whispered to Michael in a strangled voice after she had fingered them all and gathered them together again. "I never told you, but when I was little . . . I was also . . . I was also quite an . . . I wasn't a pretty child . . . That is, I was ugly."

"I don't believe you," he said, and then clasped her arm. "It's impossible. What are you talking about? And the children, they look like you, not just Eli. Are they ugly, your children?"

"You don't understand," said Tzilla. "There are girls like that . . . They think they're ugly and they're fat and even . . . maybe they even nurture that . . . or maybe sink into it, with a kind of contrariness—from so much despair, I suppose. If that's the way others see them . . . If they don't want me, then . . . You can't understand this. You, you've always been so . . . oho . . . so popular and successful."

With a half-smile, he wound his arm around her shoulders. They had been working together since he first came to the police, and he could remember how he had listened for days on end to Eli Bachar's litany about how he was doing "everything possible to avoid a serious relationship." Then he had encouraged him and later he rejoiced at their wedding and was the godfather of her firstborn son, and though he never talked to her about his life he knew that she was concerned about him in her own quiet way. She never tried to pair him off with any of her girlfriends, and when she heard about the purchase of the apartment she congratulated him without a trace of criticism and dismissed Balilty's complaints as "a collection of old women's fears and especially now, when the market is completely dead and everyone is fleeing Jerusalem and there's no better time to buy an apartment." She was gentle with him, as if she knew what he was feeling at the many moments when he withdrew into himself.

She replied to him with a smile, over the carton they had brought from the shelter, a cardboard box that had once held a television, and wiped her eyes. "This girl, Nessia—and what a name they gave her, Nessia—is just . . . I also stole things when I was a girl. Not so much, but I did take things, so that no one saw . . . Did anybody really need this? You see her whole fantasy life inside this box here, with the purple and the gold, and the panties and the bra and this wallet."

"She didn't use them," Michael commented, and removed his arm from her shoulders. "Everything's brand-new. I don't entirely understand it, why she didn't—"

"Of course she didn't use them," interrupted Tzilla. "If she were . . . How could she? Not a thing here, not a thing, do you hear me?! Nothing here fit her life, or her measurements. These aren't things that a person steals in order to use. It's just to have something, a box like this of pretty things . . . A treasure."

"Where's Eli?" asked Michael after Tzilla had recovered herself and closed the carton, folding over the cardboard flap that had begun to grow ragged.

"Didn't you send him over to the Criminal Identification lab? I thought that he was sitting with them there all day. That's what he told me . . ." She looked at him worriedly. "And when I phoned him, his mobile wasn't on, so I thought they were in the middle of something. Didn't you send him there?"

"I-I . . . ," stuttered Michael, who had not seen Eli since the moment he'd left the special investigations team meeting while they were talking about the newspaper article. "That is, I asked him to do something, but I thought that . . ." He was embarrassed for a moment, because he worked with both of them and he loved them both, and now he felt that he was required to support the cover story that a husband had told his wife. Not only had he not sent Eli to the Criminal Identification lab, but he also had no idea where he was.

"Well," said Tzilla, "it's been hours. I thought he was waiting . . . He said something about the DNA and I thought . . . I thought he would come back to question Netanel Bashari, but in the end you were the one who . . . He doesn't even know yet what a scene there was. Wasn't that something?" she said, and sighed. "Did you see what a scandal there was? And like that, in front of everyone, with no shame, I couldn't . . . I couldn't have done that," she said. She pulled her sharp nose and examined a loose button on her striped blouse.

Michael began to examine closely the memo that was on his desk, lowering his eyes so they would not disclose the lie he had told for Eli's sake, even though there was no reason to think that another woman was involved in his disappearance. In his mind's eye he could still see his evasive look as he replayed portions of what Hagar Bashari had said. Some of them were shouted—"Five years! My God, five years and I had no idea!"—and others slipped out between clenched teeth—"That whore, just because she . . . goes around like that . . . with all her . . . Making eyes at all her clients, an 'agent' they call her . . . And it's a sure thing that Zahara knew, a sure thing! She's her friend . . ." And there were things that were said quietly, after her husband had left the room. And while Netanel Bashari was still sitting there opposite her, defending himself by clasping his fingers together and at the same time abandoning himself entirely to her outburst, the red marks of her fingers still visible on his cheek, Hagar said: "It's all because of that synagogue and all that politicking, all those people . . . 'Community life,' they call it, a 'community' . . . Maybe I should just be thankful that there was only one woman?"

It all began at a meeting at the synagogue, where Michael had intended to go down into the basement with Netanel Bashari to look at the objects his sister had collected there and try to learn something from them about the slips of paper that were found in the Beinisches' garden. When he and Tzilla arrived there, the synagogue gate was locked, and no one answered when they rang the doorbell. Several minutes later, after they had given up, Tzilla said, "Here they are," and before he could wonder aloud about the plural, he saw Netanel and discovered that he had not come to the meeting alone. His wife, Hagar, walked next to him with bustling steps and demanded to know from the person responsible for the investigation in person, and in the presence of witnesses ("Will Tzilla suffice as witnesses?" Michael asked half-sarcastically), where exactly her husband had been while they had been looking for him all those hours on the eve of the holiday and the night Zahara was murdered. Michael had no intention of answering this, but Netanel, though he had begged them to keep his secret, had already caved in to her demand like someone who in an instant forswears all lies and deceptions.

"At first he said he was at the university and out shopping," said Hagar, "and yesterday he suddenly told me that he had been with Linda O'Brian, so I want to know: Is that true? Was he with Linda? I'd rather know and not be told lies, because I can't stand lies . . . And he, the good citizen of the community, Mister Civic Responsibility." At these words her voice shook. "So he was with Linda?"

After he looked at Netanel Bashari for a moment, Michael opened his hands to the sides instead of replying, and then Hagar asked the predictable questions and her husband, with restraint but firmly, answered each of them in turn ("Did you have a thing with her?" "Yes, if you want to call it that." "How long?" "Nearly a year." "Nearly a year?!" "What can I do? I fell in love. I couldn't control it."). Then Hagar began to shout and in the big hall of the synagogue, where they were sitting on the benches, her reproaches echoed. For lying to her, for exploiting her and for the opportunism that had guided him all his life, for the inferiority complexes of people from the eastern Jewish ethnic groups that were the only reason he had married her, because she was Ashkenazi. She cursed the neighborhood and that real estate agent whose behavior with her clients everyone knew about and she went on to curse the community synagogue that was the only reason—"a brothel disguised as a members' club"—all this had happened. There was no other way he could have met so many "Americans and French people and white Europeans," and even whites who listened to him the way he likes, because all that interested him was captivating the Ashkenazim, especially the Ashkenazi women, even if they were just aging whores like that one.

Then Netanel rose from the bench and with a sealed face and complete serenity said to her: "Listen, Hagar, for years I've been hearing that nonsense from you and I haven't said a word. You should know by now that there is nothing that disgusts me more than the exploitation of ethnic oppression, and you can't say that I'm some archetype of the screwed oriental Jew. You yourself have heard me get angry at Zahara about these things exactly. So now you're transferring them to me? I have enough screwed-up things about myself, from here till doomsday, and I really don't need any help from anyone. What I do need . . . Never mind, you wouldn't understand anyway if you haven't got it into your head after all these years." He pushed the bench back hard and stood up.

"Excuse me," he blurted to Michael and Tzilla, who for the past few minutes had kept her eyes glued to the heavy, closed wooden door, until Netanel Bashari walked out and it slammed behind him.

Against their will, for a long time after his departure they listened to accusations and curses, insult and anger, and when Michael tried to rise from his seat and gestured toward his watch for Tzilla's benefit, Hagar looked at him pleadingly and into the synagogue's silence, which had returned for a moment, she said in a voice from which all the strength had drained out: "What is going happen? What am I going to do now? What does he think I'm going to do? He's the only person who's close to me . . . I don't have other friends. I don't have . . . Even this synagogue, they don't appreciate me, and if it weren't for him they wouldn't even have . . . They accept me only because of Netanel, and now what does he think I am going to do? Do you think he will leave me?" She asked this in a childish, pleading tone, and because of that it was hard for Michael to find an answer.

It was Tzilla who answered in his stead: "That's not at all certain. Men have crises sometimes, midlife crises, and afterward they come back home with their tails between their legs."

And then, on the synagogue bench, in the dimness that held the scents of paper and havdalah spices for the end of the Sabbath and apples for the holiday, Hagar Bashari wept bitter tears of insult, like a child who suddenly discovers the injustices of the world and is amazed by them. Weeping silently, she rose and walked toward the large door, and only there got a grip on herself. "I don't intend to give up so fast," she said to the carved squares of wood on the door. "I'm going to fight for my love. I'm going to fight for it," she said, and went out, and the door remained wide open.

"She's going to fight for her love, did you hear?" said Tzilla. "Is it possible to fight for love?"

Michael looked at her and tried to discern traces of ridicule on her face, but she was serious and thoughtful. "Maybe it's possible to fight, but it doesn't have much connection to love," he said to her after a moment. "It even seems to me like a total contradiction—how can you fight for a thing like that? It's something that comes like a gift or a miracle. Either it's there or it isn't."

Tzilla looked into the mirror of the powder compact she pulled out of her bag. "In your opinion, does she love him? Are we going and leaving the building open like this?" And after she wrinkled her nose and patted her face a few times and returned the compact to her bag and they had gone out and slammed the door behind them, she replied herself to her first question.

He was looking at the small house across the street, and at the brown gate and at the big pile of trash that had accumulated on the crumbling wooden bars of the railroad tracks, and she said: "It's impossible to know. In a situation like this you can't distinguish between love and insult and habit. That's my opinion, and you know what I would do in her place? If I were to catch Eli in . . . in a lie like that? I would just get up and leave without a lot of talk. I know what people say, 'Don't judge until you've . . .' and thank God, I'm not in her place yet, but I wouldn't stay even for a moment. Without scenes and without any explanations."

The water that flowed over his head and his back and his closed eyes was no longer as hot as it had been. He was attacked by a sudden chill, and he shivered and turned the water off.

"Are you alive in there?" asked Ada outside the closed door. She opened the door with a strained smile and he saw her through the steam. "You've made a little inferno for yourself here," she commented as she waved her hands about and tried to dispel the steam that surrounded him, "and you've been scalded by the water." She pulled him gently into the bedroom.

In total darkness, from within a heavy fog of drowsiness or dream, he suddenly heard Ada's voice very close to his ear. "It's your beeper going off," she whispered to him. "It isn't stopping. Here it is—I've brought it to you so you can see."

And from within the total darkness he asked, "Who is it?" and he still wasn't sure whether they were really having this conversation, in this bedroom where he had dropped his clothes on a small straw chair, or whether he was just dreaming it inside his head.

"Should I look?" she asked, and turned on the night-light. Even its soft yellow light hurt his eyes.

On the illuminated face of the beeper, which she had brought from the chair to the bed, he saw the number of Balilty's mobile phone and next to it the world "Urgent."

In the dimness of early morning he sat in the intelligence officer's car and listened. The garbage truck rumbled forward from the end of the street and stopped and went on and stopped again in front of the next building. In the chill between night and morning, Balilty was running the motor in order to warm the car. A police car drove by, slowed down for a moment and immediately moved on. And when the windshield was all steamed up, Balilty lifted his hand to wipe away the steam with an energetic motion, but there was no vitality in his voice when he said: "So it's like this. I'm not going into all the details, just the main points." Nevertheless he went into all the details and one after the other he set them out for Michael after he again wiped off the windshield with his hand. "I didn't want to call you directly to her house," he began. "I said I'll give him at least an hour or two. I wouldn't have woken you up like that at five-thirty. I have a heart, don't I?"

Michael said nothing.

"It's a small city. Everyone knows everyone else, even though it has grown so much and all that. In any case, I go over to my sister-in-law's— Matty's sister? At twelve o'clock at night she has a flood in her house. Not at eleven, not at ten, but at exactly twelve midnight, by the clock. So I go over to her place because she's by herself, and you know how it is . . . And I'm fiddling with the pipe there, and you should know that you are going to have to replace all the plumbing if you don't want troubles like that, because here the pipes rot within a few years. The water's too hard . . ."

As in a dream Michael heard Balilty's prolonged chatter about the plumbing in his sister-in-law's house and the experience he has with all kinds of plumbing and what happens when there are rotten pipes under the sink and under the tile floor. And he didn't let up or slow down his talking, which Michael supposed was going to lead to something that would better remain unsaid at this hour, and which he also knew he would have to reply to.

"So she's standing there and handing me the pipe—a person needs a helper in a complicated job like this, and she doesn't have another piece of pipe and anyway, where would she get one?" said Balilty. "And suddenly she says to me, right in the middle of the job, 'Tell me, that Eli Bachar who works with you, isn't he married?' and I look at her and I say to her, 'Married? Of course he's married, with two children. What happened? Do you have the hots for him?' And she gets annoyed with me, not because she doesn't have the hots for him—she does if you ask me and that's really why she got annoyed—but she says to me, 'What are you talking about? You always think I'm looking,' and believe me, her whole life she's been looking for someone and hasn't found anyone. She has requirements, that one! Oho, what requirements she has. You might think she was the Princess of Kamchatka. Big deal, she was the most popular girl in her class, and that's only according to what she herself says and in any case there's been a lot of water under the bridge since then, believe me. 'So why are you asking?' I ask her, and she says, looking down at me—my head was under the sink, you should understand—and she says, 'I saw him in Simha's café a few days ago, with a girl. And Simha told me that she doesn't look like much, just some girl, but she's not just some girl. Simha says she's an important journalist and she'd seen her once on television. Just looking at her, she doesn't look like anyone special, just some girl, but Simha says that if it wasn't for her she would have gone broke a long time ago and it's only thanks to her that the café caught on. Ever since she did an article about her, people are just standing in line to get in in the evening. You remember, we sat there once. She has a poppy seed cake that . . ."

Michael buried his head in his hands. More than insult, he felt the strength of the exhaustion that silently called him to lay his head on his arm, lean on the door and close his eyes. But he rubbed his cheeks and his forehead and sat up straight and said: "I don't get it."

"You think you know a person and suddenly it turns out that he surprises you. Apparently he had a big grudge against you," said Balilty, and his voice rang out like Job's companions, the self-righteous and annoying tone of which he still remembered from high school, in the voice of the Bible teacher who made them learn whole portions of these people's speeches by heart.

"You're not saying anything," said Balilty. "I know you. It's probably the shock. You're in shock, aren't you? That's how it is. You think someone is a good guy and he likes you and then . . ."

Michael looked around and said nothing. Opposite the street, which had emptied and was quiet, he saw the face of the Bible teacher, a completely secular man who one day began to wear a skullcap—they said he suffered from battle trauma—and after the summer vacation came back with a fringed garment dangling out from under his shirt, left the school and moved to a Jewish settlement near Hebron and started to study in a yeshiva. He saw his face and heard his voice echoing in the classroom even before the skullcap and the fringes, and the words of the prophet Jeremiah that the teacher repeated with total identification—"Can the

Ethiopian change his skin or the leopard his spots?"—until Michael sat up straight in the passenger seat and looked at the round face of Balilty, who moistened his lips and loudly cracked the knuckles of his hands over the steering wheel. "I have to talk to him first," Michael finally said. "I'm sure there's an explanation."

"Yes," agreed Balilty. "I'm also sure. But I'm also sure that our explanations are different. I'm thinking it's revenge, and you . . . I have no idea how you can straighten this out in your mind, but remember that there isn't a single bad word about you in that article. He only said good things about you, and maybe there's no need to make a fuss about a thing like this."

"I don't care what he said to her. It's simply the fact that he spoke to her at all that's the issue here," Michael said, and rubbed his face with his hands.

"But nevertheless, it does make a difference what he said, doesn't it?" Balilty asked and wiped the windshield with his hand.

"No," said Michael decisively. "I don't want people who work with me to talk with journalists. Can't you understand that?"

Balilty popped his finger joints and looked around in embarrassment. It was obvious that he regretted what he had done or was frightened by its results. "I'm not saying," he muttered, "but sometimes people . . . Sometimes you maybe even have to . . . There's no point making a fuss about someone if . . . You don't have to be such a fanatic."

"First of all I'm going to talk to him," insisted Michael. "I have to hear his version."

"Talk to him, talk to him." Balilty sighed. "Of course you'll talk to him. It's necessary to talk, only . . ." The beeper went off and the mobile phone rang. "What good is it going to do you?" Balilty said, and picked up the mobile phone, listened for a moment and said: "Good for you. Talk to him yourself. He's here next to me in the car, and stop signaling on the radio. Do you want more journalists to get involved? I'm not even putting you on the speaker. Here, take it," he said to Michael, and handed him the phone. "She has news. It's Tzilla," and he hissed her name meanly, as if blaming her for what her husband had done.

"What?" said Michael with an effort into the telephone. "What's happened?"

"Two things," said Tzilla quickly. "One—there are signs that the girl is waking up. Not entirely, but she's moving her legs and sighing as if she were just asleep, and Einat says that the doctor said that it's a matter of a few hours until she—"

"Got it," said Michael. "And the other thing?"

"Mr. Beinisch is waiting for you here. The father."

"Now?" said Michael in astonishment. "At five in the morning?"

"It's already six," corrected Tzilla. "He has something to say, but he's not prepared to talk to anyone else, just to you," she whispered. "I'm holding him in the storeroom. Yair is with him."

"Where's Eli?" asked Michael, and out of the corner of his eye he could see how Balilty's fingers were gripping the steering wheel.

"He's here, talking with the Criminal Identification guy," said Tzilla. "Why? Do you need something from him? I can call him . . ."

"Don't call him," said Michael, and to his left Balilty's fingers started to drum on the steering wheel. "Just tell him that I want to have a word with him."

"Okay," she said crisply. "Before you talk to Beinisch or after?"

"Before," said Michael. "Beinisch can wait a while longer. It doesn't make all that much difference anymore."

"So I'll run you over there?" Balilty asked, and turned the key in the ignition. "Or what? Maybe you want some coffee first or a bite to eat? There's a place on—"

"Balilty," threatened Michael.

"Okay, okay. I was just asking. A healthy mind in a healthy body. I'm not the one who first said that," he pointed out, and released the hand brake.

Chapter 16

First there was the smell. At night it was bitter and dry like the air in the house in the bedroom during the months before her father died, the air because of which Nessia tried to remain in the doorway when they—usually her mother, but sometimes her father, in a whisper that was frighteningly hoarse—called her to come in and talk to Daddy. ("Come in, Nesseleh, come in, darling," her mother would beg her, but she was afraid to see the tubes, and the emptiness in the place where there was supposed to be a leg, and afraid that she would not be able to hold her breath and would have to breathe that smell, bitter and dry, which she could not escape, even at night in her bed, for a long time after he died, and even today you could smell it if you buried your head in Mommy's bed.)

Gradually her eyes grew accustomed to the dark. Someone was sleeping next to the door, on the chair. In the faint light from the corridor—corridor?—she could see that the person had white hair, and in the distance she heard a phone ringing, a high, loud ring, not like at home. The sheet is white and the bed is high. There are two pillows, big ones, not like at home. If you stick your arms out to the sides you discover that the high bed is narrow and you can't touch the floor with your hands, not only because the bed is high but also because your hands are tied. A needle is stuck to it with brown sticky tape, and a thin tube leads from the needle, and the tube leads to a bag, and the bag is hanging on a pole. A pole like the one that was next to Daddy's bed, where every so often Nurse Varda or the Arab male nurse Wahid would go over and feel the bag, shake it and sometimes take it off the top of the pole, throw it in the trash can and bring another one. And it was Nessia's job, ever since the business of the leg, to let her mother get a bit of rest every afternoon—she and her brother Zion—and watch that the drip didn't stop and that the drops made their way from the bag to the tube. When it emptied they would call Nurse Varda and hear her nylon stockings rubbing together when she moved her legs around the pole or they would call Wahid and look at his large brown fingers and the brown stain on his white athletic shoes. Sometimes Nessia would spend hours watching the drops making their way from the top of the thin pole into the narrow tube, and Varda explained to her that in one bag there was medicine and in the other fluids ("So he won't dehydrate. Your father can't drink from a glass anymore, isn't that so, sweetie?").

Now she too has a tube like that and a pole, but there is only one bag and there is no way of knowing whether it is of medicine or fluids. This room where she is lying alone in the dark is a room in a hospital, yes, a hospital, and apparently, she, Nessia, will die soon, just like her father, who first was in the hospital with a pole and a bag and drops that came down and then he died.

The door is open and the corridor is lit. A nurse in a white uniform walks past, stops in the doorway very close to the person who is sleeping in the chair and peeks inside. This is not Nurse Varda, because she does not have blonde hair and she is not fat, but you can also see the lines of her underpants through the white uniform, where they end exactly, and her white shoes also squeak on the floor. She does not see that Nessia's eyes are open, because Nessia is lying in the dark. She wants to scream but she holds back. She knows how to keep quiet. Even if she is going to die soon. She is already used to keeping quiet and holding back and keeping everything inside, until it is perfectly clear where she is and what is going on. "What's new?" asks the nurse in a whisper, and without waiting for an answer she comes into the room.

The man sitting in the chair next to the door wakes up and says in Peter's voice: "Sorry. I fell asleep for a moment."

"It doesn't matter," the nurse says. "Sleep, sleep a little, it's been hours since you . . ."

Nessia shuts her eyes again. "Before, it seemed to me," Peter tells the nurse, "that she moved, and maybe I even heard sounds. Maybe in a dream."

"She's not quiet," agrees the nurse, "but that's a good sign. We want her not to be quiet, to come out of the coma, to regain consciousness."

Only Nessia knows that she can keep her eyes open. She can also move her hands, and scratch her head, but she will wait until there is no one in the room, until there is no one standing there and watching her like that nurse is standing there now. Now she hears the squeaky rubber shoes close to her. The nurse is approaching the bed. She stands there. She bends down over Nessia. And it isn't dark anymore, there is a little light that goes on. Nessia squeezes her eyelids shut. The nurse is standing very near, and she also has a smell, of soap, but a good smell, a green smell. On Nessia's wrist a cold finger tightens and presses hard. She stands there, that nurse, for a long moment and then she sighs and apparently writes something down, because this noise is the sound of a pen scratching.

"Vera, Vera," somebody calls from outside, and the nurse drops something on Nessia's leg—a clipboard?

"I'm here, with the girl. I'm just taking her blood pressure," she says from a distance, and again the rubber soles squeak and Nessia hears the sound of something inflating and then there is pressure on her arm. It hurts, but she doesn't make a sound. Suddenly there is the sound of air rushing out all at once, and someone else is standing in the room very close to her. She feels him above her and also on the sides and also from behind her, even if she is lying in the bed. Her eyes are shut, but she feels. Someone is holding her tight from behind and there is a heavy hand on her mouth, blocking, suffocating. A smell of perfume, a strong, bitter smell of something else, a blow and all at once her legs are on the ground and she is coughing terribly, wants to throw up. Her legs are dragged along the ground. He pushes and pulls her along the sidewalk under his arm into a smell of plastic. The smell of a car. He folds her legs. It hurts. Another blow, on her head from behind. Large hands around her neck. They are carrying her. Her eyes are covered. A hand on her mouth. A large hand but not hard. Rosie whines. It is dark all the time. It is dark and the floor is cold and it is dark and there is heavy breathing above her. She is thirsty and she is nauseous, and it is dark all around, the kind of darkness you can't see anything in, not even your own hands. She wants to throw up but nothing comes out. She wants to scream, but no sound comes out. Not even a groan. She cannot move her hands. Something is restraining them. At the wrists. Tied. Squeezed. Her arms, too. A heavy hand is laid on her mouth, blocking, pressing. Two hands. The horrible smell enters her nostrils and her mouth and her skin. It overwhelms her completely. The nausea. Again she wants to throw up. And then darkness again.

For a moment she opens her eyes and again stares at the faint light in the corridor. Next to the door, the empty chair. No one is sitting in the empty chair. Anyone could come in. Her eyes close again and then she reopens them. For a moment, as she blinks in the dazzling light, the night smells mingle with another smell, familiar, delicate, of flowers, maybe roses. A smell that reminds her, after she shuts her eyes again and concentrates, of the white bottle with the blue ship that stands on the shelf at Yigal's place. And once she opened it and sprayed a bit on herself, as if his shaving drops were perfume. A smell of sweat, and bleach also, come very close to her face, and a little cloud of heavy breath, all of which tell her that her mother is leaning over her. And then come the voices. Her mother's voice, whispering very close to her: "You who hold every living creature in Your hand and the spirit of every man's flesh, in Your hand is the power and the force to raise and strengthen and heal mankind," just as her mother used to whisper next to Nessia's father's bed until he died, just like she, Nessia, would also die; and another voice, young and gentle, a woman's voice: "Doctor, I've been sitting here for several days now. There's a change. I'm not just . . ."; and a new, completely strange voice, of a person standing close to her and maybe he is touching her arm—the touch hurts, as if there are needles there and as if something is bearing down on her arm—and the voice says: "Excuse me a moment, Mrs. Hayoun," and he presses something, maybe a finger, yes, a finger, on her wrists and there too it bears down and hurts (but Nessia doesn't utter a sound, not even a sigh) and the voice says: "There is movement, there are spasms." He rolls up her eyelids and she holds her breath. She takes in "spasms" and "sensations" and "It could take a another few days," and a thick voice calls over the loudspeaker: "Dr. Sela, Dr. Sela, to Internal Medicine B," and someone runs out and inside the room Peter's voice is also heard, very close to the bed. What is he doing? He is singing to her. She never knew that he knows how to sing. He sings to her very, very quietly, into her ear, and it tickles. But nevertheless she does not move and just holds her breath. In English he is singing her a song she does not know, but the words "my love," she knows. And again the young voice, the woman's voice, saying: "Her eyelids are moving. Look, they're fluttering." Nessia squeezes her eyelids tighter. She does not want to open her eyes. If she opens her eyes, they will ask her things. She is sure that they have found her things. They will ask her about the carton and maybe they even found the makeup kit. And she has already woken up once to the smell of mold and mildew, the smell of pee-pee, and she was nauseous. She wanted to throw up and it didn't come out. But then she was on a hard, cold floor, and there was the smell of a wall and darkness, and now it was morning. And she feels the light through her closed eyelids. She hears Peter's voice that is singing to her, and her mother's hoarse voice: "You who hold every living creature in Your hand and the spirit of every man's flesh," and the voice of the girl, who is saying: "I saw it. I tell you, I saw it, a kind of shudder, sort of, like a tic."

Her body is not obeying her. Her body is rebelling. It wants her to open her eyes despite her decision, despite everything that will come afterward, all the questions and the talk. Her eyes want to open and she is struggling with them and feeling how something down in her legs is shaking, tickling her feet. But she thinks about the carton and the blow on the back of her head, and about the hands around her neck and on her mouth, and again she feels the throttling and the darkness and the smell of mildew and the nausea and the smell of the perfume and the strong hands and the cold floor. Rosie howls. As if from far away. A body is pulled. Something has happened to Rosie. Who is taking care of Rosie, if Nessia is here and Mommy is here? How hard it is to keep her eyes closed and not to move, to breathe quietly without moving. "Her leg moved," says the voice of the woman who was talking to the doctor. "I'll be right back," she calls from far away, maybe from the corridor, and Nessia feels the large, chapped hand that is touching her knee and under her knee. Her mother's hand.

"She's lost weight," she hears her mother's voice almost wailing as she pinches her flesh. "Her leg is like a matchstick." And then strangled weeping, in an unfamiliar voice, and a face very close to hers and a smell of cilantro. The hand on her face is her mother's hand, and the smell is her smell, but this voice, wailing like that, hoarse, can't possibly be her voice.

When in one swift movement Michael opened the door to his office— first he had run up the steps, two by two, leaving Balilty behind him to call out: "Wait for me, wait for me a minute, where are you running?"— Eli Bachar was startled. He was sitting there in Michael's chair as he often did when the room was empty, and as the door swung open he laid his hands on the pile of notes and papers that were scattered in front of him on the desk, as if protecting them.

"So there you are,'" he said at the sight of Michael. He squinted with his narrow green eyes and scratched his cheek with his hand, and then went back to looking at the papers as if he could not drag himself away from them. "In the end you show up. I heard that the little girl has woken up, or almost woken up," he added, and carefully piled the notes and the papers into one stack. The sound of his voice, the lightness with which he spoke, the careful movement of his hand as he smoothed out paper after paper—all seemed forced and fake to Michael. This sense of counterfeit rustled in the air; there was something embarrassing and disturbing about it, and that was another reason he wanted to get the matter over with quickly, even though he already knew that nothing could be finished here, unless it turned out to be something altogether different, but that was unlikely.

"Look at this," Eli said, and picked up a slip of paper from the metal surface of the office desk. "Look what it says here," he said, and began to read slowly and emphatically: "'To imprison someone: Take a new piece of pottery and on it write these names and put it in the oven during baking: Assir, Aviyus, Batim Batim, Aviness, Asiruhu Belachashim.' They're really something, these spells and amulets, aren't they?" A kind of forced cheerfulness was in his voice as he held out the slip of paper to Michael, who was still standing on the other side of the desk. "Look. Get a load of this. I read it to you word for word."

Michael cleared his throat and sat down heavily in the visitors' chair, and opposite him the hand was still held out with the slip of paper.

"Do you need your seat?" Eli asked, and rose from the chair. "I'm just waiting here for a message," he apologized. Since when had Eli ever apologized for sitting in his chair at his desk? "Any moment now they're supposed to inform me of the results of the DNA test. They said that it takes a while, because just going by the hairs that we found . . . ," and at the sight of Michael's dismissive wave, he sat back down in the desk chair.

Michael had a few openings, three or four. He had intended to approach the subject gradually and say something noncommittal like: "Where were you yesterday? Tzilla and I were looking for you," or: "What do you think of Miss Shushan's article?" and to get Eli Bachar to talk of his own initiative, but it all collapsed before those familiar green eyes that were now systematically evading his. It was impossible to plan a cautious move against a person whom you had considered your best friend, whom you had never thought to doubt. Thus, in what he finally said there was not a trace of the things with which he had planned to open.

"Tell me," said Michael after he suppressed the "Have I done you any wrong?" that would have escaped him had he not lit the cigarette he rolled between his fingers. There was no tremor in his voice, and his fingers, when he looked at them, looked like they always did, completely steady. "Did you meet with Orly Shushan?"

For the first time, Eli looked him in the eyes. For a long moment he looked and did not reply. His eyelids fluttered, and there was also a limp nod.

"I want to hear it from you, exactly," said Michael throatily. "All the details."

Eli Bachar cleared his throat, twice. "I meant to talk to you about this. I didn't know that . . ." His voice faded as he glanced around, as if looking for something, but Michael said nothing. And as if the silence was too hard to bear, anxiously and apologetically, Eli Bachar said: "I didn't know that you would see the article so soon. I meant to . . . Do you want some coffee?" he asked. He took a sip from a plastic foam cup and wiped traces of the muddy beverage from his lips. "I meant to speak to you later, after the DNA," he said, and set the cup down on the desk.

"So speak to me now," Michael said, and this time *he* looked aside. It was one thing to look at a suspect during an interrogation, and another to look into the eyes of someone whose behavior causes you deep shame.

"Don't talk to me like that, in that tone of voice," Eli said, and carefully rolled the slip of paper he had read from earlier into a little scroll, rolling it and rolling it until it was as thin as a toothpick. "You haven't heard it from me yet, and definitely the person you heard it from doesn't know what I know."

"I'm listening," said Michael, "and they're waiting for me in the little room."

"I heard. I saw. He can wait for a few more minutes," said Eli Bachar with the calm of someone who has nothing to lose. "I told you, don't talk to me like that. I'm not just another one of your suspects."

Things that Tzilla had said, on their way from the synagogue, echoed in his mind now—"Did you see how she talks to her husband? That's the worst, when you talk in such an ugly way to someone close to you, and that's the way she talked even before she knew he was lying. People . . . People don't understand that even between people who are close there has to be respect and courtesy. What am I saying 'even' for? Even more. Between people who are close there has to be even more respect and courtesy"—as he looked at Eli Bachar's face.

"You met with Orly Shushan," said Michael.

Eli crumbled the rim of the plastic foam cup he had pulled from the edge of the desk. "And I can also imagine what they said to you, and who said what to you. And I also know who told you. And the person who told you"—he looked at Michael with an insulted expression—"whose name I don't want to mention now, no doubt told you that I did this because of some . . . because I was annoyed or angry or to screw everything up."

As Tzilla fastened her seat belt, she was still shaking her head and saying: "People act disgustingly to the ones who are close to them. They're sure they have them in their pocket, and that's what's nice about you. Maybe the thing I love about you," she said, and her silver earrings tinkled as she leaned over to pick up the bottle of mineral water on the floor of the car, "is that you never think you have anyone in your pocket. What I hate most is when people think . . . that they don't need to make an effort anymore. You'd never talk that way to anyone you love," she said, and took a long sip from the bottle, then wiped its rim and offered it to Michael. "People just don't like it when people relate to them as if they're taken for granted. You must never stop making an effort for someone who is important to you."

Making an effort now meant not to be mean and sneaky, he reminded himself as he looked at the open window behind Eli's back. From the direction of the entrance to the Russian Compound came the distant, threatening roar of a chorus of rhythmic voices. Seven o'clock in the morning and the Arab women from Sakhnin and Nazareth were already standing and shouting into the Russian Compound. All night long they sat there with their bundles next to the wall, after they had come from their cities to protest the arrest of the men who had participated in the demonstration: their husbands, their brothers, their sons. Then their voices were swallowed up in the sirens, more and more sirens, as if all the police cars were sounding their sirens, one after the other. The place is going up in flames, he mused, and he is busy with one journalist and an ugly, petty story.

There is no point in beating around the bush with a person who is close to you. There was no call here for the cunning that Balilty had recommended. He would gain nothing from it, and anyway it was impossible to turn back the clock. And if there was some chance of working things out with Eli, even the shadow of a chance, it would be better to do it the right way.

"Balilty heard from his sister-in-law who heard from the woman who owns the café," said Michael finally. "I have no intention of interrogating you or anything. Cards on the table. I thought we were close. I didn't know that I had to be careful about you, too."

"Close?" Eli Bachar repeated the word with sarcastic emphasis. "Apparently we don't think the same thing about what closeness means. There are people who think you can do anything to someone who is close to you. Not I. But that's a different story and it doesn't have anything to do with . . ." He stopped speaking for a moment, took a long breath and exhaled noisily. Then he turned around and shut the window. "I'll tell you exactly how it happened," said Eli Bachar, "and I'll tell you the whole truth. I haven't got anything to hide. This wasn't the way that I intended . . ." He wriggled uncomfortably in the chair.

Michael crushed out the cigarette before he had smoked it halfway. Eli Bachar had respiratory troubles, and the room was already filled with the smell of cold smoke when Michael crossed his arms.

"She came here, that Orly, looking for you and you weren't here. I don't remember where you were, maybe with the girl's mother, maybe with Yigal Hayoun's Arab . . . No, I think you were talking to the couple who live opposite, the architect and the ceramicist, *nu*, Shalev, or with . . . It doesn't matter. I can't remember, but you couldn't be disturbed. She came here and sat down in the corridor. I didn't want her to see us running around like that and all the details, she . . . I went up to her, I spoke to her and she asked to accompany me on the investigation. I told her to forget it. She said that she had received a complaint about a humiliating attitude toward an Arab. She knew he was called Imad and she knew that he was from Ramallah and with Yigal Hayoun and that he had been arrested because he didn't have a permit to be here and that this, she said, was just an excuse. She had been told, she said, that you had beaten him during the interrogation and had extracted information from him by force, just because he's an Arab, and even from before that she knows that you're a tough interrogator—'brutal in interrogations,' that's what she said. I saw that we weren't going to get out of this if I didn't give her something . . ."

"I don't get it," said Michael in a strangled voice, not from fear but from anger. "If all those years that we've been together . . . You couldn't come and ask me? You couldn't have waited? She scared you so much?"

"Yes. No, she didn't scare me, but I didn't want . . ." Eli Bachar looked around, and his eyes scurried from side to side just the way Balilty's did when he was caught sinning. "If I hadn't. . . . She said that in any case she was going to mention you and that whole story with Imad in the article, and that she also has connections with the television, that she could make a big deal of it and that it was better if you cooperated, because otherwise she will write whatever she knows, and I . . . I didn't want her . . ." Eli lowered his eyes and did not speak.

Michael did not manage to control the sarcastic tone of his voice. "Uh-huh," he said with deadly calm. "I get it. It's only because . . . So for the sake of my reputation you met with her alone, and for my own good you gave her the entire story of my life and—"

"That's not so!" protested Eli loudly. "That's not how it was. I didn't tell her all the things that are in the article, I just—"

"What do you mean you 'didn't tell her'?" shouted Michael. "It's written in a way that it's clear that everything came from someone, and from inside."

"Tell me," Eli asked, and leaned toward Michael from the desk chair that was his, "how come *you*—aren't giving *me* any credit? What am I? Someone off the street? I'm telling you something, I'm telling you that. . . ." The questioning tone turned accusing. "You're considered an intelligent person, but in certain things you act like . . . a baby. Where do you think you're living? Have you ever even read anything she's written?"

"No, never. I never have," admitted Michael. "I've never . . . Until this thing."

"So you don't know anything," Eli said, and turned around and this time opened the window wide. "It's a technique," he said, and glanced outside. "That's the way they write. You don't say anything and she gets to it through her sources and puts it in as though you've said it. Even me—if Balilty hadn't told me how she works, I wouldn't have known that it . . . it's slanted so that people will think that you spoke to her yourself and gave her all the information."

"You've read this trash. There wasn't a single word there about Imad or about my brutality in the article," argued Michael. "Nothing about beating people up or interrogations or anything. Not a word about the whole thing."

"I fell into a trap," Eli said gloomily, and crushed the cup, "and believe me I've really been eating my heart out about it since then."

"So what did you say to her, then? And why did you fall into the trap? What are you, a little kid?"

"I was tired," Eli said, and turned his eyes away.

Michael lit another cigarette and with a mouthful of smoke he said: "I want us only to tell the truth—let's say not all of it, but with no games. You're talking with me, not with some . . . And don't tell me any stories."

In silence Eli spread out the thin scroll he had rolled and smoothed it with his hand in rhythmical movements as he spoke: "I gave her just the main details—that you're divorced, that you have a son, that women adore you, that . . . I said . . . I made you a star . . . I thought . . . I thought that if we ever really do leave here and set up the partnersh . . . and set up an office or something . . ."

"You thought you would use this for public relations?" said Michael in astonishment. "Is that what you thought? That if you gave her a piece of my love life or about how successful I am, you could cut it out of the newspaper and hang it up in the office? How exactly did you think that—"

"No," protested Eli. "I'm not an idiot. I can't tell you exactly. Maybe it was also because I was annoyed just then, and tired, and she pressured me, so I told her I would talk to her later, and I thought I wouldn't have to tell her anything, just general stuff and she got the rest out of—God knows whom. Not from me, I swear to you. You can ask her if you don't be—"

Michael snorted scornfully. "Ask her? Have you gone completely out of your mind?! You're talking like . . . as if you haven't understood a thing. I mean, you yourself have seen what she does when you're nice to her."

"She really is a bitch," whispered Eli, "and this is just the first article in a series."

"She's not even a bitch," said Michael. "She's just your average survivor. That's what your average survivors look like. She does her job, she thinks it's what they want from her and she goes for it with all her might, just like us. She puts her hands deep into the shit . . . Never mind, she doesn't matter to me at all." He heard his voice break. "She's not the issue. You're the issue. And even though it won't clear things up, I have to tell you that for

me . . . that as I see it . . . that I feel that this thing, what you've done, as violence. Just plain violence. And I'm asking myself how thick-skinned I can
be if I didn't know that that's how you feel and that—"

"Like that? So simple?" Eli interrupted him. "Since when are you so
simplistic? That's *your* question, isn't it? Isn't it you who's been explaining
to me from the beginning how people don't act out of a single motive,
especially when it's a matter of something out of the ordinary? You
yourself always explain to me—"

"Yes," admitted Michael. "It's simplistic, but when people hurt you,
the first thing you ask yourself is why they hate you, why they betrayed
you . . . what you've done to deserve it and how you ignored A and B and
C that were . . . Never mind, it's not important . . . No, in fact it is important, but we aren't going to resolve this right now. I don't know what I
did to make you . . ." However, he felt that in fact he did know, but this
knowledge, which was vague and refused to be put into words, embarrassed and shamed him; and it necessitated the recognition of an infan-
tile side that had been revealed in Eli Bachar and the recognition of his
own insensitivity. "What else did you talk to her about apart from my
love life? I want to know what is going to be in the next articles."

"I told her," said Eli Bachar, and a ray of sun illuminated locks of gray
in his curly black hair, "the truth about the Arab, that you . . . I told her
how angry you were at Balilty when . . ." His voice faded. "But I didn't
tell her who . . . I didn't say 'Balilty.' I didn't mention any names to her,
only . . . only that you really didn't . . ."

"But she somehow understood that it was Balilty?" said Michael
coldly. "I'm sure she figured it out somehow."

"She asked me whether it was someone from the special investigation
team," admitted Eli Bachar, "and I said . . . I think I didn't answer . . ."

"Did she record the conversation?"

"What am I? A child?"

Michael tilted his head. "They always record, just to be sure, for
backup and in case there are complaints . . ."

"I told her," said Eli heatedly. "That was my condition for talking to
her at all and she took notes the whole time about what I agreed that—"

"That you didn't see a tape," Michael interrupted him, "doesn't mean
there wasn't any."

"I looked really hard," insisted Eli Bachar. "I saw that she put her bag
aside, really far away."

"But she wears those big shirts. There's room for—"

"What do you want from me? To do a body search on her? And anyway, she was wearing a tight sweater, black, with a low neckline," said Eli Bachar. "She even made eyes at me, or at least it seemed to me she did, stretching and giving me sidelong glances, asking how it was for me and my wife to work together, being together all the time, but I didn't take it personally. I thought it was part of—"

"You could at least have exploited the situation to get something out of her," Michael said bitterly, and glanced at his watch.

"She digs into everyone's life there," said Eli. "I don't think she has anything sensational. You see what she writes there—she doesn't even mention Avital by name, just a married man who is one of the suspects, with whom Zahara Bashari purportedly had an affair, and that we questioned him and arrested him. I asked her about that and she said, 'I was told,' but she wasn't prepared to give details and I'm sure that she doesn't know any more than that."

For a moment there was silence, and Michael was aware of his temple throbbing and the dryness in his throat and mouth. This conversation hadn't brought any relief, any sense of release. Maybe it would have been better had he said something about Eli's jealousy, but he couldn't bring himself to speak about this because of the embarrassment, and because he could imagine Eli's voice, scornful and dismissive, saying to him: "Jealous? Me? What woman?" Or he would say to him: "What do you think you are?" He undid his watch strap, set the watch down in front of him and rubbed his wrist, and instead of asking whether Eli was jealous of his relationship with Yair, he heard himself, despite himself, because he felt that the question would be invasive and insulting, ask: "Tell me, what really happened? Tell me what . . . What have I done to you?"

Eli Bachar shrugged. "To me?" he said. "You haven't done anything to me. Not a thing."

"I thought that we'd manage to talk truthfully, frankly," said Michael without disguising the note of disappointment. He put his watch back on, stuck the cigarette packet in his jeans pocket and pushed back the chair.

Eli also got up. He put his hands in his pants pockets and looked as though he had something else to say. Michael looked at him for a moment without speaking and went to the door.

"Do you think that this is it?" burst out Eli. "That we're done with it?"

Michael stopped and turned around. Astonished, he looked at Eli's narrow, tanned face, which had now faded, and at the two dark circles under his eyes. "Do you think that between one thing and another, for the meantime, it's possible to make everything all right?" whispered Eli without looking at him. "Do you think that first you're going to make air out of me and promote . . . that baby and leave me . . . and put me on the shelf and then you're going to come along and tell me you're 'hurt' and 'aggression' and 'violence,' and I'm going to go down on my knees? You've put me aside—so I'm sidelined. What do you think, huh? To 'talk truthfully'? That I'm in your pocket?"

"Oh, so that's it. That's what's the matter," said Michael quietly. "In the end you let it slip out."

"It has nothing to do with it!" yelled Eli in a higher voice than ever. "It has nothing to do with it. It was just a coincidence that—"

"There is no such thing as coincidence," said Michael, and suddenly he sensed something else in his own expression, something he did not understand and had not expected. A kind of film was shed from his eyes, and sorrow looked out from them, and some other deep emotion, as if in Eli's hurt he had heard something else, more important and heart-breaking than all that had been said between them. And then, with embarrassment, and as if with no strength, he held out his hand and softly touched Eli's shoulder, and left.

The corridor was not empty and his footsteps were not the only ones that echoed. Doors opened and telephones rang and people hurried past him. Somebody tapped his arm and someone else said, "What's up, Ohayon?" Apparently what had happened in his room was obvious on his face, because there was no doubt that Tzilla, who was standing in the corridor with her hand on the door handle, was alarmed when she asked as he came up to her: "What happened?"

"Nothing. Nothing new," he promised in a faint voice. "Is he still there?"

"He hasn't budged," said Tzilla. "With Yair, and I didn't let Balilty . . . Tell me, what happened? Do you feel okay?"

"Perfectly fine," he said to her, and even contorted his lips into what he hoped would look like a smile. "I'm just tired."

"Maybe we'll postpone it for a little . . .?" She hesitated and nodded toward the closed door.

"Nonsense," dismissed Michael. "We're not postponing anything, I'm just wondering whether . . ." He looked around and thought about the other rooms. "Never mind," he finally said. "I thought maybe we would sit in some other room, but . . . Maybe it's best in the little room after all. There's an informal atmosphere there and this might . . ."

"Where should I put this for you?" Tzilla debated, and moved her eyes from Michael to the miniature tape recorder she was holding. "I've already recorded the date and the time on it, but where should I put it? Have you got a shirt on under the sweater?"

"Just an undershirt," apologized Michael, and suddenly he felt like a child under the efficiency of her fingers, which surrounded his waist. "In the belt of your jeans. There's no alternative," she said, and rolled up the bottom of the blue sweater. "Here. Like that, and there's also another tape in the drawer. If he agrees, put that one on the table. You haven't had anything to drink yet," she scolded him. "Go ahead in and I'll bring some coffee, or would you rather—"

"Bring it, bring it. Why not? Also for Mr. Efraim Beinisch, and bring some water, too. Never mind. All the bottles are stored in this . . ."

"Einat phoned again," reported Tzilla as she touched the door handle.

"*Nu?* Has she regained consciousness?" he asked impatiently.

"Not really," said Tzilla, "but it's a matter of hours, the doctor said, and I thought I should go over there."

"Not yet," said Michael. "Wait for some progress. In any case no one is going to let you talk to her now."

"I told you," he heard Efraim Beinisch say as he opened the door. "I don't tend the garden, only Mrs. Beinisch, my wife, and there's a gardener . . ." He stopped speaking and stood up when the door opened and looked at Michael anxiously. On the table, between two bottles of mineral water and two colorful paper cups, beneath the old desk lamp with the cracked plastic shade, lay a large color photograph of a climbing rosebush. Packets of coffee and plastic spoons were in the open cardboard box under the table and a carton of bottled mineral water stood on the table, near the closed window. The lamp illuminated the surface of the table and picked it out of the dimness of the room. Faint autumn sunlight came in through the slits in the brown iron shutter. They sat next to each other, facing the table that stood next to the wall and concealed the bottom half of the window. On the wooden frame around the dusty, stained windowpane, traces of peeling green paint were still visible.

"Mr. Beinisch is not prepared to speak to anyone else, nor does he agree to our recording the conversation," said Sergeant Yair with no preliminaries. He rose from his chair and buttoned the top button of the light blue shirt with sleeves rolled up to the elbows ("Did he always dress like that, or did he learn it from you?" Balilty's scoffing voice echoed in Michael's ears) and tucked the shirttails into his narrow black belt. "So in the meantime I've been asking him a few things about the antique rosebush. He says—Mr. Beinisch says—that to the best of his knowledge they never had a bush like that in their garden, and not in the garden next door, it seems to him, but he really isn't knowledgeable about flowers."

Efraim Beinisch said feebly: "I'm not knowledgeable, but there isn't one." He turned to Michael and explained apologetically: "I came here before six o'clock in the morning. I've been waiting for more than two hours, but I didn't want . . . I don't like to impose and they told me . . ."

Michael shook his head and Yair looked a question at him. Michael shook his head again. "So maybe I'll go help Eli now with all the material—"

"No, no," a tense Michael interrupted. "There's no need. He'll manage on his own. Ask Tzilla . . . She knows exactly what needs to be . . ." Yair nodded obediently and left the room.

The darkness of the room and the thick, oppressive air in fact suited him at that moment. A kind of paralyzing obstinacy led him to sit beside Efraim Beinisch, with his back to the window, and with all the oppressiveness and discomfort that were obvious on the man's face. The accountant kept patting the sleeves of his suit jacket as if trying to rid them of invisible dust. Side by side they sat, with the table in front of them and their backs to the window like two schoolchildren. "They told me that you wanted privacy," Michael explained, and turned his chair toward Beinisch.

"Privacy, yes," Efraim Beinisch muttered, and ran his large white fingers through his hair. The light of the desk lamp gave a gray tone to the yellowish color of his hair, a remnant of its former red. He laid his hands on his knees and leaned forward, and Michael looked at the large brown birthmark on his right hand and the freckles that ran to his knuckle, where his wedding band gleamed. He was touched by something about this hand, with its freckled, wrinkled skin and the small age spots that were scattered among the wrinkles, and the way he twisted the wedding band and irritated the flesh that swelled around it.

"Has something happened?" asked Michael, and he himself was surprised by the note of patient pity in his voice as he asked the question.

Efraim Beinisch wiped his round face, which was gleaming in the light of the desk lamp. Then he turned his head toward the window, as if listening to the sounds of thunder outside, and he sat up straight in his chair and asked: "What was that? Did you hear that? Is that thunder or shooting?"

"I think it's thunder. They said it would rain today," said Michael reassuringly. "Look, here comes the lightning."

"No, all last night there were . . . Where we are we hear everything that happens in Gilo," Efraim Beinisch said, and examined his hands. "But that's only at night."

Michael said nothing.

"These aren't good times," Efraim Beinisch said, and cleared his throat. "There's no quiet. Difficult times . . ." He stopped speaking and looked toward the closed window, touched his Adam's apple, ran his fingers around his thick neck and touched the knot of his blue tie.

"Mr. Beinisch." Michael sighed after a long moment of silence. "You came here because you wanted to tell me something."

"Yes, yes," said Efraim Beinisch in a thick voice, "but it's difficult. This is difficult for me."

"It's difficult for you to talk?"

"Not to talk," said Efraim Beinisch. "Talking isn't difficult. It's what to say that's difficult," he explained, and lightly tapped his knee before grasping both sides of the chair with his hand.

"Does it have to with Yoram?" guessed Michael.

Efraim Beinisch nodded his head. In the light of the lamp Michael noticed the nervous blinking of his eyes as he stood halfway up and took a packet of paper tissues out of the back pocket of his trousers. "My wife, she puts them here," he apologized, and blew his nose noisily.

Michael crossed his arms on his chest. "Have you found out something new?" he asked gently. "Something about Yoram?"

Efraim Beinisch opened his mouth, but didn't utter a sound. For a moment he looked like a large fish out of water, and finally he shook his head as if giving up and took a small package wrapped in newsprint out of the inner pocket of his jacket. He unfolded the paper and pushed it aside and examined, as if seeing it for the first time in his life, the small notebook bound in brown leather. He looked at it, and looked some more, before he handed it to Michael.

Michael felt the soft leather and undid the yellow cord that held it together. He got closer to the desk lamp, set the notebook down under it and paged through it slowly, reading what was written on the first pages, and then he ruffled quickly through the pages, stopping at a page that was completely covered in big round letters that said: "To lift all kind of spells: Write on a parchment that has been ritually purified: May it be Your will, the Holy Name, Lord of Israel, that You lift from the bearer of this amulet all manner of spells, be they in writing or be they spoken . . ."

He turned and looked at Efraim Beinisch. "Where did you find this, Mr. Beinisch?" he asked, and tried to make his question sound matter-of-fact and to ignore the throbbing that had grown stronger in his temples.

Efraim Beinisch shook his head a few times and looked down. In a broken voice he said: "It's this. Because of this I wanted . . . God . . . In Yoram's room, in the sock drawer."

"Is it his, this notebook?" asked Michael, and he was immediately concerned lest his playing innocent was too artificial and caused Beinisch to immediately clam up.

"I wish it were," said Efraim Beinisch. "I wish it were. God help me, it's the girl's."

"The girl's?" asked Michael. "Which girl?"

"The girl. The girl that . . . Nessia. It's hers. Don't you see that it's a child's handwriting? It says here . . ." He rifled through the notebook quickly to the last page. "Here we are. 'Peter brought a golden ball to decorate the sukkah' . . ."

"And this was in Yoram's room?" asked Michael carefully, restraining his voice so as not to frighten Efraim Beinisch, who could just stop talking and walk away the same way he had suddenly appeared of his own free will.

"In the sock drawer, and that's the truth," Efraim Beinisch said, and laid his hands on his knees and examined them with interest.

And instead of proceeding as if tiptoeing on eggshells, instead of listening to that anxiety, Michael gently set the brown notebook aside on the corner of the table, laid a hand on Efraim Beinisch's arm and said simply: "You searched his room."

"I . . . I looked through his things . . . God, God in heaven." Efraim Beinisch sighed.

"Before our search?" Michael asked, and watched him nod limply. "You looked through his room before our people searched there?"

"I . . . I don't know why," said Efraim Beinisch, and he raised his round face, which had turned yellow. "I know that he . . . that he tells lies, and I thought . . . But he wasn't . . . He . . . I knew he had gone out that night. I thought then that . . ."

"What did you think?" Michael asked, and poured some water into the pink paper cup—how odd it was, suddenly, this bright pink—and handed it to Efraim Beinisch, who didn't move. "Drink, drink," he urged, and he watched the man slowly lift his head, shaking it from side to side and extending a trembling hand toward the cup and bringing it to his twitching lips. The sounds of his swallowing were heard in the silence of the room, and then came the rumble of approaching thunder.

Efraim Beinisch wiped his lips with the back of his hand. "God," he said, "his mother doesn't know I found anything. I didn't say anything to her. She would die if she . . . I'm dying myself."

Quickly, so as not to lose the moment, Michael brought the conversation back to the place it had stopped. "You thought he went out to have a good time the night the girl disappeared?"

"I don't know what to think anymore," explained Efraim Beinisch. "Sometimes you don't want to think. You don't want to see what you're seeing."

"But you searched his room," Michael reminded him, "without anyone knowing. So you did want to know."

"I had no alternative," Efraim Beinisch said, and looked at him with supplicating expectancy. "I had no alternative. Sometimes there's no alternative, and you have to know the truth."

"Yes," said Michael. "Sometimes there's no alternative."

"Especially," said Efraim Beinisch, "if you know you've raised . . . that your child, your only son . . . your only son, whom you love, the son you thought was . . . everything . . . And you discover that . . . that he's rotten." The last word echoed in the room, and Efraim Beinisch sat up straight in his chair. "Rotten," he repeated. "Completely rotten. Only God knows how. Like an apple that's red and beautiful on the outside. On the outside, like a red apple, bright, and inside—a worm. All rotten. In fact . . . sick. Very sick."

At that moment there was a knock on the door and it immediately opened and Tzilla stood there, bending over the threshold to pick up a cup of coffee she had set down to free her hand to knock. Michael rose and hurried over to her, took the two glass mugs from her and murmured, "Thanks, and do not disturb," then pushed the door closed with his shoulder before she could say another word and carried the two cups to the table. Then he dug into his pants pocket, took out the packet of crushed cigarettes and offered one to Efraim Beinisch, who looked at him in confusion, raised his head and with a resigned expression put the cigarette between his lips and waited for Michael to light it.

"I haven't smoked for thirty years," he said. "Blood pressure. But now nothing matters anymore." He looked at the cup of coffee as if astonished. "I don't drink coffee, either. My wife doesn't let me . . . ," and he immediately took a long, noisy sip.

"Mr. Beinisch," said Michael without taking his eyes off the other man, who had leaned his elbows on the table, one hand encircling the cup of coffee and the other holding the cigarette, from which gray smoke curled, thickening between the two men. Beinisch's watery eyes followed the spiral of smoke, which first curled upward alone and then joined the other and thickened into a cloud above the cracked lamp.

"Do you think Yoram abducted the girl?" asked Michael.

Without taking his eyes off the cloud of smoke, Efraim Beinisch nodded.

"Why do you think he abducted her?"

Efraim Beinisch looked at him silently.

"Do you think the girl knew something about him? That there's anything . . . in the notebook?"

Efraim Beinisch lowered his eyes and coughed, but did not speak yet.

"Do you think he murdered Zahara Bashari?" asked Michael simply.

Heavy rain pattered on the iron shutter.

Efraim Beinisch wrapped his hand around the glass mug. "This is the end of us," he murmured. "I thought that we would have quiet, that he would get married and go to America, that he would . . . But God didn't want this. I'm not a religious man, Mr. Ohayon. You should be aware that I'm not a religious man. I finished with God . . . Anyone who was under communism in Hungary doesn't . . . can't . . . The Russians killed my whole family. My father died in a camp . . . Like the Nazis, but people don't know . . . But now I'm asking, what more does He want? What did I do wrong? Where have I sinned? We just had one son. My wife couldn't . . . and she didn't want to, and we gave him everything, really everything, and here we are drinking coffee as if . . . ," he muttered, "as if nothing has happened."

"I can imagine how hard it was for you to come here," said Michael.

"It was the most difficult decision I ever made in my life," said Efraim Beinisch, "but I had no alternative. I'll tell you the truth: I thought, either I put a bullet through my head or drive the car off a cliff, or else I do what needs to be done. I can put a bullet through my head *later*, too, but first I had to do what needed to be done." His voice rose. "I'm not talking about the law, Mr. Ohayon. I don't give a damn about the law. I'm talking about something bigger."

"Do you think he had a relationship with Zahara Bashari?" probed Michael. "Do you think he is the father of her child?"

"Did he have a relationship?!" said Efraim Beinisch. "With him, it's impossible to know anything. He doesn't tell. Ever. Even when he was a child, Yoram never said anything. He just spoke about . . . peripheral things. I never understood what really happened. Even at school, when the teacher called us in, that they caught him, he said . . . he told stories . . ."

"What did they catch him doing at school?" asked Michael.

"He . . ." Efraim Beinisch looked at him in embarrassment. "What does it matter now? But maybe you're right. Maybe it is important. He . . . There was a girl at school. I don't know exactly what . . . He captured a cat with its kittens and . . . he showed the girl . . . She watched how he killed the kittens, with a stone to their heads. The girl . . . She . . . Her mother . . . She had to be taken to a psychologist, but . . . it never happened again or, if you ask me, he learned how to conceal . . . he didn't show anyone anything. His mother doesn't allow it to be mentioned. We never talk about it anymore. At home she said to me, 'What do you want from him? He's just a child.' So I let it drop. I'm to blame. I should have . . ." His voice faded and he looked with astonishment at the burning cigarette and dropped it into the pink paper cup.

"Did he have a relationship with Zahara?" asked Michael again.

"I . . ." Efraim Beinisch leaned forward and looked at Michael. "I don't have . . . I didn't have anything against those people, the Basharis. But understand, it was the women. It's a women's affair. When we first moved in there was a common entrance. There was a porch at the entry to the house with a window on the Basharis' side. On the first day we came we said hello nicely and we introduced ourselves and everything. We shook hands and they said congratulations. But after a few days the problems started. You never know what the first thing was. My wife hung out her laundry in the yard, on the clothesline, and Naeema Bashari threw all the laundry next to the door. It was her clothesline.

How could we have known? She didn't come to talk, just threw down all the laundry. Then she threw things out of the window onto the entry porch, peels and garbage and . . ." He stopped speaking for a long moment and stared as though he were seeing scenes from the past. "Had it been just between me and Mr. Bashari, believe me, everything would have been sorted out long ago, but a quarrel between neighbors is a quarrel between women and it wasn't possible to reason with Naeema Bashari. I could feel how she wanted to get rid of us in any way possible, no matter how—she just wanted us to go. I wanted to, I wanted to leave. But my wife . . . she didn't want to give in. She wanted war. To win. To teach her a lesson. Like"—he nodded in the direction of the window— "like with the Arabs, but here it's with women . . . Believe me, Mr. Ohayon, a quarrel between neighbors is a quarrel between women."

"And the children?" asked Michael, who wanted to get the conversation back to the question from which it had started.

"Yoram was born after we had already been living here for many years. After we had already despaired. It was like a miracle." Now he snorted and shook his head. "You think there's been a miracle and God laughs in your face. I invited them to the circumcision. I went over there, and for once I spoke to Mr. Bashari. To this day my wife doesn't know. I thought . . . an opportunity. And they didn't come. Nothing. No congratulations, no explanations, no apology, after years that we'd been living there without . . . And they, with all their four children . . ."

"But I understand that as children your Yoram and Zahara Bashari would . . ." Michael did not complete the sentence and allowed it to hang in the air.

Efraim Beinisch wiped his broad hand over his eyes for a moment, as if to eradicate from them sights that he could not bear. "They were such beautiful children," he said, and spread his palms as if in supplication. "Both of them were so beautiful. Even she, Zahara . . . I have nothing against Jews from the oriental communities, Mr. Ohayon, believe me. Had it been up to me . . . But their mothers didn't let . . . First the mothers and then everyone, her brothers and her father, and I—what could I do? Argue with them all? 'Let them, let them play together.' She could have been good for him, a good influence on him. But her big brother caught them together. They were so little and there was . . . I want to tell you, precisely because of the feud, and precisely because his mother hated her parents so much—this is exactly why he fell in love with her.

But we killed it for them. Yoram, he loved her, but the hatred was bigger. What could he have done when the families . . . hate each other like that? And Yoram is his mother's son and he'd never go against her. And Clara, it's impossible to budge her from this, even in the smallest things and certainly in a thing like this. That her son should go with the daughter of . . . Yoram was a mamma's boy . . . They say that in the old days everything was different here, that everyone was poor but together, that there weren't . . . But that's incorrect, Mr. Ohayon. In the old days things were also bad. Everyone was poor, and everyone was a new immigrant and . . . they didn't let you live, there wasn't solidarity and mutual aid . . . You don't know what a child . . . So good-looking, like his mother . . . She looked like that when I first met her in our city. Just like that, with those huge eyes . . ." His voice faded and he looked around as if trying to understand where he was, until finally he gathered his wits and tightened his lips.

"But nevertheless they were in love and had a relationship," said Michael. "You saw them."

"One time I saw everything with my own eyes, just once," said Efraim Beinisch. "I was the one who saw it, and not my wife. And I didn't say anything to anyone. No one in the world knew, even his mother. No one . . . God almighty, a person has an only child . . . one . . ."

"When was that?" insisted Michael.

"Before . . . Yoram was in the army and she wasn't yet, I think. He was in computers in the army and he came home every day. An only son, came home to his mother. And once we were . . . His mother wanted us to check our gas masks because we'd received a notice that they were out of date and they had to be checked. They were in the shelter. The shelter is shared. It . . . During the Gulf War . . . Never mind. What happened during the Gulf War in . . . In the end, I built a sealed room inside the house. But there, in the shelter, were the gas masks, and I went down there at night—not late, but it was already dark—to get the masks. The door was closed, with a lock. I didn't find a key. There's one small window. The shelter is half underground and half aboveground. I thought . . . maybe burglars . . . I went down on my knees and looked in. There was a rag on the window, but there was a little gap in the rag. I looked through a hole. There was a bit of light, maybe a candle. I saw . . . They were . . . together." Efraim Beinisch crossed his two fingers as if to explain by the gesture what he had seen.

"And only that time?" asked Michael.

"I didn't see anything more than that, but I know things."

"And it was Zahara?" confirmed Michael. "You're certain?"

"Her face was in the light, and she was naked—the upper half of her body, her face in the light. She didn't see me—I was in the dark."

"And you think they had a relationship like that all those years?"

"Of course they did. All those years. I know it here"—he pinched his arm. "I know it on my flesh. The whole time. It was because of the hatred that they fell in love. We made him sick. I don't know exactly where they met and there are many more . . . things that I don't know . . . Even about Michelle. He's going to marry her. When I met her parents and . . . Doesn't she see anything? Tell me, how can a woman be with a fellow and not know anything? How can you know anything about anyone? I used to think that you could know about your own child . . . But you only know if you want to know."

"Or if you look in his sock drawer," noted Michael.

"Believe me," said Efraim Beinisch. He looked at his large hands and then rose a bit and pulled the packet of paper tissues out of his back pocket again and very carefully pulled out one tissue and used it to wipe his face and then his hands. "If only I hadn't had to look there, if only I hadn't needed to know what I know. God, I just think about his mother and she . . . She just won't believe it."

"What won't she believe?"

Efraim Beinisch pointed to the small leather notebook that was lying on the table near Michael. "God almighty," he said, and shook his head. "I gave that boy so much—going places with him and talking to him and the zoo and karate lessons, and the computer, one of the first ones in the country. There wasn't anything . . . But it didn't help, Mr. Ohayon. Believe me, you can't know . . . When the air is full of hatred—what can possibly grow there?"

"Mr. Beinisch," Michael said, and turned his chair to face the other man. "Where was Yoram on the night Zahara Bashari was murdered? Where was he really?"

Efraim Beinisch wiped his brow again and then laid his hands on his knees and arched his back and said: "He went to pick up Michelle from the airport. That's what he told us. We thought she was supposed to arrive at two o'clock in the morning, but in the end she only arrived at six."

"We checked," said Michael gently, "and she wasn't supposed to have come on the KLM flight. She wasn't on the passenger list. From the out-set she was on the passenger list for the El Al flight that comes in at five in the morning."

"Yes," protested the father, "but at the time we didn't know that. He said that . . . You already know what he said."

"And even at two in the morning. Even supposing she was coming in at two in the morning, when did he really leave the house?"

"Yes, this is what I came here for . . . ," said Efraim Beinisch miserably. "I wanted to tell you . . . he wasn't at home. My wife thinks I was asleep, and my son thinks I will say what I'm told to say, but I'm telling you: I wasn't asleep, I hadn't taken a pill, and he wasn't at home. I don't know where he was. He has a car and he's independent and he never tells me anything because I don't ask. Why ask? And if I did ask, would he tell me? And if he does tell me anything, there's not a chance it's the truth. That's the truth, Mr. Ohayon, may God forgive me. What would you do in my place, Mr. Ohayon? You're an intelligent person. Tell me, what would you do?"

"It really is very difficult, your situation," Michael murmured, and for a moment he saw his own son's face in his mind's eye. "I," he would have said to Efraim Beinisch, "would not have been able to be in your situa-tion," and he immediately reprimanded himself for this certainty.

"There are people who will tell you," said Efraim Beinisch, "even my wife, that it doesn't matter what your child does—he's always your child."

"You aren't denying Yoram, Mr. Beinisch," Michael promised him. "These are two quite different things."

"Exactly," said Efraim Beinisch. "That's what I thought. I'm not sever-ing anything with him, but I can't protect him by lying. I should have protected him a long time ago. And not with a lie. Only there isn't any-thing I can do if he . . . if it turns out that he really did . . ." His voice faded and his gaze blurred. The room was silent, save only for the rain that beat down hard on the iron shutters.

"And on the eve of the holiday?" asked Michael after a long moment. "Where was he when the little girl disappeared?"

"He told us that he was with Michelle, that they'd gone to Tel Aviv. I'm telling you the truth," whispered Efraim Beinisch. "That's what he told us, but later it turned out that Michelle had gone to visit a friend of hers at a kibbutz, some kibbutz near Netanya; I forget what it's . . . He drove her there and said that he had to go back to take care of something, and apparently he came back here . . . We didn't even know he'd come back . . . I . . . didn't . . . want to think . . . I took a sleeping pill. A person can't be thinking like that all the time, Mr. Ohayon, don't you see?"

Michael nodded his head, pondering the face of the fiancée, who had not batted an eyelash when she stated that Yoram Beinisch had been with her the whole night at Kibbutz Yakum. He wondered what Yoram had told her so that she would lie for him so brazenly. "A person can't . . . ," continued Efraim Beinisch, but he stopped suddenly in alarm when the door handle squeaked. Eli Bachar was standing in the doorway. "I need you for a minute," he said when Michael looked at him questioningly. "Could you just step outside with me for a moment?"

Michael hesitated for a moment and then rose, asking himself whether Eli would take him out like that from a conversation with the father of a murder suspect because of what had happened between them earlier. And Eli, reading his look, said: "It can't wait."

Michael laid his hand on Efraim Beinisch's arm. "Just a moment," he said to him, and hurried out.

"There are results," said Eli Bachar, "and I've already phoned his mother. I've asked her to come here, but she said she couldn't, she wasn't feeling well. Her voice . . . It was as if she already knew. I asked her where her son was and she said he was there, at home, but I'm certain she was alone . . . I told her that we were on the way to their place. I didn't say that the father was here, I didn't want to . . . I have a feeling that . . ."

"We'll take him with us," decided Michael. "The two of us will take him with us and there, in the house, when the three of them are together, there will be . . . Things will become even clearer." For a moment he hesitated as to whether to say anything to Eli about what the father had confided to him, but instead of speaking he opened the door and went up to the large, heavy man, whose shoulders slumped. "Come, Mr. Beinisch," he said to him. "Let's take you home. We have some news that isn't very—"

"Has something happened to my wife?" said Efraim Beinisch in alarm, and he rose from his chair. "She wasn't feeling so well last night—all these things with her blood pressure and her heart condition aren't . . . Has something happened to her?"

"Your wife is fine," promised Michael, "but we have the lab results, and the picture, I'm afraid, is not so good for your family."

"It's the genetic test," said Efraim Beinisch. "It's his child, isn't it?"

Michael nodded, and without speaking the three of them walked down the corridor, Eli Bachar in the lead, Efraim Beinisch behind him and Michael in the rear, looking at the broad ruddy nape, in the wrinkles of which beads of perspiration gleamed. When they reached the car, Efraim Beinisch looked helpless. He turned to gaze at the building as if he were seeing it for the first time, raised his eyes to the dome of the Russian church and then sank into the backseat and sighed loudly. "God almighty," he muttered, and shrank even more into the seat as Eli Bachar shifted into reverse and turned the Toyota around, listening to the squeal of the tires.

"The tires need air," said Eli. "Remind me to fill them up."

Chapter 17

I t's locked. Maybe she's not home," said Efraim Beinisch, and with a trembling hand he grasped the key ring he took out of his pocket. He anxiously fingered one of the keys and finally fitted it into the keyhole with a decisive gesture. Michael followed him into the living room, and from there to the kitchen and the bathroom, and saw how he was trying to restrain the frenzy in his movements, while Eli Bachar's footsteps receded in the direction of the other rooms. They heard him call out from the other end of the apartment, just as both of them were looking at their reflections in the bathroom mirror. "There's one room here that's locked," Eli Bachar called to them, and immediately the two of them rushed back to the dim corridor.

"This is our bedroom," said Efraim Beinisch in a shaky voice. "We never lock it," and he pushed the handle down once or twice and tried to force the door open with his shoulder and called out in a panic: "Clara, Clara. Open the door, Clara. It's me. It's only me." Not a sound came from the locked room.

Eli Bachar looked at Michael, then took a Swiss Army knife out of the inner pocket of his windbreaker and selected one of the blades. "I'm opening it," he warned, and Efraim Beinisch obeyed his voice and stepped back.

"It's open," said Eli Bachar after a moment, and he carefully laid the metal frame that had been around the keyhole on the floor. Only then did he move aside and let Efraim Beinisch go in. In the space between his body and the doorjamb, in the illumination cast by the night-light next to the bed, Michael saw only the bare white legs swinging in the middle of the room, in which the shutters had been closed, tinted in the yellow light and swinging away from it, changing from light to dark as they swung almost to the old wooden ladder that had been positioned there. And because of Efraim Beinisch's large body standng in front of him, and then collapsing into his arms, he did not have time to lift his head to the high ceiling and to the shadow that moved back and forth across her face.

He lay Efraim Beinisch down on the flowered carpet and was wondering whether to awaken him from his faint when Eli said to him: "Hold the legs of the ladder for me. It's pretty rickety." Only when he had thrust the weight of his body on the base of the ladder did Michael look up and see, as Eli climbed quickly up the rungs, the iron hook stuck in the middle of the ceiling—there was one like that in his new apartment, and if it wasn't used, as Linda had said, to suspend a lantern or to dry strings of garlic or peppers, it had probably been used to hang large cuts of meat after slaughter—and the synthetic laundry line that was dangling from it, white and shiny, and after that he saw the bluish-blackish hue of Clara Beinisch's face and the pinkness of the tongue protruding from her mouth.

"Help me get her down," groaned Eli Bachar from the top of the ladder, which was swaying now that he had cut the cord and was holding the body in his arms. "She's heavy as a . . ." He puffed as Michael held the legs. "Heavy as a corpse . . . How long has it been since we called her?" he muttered as he laid the body on the pink bedspread. She was not cold like other corpses, and it would have been possible to think for a moment that she was still alive had it not been for the face, which was blue and distorted, and the astonished-looking open eyes and dangling, broken neck. Lest he become nauseous, Michael looked away before he began imagining how he himself would look had he hanged himself by the neck like that from the iron hook.

"Just look at how she arranged everything. It couldn't have been because of my phone call. She had planned it before then," said Eli Bachar, who surveyed the room as Michael picked up the phone beside the bed and called an ambulance. "You don't do a thing like this on the spur of the moment," said Eli Bachar. "It needs preparation," and as he leaned over the bed and stubbornly but futilely tried to find a pulse in Mrs. Beinisch's wrist and neck, Michael pulled the mobile telephone out of Eli's belt and called the Criminal Identification lab vehicle.

"Too late," Eli muttered, and dropped her left arm. "It's been half an hour since I spoke to her, maybe even an hour. Apparently she went

right afterward and . . . And there's no sign of a note or a letter or anything," he complained, and looked around.

Michael now knelt beside Efraim Beinisch, patted his cheeks and called:
"Mr. Beinisch, Mr. Beinisch, Efraim, Efraim," and Eli Bachar walked
around the double bed and examined the chest of drawers next to it. From
a small jewelry box on top of the bureau he drew out a string of white
pearls that had been coiled like a snake, the gold clasp sticking up, and only
then did he notice the book that was lying next to the jewelry box.

"I don't know what language this is," wondered Eli as he paged
through it, "but there isn't a note inside it, either." By the light of the
night-light he opened drawers and peeped under the bed. When Efraim
Beinisch opened his eyes and looked with an unfocused expression into
Michael's eyes, Eli Bachar had already opened in turn all the doors of the
large wardrobe, all of which were embellished with a thin gilded frame,
and each of them in turn had squeaked until it bumped into its neighbor.

Michael opened the shutters. Pale light came in through the large
window, muddied by the streaks of raindrops, and the light brought into
relief the black dress Clara Beinisch had been wearing before she
climbed the ladder and tied the laundry line to the iron hook. "I'm just
getting some water," he said to Efraim Beinisch, who was still lying on
the carpet at the foot of the double bed, with the pink satin fringes of
the bedspread above his head.

The kitchen was tidy and quiet, as if nothing had happened, and on the
marble countertop, on a very white towel that had been spread next to the
sink, cups that were still damp inside had been placed to dry, and it was
clear that they had been washed not long ago. After Michael examined
them, he filled one of them with water from the tap, and on second
thought filled another glass as well and brought both of them with the
damp towel into the bedroom. There, at the foot of the bed, he knelt again
and dipped the edge of the towel into the water and patted Efraim
Beinisch's cheeks with it. As he did not move, Michael folded the towel into
a narrow rectangle and laid it on the forehead of the man who was lying
there and watched the drops of water trickling from its edge onto his large
ears and from them onto the white ceramic floor. And at the same time he
wondered what the original floor had looked like, and immediately tried to
rid himself of this thought, unsuccessfully. Then he heard Efraim Beinisch
muttering, as he slowly lifted his hand to his forehead: "If I had been at
home, this wouldn't have happened. This wouldn't have happened."

Efraim Beinisch slowly wiped his forehead with the towel and his eyes closed again halfway. "Can't anything be done? Is she dead?"

Michael nodded, and Efraim Beinisch opened his small, pale eyes wide and fixed them, defeated and desperate, on Michael's face. Michael tilted the second glass of water to his lips and supported his head from behind and said: "Drink, Mr. Beinisch. The doctor will be here soon." After he had taken a few sips, Efraim Beinisch sat up, grasped the edge of the bed and tried to stand.

"Sit for another minute. Not all at once," Michael warned, and out of the corner of his eye he saw Eli pulling the drawers, which were also embellished with a thin gilded frame, out of the wardrobe. "I thought we would find Yoram at home," Michael reminded Efraim Beinisch.

Efraim Beinisch leaned on the bed, his legs sprawled in front of him. "They should be in their room, he and Michelle," he said in a limp voice, and turned his head a bit, until he noticed the naked feet and buried his head in his hands, "but maybe they went out for a while. It seems like there's no one in the house . . ." He stopped talking, held his breath and stood up all at once, supported by the edge of the bed. "We have to check Yoram's room. Who knows what . . . ," he said, and hurried out of the bedroom. Michael followed him to the end of the corridor and stood beside him as he opened the door to his son's room. Here too there was a large wall closet, and all three of its doors were wide open. In one of the drawers, all of which had been emptied, only an orphaned sock remained. Efraim Beinisch looked at the red stripe embroidered on the cuff, raised his hands to his chest and whispered: "He saw that the notebook was gone. He understood."

On the floor, at the foot of the closet, and on the rumpled bedding and the small rug there were piles of clothing and other items. "They're not here," repeated Efraim Beinisch, and this time there was a note of relief in the sentence, but he still had his hands clasped to his chest.

"It looks as though someone has packed everything up and hit the road," said Michael.

"Michelle's large suitcase isn't here," agreed Efraim Beinisch, sighing, it seemed, in relief.

"Had they been planning to go anywhere?" asked Michael. "I thought we had agreed that Yoram wasn't to leave the house," he reminded the father, who was still standing in the doorway, leaning on the doorjamb.

"He didn't ask me and he didn't tell me anything," said Efraim Beinisch. "I told you, he does whatever he wants, Yoram, and now we have to . . . When his mother . . ." His shoulders shook in a spasm, and for a moment Michael was afraid that he would collapse and fall, but he only swayed where he was standing and supported himself on the door-jamb. "She put on a dress to do this," whispered Efraim Beinisch, "and took off the necklace." With labored steps he entered his son's room and dropped his heavy body onto the mattress of the futon and buried his head in a pillow. "She didn't show any sign," he said to the corner of the mattress. "No sign at all. Last night she was as usual. She didn't want to hear what I wanted to tell her . . . I thought that she really didn't know anything. I didn't think . . . Apparently she woke up and realized where I was. She always said that if anything happened to Yoram . . . She . . . She didn't say anything to me," he mumbled, and sat up straight. "People leave . . . Did she leave me anything? Did you find a letter? Did she leave anything for . . ."

"We haven't found anything yet," Michael said, and cocked his ear to the corridor. "I think that the doctor has arrived, Mr. Beinisch," he said reassuringly, "but you have to tell me the whole truth: Do you think Yoram has left the country?"

Efraim Beinisch looked at him miserably. "I have no way of know-ing," he muttered. "He was here last night and in the morning before I left I didn't check whether they were in their room, he and Michelle. It could be that . . . I told you—I don't know."

The front door was flung open, footsteps approached, something heavy was carried through the corridor and against the backdrop of the voices coming in—"Are you bringing the stretcher?" called one; "Wait till the doctor is finished," called another—Michael went over to Efraim Beinisch, leaned over him and looked into his eyes. "We've already seen that you know your son. You're the only one who really knows how Yoram operates," he said to him, "and now I'm asking you: In your opin-ion, is it possible that despite all the promises and threats he has left the country with his fiancée, Michelle? In light of what has happened," he said, indicating the corridor with his head, "it's really a good idea not to hide anything, because there's really no reason to."

Efraim Beinisch shook his head, looked around as if an answer might be found in the open closet and then spread his arm and said: "God almighty," and was silent for a moment before he added: "It could be. To America. With Michelle. God knows what he told her. But you're right. There's no reason anymore."

"Wait here. The doctor will speak to you in a few minutes," Michael instructed him, and hastened to the kitchen to telephone from there. Next to the refrigerator, on the wall, a telephone had been installed to match the refrigerator. He dialed the number of Balilty's mobile phone three times, and three times he got the recorded announcement: "The subscriber is not available. Please try again later."

So he called Tzilla, and the moment she heard his voice, she scolded him: "Tell me, why aren't you answering calls on the beeper? For half an hour now I've been trying to . . ." He had to shout at her to silence her to tell her what to do and then cut off her complaints ("What do you mean, roadblocks?" she said impatiently. "Who's going to give me personnel for that? At the airport will be enough. I'll talk to Balilty. We'll figure out what to do") before she said to him: "I've been looking for you like crazy for half an hour. The girl, she's woken up. She's opened her eyes and she's conscious but she's not prepared to talk. She's not talking to anyone, and Einat is going crazy. She hasn't said a word and I thought that only you—"

"Not now," Michael told her, and looked at Eli in the doorway of the kitchen. "Not now. In a while I'll go over there; you stay where you are, and don't get any ideas or take any initiatives."

"The crime lab people are here, and so is the doctor," said Eli as Michael hung up. "They want to talk to you and to the husband. They'd also like to talk to the son, but there's no son, is there? Our Yoram has vanished. Didn't stay to wait for the DNA. Vanished and killed his mother." Michael followed him out of the kitchen.

"There are all kinds of ways to kill," muttered Eli Bachar as they stood again in the doorway of the bedroom and watched the doctor, who was leaning over Clara Beinisch's corpse. "All kinds of ways, believe me. You can kill without even touching a person. That's what Balilty would tell you. And I bet you that this fellow is already outside our territorial waters."

In silence they retreated to the window, along with the doctor, who also moved aside to make way for the stretcher bearers. In silence they watched Yaffa from the Criminal Identification Unit, as she gathered the contents of the drawers into the black plastic bag, and Alon, as he took photograph after photograph: the corpse from the left and from the right and from above, the iron hook, the ladder. "It's too bad you moved it," Alon said, and immediately bit his lip, "but you probably thought that it was still possible to do something." He didn't take his eye from the viewfinder of the camera. "You probably thought it was possible to get her down and give her mouth-to-mouth resuscitation or something."

"No," said Eli, "her pulse was already gone. Her neck was broken—even I can see a thing like that—but you can't leave a person there like that, hanged."

Alon took a few more pictures, the camera giving rhythm to the silence. Then he stifled a yawn and said: "Okay, I'm done here. You can take her out," and the two young men in the white coats laid the stretcher on the bed.

From outside the room came the sound of heavy footsteps, and Efraim Beinisch entered and covered his eyes as they laid his wife's body on the stretcher and lifted it. "The doctor said that she died instantly, with no . . . with no . . . ," he said, and looked around. "And her child isn't here, he doesn't even know. The doctor gave me an injection," he added in a tired voice, and sat down on the edge of the bed. "I don't know what . . . I don't know what to do," he said, and lay down on his side and stretched his legs. "God almighty, what have I done to deserve this? What?" he said as he curled his knees to his chest and all at once stopped talking. His body relaxed and his breathing became rhythmic.

"He's fallen asleep," Eli said, and looked at Michael helplessly. "What shall we do? We can't leave him here like this alone. He'll wake up and . . . Is there someone we can call for him? Someone from the family or from—"

"There's no one, as far as I know," mused Michael aloud. "They don't have anything to do with the neighbors and they worked together, so he doesn't even have a secretary."

"Wasn't there something about a brother-in-law? Or a sister-in-law?" said Eli, making an effort to remember. "Wasn't there some talk of them being at a family celebration of some sort? We have to at least inform . . . take care of . . . I'm calling Tzilla," he finally declared. "She'll know what to do," and immediately pushed the buttons on the mobile phone in his hand.

Distractedly, still looking at Efraim Beinisch's large body, the knees curled to the chest and the head hidden in the arms, Michael heard Eli's choppy sentences—"I have no idea . . . How long will it take? As quickly as you can"—and wondered who would be called to sit beside his own bed, when he would need watching and afterward when it would no longer be necessary, and who would make the funeral arrangements. In his imagination he saw his son Yuval burying his face and weeping, and in this bedroom he was filled with great sorrow and pity for Yuval and for himself and when he shut his eyes he saw Ada's face.

"It'll take her a few minutes," said Eli to Michael, "and from here she'll find whoever needs to be informed, but she asks that you go up to Mount Scopus. There's nothing for you to do here now. Take the car. I'll wait for her here. It's more important now that you be at the hospital."

Only as he drove past the apartment, which during the past few days he had forgotten he had purchased, did it occur to Michael that there had been a new note in Eli Bachar's voice—a calm and authoritative note, from which the bitterness had disappeared like a boil that had been lanced and drained and didn't hurt anymore.

Were it not for all he had been through during the past several days, he might have smiled at the sight of the girl's shut eyes—shut so tight, there was a furrow between her eyebrows—and the lips she curled into her mouth. She lay on her back without moving, even though there was no doubt that she heard everything that went on around her. He knew that she heard her mother protesting when he asked her to leave the room, and the psychiatrist's pessimistic remark—"You can lead a horse to the water, but you can't make him drink. It's an English proverb"—and even the shuffle of Peter O'Brian's feet walking around the bed as he muttered: "She has really gone through hell." Now, when he was alone in the room with her, he sat down on the edge of the bed near Nessia's legs, crossed his arms and waited.

Had he been asked what he was waiting for, he would have shrugged and said, "For a moment of inspiration," but the truth was that he hoped that this young girl, because of her great curiosity, would want to know who had sat down on her bed and would open her eyes to take a peek at him. The big hand on the large wall clock ticked and made a full circle, and then another, and not only did the girl not open her eyes but she squeezed her lips even tighter and for a moment even bit her lower lip as if to declare: "On no account," or "Nothing is going to open me." Michael examined the pale, freckled face that had lost its awkward fleshiness and looked so vulnerable. He also examined the kinky brown hair that surrounded her face like a halo. Now that the hair wasn't imprisoned in a rubber band her face suddenly looked narrow and delicate; he saw strands of gold in those curls and he also saw her hand, lying beside her still body as if it had finished shedding a skin and had been renewed. And silently he said to himself that this crisis, because of which she was now lying on her back and sealing herself off from the world, had caused a change in her and had given her face, and perhaps her body as well, a vulnerable delicacy that had not been visible in them before. He looked at the large book that was lying on the bed next to her—Peter had set it down there before he went out of the room—and opened the shabby binding and read the large, curly letters, "Shakespeare's Tales for Children," in English. (Every night, before the lights went out, Peter read from this book to Nessia or crooned songs to her, to bring her back to consciousness. Perhaps it had worked, and more than the reading or the singing, the persistence in his voice; people's refusal to be in the world is softened more than anything by the melody of a voice and the loving and devoted intention in it.) Had Nessia been a very small child, he would have told her the story of the ugly duckling, but after she had seen what she had seen, she did not need fairy tales, and certainly not fairy tales in which there was a moral.

"Why doesn't she want to open her eyes?" he had asked the psychiatrist before they entered the room. "I don't have enough data," the psychiatrist had replied. "The mother couldn't exactly explain. But this is a possible reaction after a trauma like the one she suffered. People are afraid to be conscious."

"But she *is* conscious, at least partly conscious," argued Michael. "Even a layman like me can see that, so that's not what she's afraid of."

"Yes," agreed the psychiatrist unenthusiastically, "but we have no way of knowing what she remembers and what is frightening her."

Now Michael looked at her cracked lips—her mother had told him before she went out to moisten her lips with a swab wrapped in gauze, but he held back—and the squeezed eyelids that fluttered from time to time and he asked himself how he could reassure her.

"We've caught him," he finally said in a tone used for speaking to adults—he knew no one had told her that before him. "We've caught him, and he can't do anything to anyone anymore."

He thought he saw a very slight movement, a kind of dismissive shrug.

"You don't even know who you're talking to," said Michael. "I'm

Chief Superintendent Michael Ohayon. We spoke in the street on one occasion and I know that you remember me. I'm the policeman who asked you to tell me what you knew, anything that would help the investigation, and you didn't say a thing. But nevertheless you helped us, without saying anything, only it's a pity that you had to endanger yourself so much and get hurt." Her upper teeth covered her lower lip, but apart from that there was no sign that she had listened to him.

"I want to tell you something," he finally said, "but first I'm going to lock the door, because it's absolutely just between us. It's a big secret and I don't want anyone apart from you and me to know." He spoke the last words as he rose from the bed and very noisily walked to the door and locked it and immediately turned around and managed to catch sight of her eyelids a second before they were tightly closed again. Nessia breathed flatly and rapidly and tightened her lips. He went back and sat down on the bed closer to her head and spoke softly and slowly.

There are children, Michael told her, who don't have things, who have a feeling that no one in the world loves them. And they are certain, these children, that they are ugly and stupid and repulsive and, he continued, they make a private world for themselves, a world that is only theirs, a secret world with pretty things. Sometimes they also make a secret hiding place, just for them, and bring things to it. They can't always get these things easily, but they have their methods, all kinds of methods, and here he stopped and asked if she knew why they had methods.

Even though Nessia did not move, Michael could tell from her head, which moved ever so slightly, that she was listening and taking in every word. They have methods, Michael explained, and crossed his arms, because in fact they are not at all stupid and maybe they are more intelligent than other children. And therefore they know, these unusual children, how to get the pretty things that they need to have for the beautiful secret world they invent. These children are not only imaginative, they are also inventive. Inventiveness, he explained, is finding the right, special way to do something. And it is clear that these children are unique and extraordinary, because it is known that not everyone can bring his imagination to life. He looked at her face and said: "There are very few people who know the truth about these children, very, very few." And after that he said nothing. If the girl really was fully conscious—and perhaps it was enough if she was only partially conscious—then she was burning with curiosity. Burning, but very cautious. She won't open her eyes until she knows that his knowledge will not bring her shame and disgrace, Michael reflected, because shame and disgrace frighten her more than ordinary punishment. She will open her eyes only if he promises her in an indirect way, implicitly, that no one will shame her anymore, that no one will shame Nessia anymore; she has shamed herself enough.

Then he told her that if he happened to meet a boy or a girl like that, especially a girl who knows how to observe things and remembers everything she sees and hears and in addition to that understands the significance of things, he would do everything he could so that this child would talk to him and be his friend, like—and here he hesitated a moment—"like you and Peter."

Someone tried to open the locked door and gave up. Michael looked at the small fingers that drummed once on the sheet, and did not know whether she was signaling him to continue or objecting to the comparison to Peter, but nevertheless he risked saying that if by any chance the treasures that a boy or girl like that had secretly collected were to come into his hands, he would not show them to anyone, nor would he tell anyone about them. He wouldn't say a word about them to a living soul—when he said that, the small fingers fluttered—and even if something in the treasure trove could help solve a murder, even then it would not occur to him to share this secret with a living soul.

"Peter doesn't know anything," Nessia said, and her voice —for which he had been waiting for a very long time, though he had not imagined that he would hear it before she opened her eyes—was limp and weak.

"And he won't know, either, if you don't want him to," promised Michael solemnly.

"He killed her," whispered Nessia. "Handsome Yoram killed Zahara." Only then did she open her golden brown eyes and look at him, as if her entire life depended on what she saw in his eyes.

"Yes," said Michael. "He killed her, but he will never kill anyone else again."

Her narrow eyes now regarded him suspiciously, and he repeated his promise in a low, calm voice that brooked no doubt.

"He found me," Nessia said, and coughed. "He found me in the shelter, and he also found the handbag."

"But you found that handbag before then," said Michael. "You knew something even before then."

She rolled her head on the large pillow and licked her lips, and

Michael dipped the gauze in the glass of water and handed her the swab. She examined it from top to bottom for a moment before she put it between her lips and sucked. "No, I didn't know," she said. "I only saw . . . I saw them once near the haunted house."

"The haunted house on Bethlehem Road?" Michael risked guessing.

"They didn't see me. No one saw me," she said, and there was a glimmer of pride in her words. "I was in the yard," she explained.

He nodded without taking his eyes off her.

"A girl like you," said Michael with careful seriousness, "already knows that people, even grown-ups, do things the other way around from what they feel or want."

"The other way around? Like not showing that they love someone?"

"That too," agreed Michael.

"Yes," said Nessia, "but not Handsome Yoram. Why did *he* do it the other way around?"

"Out of fear," said Michael. "He was afraid."

"Do you mean he was afraid that she would tell his parents and her parents?" Nessia shut her eyes, and he saw the discharge that had accumulated in their corners.

"And also he already had . . . he already had a relationship with another woman. He was engaged," he explained to her.

Nessia rolled onto her side, facing him and he quickly moved to the edge of the bed. "Because of the fiancée from America," she whispered and frowned. "Because of her."

"Does it hurt?" asked Michael in alarm.

"No. Yes. A little, but . . . but right now," she demanded, "first you tell me . . . explain everything to me . . . Because of the fiancée from America, the blonde. I saw her. Mrs. Jesselson told my mother that she's rich."

"Yes," said Michael. "His mother liked this fiancée. It's like if you have a friend your mother doesn't like and doesn't agree that you can be her friend, and instead she prefers a different friend."

"All right," said Nessia, and slowly and carefully she rolled over to lie on her back again. "But I don't have any friends. They don't like me, the girls in my class."

"Now everything will be different," promised Michael. "Now you are a different person—you've been through things. I think that if someone learns what you have learned recently, he develops and his life doesn't stay in the same place."

She gave him a long, searching look, and because of it he hastened to add with utter seriousness: "If someone, especially a young person, goes through such a difficult crisis like you have, and if he remains alive as luckily happened in your case"—now he dared to stroke her arm—"then he comes out of it stronger than before."

"My body is awfully weak," said Nessia doubtfully. "I can't lift my leg."

"Your body will get stronger," Michael promised, and removed his hand from her arm, "but I was talking about *you*, about *Nessia*. You will look at the world differently, and also at yourself."

"But if I did have a friend like that, and I had to tell her that my mother didn't allow me to be friends with her, I'd just tell her and that would be the end of it. Why would I have to kill her?" she wondered. "Isn't it the same for grown-ups?"

"Not exactly, not always. Most times it's like you say, but . . . ," said Michael. "In this case . . . There were more complicated things in this case.'"

"Why?" demanded Nessia, and Michael looked at her helplessly. He did not know whether to tell her about the pregnancy. What does a girl of her age know about sexuality?

"Now you're going to tell me that I'm too young to understand," she challenged in a voice limp from weakness. "Now you're probably going to tell me that when I grow up I'll . . ." She gazed at the ceiling and peeped at him surreptitiously from the corner of her eyes without moving her face.

"They . . ." Michael cleared his throat. "They had already . . . He had promised her and she . . . Zahara . . . He had promised to marry her and she wouldn't have kept quiet . . ." Nessia looked at him suspiciously, and finally he said: "They had already been like man and wife. Zahara was pregnant."

"Ah," said Nessia. "Now I understand. That is," she continued without embarrassment, "it's like in *The Young and the Restless*. I understand that. There was this woman there—do you know it?" He shook his head and intended to say something about how he didn't have much leisure time. "Okay," said Nessia without waiting for an explanation, "there's this girl there, it doesn't matter what her name is, and she's pregnant from this man, because they had sex." She looked at him to make sure that he was listening, or to see whether he was shocked by what she was saying, and as he looked straight back at her, she continued, weighing the syllables one by one: "The school nurse explained to us about sexual intercourse, and anyway I already knew about it. In *The Young and the Restless* the girl tells the man that she's going to tell everyone. She's really annoyed with him, and he says to her: 'That's blackmail. That's what this is, blackmail.' So Zahara also blackmailed him, Yoram?"

"You could say so," said Michael, "but we don't exactly know this as yet."

"I . . . ," Nessia said, and closed her eyes as if she was feeling very weak. "I once saw him run over a cat. He ran over it with his car and the cat was lying there on the street, completely crushed. And he, he got out of the car and looked at the tires, to see if they had gotten dirty, the tires on his car. He didn't care about the cat at all. He left it lying like that in the middle of the street, like some . . . like a carcass."

"Did you go out with the dog, on the eve of the holiday?" he asked as if incidentally, and saw her fingers flutter.

"You don't want to tell me?" asked Michael.

"Not now," whispered Nessia, and her eyes, which had opened for a moment, shut again. "Some other time—maybe tomorrow. Tomorrow I'll tell you."

Michael nodded. He thought that he should leave the room and let her rest, but when he began to move Nessia looked at him and asked: "So he didn't love her?"

Michael sighed. There are people, he told her, who don't know how and are unable to love anyone, because there is something in themselves that they hate so much.

"But he was so handsome," insisted Nessia. "How could anyone so good-looking not love himself?"

"Beauty is inside, first of all," said Michael, "and beauty begins from a person not thinking only bad things about himself."

"In your opinion," whispered Nessia thoughtfully, "could it also be the other way around? That somebody who is ugly could think good things about himself?"

Outside someone knocked on the door, at first gently and then with a whole hand.

"That's my mother," said Nessia with a small, forgiving smile. "You can open the door for her now. She wants to see me."

Chapter 18

Three times the small truck came around and drove away. And each time the workers piled on five water tanks they took out of the attic space. Ada and Michael stood by the window with its wrought-iron grille on the ground floor and watched them coming down the ladder, the one worker carrying the tank on his back and the other holding it from below, to ease the weight. Ada got alarmed a few times and asked whether the ladder was really steady, and then commented on how they were clearing out the scene of a murder and turning it into a bedroom. She didn't say "my bedroom" or "our bedroom," and before he had time to consider this she said: "Has the Rosensteins' daughter arrived yet? Have they done the DNA test?"

"She's here. They've done it, but not within a day. It takes a few days for DNA."

"And did Zahara's parents agree to compare . . . Are they cooperating with this?"

"They agreed. In the end, they agreed." Michael sighed as he remembered attorney Rosenstein's pleading and the stern face of Naeema Bashari.

"What do you want to bet that she's not their daughter?" said Ada without smiling. "I just know that she's not their daughter."

"I'm powerless to speak in the presence of such knowledge," said Michael, "even if you've never seen her. Even if you've never seen any of them. Neither Naeema Bashari nor the Rosensteins nor Tali Rosenstein, so how exactly could you know?"

"I know it, and it's not mysticism," said Ada. "You told me yourself about the difference in the dates. One was born in January and one was born in April. Right?"

"I think," said Michael pensively, "that what is bothering you is this order. It's overdone—this closeness between the intersecting stories, as if everything were too contrived."

"So, is it coincidental in your opinion?"

"That's not the point," he replied to her. "I just want to tell you that even if all the coincidences came together at once, it wouldn't mean that there's 'the hand of God' here or anything. Even what looks like order is disorder, and even what looks like regularity is chaos. She could be the Basharis' daughter and even that wouldn't mean anything."

She regarded him with interest, shook her head and touched his arm. "How long can it take before the Americans extradite him?" she asked.

"It could take months," said Michael, "but maybe his father's visit there, in Baltimore, and his conversation with Michelle's parents will speed it up. Maybe his father will have a confrontation with him, for once in his life, really confront him. Stand in front of him and . . ."

"The main trouble," said Ada without taking her eyes off the worker who had now arrived on the sidewalk carrying the rusted tank by himself, with careful steps and a bent head, "the main trouble is the fear." She ran her slender fingers through her soft, cropped dark hair. "Because there are parents who are afraid of their children, from the beginning, when they're babies, and they transmit this fear in the way they touch their children. Parents who are afraid of their children are even more dangerous than parents who neglect them. In my opinion, at any rate. Were you afraid of your child?"

"Sometimes," admitted Michael. "When he was little, after I got divorced and when I would bring him to my place when . . . Sometimes he would cry and I . . . I would get scared, but I got over it."

"He was afraid of him and he spoiled him, Efraim Beinisch. He spoiled his only son. He corrupted him."

"He didn't do it alone," said Michael. "He was even more afraid of his wife. She was the main spoiler there, and I don't know whether she was afraid of him or simply refused to see what kind of child she was raising."

"I can't think of anything more horrible," Ada said, and shivered. "I can't imagine what a person feels like when he finds himself turning his son in to the police, and even more I can't imagine what a person feels when he knows—and it doesn't matter whether it's an only child or one of three—that his son is a cold-blooded murderer. But I can't stop asking myself whether . . . What I would have done if . . ."

"It wouldn't have made any difference," Michael said, and lit a cigarette. The high wooden ladder stood in the center of the big room, leaning on the edges of the hole they had torn in the ceiling, and the workers walked past them before climbing up into the space under the tile roof. The older worker, who was already on his way to the ladder, looked at Michael's hand, and Michael extended the cigarette packet to him. "Would you like one?" he asked, and the man smiled and very carefully pulled out one cigarette, thanked him with his eyes and waited for Michael to light it. Then he took a long, hungry drag, coughed, cleared his throat and paused for a moment before he began to climb the ladder.

"It wouldn't have made any difference at all. It wouldn't have mattered, because in any case there were the DNA results and in any case it turned out that fetus was his and it was already clear that his alibi was . . . that he didn't have an alibi."

"And that story with his mother, and the fiancée and all that," said Ada. "She didn't even wait for the trial, the mother. Nothing."

"That's how it goes," said Michael. "The father said he would put a bullet through his head, that he would drive his car off a cliff, and in the end it was she. You should know that the one who keeps quiet, that's usually the one who . . . What should I have done? Put a watch on her? It didn't even occur to me . . ."

"Do you think that it was because she knew?" asked Ada. "Because she couldn't live with that knowledge?"

"Who knows," said Michael. "She didn't leave anything, not a note and not a letter. But I think something else. I'm thinking . . ." He looked out the window. "There are birds on that carob tree," he muttered.

"What are you thinking? You said you were thinking something. Don't stop now," demanded Ada.

"It's just a thought." He hesitated. "I think she could have managed with that knowledge if she were the only one who knew and no one else discovered it. I think that she realized that her husband also knew and she knew or felt that he wouldn't just pretend he didn't know. She realized that Efraim Beinisch would talk, and even if he didn't talk, I think the fact of the knowledge that her husband knew, and knew that *she* knew, would have been enough. She wouldn't have been able to live with this shame if anyone shared it. You asked what I'm thinking? Here's what I'm thinking: How much longer do we have to wait for that contractor?"

"He'll be here in a minute," Ada promised, and patted his arm. "You've got dirty from the whitewash." She patted his shirt again and then stood on her toes and ran her finger along his cheek and looked into his soft brown eyes. "Why? Are you in a hurry?"

"No. I'm not in a hurry," said Michael. "Just terribly hungry. For two days I've been eating at the hospital cafeteria, and the time has come for a serious meal, no? Do you have any wishes?"

"As a matter of fact, I do," Ada said, and lowered her eyes, "but it will delay the meal for a while."

He crushed the cigarette with his heel. "What? Tell me exactly what you want," he said, and looked at her, smiling.

"It's not what you think." She laughed. "You're not even warm," and both of them looked for a moment at a blackbird that flew out of the carob tree as the water tank banged against the bottom of the truck.

"I want to meet your son. Don't you think the time has come for you to show him to me?"

"Indeed it has," said Michael.

BATYA GUR's stunning novels probe the depths of human emotion in one of the richest, most fascinating parts of the world. Giving the reader a glimpse into the troubles and triumphs of Israel's land and people, they tell of the contradictions and conflicts that pull it apart on a daily basis, yet at the same time "reveal the incredible love of life in this little country that dances on a volcano" (*Elle* magazine [French edition]).

Turn the page for a glimpse into other wonderfully complex and absorbing books in Batya Gur's Michael Ohayon mystery series, including:

The Saturday Morning Murder

Literary Murder

Murder on a Kibbutz

Murder Duet

AND

Murder in Jerusalem

The Saturday Morning Murder

In *The Saturday Morning Murder,* the first in Batya Gur's beautifully written series, the reader meets Chief Superintendent Michael Ohayon, as he investigates the shocking murder of a Jerusalem psychiatrist. Dr. Eva Neidorf was set to deliver a lecture on the ethical problems in psychoanalysis—making her murder quite opportune for some of her colleagues, and the investigation quite complex for Ohayon. The list of suspects is long, and Ohayon follows a trail through the psychoanalytic community—patients as well as analysts—as well as the bustling Jerusalem commercial district and the Israeli military. In this "flawless" (*Publishers Weekly*) debut, readers are treated to a complex plot, an intelligent and compassionate detective, and a beautifully realized description of Jerusalem.

MICHAEL OHAYON LOOKED AT HIS WATCH and saw that it was eleven o'clock. A strong wind was blowing, blotting out the sound of the rain. He rose from his seat, and the old man stood up, too, and asked him if he was going to go to Neidorf's house now. Michael took the hint and asked if he would like to accompany him, adding something about the lateness of the hour and the bad weather. Hildesheimer brushed his reservations aside with a sweep of his hand and said that he had already lived quite long enough, in his opinion, and that in any case he would not be able to sleep tonight. As he spoke, he led Michael to the coatrack in the corner of the long hallway, took down a heavy winter overcoat, and put in on. The house was dark and silent, and the two of them let themselves out. Outside it was very cold. Michael, who had kept his jacket on all the time he was sitting in the study, felt the wind like an icy blow and was glad to get into the police Renault.

He activated the radio, which responded immediately. Control tried to tell him something in a tired female voice; he listened patiently. Everyone was looking for him, everyone said it was urgent. "Okay; tell them I'll be in touch later. And tell my team that I'm in the middle of something." Control sighed and said, "Will do."

Hildesheimer sat next to him, sunk in thought, and Michael was obiged to repeat his question twice before the old man nodded and gave him Dr. Neidorf's address, the same address that Michael had seen on the identification card in her bag in the course of his repeated rummagings through its contents that morning.

It was a little street in the German Colony. Almost every time Michael passed Emek Refaim Street, he thought of the Knights of the German Templars who founded this neighborhood in 1878. How pathetic were their hopes for redemption, symbolized by the remnants of their flour mill, still visible on the corner. Michael maneuvered the Renault through the narrow alleys and parked carefully. He opened the door for Hildesheimer and helped him out of the small car. The two of them went through the little gate and walked up the path leading to the front door, where the old man stepped back to let Michael open the heavy wooden door.

Michael tried all the keys, at first in the light of the streetlamp and then in the light of all the matches left in the box, which Hildesheimer lit one after the other with an admirably steady hand. Finally they both resigned themselves to the fact that the key to the house was not on the ring. Neither said a word about where it might be.

Michael went to his car and came back a few seconds later, a sharp object in his hand. He mumbled something to Hildesheimer about the skills one acquired during the course of one's life, then he set to work on the lock. Hildesheimer went on lighting matches—Michael had brought a new box from the car—and ten minutes later they were standing in Eva Neidorf's house.

Michael shut the door.

In the bright light illuminating the entrance hall, he saw the old man's pale face. His grimly pursed lips expressed what they had both already realized: someone had preceded them.

~·~

Literary Murder

The next book in this engrossing series once again finds Chief Superindendent Michael Ohayon investigating a crime among insular intellectuals. In *Literary Murder*, two rival literature professors from Hebrew University in Jerusalem are murdered on the same weekend. The upstart Iddo Dudai is poisoned while vacationing in the beautiful beach town of Eilat, and the prominent poet Shaul Tirosh, whom Dudai had recently challenged in public, is found bludgeoned in his office. Since each of the victims would have been the most obvious suspect in the other's murder, Ohayon must divine whether these two rivals' murders are a coincidence, or the result of a conspiracy. And when he uncovers a love triangle and a profound betrayal, the chief superintendent learns that the dark secrets of a respected literature department run deep.

WHEN HE WOKE UP THAT MORNING, he had told himself that the first day was safely over, that Uzi was taking care of Yuval personally, that he had the finest apparatus available, that there was only one more dive to go, and that tomorrow it would all be behind them and he would be able to drive home with an easy mind.

But then he saw the title "Do You Have a Regulator?" and he began to read the article below it. "There are no rules governing the examination of the tank valve and the regulator; the sole responsibility belongs to the diver," it said. He went on reading to the end of the article and decided to show it to Yuval as soon as he came out of the water. ("During the dive, immediately after the diver had executed the underwater somersaults, a fault in the air supply was discovered, necessitating an emergency haul to the surface, while I gave him buddy-breathing," reported the diving-instructor author of the article, and Michael found himself reading with intense concentration. "Observation of the underwater pressure gauge showed a drop in atmospheric pressure from 100 lbs to close to zero, during inhalation from the regulator.")

Michael Ohayon looked at his watch: the practice session was due to end in fifteen minutes. He stood up and approached the sea. The Diving Club was crowded. No father had ever abandoned his son to his fate like this, he thought in a panic, and then he saw the figure in the black rubber suit being carried from the boat by two people and laid on the beach.

The first thought, of Yuval, was immediately dismissed, because the youngster removing the diving mask from the supine figure was not Guy, the diving instructor who had gone out with Yuval, but Motti, to whom he had been introduced the previous evening. With him was a woman in a diving suit, one of the students in the course, Michael thought. From where he was standing he was unable to see the expressions on their faces, but something in their movements, as they bent over the figure in the diving suit lying on the sand, proclaimed catastrophe.

The premonition of disaster immediately turned into a certainty when he saw Motti rapidly pulling out his knife and ripping open the recumbent figure's diving suit. The woman ran in the direction of the office, a small stone building on the beach not far from where Michael had been lying.

Motti began mouth-to-mouth resuscitation, and Michael couldn't take his eyes off the spectacle. Without knowing how he got there, he found himself standing next to them, waiting for the chest to rise and fall. But nothing happened. Together with Motti, Michael counted the breaths to himself.

It was a young man. His face was pink and swollen.

Superintendent Ohayon, who had seen a lot of corpses during the course of his career, still hoped that one day he would achieve the callousness of the police investigators and private detectives on television. Every time, he was astonished anew, always after the event, by his feeling faint, by the nausea, the anxiety, and sometimes the pity too, that he felt in the presence of a corpse, precisely when scientific detachment and attention to detail were called for. Nothing at all would be demanded of him here, he consoled himself when he realized that all the attempts at resuscitation would be unavailing.

The woman came running back with a young man who held a doctor's bag. Michael drew closer, silencing the inner voices reminding him that he was on holiday and that it was none of his business.

Murder on a Kibbutz

The third book in the Michael Ohayon mystery series, *Murder on a Kibbutz*, is another "meaty story, dense with character and plot" (*Chicago Tribune*). Chief Superintendent Ohayon is seasoned at penetrating complex and insular societies, but when a secretary is murdered on a kibbutz, he encounters barriers that even he has never seen before. The young victim, Osnat Harel, was carrying on an affair with an outsider, and the jealousies, prejudices, and inflexible attitudes of the agrarian kibbutzniks, along with their general distrust of outsiders and their fear of losing their toehold on tradition, make this the determined superintendent's most difficult case yet.

THE KIBBUTZ ITSELF WAS NOW FIFTY YEARS OLD. A half century had passed since the oldest members had settled on this land. It was not the oldest kibbutz in Israel, but it was certainly well established. The atmosphere today was festive, but at the same time it was clear that nobody was taking the celebration too seriously. Only the children looked excited, but they were drawn to the lineup of agricultural machinery, and none of them paid any attention to the platform and the little choir standing on it. And apart from the members of the choir, hardly anyone was wearing blue and white. Not even the kindergarten children, Aaron noticed with a trace of disappointment that then amused him, and there was no sign anywhere of the national flag. He would have to ask Moish about that too. And at the same moment he thought of the nostalgia that would overcome him on national holidays, and of the excitement with which he would look forward to Shevuoth, the Festival of Weeks, in particular, the feeling of participation in great and important events that had really and truly pervaded him then.

He could not entirely suppress the feeling that once you took away the blue and white and the flags on the Caterpillar, the whole ceremony seemed archaic and foreign, as if it were taking place on a collective farm in Soviet Russia. And yet, he thought, chewing a straw reflectively, he felt that time had stood still, as if he were watching documentary footage from a movie about early Zionist history. But now it was the farce of an agricultural ceremony in a place where agriculture was almost bankrupt—a kibbutz, a Zionist agricultural commune, that derived its income from an industrial plant that, of all things, manufactured cosmetics, having given its name to an international patent for a face cream that abolished wrinkles and rejuvenated skin cells and was advertised in all the newspapers with two photographs of the same woman captioned "Before" and "After." No one else seemed to be showing any recognition of the absurdity of celebrating an agricultural rite where only the manufacture and sale of face cream made it possible to go on working the land. It could, he thought, be why Srulke hadn't appeared. When Aaron had looked for him in vain in the dining hall in order to greet him, Moish had assured him that he would show up for the ceremony, "if only," he said, grinning, "to inspect what they've done with his flowers."

As he looked around, ostensibly keeping an eye out for Srulke but actually trying to catch a glimpse of Osnat, Aaron concluded that at least one sector of the kibbutz economy was blooming: There were so many children that a stranger might be excused for wondering how anybody had time for anything else. The products of this intensive reproductive activity scampered about, and the apparent contentedness and good humor of the large families gave him a pang of vague longings. But his other voice nipped them in the bud. The little devil inside him immediately scoffed at his wish to belong, and the skeptical inner voices that had grown louder over the years now asserted themselves and conjured up the image of a herd of placid Dutch cows, spoiling his sense of festivity beyond recovery. He tried to suppress the feeling that there was something stupefying about the tranquility here, recalling the rage that would seize hold of him in the past and that had attacked him today too, on his way to the dining hall with Moish for lunch.

It was only a short distance from Moish's room to the dining hall, but it had taken a long time to get there, what with having to greet everyone they met and with Moish's delaying them by remembering one little chore after another, stopping at the children's houses to see if a dripping faucet had been repaired and the sandbox in the kindergarten refilled with fresh sand, and then at the secretariat to find out whether someone who was supposed to phone had phoned, and only after he had studied the notices on the bulletin board, extracted the newspaper from his pigeonhole and read all the notes he also found there, and answered the phone ringing in the big lobby on the ground floor—only then did the two of them climb the stairs to the building's second floor, to the dining hall itself.

At the door, Moish lingered to take in the scene, and an eternity seemed to pass before he picked up a tray. As they stood before the trolley holding the trays, Aaron suddenly felt fatigued and impatient with the waste of time, the idleness. He summed it up for himself: The minute you walk into the door of the dining hall, your oxygen supply drops, your productivity declines; that phlegmatic calm, that slowness, they're enough to drive a person crazy. He retreated behind the protection of the guessing game: who was who, who belonged to whom. He succeeded in identifying members of three and even four generations standing together in groups, the youngest children on their fathers' shoulders. Which of the adults had been born on the kibbutz and which had married into it he couldn't guess, but he could tell at a glance which of them were guests like himself.

Murder Duet

Jerusalem is rich with cultural history, and Chief Superintendent Michael Ohayon, an avid classical music lover, revels in the world-class performances of the ancient city. In *Murder Duet*, the solitary Ohayon crosses paths with his neighbor Nita, an accomplished cellist, when he stumbles upon an abandoned baby and takes her into his care. Nita is from a family of musicians, and her own experience as a single mother is invaluable as Ohayon scrambles to find the baby's parents, and keep her safe from harm. But when Nita's father is murdered, and her musician brother is also murdered soon thereafter, Ohayon must share his attention with the bereaved Nita. Delving deep into the competitive and complex world of the classical music community, while struggling to keep his own life together, and the baby out of harms way, Ohayon must penetrate a reticent and layered community of musicians in this "virtuoso performance" (*Booklist*).

THE TRAFFIC JAM HAD BARRED HIS WAY through King David Street and obliged him to turn on his siren at the Mamilla traffic lights. As he had pushed on toward the concert hall, he had stared, as he always did now, with astonishment at the frameworks of the luxury buildings that were replacing the razed old neighborhood, and then pushed on toward the concert hall. His astonishment—sometimes accompanied by revulsion— at the changes in the view emerging beyond the traffic lights returned whenever he stopped at this intersection. After glancing, with a sense of relief at their survival, at the Muslim cemetery on his left and the "Palace"—the imposing round edifice that housed the Ministry of Commerce and Industry—on his right, he looked straight ahead. For months he had been contemplating the systematic destruction of old buildings. They had left a building once visited by Theodor Herzl untouched, like a single tooth in an old person's mouth, while, like a set of gleaming white false teeth, the new buildings now stood behind a big sign announcing "David's Village."

They had called him on the police radio when he was already on his way to the Russian Compound, after depositing the babies with the after-noon babysitter. At that moment he was at the Mamilla intersection, star-ing at stickers proclaiming THE PEOPLE ARE WITH THE GOLAN and JUDEA AND SAMARIA ARE HERE on the back window of the car in front of him. The driver was hastily shutting his window in the face of the barrage of curses let loose by a woman in rags, the beggar woman known as the Mad-woman of Mamilla, who plied her trade among the cars stuck at the traffic lights, thrusting a filthy hand at the drivers, grinning or growling with her toothless mouth. The address given him by the dispatcher on Shorer's orders filled him with terrible panic. "He tried you first at home," she said, and her voice—a familiar froggy croak—sent a shiver down his spine, as if she had scratched with a stone on a pane of glass.

"I was on the way," he said into the two-way radio, mainly for the sake of saying something, and he turned into the right lane. The chill that had flooded in him, that had filled the pit of his stomach at the sound of the address, had not been dispelled even by the words "the body of a man" the dispatcher had added, as if urgency justified her lack of caution about reporters listening in to the police frequency. The chill increased the closer he got—speeding past the long row of cars drawn up at the seemingly unchanging traffic lights—to the concert hall.

He was chilled, his knees felt weak, and his teeth chattered. How could Shorer find him if he spent his days waiting for babysitters? he castigated himself. He speeded up. The afternoon babysitter, the one they had taken on specially for Nita's rehearsals, had been half an hour late. "Because of the traffic," she had said angrily. The bus route had been changed for the visit of the American secretary of state. "And the day before yesterday it was because of some rabbi's funeral," she panted. "Three hundred thousand Hasidim for a rabbi nobody's ever heard of! It's impossible to live in this city anymore—it's either terrorist attacks or Hasidic funerals or state visits with limousines and motorcycles. Even if they're only going from the King David Hotel to the prime minister's house on Balfour Street, they shut the whole damned city down because of them. What do they care? They're not in a hurry to get anywhere."

Between waves of the shivers he heard himself asking the dispatcher about whether Forensics had already been informed and sent to the scene. He heard his calm, matter-of-fact voice, the familiar voice routinely and automatically on tap for such occasions. Nevertheless it sounded strange to him now as he asked whether the pathologist had already been sent to the scene. When he had parked at the rear entrance of the concert hall, he turned to the radio again and asked that Tzilla be sent to the scene.

The young Magen David Adom doctor stood next to the skinny pathologist, whose checked shirt emphasized his concave chest and his thin, hairy, white arms. Polishing the lenses of his round spectacles punctiliously, he questioned the doctor briefly in his singsong voice, the silences punctuated by constant humming. He sounded as though he were practicing an endless recitative. She responded to his questions curtly and with evident irritation. When she received the call, it was already "too late," the doctor said, and now Michael heard the echo of a faint Russian accent in the phrase. "The body was in the same position as it is now, sprawled out like a rag, with all the blood, and the legs folded," at the foot of the concrete pillar. She hadn't let anyone touch it, she asserted, no one but she had approached it. She described once more, this time without the note of complaint and condemnation, Nita's hysterical fit, and that she had sent Nita to lie down in "Mr. van Gelden's office."

~·~

Murder in Jerusalem

T he crowning achievement to a magnificent career, *Murder in Jerusalem* is the final installment in the beloved Michael Ohayon mystery series.

Acclaimed Israeli director Benny Meyuhas's film production of the heartbreaking work "Iddo and Eynam" promises to be a landmark of Israeli film—until his wife and the films' set designer Tirzah Rubin are crushed under a set piece, stalling the production indefinitely. Shimshon Zadik, the head of Israel Television, is among the first at the scene, and the death of this talented and mysterious woman, a colleague of his for many years, sends shockwaves through the film and television community. But more shocking is what comes to light in the investigation— that Tirzah's storybook life wasn't at all what it seemed, and that her death may have been part of a larger network of social and political unrest. The brooding chief superintendent Michael Ohayon has spent his career surrounded by horrific crimes, but nothing has ever disturbed him more than what Tirzah's murder reveals: that the very ideals upon which he was raised, upon which the nation was raised, may have led to unspeakable crimes.

THE KEROSENE HEATER WAS OF NO USE; the room was terribly cold. It was a Jerusalem cold—dense, powerful—of old stone rooms. Schreiber stood rubbing his hands over the soot-covered grid of the heater. "She didn't want to call you people," he said casting a look of reproach at Natasha. "It took me a while to convince her, but in the end I told her she could do whatever she wanted, but there was no way I was getting mixed up with them."

"Who's 'them?' " Michael asked.

"These religious fanatics," Schreiber said. He moved to the half-open door and lit a cigarette there. "It's pretty clear they did this, don't you think? Believe me, I know those people."

The room was very small, most of the space taken up by a single bed in disarray. A few sweaters lay in a pile upon it and at the other side of the room, in a niche in the thick wall, was a clothes hook with several shirts and one skirt hanging from it. There was a pile of books on the floor next to the bed, and perched on a woven-straw stool stood a book in Russian, open-face down. A makeshift kitchen stood facing the doorway; there were water spots and mold on the wall near the electric burner, a single pot and pan hanging there, and a dish rack with three plates, two mugs, a few spoons, two forks, and a knife. Behind a half-open door there was a bathroom: a toilet, a sink, and a faucet with a shower hose.

Michael looked around the room; everything was utilitarian and meager except for a blue vase with a clutch of wilting wild daffodils that stood on the only table in the room, and a long, narrow print in a thin wooden frame hanging over the bed. The print showed a solitary and peculiar tower standing erect in an empty brown field; one side of the tower was brightly lit and the other shaded, the shadow extending from two people, small and displaced, posed in the middle of the foreground. He wondered how it was that in spite of the bright white light on the illuminated side of the tower, the picture exuded the feeling that the light did not have the power to illuminate this world, as though the shadows had overwhelmed it and the blackness in the background was about to flood the entire picture. Four flags blew loftily in the wind from the top of the tower, but even these brought no happiness. The mood of the entire picture was one of regret, of interminable loneliness. Who had painted this picture, he wondered, and why did it disturb him so? Underneath it, in a corner of the bed, folded in between the wall and the simple wooden table on which stood the vase of daffodils and a few plates with the remains of dried-up hummus and pita bread, was Natasha, huddled under a gray army blanket and shaking nonetheless. Michael looked into her clear blue eyes and saw no fear there.

"It's like she doesn't care," Schreiber said, "but at first, from the shock of it, she screamed. After that, nothing. She wanted to clean it up. It took me a long time to convince her to call the police. I didn't let her touch all the blood and filth, I wanted you to see it as it was . . . Anyway, I took pictures of it all," he said, adding in a faint voice. "It was *her* idea."

"What was Natasha's idea?" Michael asked. From outside the apartment they could hear the forensics people arriving, and Balilty's voice a moment later. "Taking pictures?"

"No, taking pictures was my idea," Schreiber said. "Calling you was her idea," he explained, lowering his eyes. "She said that you . . ."

"Schreiber, shut up already," Natasha said. Her voice burst forth from between her narrow hands, which were wrapped around her small face.

"What? What did I say wrong? Didn't you tell me to call him? You said he was the only one worth his salt."

"There's no reason to hurt people's feelings," Natasha mumbled, looking out the half-open door. "There are other people here. Everybody needs a good word."

MASTERWORKS OF CRIME FICTION
BY BATYA GUR

MURDER IN JERUSALEM

ISBN 0-06-085293-3 (hardcover)

The crowning achievement to a magnificent career, this final installment in the Michael Ohayon series is a wonderful parting gift from the incomparable Batya Gur. A stunning tale of a talented and secretive woman's murder, set against the politically charged backdrop of the Israeli media.

NEW HARDCOVER COMING AUGUST 2006

BETHLEHEM ROAD MURDER

ISBN 0-06-095492-2 (trade paperback)

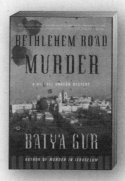

The body of a young woman is discovered in the attic of a Bethlehem Road house, in a neighborhood of Jerusalem known for its impenetrability to outsiders. Chief Superintendent Ohayon is called to the scene of the crime, where, beyond the usual horror, an old love and an unfinished romance await him.

"Gur takes infinite care with the exacting studies of the characters who give her stories their extraordinary vitality."
—*New York Times Book Review*

"Gur's outstanding police procedural . . . can hold its own with the best work of P. D. James."
—*Publishers Weekly*

LITERARY MURDER
A Critical Case

ISBN 0-06-092548-5 (trade paperback)

A shocking double murder at Israel's top academic institution brings Superintendent Michael Ohayon to the scene to probe the nature of creativity and unravel the mystery.

MURDER DUET
A Musical Case

ISBN 0-06-093298-8 (trade paperback)

Features once again the smart, charming, and lonely police officer Michael Ohayon. After his cellist friend's father and brother—who are also well-known musicians—are brutally murdered, Ohayon, a classical music afficionado, sets out to solve the crime. From the opening pages, where the detective plays a compact disc of Brahm's First Symphony, to the newly discovered music for an unknown Vivaldi requiem that provides a rock-solid motive for the crime, lovers of crime novels, as well as music, will thrill to every dulcet note.

THE SATURDAY MORNING MURDER
A Psychoanalytic Case

ISBN 0-06-099508-4 (trade paperback)

Chief Inspector Michael Ohayon journeys to the Jerusalem Psychoanalytic Institute on a quiet Sabbath morning when Dr. Eva Neidorf, a highly respected senior analyst, is found dead from a gunshot.

"Masterful." —*Publishers Weekly*

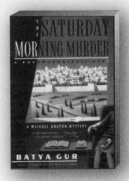

MURDER ON A KIBBUTZ
A Communal Case

ISBN 0-06-092654-6 (trade paperback)

The fourth mystery starring detective Michael Ohayon takes the brooding policeman into an Israeli kibbutz to investigate the murder of the beautiful, headstrong kibbutz secretary.

"Subtly provocative."—*New York Times Book Review*